AN EYE FOR AN EYE

THE FIXERS SERIES

A GLOBAL ESPIONAGE THRILLER OF KIDNAPPING AND TERROR

Other books by Murray Eskenazi
in The Fixers Series

An Eye For An Eye
The Pashto School
The Big Apple Bites Back
Jerusalem Farewell

AN EYE FOR AN EYE

THE FIXERS SERIES

A GLOBAL ESPIONAGE THRILLER OF KIDNAPPING AND TERROR

A NOVEL

MURRAY ESKENAZI

Port St. Lucie, Florida

The Fixers Series

Copyright © 2015, 2017, 2025, Murray Eskenazi, Delray Beach, Florida

Editing, cover, and interior design by Quantum Shift Media

ISBN print 978-0-999306-70-3
ISBN eBook 978-0-999306-71-0

Library of Congress Control Number: 2025920363

Printed in the United States of America

Third Edition

Port St. Lucie, Florida

To the memories of my father, Leon Eskenazi,
and my brother, Irving Eskenazi.
Although they are gone,
they are a constant presence.

ACKNOWLEDGMENTS

A special thank you to Keren Kilgore of Quantum Shift Media, who edited this story and made it a better book. She is excellent, and her ear for language is sure and accurate.

I also owe an enormous debt to my companion, Gerda Cohen, who has put up with my eccentric behavior while I re-wrote this book. Her opinion and advice helped me overcome some obstacles I encountered. Gerda has filled the last years of my life with love and joy.

Thank you to my late wife, Doris, who suffered through many years of my strange habits, late nights, moods, and just plain nuttiness. She made me toe the line many times, and yet she knew when to let me run loose. Doris was a tough critic and a slave driver when it came to my writing. Love is wonderful. Sometimes I wonder why Doris loved me, but I was always grateful she did.

I consider myself a lucky man to have had Doris in my life for all those years and now to have Gerda.

Capt. David N. Orrik, USN (Ret.), a Navy SEAL, my oldest friend going back to the Bronx High School of Science and Columbia, and the first person I trusted to read this manuscript. Dave's comments have made this a better book, giving it coherence and readability. Thank you, Dave; you are a unique presence in my life.

Where would I be without the many friends who have taken the time to read *An Eye for an Eye* and provided me with their insights, comments, and proofreading help? A deeply felt thank you is due to Dory Brodherson, Bob Brodherson, Bob Salem, Lenny Levey, Susan

Creaturo (who really red-lined me), Eddie Creaturo, Hank Cohen, and Axel Heyman. My partner in *Super Scrabble,* Bob Reiss, a prodigious author in his own right; Harry Levy, author of several mystery thrillers; and Keren Kilgore, my editor and publisher, have all helped me through the travails of publishing this book.

I am sure I have missed some important people who have helped me, and if I have, I apologize for any omissions.

Writing a book is a humbling experience. I have looked at the same wall for hours on end, and not once has the wall deigned to speak to me. But in the end, the wall came through. Thank you, wall.

Murray Eskenazi

TABLE OF CONTENTS

Map of Saudi Arabian Peninsula xiv

 1 A Shipping Container 1

 2 Light Sleeper 7

 3 Partners 15

 4 Jack Gets a Roommate .19

 5 Hakim Abu-Jihadi. 25

 6 Herbert Watson III 29

 7 Laura the Tourist 33

 8 Stuart J. Keaton 41

 9 Hakim Abu-Jihadi. 49

10 Phillipe d'Mosellier 53

11 Hakim Abu-Jihadi. 55

12 Jack Takes Laura to Dinner 57

13 The French Students. .63

14 Jack 71

15 Laura at Langley. 75

16 Jack 77

17 Ibrahim 79

18 Jack 89

19 Al-Nasirah Hatches a Plot 91

20   Undercover Husband and Wife .95

21   Laura 99

22   Jack in Paris 105

23   Laura, Cairo 109

24   Jack, Cairo 113

25   Sana'a 121

26   Laura 133

27   Laura 137

28   A Pickup Truck 141

29   Jack on the Road 147

30   Crossing into Saudi-land 153

31   Jack 157

32   Laura 167

33   Hakim Abu-Jihadi 173

34   Jack, Shopping 175

35   Jack, Gearing Up 181

36   Hakim Abu-Jihadi 185

37   Laura 189

38   Hakim Abu-Jihadi 191

39   Jack 195

40   Herb Watson, III 199

41   Stuart J. Keaton 201

42   Hakim Abu-Jihadi 205

43   Laura 209

44   Stuart J. Keaton 211

45   The Attack. 213

46   1ˢᵗ Lt. Henry Newman. 219

47   General Kalim Surayah 225

48   Herbert Watson, III 231

49   Jack 233

50   Hakim Abu-Jihadi. 237

51   Laura 243

52   Mickey Henderson 247

53   Herbert Watson III 251

54   Laura 255

55   President Samuel Decker 257

56   Hakim Abu-Jihadi. 261

57   Herbert Watson III 265

58   Al-Nasirah. 267

59   Laura 273

60   Jack 277

61   President Samuel Decker 281

62   Jack 285

63   Stuart J. Keaton 295

64   Jack 297

65   Stuart Keaton 311

66   Laura 315

67   General Kalim Surayah 321

68   Jack 327

About the Author 337

Map of Saudi Arabian Peninsula

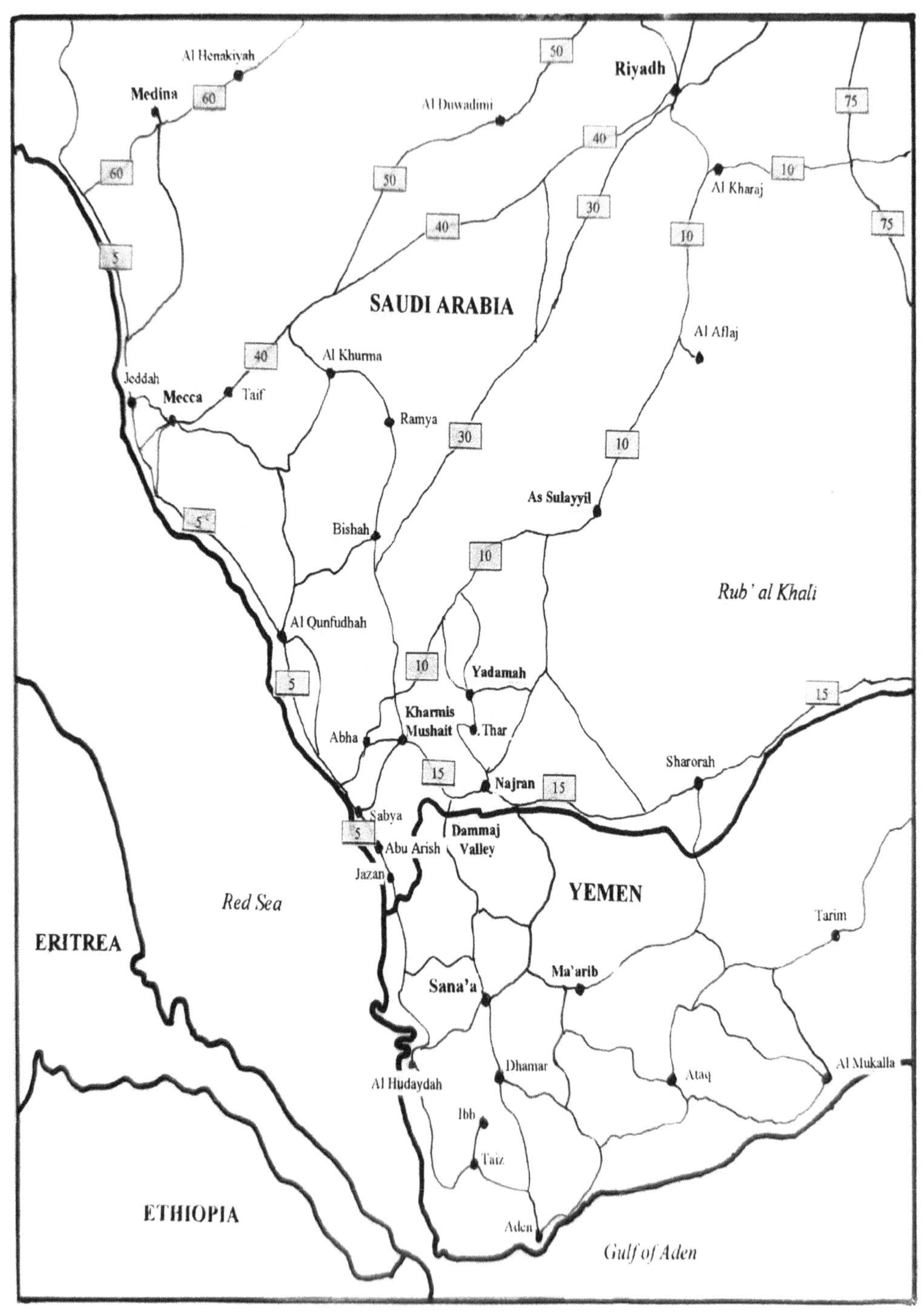

1

A SHIPPING CONTAINER

Ma'arib, Yemen
Friday, 8 August

In the scrubby desert, a 40-foot-long shipping container was sitting by the side of the road. Wind-blown trash had collected on all sides, then layers of sand piled over it, anchoring it in place. The shipping container had come from China almost three years ago, fully loaded with AK-47s, ammunition, and hand-held rocket launchers.

Like every other Chinese shipping container, it was cast aside as useless after one use. They were so cheap that they weren't worth the effort to recycle or reuse. So, they just sat wherever they got unloaded and rusted away. Port areas and warehouse storage yards around the world were filled with thousands of empty Chinese shipping containers.

This container had once been painted green, but years of constant sandblasting by desert winds had stripped most of the paint away. In the dry climate, the bare steel was covered with a thin layer of rust. The company's Chinese name, once painted in white along the sides, had also mostly flaked off. The container had lain empty and abandoned until a week ago. That was when four Yemeni members of al-Qaeda in the Arabian Peninsula (AQAP, pronounced A-Cap for convenience) and a Palestinian bomb maker from Hamas had taken up temporary residence in the shipping container, converting it into a makeshift bomb school.

The impromptu schoolroom contained two folding tables, four hard-shell air travel carry-on cases, detonators, hair-thin wires, eight cell phones, and twenty-four kilos of Semtex explosive. A small gasoline-powered generator provided electricity for the container. The Palestinian was teaching the Yemenis the fine art of committing suicide with homemade bombs while murdering unsuspecting civilians. Each of the Yemenis was going to take a one-way airplane ride.

The plan was to pack the bomb components in a hard-shell carry-on. Under the fabric liner, a thin layer of six kilograms of Semtex plastic explosive, about three millimeters thick, was to be molded to the inside contours of the outside shell of the carry-on luggage of each expectant Yemeni martyr. The airport security machines would not detect the thin layers of Semtex and the hair-thin wires.

One of the would-be bombers was to board a British Airways jumbo jet flight from Dubai to New York and put the case in an overhead compartment near the outer skin of the plane. Just before the plane landed, the Islamic hero would detonate the bomb, blowing out the side of the plane and raining bodies and airplane pieces all over the non-believers below.

If the plan worked correctly, three more bombs would also explode in rapid succession, one over London, one over Paris, and one over Washington. A call from the martyr's cell phone on the plane would trigger the bomb detonator, which was activated by another cell phone in the luggage.

That the would-be martyr would die was of no consequence since he was guaranteed a place in Paradise at the right hand of Allah (not to mention a bus full of virgins for his eternal pleasure). A major propaganda coup would result when over 1,600 infidel passengers went to hell on the same day, within two hours of each other, and with luck, some more on the ground would die from the falling debris.

The fix was in with three airport security checkers who wanted to do their bit for Islam. Fortunately, one of the security checkers, while visiting a café in Dubai, couldn't keep from boasting of his impending contribution to jihad, and word of the possible attack got picked up by one of the CIA's informers working as a server in the café. The server passed it on to his handler, who then passed it up the chain of command to his supervisor.

As a result of this report, an American undercover agent, who spoke Arabic fluently and was in Yemen on another assignment, was now sitting on a sand dune half a kilometer away, observing the five men for the past three days. The American looked like a peasant goatherd, and he smelled like one, too. Perhaps that was because he had a herd of eighteen goats under his care.

Two nights earlier, after the Yemenis and the Palestinians had left their shipping container schoolroom for the day, the American had snuck up to the container and picked the padlock securing the doors. Once inside, he took photos of everything with his iPhone.

There were four cell phones lying on the worktables in various stages of disassembly. He photographed each phone and then reassembled them so that he could turn them on and reveal the telephone numbers.

Then, referring to the photos of the disassembled phones, he took them apart again and arranged the parts exactly as they were in his photo.

Once he had all four phone numbers and was satisfied that everything was exactly as he had found it, he exited. He replaced the padlock exactly as the Palestinian had placed it.

In the desert darkness, the American climbed onto the roof of the shipping container. Using a hand-powered drill, he bored a ¼" hole in the rusty steel and slipped in a battery-powered bug that would allow him to hear all that was said inside the container by the heroes of al-Qaeda. A piece of duct tape covered the opening and kept the bug and the battery in place. From the scrubby dune where he tended his goats, the bug's signal easily reached him.

The morning after bugging the container schoolroom, he walked into Ma'areb to the local souk. There, he purchased four throwaway cell phones from four different vendors. He preprogrammed each new cell phone with one of the four numbers of the bomb makers' phones, assigning them all to the speed-dial eight key. Eight is a lucky number in Chinese culture, as the Semtex, carry-on cases, phones, wires, and schoolroom all originated from China. It seemed to be a fitting relationship. All he had to do was press the eight key on each phone for two seconds, and the calls would be dialed directly to the phones in the carry-ons in the shipping container.

The next day, the American was sitting with his goats in the dunes, his earbud connected to his iPhone, listening to the AQAP mujahideen playing with their toys. For their final exam, the Palestinian instructed each man to assemble his bomb.

Assemble they did.

Then he instructed them to arm their bombs with the cell phones off.

The goatherd was listening to every word, his four cell phones arrayed in front of him.

Each bomb was examined in turn by the Palestinian. Three bombs were satisfactory.

To the fourth man, the Palestinian said, "Hassan, you are dumber than goat shit. With the way you have this wired, the bomb will explode when you first turn the phone on." Turning to the others, he said, "Show him what he did wrong and how to do it right."

As the Palestinian watched, the other Yemenis showed Hassan what to do, and he finally got his bomb wired correctly.

"Now," said the Palestinian, "you can all turn your phones on."

Proudly, the four Yemenis turned on their phones in their carry-on luggage.

The American goatherd waited 40 seconds for the bomb phones to boot up and establish a connection to the nearest satellite, then he pressed and held the eight buttons for two seconds on two of his phones. Then he pressed the eights on the other two phones for two seconds. The four speed-dial signals began the complex process of connecting to the four phones in the carry-on cases in the container.

The Palestinian was pleased. He said, "My brothers, you have done well. We are ready to strike. On the second ring of each phone, the bombs will explode. These four bombs will bring down the infidel planes and rain death on their cities. Our sheikh, Abdel Karim Washim al-Nasirah, will personally come to see all of you before you leave on your missions. Now I want you each to turn off your phones and carefully disassemble the last connection that we just made so that the bombs are safe to handle."

Each Yemeni reached for his phone inside the carry-on cases. Two phones started to ring. Then the third. Then the fourth.

The startled men froze for a heartbeat.

The Palestinian instantly realized what was about to happen and dove to the floor as two of the bombs exploded. The other two didn't detonate—they had been destroyed by the initial blasts.

Two bombs were enough. Twelve kilos of Semtex exploded simultaneously. The shipping container was split open on all sides. All five heroes of al-Qaeda in the Arabian Peninsula died as martyrs for Allah. That ol' Hamas bomb maker really knew his stuff.

The goatherd thought, *That'll fix 'em.* Then, as he buried his four disposable cell phones in the sand, he thought, *it's time to sell this scrawny flock in the market and get the hell out of Yemen.*

He was disappointed that he hadn't been able to accomplish the primary objective of his assignment, but at least he'd managed to raise a ruckus before he left.

2

LIGHT SLEEPER

Jack
Silver Spring, Maryland
Tuesday, 31 March

I'm a light sleeper. Otherwise, I'd be long dead by now. Under my pillow, I keep a Browning 9mm Hi-Power. Thirteen rounds in the magazine and one more in the chamber. It doesn't matter where I am; if I'm breathing, the Browning is with me.

I was back from a mission to Yemen, on extended R&R, and safely asleep in my bed in my home in Silver Spring, Maryland.

It's a normal, solid, upper-middle-class ranch house, built on a concrete slab, essentially anonymous. The only thing different about my house is *me*. I live alone and travel a great deal. My neighbors think I am a salesman for a hotel supply company, so I am always traveling all over the world on an irregular itinerary, visiting hotels in many countries. It's the perfect cover for a spy attached to an agency group that is informally known as "The Fixers."

There I was, asleep in my bed at about two in the morning. My sophisticated alarm system was on. A tiny sound somewhere in the house registered in my subconscious. It wasn't one of the normal house noises like the furnace kicking in or the TV cooling down, nor was it one of the tiny creaks and groans of an old building.

It was a soft, muffled click. And it didn't belong in my house at that hour. Could it have been from my back door? Instantly, I came fully awake. I slid my hand under the pillow, gripped the pistol, and slid it down next to me, released the safety, and cocked the hammer. I put my finger alongside the trigger guard but not on the trigger and lay there listening. Nothing.

As quietly as possible, I slid out of bed and got behind the half-opened bedroom door. I assumed a low crouching position on one knee in order to be a smaller target. I waited in the dark, listening, and still there was nothing.

I felt the carpet beneath my bare feet. The air was cool on my naked body.

Maybe my imagination was running in overdrive. The only lights in the room were the soft glow of the illuminated light switch on the wall by the bedroom door and the dull red numbers of my digital clock. The light switch registered in my peripheral vision while I concentrated on listening. There was no sound.

Suddenly, a silent black shadow passed between me and the light switch and stopped just inside the bedroom. A cat burglar couldn't move that quietly. I never heard the slightest sound of this guy moving. I was sure I hadn't invited anyone to drop in for a beer.

I have never fired my weapon in my home. I don't need that kind of problem, nor do I want that kind of attention. But this guy didn't come to sell me an encyclopedia.

He was half a head shorter than me. Asian? Middle Eastern? Apparently, he had night vision goggles because he almost immediately realized I wasn't in my bed and he couldn't find me in the room. So, he must have reasoned I had to be behind him because he suddenly whirled, and I heard a knife whistle above my head.

If I hadn't been crouching down, he would have cut me across my chest, and I would be lying on the floor in my blood. I shot upward and forward with my fist, aiming for what I hoped was his throat. I hit him, but he had some kind of slippery fabric on his neck, and my fist slid off to one side. I heard him gag, but my hit wasn't as square or as hard as I wanted it to be. If I had hit him square in the throat, he would have drowned in his own blood from a crushed larynx. The knife fell onto the carpeted floor with a thud.

He tried to bring his arms up in a defensive posture, but I was already inside his defense perimeter. I grabbed one of his hands and forced his thumb back until he was kneeling on the floor, trying not to scream through his damaged throat. Then I reached out and hit the light switch, turning on the overhead lights. Because he was wearing night vision goggles, the sudden glare of lights caused him to give a hoarse scream from the pain of the amplified light in his eyes.

I put my full 190 pounds into the knee that scrunched into his spine and pinned him to the floor. The Browning was pressed hard against the back of his head.

"You move and you die," I whispered. I was really pissed off. There might be more than one attacker. This guy had to be immobilized without killing him. I wanted some answers from him.

I pressed the brachial plexus on his neck, causing temporary unconsciousness. I left him blacked out on the floor and started turning on lights, hoping to blind anyone else who might be with him wearing night vision goggles.

No one else was there. The back door had been opened by a pro— no damage, just unlocked. This character had just disarmed a highly sophisticated alarm system without triggering it.

I relocked the door. Just the two of us were in the house. If anyone had been outside, he or she was probably gone by now.

I went back to the bedroom. My attacker was still on the floor, just beginning to regain consciousness. He was dressed from head to toe in a tight-fitting black jumpsuit, including a face mask that had holes for his eyes and mouth. The suit was made of a thin black knit fabric with a slippery surface. He was a sneaky-looking, skinny bastard.

I intended to tie him up by cutting strips of cloth from his jumpsuit. I picked up his knife; it was a Fairbairn-Sykes commando knife, razor sharp and deadly. This was a professional's tool.

Using his knife, I slit his black suit up the back, intending to get a few strips of cloth.

Whoa! The back strap of a bra came into view. *Is this guy a cross-dresser, or is my attacker a woman?* I thought.

I rolled him over, and sure enough, he had boobs–pretty nice ones, too. He was a she.

Change of plans. I cut the sleeves free from the rest of her outfit and used them to tie her hands behind her back and bind her ankles together. By the time I was done, she was fully conscious again.

The mask over her head was twisted out of position, and I could see she was having trouble breathing, so I pulled her to a sitting position on the floor. I cut the mask around the neck of her suit and took it off her. She was striking—until the fury in her gray-blue eyes shattered the effect. Her soft, short, dark curly hair, almost black, was all messed up.

Our eyes locked together and held for a long instant. I felt a sudden surge of adrenaline course through me. We kept staring into each other's eyes. It felt like forever before I finally broke away. Just looking at her left me strangely shaken. It was a sensation I had never felt before. Who was this woman?

"What is your name, and why are you trying to kill me?" I asked.

Her response was to spit at me, leaving a wet spot on my chest. I looked down then past the spot.

I saw I had a full erection.

It suddenly dawned on me that I was naked. I grabbed a pair of pants off the chair and got semi-decent. I uncocked the hammer and stuck the Browning in the back of the waistband. The steel felt cold against my bare ass. "You didn't answer my question. What is your name, and why are you trying to kill me?"

No answer. Just that angry glare. I wondered whether she understood English. Even though I had come through this thing okay, I was still pissed off. I grabbed the front of her jumpsuit and hauled her up until she was sitting on the edge of the bed.

Pulling her up caused the left shoulder of her suit to tear, exposing the left side of her bra. Her bosom was better than just pretty nice. Her bra was made of sheer material, and her left nipple showed through the fabric. I've seen breasts and nipples before, but this one was having a strange effect on me. Having her hands tied behind her back pulled her shoulders back and forced her chest to project forward. This woman had exciting boobs.

"Have it your way. Let's see if my friends at the farm can get some answers from you."

"No," she whispered, "don't call them. They will shoot me full of chemicals." Ah, so she spoke English, but with a slight accent.

"Then tell me your name and why you are here. Then, I will decide what to do with you."

She said, "My name is Laura. I came to kill you."

"Who do you work for, Laura?"

"I work for no one. I am on my own."

"You have too many skills, and your equipment is too professional for a freelancer. Now tell me who you work for."

"Go to hell."

"You are stuck with me right now. I can make a call, and the experts will wring you dry. Now tell me who you work for."

"I used to work for Mossad until I quit."

"Why did you quit?" I asked. I glanced at her lovely breast and the darker nipple, then looked back at her.

"So I could kill you," she stated.

"You aren't making sense. I have done a few operations with Mossad, and we are on the same side. Why do you want to kill me?"

"Eight months ago, you were in Ma'arib. You killed five men who were working on a plot to blow up some British Airways flights flying out of Dubai. One of those men, a deep-cover Mossad agent, was my twin brother Zvi. He was posing as a Palestinian and was tasked with getting to the head man of al-Qaeda in the Arabian Peninsula. You blundered in and killed them all by detonating their own explosives. For that, you will die," she said with a tone of finality.

I was taken aback. "Wait a minute. This is the first I've heard that one of those men was Mossad. I wouldn't have been sent there if we had known. We don't clear our operations with Mossad any more than they tell us what they are doing. I was one of several agents who were all given the same assignment as your brother by the agency. I was supposed to get to the head man of A-Cap and eliminate him. If I couldn't get to him, I was supposed to disrupt their operations. Disrupting operations was all that I could accomplish."

She didn't seem to be mollified by my words.

I continued, "And why was your brother teaching them how to make bombs? They were planning to blow up four airliners and everyone on board."

Laura looked at me as if I were an idiot. "Those four were never going to get out of there alive. They were going to have a terrible accident that killed them all while they were showing the head of al-Qaeda what they were planning to do. The idea was to kill al-Nasirah and any of his lieutenants who were with him. The bombers were the excuse to get the leader to show his face."

I gradually became aware that my erection was still pressing against the front of my pants. This woman was having a weird effect on me.

"I have another question," I said. "How did you find me?"

She looked away. "It wasn't easy. First, I had to find out who set off the explosives. One of our other undercover people in Yemen was sure it was you. Then I had to find out where you live. That was really difficult. It meant hacking into a very secure computer at your headquarters. Once I was in the computer, I read your after-action reports and confirmed that you were the one responsible. I then found your address. When I knew your address, I hacked into the Building Department computer to get the plans for your house so I would know the layout. And then I had to wait until you were home and feeling safe so I could get to you. I quit Mossad, and killing you became my reason for living." Laura's eyes focused on the front of my pants for a moment, then she looked away again.

"What did you do for Mossad, Laura?"

"What difference does it make?"

"I want to know so I can decide what to do with you."

"I was a programmer and hacker for five years, then I did several field assignments, and someone later brought me in to train new agents in field use of computers. When I was in the Israeli Defense Force, I taught weapons and Krav Maga, so I did some of that for Mossad too."

My thoughts were racing. *Krav Maga? IDF and Mossad's most successful unarmed combat systems? And this woman was an instructor?* I felt impressed with her experience and nodded my approval.

"What about languages?"

"I speak Hebrew," she said.

I knew that most Israelis spoke several languages. She was speaking to me in English. "What other languages do you speak?" I asked.

"I can speak Arabic with a Palestinian accent or with a Lebanese accent," she said. "I also speak Italian and Ladino." This last admission was given grudgingly.

I continued staring at her, my thoughts racing. *Ladino is an old Spanish patois spoken by the Sephardic Jews, sort of like the equivalent of Yiddish spoken by Eastern European Jews. If she's telling the truth, this woman probably has other abilities too.*

"Words of apology from me won't bring your brother back. But I am truly sorry for what happened. Neither will killing me bring him back. I still have my assignment to complete." Her boobs were staring at me, or was I staring at her boobs? I forced my eyes to meet hers. We locked eyes again. Damn! She had compelling eyes!

I continued talking while I thought about kissing her breasts. "I believe you still want to kill me, and as long as you are out there, you will keep trying. You have too many talents. Your presence is not good for my peace of mind." Those eyes!

"An idea has just occurred to me. I am going back to Yemen in a few weeks. Let me clear this with my boss, but the basic thought is that we go together. If you could find me when I don't want to be found by anyone, then maybe together we can find the head of A-Cap. The best revenge we can get for your brother is to complete his assignment. It was also my assignment. So, let's make it *our* assignment."

She didn't give me an answer. But neither did she tell me to shove my proposal.

I had a gut feeling that the confrontation between us had ended, at least for the moment. There was no logic involved, just my instincts. Besides, I had my gun and her knife.

"You said you were an instructor in Krav Maga. I know your bare hands are a deadly weapon. I'm going to untie you, and I don't want you to try to kill me when I do. Agreed?"

She nodded her agreement, and I believed her. Using her knife, I reached behind her to cut the cloth holding her hands. She leaned into me to allow me to reach her hands. She smelled really good. Not a perfume smell, just a clean human animal smell. Her shoulder brushed against the bulge in my pants. That did nothing to make the bulge disappear.

When her hands were free, I rubbed her wrists to restore circulation. Touching her wrists felt good. I think my bulge got harder.

I knelt down to cut the cloth binding her ankles. "Don't kick me," I said. "I really am not your enemy."

After her ankles were free, I rubbed them to ease the pain I had caused her when I had tied the tight knots. Then I reached out and pulled the cloth up to cover her breast and tucked the end under her bra strap. I really didn't want to, but it was the gentlemanly thing to do, so I did it.

"What's your full name, Laura?" I asked.

"Halevi. Laura Halevi," she answered.

"Assuming I can get approval, are we partners on this assignment? I did not hear you agree to the deal."

"Let me think about it. I'll let you know in a couple of days."

Maybe was better than a *no*.

Then she pointed at the front of my pants and said, "But you'll have to keep that thing to yourself."

I swear I must have blushed.

3

PARTNERS

Langley, Virginia
Friday, 3 April

It had been three days since Laura invaded my life. Before she left my house that night, I entered her Israeli phone number in my cell phone directory. She already knew my cell phone number from hacking into the Langley computer. If we were going to be doing an operation together, we had to be able to communicate.

In my business, there is considerable leeway for independent action when I am out in the field. Forming working alliances with foreign agents when I am not on an active assignment is not something I can do without approval from a honcho higher up the food chain.

Since you have been in my bedroom when I was naked, allow me to introduce myself properly.

My name is Jack Miller. Jack is my real name; Miller is not. I chose Miller because it is one of the most common occupational-based names in the world and is the name I use most often. Every Western nation and religion has people named Miller. Using a false name protects my parents and me. I haven't used my real family name in so long that I would not respond if someone called me that name out loud.

I work for the CIA in a special group that fixes things, usually with extreme prejudice. Lately, almost everything I do involves some Middle Eastern radicals who shout, 'Death to America.'"

I am 38 years old, and I have never been married. I am 5'-11", 190 lbs., and very, very fit. My hair and eyes are brown. My face is so ordinary that no one seems to remember me. If I entered a crowded room and then left after half an hour, no one would notice that I came in, hung around, or exited.

I am of average height and appear to be of average weight. I am in many ways essentially invisible. Despite my invisibility, I have a few scars from a time when a bullet found me and when knives cut me.

I am a deadly shot with a pistol or sniper rifle. If I decide I want you dead, there is a 98% chance that you will die of unnatural causes emanating from me.

I am fluent in Spanish and Arabic, know a few regional accents, and have a working familiarity with French. I also have a smattering of German and Japanese.

I majored in computer science at Cornell University School of Engineering. Naval ROTC got me into military service, and when I graduated, I elected to join the Marine Corps. I went in as a green Second Lieutenant. Desert Storm came along, and by the time it was over, I was a Captain.

My ability to pick up local languages attracted the interest of the CIA, and my combat recon experience was also helpful. Then, while I was in the agency, I received a promotion to Major in the Marine Corps Reserves.

My IQ is somewhere above 175. I have no religious affiliation. My mother is a non-practicing Jew; my father is a lapsed Catholic. Over the years, I have studied all the world's major religions and rejected them all, although the emphasis on kindness in Buddhism has some merit. I think religion causes more trouble than any other human invention. I believe that if you go through life without stepping on the other guy's toes, then we'll all get along just fine. Essentially, I have lived a a lucky life, and as long as I continue to think outside the box and carefully plan ahead, I expect my luck and life to continue.

In the three days since Laura had gotten into my house, hopefully, she had time to recover from our encounter. I couldn't seem to get her out of my head, so maybe you could say that I haven't recovered from the encounter.

Yesterday, I called Laura for her answer regarding our working together to chase down the head of al-Qaeda in the Arabian Peninsula. She agreed to the deal if our bosses also agreed.

So today I had an appointment to see Herb Watson at his Langley office. Herbert Watson III (code-named *Beartrap*) is my boss. He's about 53 years old, a third-generation Yalie and third-generation Skull and Bones. He also holds an MBA from Harvard and a law degree from Yale. He is an old-line WASP, an uncompromising patriot, and also a hard-nosed prick. With his perfect WASP profile, pale blue eyes, and skin that never sees the sun, he would look perfectly natural wearing spats and an ascot tie at a sailing regatta. Does patrician ring a bell?

The first Herbert Watson, Herb's grandfather, was a colonel commanding a cavalry regiment in World War I. He stayed in the army after the war. Herb's father served in the OSS (Office of Strategic Services) during the Second World War, hunting Nazis. After the war, he kept at it, and when the CIA was formed, he was invited to join—only now, the targets were communists. Herb now works for the agency, and he feels like he is in the family business. Herb cannot make small talk and is always bored at cocktail parties. Abruptness bordering on rudeness comes naturally to Herb.

We get along together just fine because we respect each other for what each of us can do. I don't think he has a warm feeling or a sympathetic synapse anywhere in his body. Herb has only two redeeming features. The first is that he is coldly analytical. His brain could double as the central processor in a Cray supercomputer. The second redeeming feature is that he will move the entire U.S. government to support his people when they are in the field. That second redeeming feature is enough for him to earn my loyalty.

I was making my pitch to Herb, explaining why I wanted Laura Halevi to join me on my next mission to Sandland.

"Herb, this woman is a very resourceful agent. To get to me, she managed to ID me as the guy who blew up the Ma'arib bomb school. Then she hacked into our mainframe here at headquarters to get my home address. At my house, she bypassed one of our best security systems without setting anything off. She can pass for an Arab and speaks Arabic like a Palestinian. I had her on the range this morning, and she is a crack shot with a pistol or a rifle. She is motivated to get this job done. She has a warrior mentality. The fact that she was going to use a knife on me says she isn't afraid to get up close and personal. She said she had field experience with Mossad. If she checks out with them, I want her with me on this mission."

Herb gave me one of his why are you bothering me with this stupidity looks, but he didn't say no.

"I'll talk to our friends at Mossad and see what they have to say about her. If she is approved for this operation, she must be on their payroll, and the agency and Mossad must provide joint support. I am not letting some Israeli rogue operate under our flag. If this thing blows up on us, she must be their responsibility. I'll check her out. That is all I will promise."

I got up to leave when Herb said, "Oh, and one more thing. I want her to show us how she hacked into our mainframe so we can block anyone else from doing it the same way."

"Fair enough," I said. "That is all I am asking for right now." I left the office before Herb changed his mind.

4

JACK GETS A ROOMMATE

Washington, D.C.
Friday afternoon, 3 April

I called Laura on her Israeli cell phone and planned to meet her later that afternoon at a café in Dupont Circle. I arrived first.

While I was waiting, I realized I wanted Laura near me a lot. A scheme began forming in my devious mind. Would she go for it?

When Laura arrived, I admired the easy, athletic grace with which she walked. She was wearing a pale-yellow sleeveless blouse and navy slacks.

Laura has a beautiful face and an outstanding body. My eyes kept moving from her face to her breasts and back again. I could see the faint outline of her nipples poking through the thin fabric of her blouse. I hope I wasn't too obvious.

There were beige lace-up, low sneakers on her feet. Her tan arms were muscular. The slacks were smooth against a very shapely ass.

I realized she didn't wear makeup or nail polish, and in fact, she didn't need any.

Her short dark hair was curly. There seemed to be an internal glow to this woman, or maybe I was just imagining it.

We shook hands when we met. Laura's hands are very strong. These were working hands, capable, smooth, yet hard and deadly.

Over coffee, our conversation was relaxed and easy. I told her Herb's conditions and what he planned to do. She wasn't sure the top people at Mossad would let her back in, but they might do it for a joint American-Israeli operation. Yitzhak Nahum, the Chief of Mossad, had once been a mentor to Laura and her brother when they were both new agents, and he himself was still a field officer. As her boss, he had strongly opposed her resignation after Zvi's death. He didn't know what her plan was or why she was leaving, but he was certain it was for all the wrong reasons, and he made that clear in no uncertain terms. But he could not force her to stay when she was so determined to leave.

"Do you really think they will approve a joint operation?" she asked cautiously.

"There have been joint ops in the past, and this one is a top priority. I think we have a better than even chance that we'll get the green light," I said.

I took a sip of my coffee. I decided that now was the time to pitch my idea to Laura. "Laura, I have your cell phone number, but every time I contact you, it's an international call to Israel. Where are you staying in this area? You can't be at the Israeli embassy because you aren't on official business. So, you must be staying at a hotel."

"I am at the Holiday Inn in Arlington."

"Staying at a hotel must be straining your finances. I am going to suggest something, and I want you to consider it before immediately refusing my offer. I have two extra bedrooms in my house. One of them is a guest bedroom and has its own attached bathroom. I use the other as a home gym. You can stay with me until we get the go-ahead for the mission or, if they turn us down, until you return home to Israel. I promise to behave like a gentleman. Think about it."

"Jack, it is kind of you to offer. I think you will keep your promise, but this arrangement would not be proper."

"Proper for who? My neighbors hardly know me. No one at Langley cares. You must be spending $200 a day where you are. You are probably renting a car for an additional $75 per day. Who knows how long you will have to stay there until the powers-that-be decide for us. You could be in a deep financial hole before that happens. Accept my offer in the spirit in which it is given and move into my house. It makes sense."

Laura smiled. "OK, Jack, I can't fight against the logic of your argument. I don't know how much longer I can afford the hotel anyway. I accept. Should we do it today?"

"Absolutely. Let's go get you checked out now and return your rental if you have one. We'll need to pick up some groceries because I seldom have much in the house. You'll have to help me with the shopping."

"Done," she said. "Let's go."

*   *   *

We found an Avis office in D.C., returned her rental car, and then we drove to Arlington and checked her out of the Holiday Inn. At my house, Laura's things were stashed in the guest bedroom.

"Do you have a washer and dryer here? I travel light, and I haven't much in the way of clean clothes left," said Laura.

"There is a large closet off the kitchen that has the laundry equipment. I'll show you where it is. I have an iron, but I don't know if it works because I've never used it."

"All men are hopeless," she said, and laughed as she headed for her bedroom to get her dirty laundry.

Ten minutes later, the washing machine was working, and she came and sat on the couch with me, but not too close. My eyes kept wandering back to her breasts and her nipples poking out of the yellow blouse, and my thoughts were very ungentlemanly. But I had made a promise to behave. I wasn't about to do anything to upset her.

We discussed what we would make for dinner and who would do what. It really worked out that I would set the table, make the salad, and then get out of her way. I can completely disassemble and reassemble a V-8 engine, and it will work when I am done, but do not let me in a kitchen. For anything more complicated than scrambled eggs, I am a total klutz.

Soon, the washing machine beeped to indicate that it was done, and Laura went to put her clothes in the dryer. Delicates, like her underwear and some tops, were hung on a drying rack to air dry. It was a very domestic setting, an unusual feeling for me, but I liked it.

We left the house and spent the next hour shopping for food. Laura picked out the food, I pushed the supermarket cart and did the grunt work. I managed to drive the cart without deploying the airbags.

Back at my house, we put things in the fridge together.

Later, dinner was simple: spaghetti, meatballs, salad, Italian bread, and coffee. The spaghetti sauce Laura whipped up was superb. We opened a bottle of red wine and continued sipping in the den after I put the dishes and pots in the dishwasher. Hey, she did the cooking, and I enjoyed the meal. The least I could do was take care of the cleanup.

We sat on the couch. Neither of us wanted the noise of the TV. She was reading a paperback novel in Hebrew. I was doing the Washington Post daily crossword puzzle. Normally, I finish the puzzle quickly. Tonight, I was distracted by Laura sitting so near. I felt like a kid on a special date, and I didn't want to do anything to ruin it. I kept glancing over at her face and at her blouse, trying not to be too obvious.

She must have felt my eyes on her because she looked up at me and smiled.

I smiled back, and my guts did a flip-flop. She is special, almost beautiful. I don't know why, but the minutes seemed to both fly by and drag at the same time. I wanted to hold her in my arms and kiss her. But I had made that damn promise to behave like a gentleman. Shit!

At 10:30, Laura stood up and said, "I'll get my clean clothes from the dryer. Then I'm going to take a shower and get some sleep."

"If you need anything, just ask," I said. "There is a bathrobe in the closet that should fit you pretty well."

We both said goodnight, then Laura went into the kitchen and disappeared down the hall, carrying her clean laundry to her bedroom. I heard the bedroom door close. I sat there alone.

For the first time, I realized I was *very* alone, and it wasn't a good feeling. A bit later, I also went to bed, but I didn't sleep well at all.

5

HAKIM ABU-JIHADI

The southern hills of Saudi Arabia
Saturday, 4 April

A man with the *nom de guerre* of Hakim abu-Jihadi trudged up the almost invisible path toward the cave. *Why do we always pick caves that only goats can get to,* he wondered? The butt of the AK-47 on his shoulder was banging his right kidney with every step up the steep hill. The pockets of his Russian army vest were filled with loaded magazines for the rifle. The weight of the ammo added to his annoyance. His ankle-length *thawb* made it difficult to climb the hill. Hakim cursed under his breath as he climbed upward.

Hakim had a round face and a full, bushy black beard. His clothing was indistinguishable from that of any other mujahideen. He was slightly shorter than most Arab men, but he made up for his lack of height by being a fierce fighter who knew no fear. His ruthless ferocity, leadership, and dedication to Islam had elevated him to the position of chief lieutenant and adviser to Sheikh Abdel Karim Washim al-Nasirah, making him one of the most wanted men in the Arabian Peninsula.

Hakim had dark brown eyes. He claimed his eyes could see into men's hearts, and if your faith in Allah was lacking, he would not hesitate to kill you. Many whom he had found wanting in faith had died by his hand.

At 36 years of age, his body was as tough as twisted rope. His endurance was the envy of younger men. Even so, he was annoyed at having to climb the hill to the cave. *Our next camp has to be a cave lower down,* he thought.

Hakim had spent almost four years in Yemeni jails, and he had a slight limp as a reminder of the many beatings he had received from the guards in jail. He knew exactly which guards he would like to behead when al-Qaeda in the Arabian Peninsula finally rose to complete power in Yemen.

It was in the Yemeni prison that Hakim had met al-Nasirah. Al-Nasirah had masterminded the escape from the prison by digging a tunnel to a nearby mosque. Al-Nasirah, Hakim, and twenty others had escaped in that prison break. Many of those men were still with al-Nasirah in AQAP.

Looking upwards, Hakim spotted one sentry silhouetted against the night sky at the top of the hill. *The fool would get himself killed, and the rest of us, too. He is supposed to know better. Al-Nasirah will have his hide when I report him.*

Finally, he arrived at the cave entrance. Two thorny bushes and a boulder blocked the view of the opening. Hakim made two soft bleats like a goat. A guard hidden in the darkness of the cave opening, his rifle aimed at Hakim's chest, grunted.

Hakim gave the password, *"Subhan Allah"* (glory to God).

The guard responded, *"Allahu Akbar"* (God is great).

Hakim nodded at the guard, entered the cave, and walked directly toward the rear. A floor-to-ceiling black curtain was strung across the cave. Hakim passed behind it. Three meters further into the cave was another black curtain. Hakim passed through this curtain as well. The two curtains effectively blocked any light from escaping the cave. Now he could see a faint light further into the depths of the cave. Crates of ammunition and rockets were piled along one wall. *I am happy I didn't have to bring those up here. That was a job for donkeys,* he thought.

The cave floor sloped downwards and bent to the right. As Hakim progressed, the light grew brighter until he entered the main cavern. Twenty mujahideen were sitting in a rough circle around a pair of lanterns. Three more fighters were curled up asleep against the cave wall. The cave exhaled the sour stench of stale bodies pressed too close and rancid cooked food. Somewhere within the roof of the cave, there was an opening that let the smoke from the small cooking fire escape. The cooking fire was only lit after sundown so that the smoke could not be seen in the dark. Smoke during the daytime might reveal the location of the cave.

No cell phones were allowed to be turned on by the mujahideen. Any cell phone that was powered on could reveal the user's position to the NSA (National Security Agency), even if it wasn't in actual use. Radio traffic was kept to an absolute minimum, and coded phrases were always used to disguise the content being transmitted. This level of paranoia was clearly warranted because the cursed American NSA sucked up all electronic traffic from the area.

One fighter acknowledged Hakim, "He is waiting for you," and moved his head toward the back of the cave.

Hakim grunted and kept walking deeper into the cave. He passed a side cavern where six donkeys were stabled. Sharing the stable with the donkeys were four French university students—two men and two women—who had been abducted on the road between Karmis Mushait and Riyadh six days ago. They all wore iron leg shackles. Al-Nasirah was demanding a ransom of 400,000 euros from the French government for their release. Hakim had traveled a day away from the cave to make his telephone contact with the French ambassador in Riyadh. Now he was back to report.

Sheikh Abdel Karim Washim al-Nasirah, also known by the *nom de guerre* Abu-Basir, sat on the floor of the cave at a small writing table with folding legs. His long oval face ended in a pointed chin, covered with a black scraggly beard. His head was covered with a white Pakistani-style cap. He wore a black robe, over which was a vest filled with AK-47 magazines like Hakim's. He had sandals on his bare feet despite the cold of the hills. His gaze was intense, piercing, and commanding. Al-Nasirah was once a chief lieutenant and confidant of Osama bin Laden. Now he was the head of al-Qaeda in the Arabian Peninsula with a 10 million dollar price on his head. No one disobeyed his orders. Such insubordination could bring a flogging, and often, death would follow.

Al-Nasirah looked up as Hakim approached. "Will they pay?"

"The fools want to bargain. They will pay 100,000 euros for each man but will only pay 50,000 euros for each woman. The total is 300,000 euros."

The sheikh laughed. "They think we don't know that they value their women as much as their men. Just because our women mean so little to us, they think we will give them a discount on their women."

Al-Nasirah took a sip from a coffee cup at the edge of his writing table. "Go back and inform them that if they want a discount on the women, we will return them for 50,000 euros each, but without their fingers or toes. Otherwise, the price is 100,000 euros each, no discounts, no bargains."

Al-Nasirah took another sip from his coffee cup. "And you can tell them I am tired of feeding them and listening to their complaints. If we don't have the money by next week, then the price goes up to 150,000 euros each. In two weeks, I will give the women to my mujahideen for sport, and then we will behead all four of them as spies."

Hakim smiled inwardly at the discomfort the ambassador would have to endure. "Tomorrow I will go out again, and I will return in two days. We will get paid the full price. The French always pay."

"Make sure they wire the money to our Cayman bank account. The bank will make the required transfers until the money gets to our Qatari account."

"It will be done," said Hakim. "Now I would like some food and a little rest. One more thing, sheikh, as I climbed the hill, the sentry on the hilltop was easily visible to me. He was at the crest of the ridge, outlined against the stars and moon. He could get us all killed."

"I will deal with him. Go with God," said the sheikh as Hakim left.

6

HERBERT WATSON III

Langley, VA
Saturday, 4 April

Herb Watson was in the office on Saturday, as was his usual habit. Some of his colleagues claimed the CIA was the only love in his life. There might be some truth in the comments. Herb had no wife, no children, no pets, no plants, almost no friends, male or female; no hobbies other than being a voracious reader; no sports team interests; and he didn't care what Yale, his alma mater, was doing against Harvard or Princeton. No one knew what he did when he wasn't at work. The simple truth was that Herb Watson was married to the CIA, and America's interests were his only interests. If it weren't for the need to eat, sleep, wash, and change his clothes, Herb Watson would be at his desk 24/7.

Herb and one junior assistant hold down the Arabian Peninsula desk. His responsibilities encompass all intelligence coming from Saudi Arabia, Yemen, Oman, the United Arab Emirates, Qatar, and Kuwait. Other officers, actually teams of officers, had the responsibility for the headaches of Iraq, Afghanistan, Iran, Syria, Egypt, the Palestinians, Libya, Jordan, Turkey, North Africa, and the other Islamic nations. The cooperation among the various officers at these various desks was excellent. There was very little empire-building going on, and as a result, the exchange of information was much better than the public or the press imagined. Not that no one was ever angling for a promotion or a higher pay grade. Career advancement efforts and ego stroking were constant undercurrents, but somehow, the primary job of the CIA—protecting America—got done.

One of the irrational expectations from the press, Congress, and, by extension, the American public, is that the CIA is supposed to be all-knowing about anything and everything America's enemies are planning. Every time we are outsmarted or an enemy pulls off a successful operation or manages to keep a secret, Congress punishes the agency by cutting its budget. Every new president decides how the agency will concentrate its efforts during their four- or eight-year administration, resulting in schizophrenic changes in direction every few years.

During the Cold War, the CIA had spies, informers, electronic surveillance, and clandestine military operations. They hid defectors, blackmailed our enemies for information, and generally behaved with an any-means-justifies-the-end mindset. Each new president sets down new rules and goals, attempting to shape the CIA according to their own personal code of conduct. Every scandal or screwup resulted in more restrictions on what the agency could do. Restrictions got piled upon restrictions until the agency was almost paralyzed.

It is not enough for the agency to analyze what our enemies are doing. We also demand that it know what our allies, informal friends, and non-aligned nations will do in any situation. In recent years, in collaboration with the National Security Agency, they have attempted to accomplish this task through electronic surveillance and with the smallest possible number of field personnel. The Congress, whenever there is no active fighting by American military personnel going on somewhere, always seems to force the CIA to scale back its operations since we are living in a "time of peace." As soon as trouble erupts that catches us by surprise, the Director of the CIA is called in for congressional hearings, at which time the poor bastard cannot answer the questions asked by the congressmen and senators because to do so would let our enemies know exactly how we gather our intelligence and who our sources are. Anything he says will be in the newspapers or on TV within 24 hours (or less). So, he sits there eating humble pie, and our know-it-all Congress then cuts the budget again. Why any rational person would want to be the head of the CIA is a matter of great wonderment.

Herb checked his watch; it was 8:10 AM. It would be 3:10 PM in Israel. Even though it was Saturday, Herb knew the Mossad director would be at his desk. He reached for his phone. "Get me Yitzhak Nahum in Tel Aviv."

Within a minute, his intercom beeped, and the secretary said, "Mr. Nahum on line 4."

Herb Watson picked up, "Hello, Yitzhak." The voice transmission, despite being encrypted and scrambled, was remarkably clear and distortion-free.

In almost perfect American English, Yitzhak said, "Hello, Herbert. It's been a while since we last spoke."

"It seems one of your agents has turned up in my backyard, Yitzhak. Laura Halevi came over here to kill one of my best men."

"Is he dead?" asked Nahum.

"No, he is quite alive. It seems my guy was responsible for the death of her twin brother Zvi. He blew up their bomb school in Yemen. She was looking for revenge."

"Ah, now I understand why she quit my service. Is Laura in any legal trouble with your people?

"No, she is still a free woman, and no one is interested in pressing charges. However, in a strange twist, Halevi and my man both decided to work together to take out al-Nasirah. I don't know enough about Halevi to trust her, so I don't want her operating out of my shop. However, if you're interested in taking her back into yours, we could conduct a joint operation. The agency will finance the entire op, but she will have to be on your payroll."

"When she resigned, she would not give me any reasons for leaving. I did not want her to go. I would need three people to replace her. Of course, I want her back. She was, or now she is again, one of our best people. Give me the details of what happened with your man."

Herb explained how Laura Halevi had hacked into the computer at headquarters, the early morning break-in, bypassing the alarm at Miller's home, and how Miller had survived the attack.

Nahum chuckled on his end of the line. "Your man is lucky to be alive. He must be a formidable agent. Halevi's bare hands are deadlier than most guns. Her computer skills often leave my best techs wondering how she does some of her tricks. Together, they just might bring down al-Nasirah. If you are willing to take the plunge, we'll go along too."

"Sounds good to me. I think I'll let them stew for a while before I let them know the operation is on. If they're going to work together, they had better get to know each other a little better."

"Herb, if they will be traveling in Muslim countries, they will have to go as brother and sister, or they will arouse major suspicions among the locals. Let me consider this operation for a few days and discuss it with my team. I'll get back to you next week."

"Okay, Yitzhak. Thank you for your cooperation. Maybe we'll finally get that son of a bitch. I'll expect to hear from you on Monday or Tuesday."

"Goodbye, Herb. Thanks for letting me know that Halevi is alive and well." Yitzhak Nahum in Tel Aviv looked at his phone, realizing he was speaking into a deadline.

Watson, as usual, had already hung up without saying goodbye.

7

LAURA THE TOURIST

Washington D.C.
Saturday, 4 April

On Saturday, Jack took me sightseeing in Washington. We left his house a little after 10 in the morning. We went to his favorite places first. What surprised me was the nature of those places.

The first stop was the National Archives, and the Rotunda of this building was inspiring. The polished marble columns, the soaring ceiling, the crowds, and the documents in their special cases filled with inert gases. We examined the original, signed parchments of the Declaration of Independence, the original Constitution of the United States, and the original Bill of Rights. One of the surviving copies of the Magna Carta was also on display. Jack stood there looking at these manuscripts with a look of reverence and respect on his face.

After a few moments of silence, Jack started speaking.

"These documents set America apart from every other nation on Earth. It is the ideas in here—and the belief of the people that these words are worth dying for—that have helped America endure.

"We aren't perfect. In fact, we are very imperfect. But we never stop trying to be a little better today than we were yesterday. Sometimes we take a step backward, but there are a hell of a lot more steps forward than backward.

"The way we have treated the Indians and people of color is a stain upon our nation. But we spilled the blood of a million Americans from both sides in the Civil War to set it partly right. And we are still at it, trying to set things right.

"We mistreated our immigrants—Irish, Italians, Poles, Catholics, Jews, Asians, Africans, Hispanics. All of them had to struggle to find the respectability of equality here. However, they eventually became an integral part of the American fabric and succeeded. Some are still deep in the struggle.

"The strange thing is that even the oppressed minorities so love the idea of America that when we are attacked, they are still willing to lay down their lives for the ideals America stands for.

"We are working toward the day when the only ethnic name that will really carry meaning is 'American'. We're almost there. Just some pockets of bigotry remain, but by and large, our younger generations are color blind. They don't care what a person's sex or religion is—or if they have any religion at all. Just live by the same rules as the rest of society.

"Few Americans leave here to become citizens of another country. They may live elsewhere for a few years, but they never lose their American identity.

"Their allegiance to these documents—to the flag we fly, to the memory of those who have sacrificed so much for the idea of liberty— somehow draws them back here by the blood in their veins and the beating of their hearts.

"The air is different here. The earth is different here. The people are different here. The reasons we work—and for which we reluctantly go to war—are different here. There are those who hate us because we are different. For over 200 years, we have been leading humanity toward a better place—spreading the concepts of personal liberty and the belief that governments exist to serve the people. It all began with these four documents.

"One more thought is important. These documents were created by people who spoke English. Looking back over recent history, were it not for the English-speaking peoples of the world—Great Britain, the United States, Canada, Australia, New Zealand, and the British colonies—we might all be speaking German, Japanese, or Russian today.

"I believe there is something in the English language, and in the English ideas of justice and fair play, that creates the fertile ground where liberty can sprout and thrive. I can't put my finger on exactly what it is, but the evidence of the last two hundred-plus years tells me it is surely there."

When Jack finished speaking, there was nothing I could say. I was awestruck.

A 14-year-old girl with brown skin was standing near us with her mother, father, and younger sister. She heard what Jack had said. She looked at him and asked, "Are you a teacher, mister?"

"No, young lady. I am just an American, like you. These pages suggest that we all have the opportunity to work, grow, and fulfill the potential within us. It will be up to you how you use the opportunity and how you overcome the obstacles you will face. The color of your skin and the fact that you are a woman suggest that there will be more obstacles for you than there were for me, but you can still overcome them. Treasure the freedom you have and never let anyone push you down so that they can say they are better than you. And work your butt off. Nothing worth having ever came easy."

The girl grinned, Jack grinned, and they exchanged that silly American high-five motion together. *Why do Americans always do that? It's strange,* Laura thought.

As we walked down the front stairs of the Archives building, it occurred to me that the warrior man I was with had a much deeper philosophical side than I had ever imagined. I was two steps behind him and took the opportunity to admire his cute behind.

"How are your feet holding up?" Jack asked over his shoulder.

"We have only been to one place. My feet are very fine at this moment."

"Good, because we have a nice walk to my next favorite place."

We headed west on Constitution Avenue. The weather was mild. I was wearing tan slacks, a light green Under Armour T-shirt, Nike running shoes, and carrying a light sweater. Jack had on gray chino slacks, a blue plaid short-sleeve shirt, and black leather sneakers. We looked like a pair of tourists.

As we headed west, we passed the back lawn of the White House. I was surprised at how small the building looked from a distance, considering the amount of power it exerts.

We continued west until we were at the end of the National Mall, where the Lincoln Memorial stood. We turned left, and as we stood before the massive memorial with its many steps, the statue of Abraham Lincoln seated in his marble chair stared out over the Mall.

Jack looked up, and as we climbed the steps, he began speaking. "It is odd that he sits on a chair that looks like a throne. He was the most humble man who ever held the office of president. He led the nation through its most turbulent times, preserving America as one nation, indivisible, despite a significant portion of the population wanting to dissolve the Union. If he had lived in the aftermath of the Civil War, the Reconstruction would have gone better, and the bitterness of the war would have been lessened. He would have led a kinder government. But his assassination caused the North to want to punish the South, and the Northern occupation was harsher than it had to be. The resentments of the South led to the Jim Crow laws and the segregation that, even today, continues to plague our nation.

"Some people in the South refer to the Civil War as the War of Northern Aggression. They conveniently forget that the war was started by Confederate forces attacking Fort Sumter in Charleston, South Carolina. I often wonder if the South hadn't made the first aggressive move, whether a compromise to avert the war might have been worked out. But there's no changing our history now."

Jack looked at the dedication inscribed on the wall behind the statue of Lincoln. "Lincoln had the gift of using the fewest words to say what he thought, and those thoughts have resonated through generations of Americans. His simple address at the Gettysburg cemetery is still as meaningful today as it was in 1863. Schoolchildren and adults still repeat and memorize his words, and they still stir us to great deeds. 'Government of the people, by the people, for the people.' Such a massive idea in so few words.

"This humble, homely man was one of the greatest men humanity has ever produced. We were lucky we had him and that he had the courage of his convictions when we needed him the most. Harry Truman was a humble and courageous man. Everyone since Truman has been just a politician who managed to get elected."

By now, we had reached the top of the stairs. We stood there together looking up at the mournful face of Abraham Lincoln. Crowds of visitors passed behind us, around us, in front of us, but Jack didn't notice any of them. Every hand seemed to hold a cell phone or a camera, taking pictures. Jack's attention was so focused it was almost trance-like, even holy.

Finally, Jack turned to me and said, "There are a few more places to visit. Look down there at the Capitol building at the end of the Mall. A few great men and women have served in the House and Senate there, plus many others who have proven to be a major embarrassment to the nation. I try never to waste time there. I suggest we return to the Vietnam Veterans Memorial. That memorial wall with all the names is very moving. Then the Korean War Memorial, and then we'll go to Arlington to the Marine Corps Memorial, and the Tomb of the Unknowns. The common theme in all these memorials was that America fought for a principle and not to claim territory. The only land we ever took was enough space to bury our dead. When the wars were over, we were happy to come home to America."

As we walked down the stairs, Jack held my hand so I wouldn't fall. There was no chance that I would fall, but the touch of his hand was exciting, and I wasn't about to make him let go. It seemed so natural to hold his hand.

We spent the rest of the day visiting the memorials, and Jack had a mini-lecture for each one of them. Not the standard type of lecture about the greatness of America, but thoughts focused on the sacrifices made by ordinary men and women in defense of liberty and freedom for people half a world away from home.

"As an Israeli, I get it," I said, "this hunger for liberty and freedom. We've fought for our survival against insane odds, and somehow, we've succeeded. Our society is more like America's than anywhere else, though we've got our own quirks, for sure."

Jack and Laura stopped at a row of food trucks, the smell of frying onions and grilled meats drifting through the air. Laura handed over a few bills for falafel and shawarma. "Lunch and dinner—street style," she said with a grin. "I would guess most of these trucks never actually move from their parking places. They're like restaurants on cinder blocks."

She took a bite, then lowered her voice. "You notice how many of these guys are Middle Eastern or North African Arabs? At least half of the trucks claim they are *halal*. Makes me wonder, is there some kind of slow, sneaky takeover of the street food scene? Maybe Congress should look into it—though knowing them, they're too busy doing absolutely nothing useful."

After we ate standing in the street, we drove back to Jack's house in Silver Spring. I reflected on the day. Jack's passion for America was certainly evident. He behaved like a perfect gentleman, and yet every time we touched by intent or accident, a tingle went through me. I was happy just being with him. I kept wondering what he was feeling, but I was too afraid to ask, fearing what the answer might be.

Later that evening, we watched the late news on TV. Why is the news almost all bad news except for the sports and weather?

At 11:30, I stood up from the couch. "Jack, I had a wonderful day. Thank you for showing me the parts of Washington that you like the best. I know there is so much more. Maybe we will have another day to visit some museums."

"Laura, I enjoyed spending today with you, too. It has been one of the very best days I can ever recall. Thank you," Jack replied as he reached out and lightly touched my hand.

"Goodnight, Jack. Thank you again." I turned and walked to my room.

My emotions were all fluttering from one feeling to another. He was certainly sticking to his promise to behave like a gentleman. But I had to admit to myself that wasn't what I wanted. I came here intending to kill this man. That first night, I was amazed when he untied me. He decided he *trusted* me even though I had invaded his home to kill him. His kindness and sincerity were changing my views. He was a warrior, but he was one of the good guys. I believe that at this point, I would fight to the death in his defense. What a strange turn of events.

And it didn't hurt that he was attractive. Nothing really special about him, just a nice-looking guy that you knew you could depend on. Being near him seemed to flip all my switches to "on."

8

STUART J. KEATON

U.S. Embassy
Riyadh, Saudi Arabia
Monday, 6 April

Stuart James Keaton—who carries the unwieldy title of Ambassador Extraordinary and Plenipotentiary—is an early riser. By 6 AM every day, he is usually at his desk, having done his exercises and eaten his ascetic breakfast. Keaton can function effectively on only four or five hours of sleep a night.

Keaton is a disciplined, meticulous man in his mid-50s. He is a successful multi-millionaire oilman, originally from Oklahoma, who is fluent in Arabic, having spent 17 years in the Middle East. His obvious intelligence shines through in everything he does, impressing everyone he meets.

At 6'-2" tall, he is ruggedly handsome with deep brown eyes that seem to look into the heart of whoever he is speaking to. His dirty blond hair is just beginning to gray at the temples. His body is just as vigorous today as it was when he worked in the oil fields after college.

Most people would expect an oilfield millionaire to be rough around the edges, but Keaton carried himself with a modest, almost regal bearing. He treats everyone with respect—Saudi princes, career diplomats, embassy staff, journalists, politicians, waiters, chauffeurs, chambermaids. Respect given, respect returned.

In Riyadh, they call him a man of inner strength. In Washington, they call him the right man for a delicate job. And in both places, they are right.

This morning in Riyadh dawned as all Saudi mornings do, with the overnight chill quickly turning to a broiling, glaring day that will tax a person's endurance and a sun glare that will blast a person's eyeballs to jelly.

Saudi Arabia is an absolute monarchy ruled by an extended royal family. The King owns everything and everyone within his kingdom. Islam of the Sunni Wahhabi sect is the only faith, and Sharia is the only law. Twenty-eight million people reside in Saudi Arabia, comprising twenty million Saudi citizens and eight million foreign workers. The eight million visitors are exploited and do all the work, and when their visas are up, they must leave the Sharia paradise that exists within the kingdom.

The desert is an abiding presence everywhere in Saudi-land. Saudi Arabia has the second-largest land area of all Islamic countries, and almost all of that land area is desert. Within its borders are the cities of Mecca and Medina, the two holiest cities in Islam. Every Muslim man and woman is required by the Koran to make a pilgrimage to Mecca at least once in their lifetime. If a Muslim has fulfilled his duty and visited the holy mosque of Al-Masjid al-Haram in Mecca, he can then add the word *hajj* to his name.

Underneath all that Saudi sand lies the world's largest known oil reserves—and it all belongs to the King. Fortunately for Saudi citizens, the ruling House of Saud has wisely decided to share a portion of its enormous wealth with the ordinary folks who comprise the 20 million native Saudis. It is an easy way to prevent a revolution.

Behind the U.S., China, and Russia, Saudi Arabia has the fourth-largest annual military expenditures in the world. Almost all of the vast store of military hardware comes from the USA, which makes Saudi

Arabia one of America's most valued customers. Decision-makers take great pains to keep the relationship with the House of Saud amicable and congenial. Keeping the waters unruffled and the King's demeanor serene is the primary job of Stuart J. Keaton, Ambassador Extraordinary and Plenipotentiary of the United States of America to the Kingdom of Saudi Arabia.

Behind the facade of serenity, the Wahabi branch of Islam is training hundreds of thousands of young Islamic minds all over the world, in Saudi-financed *madrassas*, to hate the West and to follow Islam heart and soul, and if necessary, to throw in their bodies for martyrdom. Paradise awaits true believers.

Keaton's wife, Adelle, and his daughter, Susannah, are both late risers by his measure, usually appearing ready for their day's activity by 7 AM. Adelle was once a fourth runner-up to Miss Oklahoma in the Miss America Pageant. It seems she told one of the local judges, who had grabby hands, to shove his dick up his ass, so she never made it to the big time in Atlantic City. Now in her 50s, she remains a beautiful, intelligent, educated, athletic, cultured woman, a gifted musician, and not at all full of herself.

She and Stu Keaton met at a party at the University of Oklahoma in Norman. Stu pursued and wooed her nonstop until she finally agreed to be his steady date. Thirty years later, she never regretted becoming Mrs. Keaton. At 5'-10", with natural blonde hair, gorgeous blue eyes, a beautiful face, and a knockout body, she could stop all conversations just by entering a room. Except in Saudi Arabia, she makes it a point to cover up her natural beauty because of local customs. Loose-fitting garments and flat-heeled shoes are her usual attire. When she goes out, she adds a headscarf in deference to Muslim custom.

Andrew, the Keaton's firstborn, is 24 years old, a lieutenant in the U.S. Navy aboard an Arleigh Burke-class guided missile destroyer in the Persian Gulf. An Annapolis graduate, he excelled in electronic engineering while also earning varsity letters in football and lacrosse. He, too, has inherited the best genes from both parents. He could have been a poster boy for Naval recruiting. 'Drew' Keaton looks so terrific in his uniform that it is almost as if his body had been designed by nature for the U. S. Navy. Girls chase him wherever he goes, but so far, he has remained free of their clutches and uncommitted.

Drew Keaton has it all going for him: good looks, an exceptional mind, and natural athletic ability. Other officers mark him as a comer and as a friend. The men he commands respect him not only as an officer, but as a man; they trust his decisions and know he will treat them fairly.

Susannah Jean Keaton, the Keatons' second child, was a late baby. She is 11 years old. Suzy is full of life and destined to be as beautiful as her mother. She has inherited the blonde hair, high cheekbones, perfect features, intelligence, and grace, as well as the luminous blue eyes. She attends the American International School, and several young boys in her class are already in love with her. Susanna is tall for her age and already taller than all the boys in her age group. She is also one of the best soccer players, boy or girl, in her school. Unfortunately, in Saudi Arabia, when she is not on the school grounds, girls cannot compete in athletic competitions as masculine as soccer. So, she is forced to settle for beating all comers at tennis.

Riyadh is 7 hours ahead of Washington, D.C. When normal people ended their day, Ambassador Keaton would still be on the telephone to Washington or attending endless meetings via electronically scrambled teleconference. The government's insatiable need to get everyone on the same page is a major time waster for Stu Keaton. Every minor event requires a policy review and re-emphasis of where the U.S. stands on issues of importance—and every issue is *really important* to some Washington paper pusher.

Saudi Arabia is supposed to be a steadfast ally of America. The U.S. government clings to this fiction as if it were written in stone, refusing to recognize the obvious truth that Saudi Arabia's only ally is Saudi Arabia. The fiction has been convenient for both sides since the end of World War II and will continue into the foreseeable future.

Mondays are always extra busy for the ambassador. All the urgent events that occurred over the previous Saturday and Sunday, while the Washington bureaucrats were enjoying their weekend, now need to be addressed *immediately.*

Street riots in Egypt, ISIS gains in Syria, Syrian refugees in Turkey and Europe, terrorists in Libya, independence minded Kurds, AQAP in Yemen, nuclear saber rattling in Iran, suicide bombers in Iraq, corruption in Afghanistan, temper tantrums by the King of Saudi Arabia, all need to have the attention of the ambassador and he and the CIA Head of Station have to report the latest intelligence that has been gathered over the weekend.

Mike "Mickey" Henderson is the CIA Head of Station in Saudi Arabia. Mickey Henderson is a big man with a big intellect. Henderson is an ex-Marine major who had been recruited by the CIA while he was serving in Afghanistan. He still wears his hair in a high and tight Marine cut. Before joining the Marines, he had once been an amateur heavyweight boxer. He took a couple of severe beatings in the ring and decided that he had better stick to *Scrabble.* His nose never quite looked right after he quit boxing, so he had reconstructive surgery. Still, it would be foolish, bordering on suicidal, to mess with Mickey in a barroom brawl. Mickey Henderson's formal title is Cultural Attaché, but all of Saudi Arabia knows what his real job is. His cover is almost a joke among Saudi government people.

Mickey dropped into the chair opposite Stu Keaton's desk, six sheets of double-spaced computer printouts in his hand. Three contained top-secret intelligence bound for Langley and the president. The other three held Mickey's modified version—crafted for those trusted to keep their mouths shut, but who never could.

Information and intelligence that was supposed to be kept secret was regularly leaked to the press by congressmen and senators who couldn't hold a confidence if their lives depended upon it, and by Cabinet members trying to augment the public's perception of their importance to the administration. Langley first looked at the intelligence and then decided what it could live with if the intelligence were leaked.

Occasionally, Langley would slip in a piece of disinformation that it wanted the various Islamic enemies of America to believe. Trying to keep it all straight in his head was a daunting task. Mickey sometimes felt as if he were juggling twenty razor-sharp butcher knives in a room with mirrored walls, while blinding strobe lights flashed in a random pattern. He thrived on the tension and the stress of his job and wouldn't change it for any other in the world.

Keaton and Henderson made a good team. There was complete cooperation, totally devoid of rivalry. Each man understood the other man's duties, priorities, and imperatives. They worked almost seamlessly together, neither man seeking any petty advantage over the other, with only the best interests of the United States as their goal.

"Let me have the straight poop first," Keaton said.

Mickey slid the top three pages across the desk. Keaton already knew most of it; his eyes skimmed the lines, confirming what he'd suspected.

When he was done, he looked up at Mickey. "ISIS is pounding the hell out of everyone in Syria. Our airstrikes aren't making a dent."

"Air power alone almost never wins a war," Henderson replied. "You need boots on the ground to turn the tide. And since we're not sending ground troops, I don't see us getting the results we want. Honestly, I'd let them fight until they're too exhausted to pick up a rifle. If it were up to me, I'd keep both sides supplied just enough to keep killing each other for the next twenty years."

Keaton's mouth tightened. "As long as civilians are dying—and as long as dead babies make the front page—we'll keep trying to stop it. Assad's troops and ISIS can slaughter each other for eternity, but they both use civilians as shields. Now the Russians are sending in advisers. There are no good guys left, only bad ones. But if we kill civilians while hitting the bad guys, the people sitting safely at home are the first to call us baby-killers."

Keaton shook his head in disgust. "They hide fighters and weapons in schools, mosques, hospitals, ruins, daycare centers, U.N. camps—then scream 'war crimes' when we blow the bastards to hell."

"That's the price for sticking to a moral code no one else seems to follow," Mickey said. "And we let reporters embed with our troops. Half of them are just hunting for that 'Gotcha!' moment so they can grab a Pulitzer."

Keaton tapped his pen against the top sheet of paper. "The civilians getting killed aren't always innocent—or even neutral. The very people we're trying to protect can turn on us in a heartbeat, assuming they haven't already decided we should be wiped out and damned to hell.

"Sooner or later," said Keaton, "we'll have to face the fact that Islam is on the warpath, and stopping it will take an all-out fight. It will be a guerrilla war, with fighters vanishing into civilian crowds and civilians becoming fighters in minutes. And the peaceful Muslims? Indistinguishable from the fanatics. The battles will be fought in the worst places imaginable, by small units, and it will drag on for decades."

"It's already been going on since 9/11," Mickey said. "There's no end in sight. Osama wanted a war with the West, and he got it. There will be no easy end, no formal peace treaty, no peace as we've known it—not in our lifetimes. We'll be fighting fanatics forever. Any crackpot ayatollah can restart it with a single *fatwah*. The one thing we can't let happen is them getting nuclear weapons. These people," he said, shaking his head, "are like the scorpion riding on the frog's back."

Keaton smiled. "I'm guessing there's a fable in there somewhere. Let's hear it."

"Of course, there is," grinned Mickey. "One day, a scorpion came to a wide stream that he wanted to cross. A frog was sitting on the bank, sunning himself. 'Take me across the stream on your back,' said the scorpion to the frog. The frog replied, 'If I let you on my back, you will sting me and I will die.' 'Do I look stupid?' said the scorpion. 'If you die, then I will drown and I will be dead too.' The frog thought that this argument was logical, and he would be safe. So, he let the scorpion climb on his back and started to swim across the wide stream. Halfway over, the scorpion stung the frog. The frog looked up at the scorpion and said, 'You fool! Now we will both die. I will die from your poison, and you will drown and die in the stream. Why did you sting me?' 'Because,' said the scorpion, 'it is what I do.'"

Mickey looked at Stu Keaton. "These jihadists are like the scorpion. They will kill everyone, even if they die in the process. They are already programmed to die from childhood. Like the frog, our job is to avoid trusting them. If these loonies ever get nukes, the fact that they know we would surely blow them away does not stop them from using the nukes to kill us. Killing is what they do."

"I agree with you there," said Keaton. "Sometimes I think our Saudi friends are scorpions pretending to be frogs." Keaton motioned toward the intelligence papers that were on his desk and those still held by Henderson. "We had better get these on their way. It is surely going to be a long day today."

9

HAKIM ABU-JIHADI

Najran, Saudi Arabia
Tuesday, 7 April

Hakim pulled his pickup truck to a stop in a parking spot on King Abdulaziz Road. He was in the city of Najran, a four-hour journey from the cave in the desert hills. Hakim opened the back of his old mobile flip phone and inserted a new SIM card, effectively giving him an untraceable phone. Then he inserted the battery, turned it on, and as soon as it booted up, he dialed the French embassy in Riyadh.

A male operator, probably a French soldier, answered. Hakim knew that the embassy's operators were all bilingual in French and Arabic. Hakim spoke clearly and slowly in Arabic. "Tell the ambassador that I will call back in exactly 25 minutes regarding the four students. 25 minutes." Before the operator could answer, Hakim cut off the call and shut down his cell phone.

He opened the back of the phone, removed the battery, and extracted the SIM chip from beneath the battery case. He threw the chip out of the driver's window into the dirt. It would take the NSA more than the ten seconds the call lasted to trace and locate him by triangulation from the nearest cell towers. Hakim inserted a new SIM chip into his phone, replaced the battery, but did not turn the phone on. He had, in effect, a brand-new cell phone.

Hakim put the truck in gear and drove the few miles to the parking lot of the King Khalid Hospital. He parked as close to the entrance of the emergency room as he could. Hakim removed his vest filled with AK-47 magazines and stowed it along with his knife and pistol under the driver's seat. He exited the truck, locked it, and walked around to the main entrance of the hospital.

Visiting hours were just beginning, and several people were entering the hospital at the same time. Security in the lobby was lax; two bored police officers worked at a metal detector. Hakim passed through the detector with no problems.

In the lobby, he found a seat in the waiting area. Only one other person was sitting nearby, and he was speaking on his cell phone, totally engrossed in his own conversation. The clerk at the reception desk was busy issuing passes to the hospital visitors. At 25 minutes on the dot, Hakim turned on his brand-new cell phone. When the phone booted up, he dialed the French embassy.

"Let me speak to the ambassador *now*. If you delay, we will kill the four spies immediately," said Hakim.

The operator knew his instructions. He said, "*Oui*," and immediately put the call through to the ambassador.

Ambassador Phillipe d'Mosellier picked up the phone on the first ring. Present in the office with d'Mosellier were the embassy's head of security, military attaché, and a colonel from the Saudi army. The call was simultaneously routed to the U.S. Embassy and to NSA headquarters in Bethesda, Maryland. Stu Keaton and Mickey Henderson were listening too. The call was on speaker, so all could hear, with a recording being made to try to identify the caller through voice analysis later. No one listening had any genuine hope that the effort would yield the name of the caller.

All this was possible because the diplomats out in the boondocks worked much closer together than their counterparts in national capitals did.

Hakim was certain the call was being recorded and that the American NSA was trying to trace his location. The tracing process would take about three minutes. They would also try to get a satellite to take pictures of wherever the triangulation told them he was calling from. Hakim said, "There will be no bargaining for the prisoners. If you refuse to pay the full price for the women, we will return them to you without their fingers and toes. If we have not received the money by next week, then the price goes up to 150,000 euros each. You have 60 seconds to decide. Delay beyond 60 seconds, and I will end this call, and we will behead them as spies for the Americans. But before we do that, I will give the women to my fighters for their mutual pleasure."

The ambassador said, "Do not harm them. We will pay what you ask. *DO NOT* harm them! The 400,000 euros will be transferred this morning."

Hakim snarled, "There had better be no trickery. Two days after we confirm receipt of the money, we will free them. We will let you know the location where they are released. I have already given you the account number for the transfer. No tricks, or they will all be beheaded. *Allahu Akbar.*" Hakim disconnected the call. He did not bother to shut off his cell phone. Instead, he opened the battery compartment and removed the battery and the SIM card. The phone was now totally dead.

In the unlikely event that the Americans or even the Saudis could trace his location, they would have a hard time determining who made the call or where within the hospital it originated from. Hakim would wait for many people to exit the building before he left. Even assuming the Americans could get a satellite overhead taking pictures, they would never know who made the call from inside the hospital. Tracking 40 or 50 people as they left the hospital was beyond their ability. There was no way the Americans could or would get a drone in place to shoot Hellfire missiles into a hospital in Saudi Arabia.

Hakim rose and calmly made his way through the ground floor of the hospital to the emergency room. He dropped the SIM card in a wall-mounted, red plastic sharps container for biological waste. When the container was full, the hospital would incinerate the waste, and the SIM card would go up in smoke.

Hakim put a third SIM card in his phone. This was the card he used only to communicate with al-Nasirah. He dialed al-Nasirah who answered on the second ring. The message was short: "I sold the camels for the agreed-upon price," was all he said. Then he ended the call, removed and pocketed the battery and the SIM card. Hakim knew al-Nasirah was doing the same thing with his own phone.

Fifteen minutes later, Hakim finally exited the hospital from the ER. He walked calmly to his truck, got in, and drove away, just another ordinary Toyota pickup truck on the landscape of the Arabian Peninsula.

10

PHILLIPE D'MOSELLIER

French Embassy
Riyadh, Saudi Arabia
Tuesday, 7 April

D'Mosellier lost no time in calling the Élysée Palace in Paris. His conversation with the President of France was very direct and very simple. "*Bonjour,* M. President. There has been further contact with the kidnappers. I attempted to negotiate a lower price with the kidnappers. Those animals are threatening to cut off the fingers and toes of the women if we do not pay the full ransom. They have also threatened to allow their mujahideen to rape the women for sport. If we do not pay the ransom at all, they will behead the four of them and broadcast the videos to the world. I have agreed to pay the ransom they demand."

"I agree with your decision," said the President. "400,000 euros was their demand, was it not?"

"*Oui, oui.* They have provided us with an account number in the Cayman Islands to which we must wire transfer the funds. I promised them we would send the money today."

"It shall be transferred within the hour. Have we ever tried to trace the route taken by previous ransoms?"

"*Mais oui* (of course). From the Caymans, it goes to two different banks in Switzerland, and from there to Bahrain; after that, we lose track of the trail. It is our guess that the money ends up in Dubai or Yemen."

"We must stop this bandit reign of terror."

"Our good friends the Saudis could do it, but they are not willing to commit their military to chase down the bandits. They allow them to operate without fear of punishment. I think they actually get some pleasure from our embarrassment."

"Send a formal letter of protest to their government expressing our outrage at their lack of action."

"*Sûrement, mon President.* And the Saudis will ignore us and laugh at this letter, as they have ignored and laughed at every past letter. But I will do as you order."

"It does not matter if they laugh. Do it anyway. Get those four children home safely. *Au revoir,* Phillipe."

"Transfer the ransom money, and we will get them out of here within a few days. *Merci M. President. Au revoir.*" As he hung up the phone, d'Mossellier thought to himself, *Where will it end? When will we say we have had enough and finally do something about these religious fanatics?* Disgustedly, he answered his own question: *Not today, not tomorrow, not ever.*

11

HAKIM ABU-JIHADI

The southern hills of Saudi Arabia
Wednesday, 8 April

Hakim waited overnight at the home of a dedicated sympathizer to the cause of al-Qaeda before returning to the cave, lest someone single him out and track him to the hideaway.

During his drive through the desert, Hakim was once again struck by the harsh beauty of his homeland. He was a Yemeni, not a Saudi, but he was a child of the desert, and he considered all the lands occupied by Muslims to be his homeland, especially the deserts. Once the lands were freed from the Christians, Jews, and the accursed Shi'a, and once the laws of the Prophet were restored to the world, *insha' Allah,* the desert would be a Paradise again. Then, the truly righteous ones would rule the world. Until then, it was his sacred duty to fight in the jihad even if it cost him his life.

He parked his truck in a spot under a rock overhang and covered it with camouflage netting. Once the engine cooled to the surrounding temperature, the heat-sensing infrared sensors of the American drones could not detect it at all. Then he began the two-hour trudge into the hills where the camp-in-a-cave was located, and the half-hour climb up to the cave entrance. Security was necessary, or the drones would find them.

Hakim finally reached the entrance area of the cave. He bleated twice like a goat. Once again, the sentry grunted, and once again Hakim gave the password, *"Subhan Allah"* (glory to God).

The guard responded, *"Allahu Akbar"* (God is great).

We ought to change the password every day, thought Hakim. *But then these fools would forget the password, and we would wind up shooting our own men. At least the guard on the hillcrest is finally out of sight.*

Hakim passed through the two black curtains. The sheikh was standing in the large main area, giving orders to several mujahideen. He nodded to Hakim to go to the rear of the cave.

On the way, Hakim stopped to get a cup of tea for himself, then settled onto the floor in the sheikh's private area of the cave. He waited a few minutes, and Abdel Karim Washim al-Nasirah appeared.

"The money has arrived. You did well."

"Thank you, sheikh," said Hakim, and he bowed his head slightly.

"We will release the prisoners tomorrow night at Wadi Alaf'a in the desert. Then in the morning, we will tell the French cowards where their precious children are, and they can send the Saudis to pick them up, if they are still alive."

Hakim laughed as he thought about the desert nighttime cold killing the prisoners after the ransom payment. "These Westerners are soft. They do not deserve to survive. *Insha'Allah* the desert will kill them, so we don't have to waste our bullets on them."

"Frenchmen are better than Americans or Japanese. The French always pay, and the damned Americans never do. The Japanese are just as bad. Kidnapping Americans is a waste of our efforts. The only good thing is that we get to kill them and show all of Islam how we behead them on television. Then, their president makes a speech promising to bring us to justice, and nothing happens until the next kidnapping. They talk hard words, but they are such weaklings."

"Every infidel we kill brings us more fighters. Soon, all of Islam will fight the unbelievers. They will all perish by our hands, *insha'Allah.*"

"*Insha' Allah*" echoed al-Nasirah.

12

JACK TAKES LAURA TO DINNER

Silver Spring, MD
Thursday, 9 April

Laura fills my home, my days, my nights, my mind. We are proposing to go out together to hunt and kill AQAP bad guys. Meanwhile, we are marking time, waiting for our bosses to say "yay" or "nay" to our requested operation. She has been here for six days. Normally, when two strange people live together, there are times when they metaphorically rub against each other, and the resulting friction causes annoyance. I have not experienced any of those friction points with Laura, and I am really hoping I haven't caused her any friction.

We do almost everything together, including physical workouts in my gym, running every day, cleaning the house, yard work, reading, and eating our meals. She does the cooking, and I do the cleanup. And we eat out quite a bit, too. When we eat out, she insists on paying half of the bill.

I made a promise to behave like a gentleman, and it is really an effort to maintain my distance from her. Laura is a very attractive woman, devoid of artificial mannerisms and feminine wiles. She just *is* what she *is,* and I really like what she is.

When Laura moves or does anything, there are almost no wasted motions. She has the natural efficiency I associate with top-tier athletes.

She is very smart. We have had some philosophical discussions regarding newspaper articles and politics. Her analyses sometimes go deeper than mine. We are mainly in agreement on most topics, which brings me to the conclusion that if she agrees with me, she must be very perceptive. (Not that I'm biased or anything.) She doesn't have a solution to the Israel-Palestine problem, but then again, neither does anyone else. Until there is some goodwill on both sides, the conflict will continue.

Thursday morning was like most of our other mornings. We worked out in the gym/bedroom. We finished up with a six-mile run through the streets of Silver Spring. When we got back, we ate breakfast. Then we each took showers.

Over breakfast, the newspapers droned on rehashing the same global crises and reciting the usual litany of crimes and accidents. I decided it was time for fresh reading material, which for me means only one thing: a trip to the Barnes & Noble in Bethesda.

"Laura, I've just about run out of things to read. How would a trip to a nearby bookstore sound? If we go late in the afternoon, we can then eat dinner at *Mon Ami Gabi* across the street."

"That sounds good. I need some new books too. The name of the restaurant sounds French. Is it?"

"It's an American-run place, part of a chain, but you would never know it. It offers great food, superb service, and an ambiance reminiscent of a French bistro. They even honor their reservations. The food can be described as French with American touches or American with a French accent. Either way, it is one of my favorite places. I'm always satisfied there."

"Sounds good. Would 7 o'clock be a good time?"

"Yes, I'll call them. If we get to the bookstore around six, then we'll have an hour of shopping and browsing, and then we can walk over to the restaurant."

The rest of the day was filled with household tasks. I was looking forward to a shopping spree in a bookstore and dinner at *Mon Ami*

Gabi. Around 5 o'clock, we each changed into nicer clothes. I wore tan slacks and a long-sleeved shirt under a navy V-neck sweater, no tie. Laura put on a gray skirt (I didn't even know she had a skirt here. I have only seen her in pants) and a pink long-sleeved blouse. She finished her outfit with a lightweight cream-colored jacket.

"You look really great, Lady Laura," I said.

"Thank you, Sir Jack. You look rather elegant yourself."

We got into my car, and as we were driving to Bethesda, I kept glancing at Laura. I felt like a teenager out on a first date. Laura was a special person in so many ways.

In Bethesda, we parked in the Montgomery County Parking Garage. The first and second levels are limited to a maximum of two hours each. The third and fourth levels are for parking up to four hours. I figured we would be in town more than two hours. We found a spot on the third level.

We arrived at the store around 5:45 and promptly dispersed in different directions. For me, bookstores are like a toy store to a kid. I want everything in sight, even though I know I won't like most of it. I wound up in nonfiction/history. The first thing I selected was Ron Chernow's biography of *Alexander Hamilton.* Then I chose *Soldier* by Colin Powell (now there is a man who should have been our president).

I knew the story behind *Operation Mincemeat,* but to read it from the pen of one of the main actors was too much for me to pass up. *Operation Mincemeat* was the British effort to fool Hitler into thinking the D-Day invasion of Normandy was a feint and that the actual invasion was to be at Calais. If it worked, the Nazis would concentrate their forces in the wrong place. Strangely, it *did* work. I added the book to my pile. Then I added a biography of Napoleon.

Laura found me later. She had a history of modern Turkey, a book on mixed martial arts, a book about the Louvre's collection of Renaissance paintings, and a volume containing three novels by Nelson DeMille.

I knew I'd be borrowing the DeMille book from Laura. He is one of the few fiction writers I admire. He makes me laugh, and I can relate to John Corey's problems with authority. Yes, I definitely must borrow that book from Laura.

It was a few minutes after 7 when we exited Barnes & Noble and walked across Woodmont Avenue to *Mon Ami.* Each of us was carrying a heavy bag of books, at least six each.

Dinner was my treat. For starters, Laura had smoked salmon, and I had the crab cake. Delicious. Maryland is famous for its crab cakes. We sampled each other's appetizers. Both of us ordered the warm goat cheese salad. We shared a bottle of hearty Tuscan red wine for the main course of filet mignon Bordelaise with caramelized onions for Laura and a ribeye steak with *sauce bérnaise* for me. The sides of pommes frites and sautéed mushrooms were a perfect complement. We finished our meal with heavenly profiteroles, vanilla ice cream inside a puff pastry, covered with dark chocolate sauce and whipped cream. We were both feeling wonderful as we left *Mon Ami Gabi.*

As we crossed the road, toting our books, heading back to the municipal parking lot, I was really content with Laura's company. I wonder what she was thinking.

Very few people were on the street. We took the elevator up to the third floor of the four-story garage, where we parked and began walking toward the central ramp to my car. I walked to the driver's side. Laura walked to the passenger side.

A young man stood up from in front of the car next to ours and approached Laura with a knife extended in his right hand. "Gimme your purse, bitch, or I'll cut your face."

Laura dropped her purse and the bag of books on the cement. The attacker's eyes followed the purse. Moving like lightning, with her left forearm, she pushed his knife hand upwards and jammed the heel of her right hand under his chin, forcing his head and neck painfully up and back. Her right leg swung up between his legs and crushed his groin. All the air escaped from his lungs, and as he bent forward in pain, Laura smashed a karate chop on the back of his neck. Amazingly, he still held the now-useless knife in his right hand. Laura grabbed his knife arm in both hands and wrenched his arm upwards and backward with a twisting motion, dislocating his shoulder. The would-be robber fell to the cement floor, and Laura finished her defense by stomping on his right hand, crushing his fingers. If the attacker had had any air in his lungs, he would have screamed. As it was, all he could do was let out gurgles of pain. The entire encounter occurred in less than five seconds. Laura never made a sound during her defense.

When the attacker was lying in a heap on the cement floor, Laura picked up her purse and retrieved her bag of books.

I had run around the other side of the car to assist Laura, but in truth, she didn't need any help at all.

"Back the car out, Jack," Laura said. "I'll keep him clear of the wheels."

"Are you OK?"

"I'm fine, but this guy is going to be hurting for a long time. Should we call the police?"

"No. After they arrest him, he will only wind up suing us because you hurt him. Let's get out of here." I backed the car out of the spot, and Laura got in.

We drove down the ramp and onto Arlington Avenue. A Montgomery County police car was parked at the corner. Jack stopped next to the police car and lowered the passenger window. When the police officer lowered his window, Jack told the officer, "There is a person on the ground on the third level of the garage. It looks like he isn't feeling well, and he might need assistance."

"I'll call it in and go have a look," said the police officer.

"Thank you, officer," said Jack. The signal light was green, and Jack continued on his way before the officer could ask questions. We looked like a pretty respectable couple. Not the type to rouse suspicion or cause trouble.

As we drove home, Laura asked, "What was that about suing us? He tried to rob me."

"Strange as it may sound to a logical person, in the U.S., a person committing a crime can sue his victim for damages if he gets hurt on the victim's property or if the victim uses force to defend themselves and the criminal gets injured. The rules vary from state to state. More than half the states have enacted Stand Your Ground Laws, which make you immune from liability if you hurt the criminal. Maryland is not one of those states. In Maryland, you have a duty to retreat from the criminal even if you have a legal right to be where you are or you are in your own home. Since you are a Krav Maga instructor, your hands are technically a lethal weapon. You could be arrested for assault with a deadly weapon, along with that creep lying on the floor. Since he came out on the short end of the fight, he could sue you for damages and probably win in court. Further, with his torn shoulder and crushed fingers, he won't be able to hold his knife, and you have now deprived him of the means of earning his livelihood."

"America has some strange laws," observed Laura.

"Thank our armies of lawyers for standing reason on its head. Whenever they tire of practicing law, they run for elective office so they can make more laws to keep their old law partners in business."

"As Alice said, 'Curiouser and curiouser.' If I tried to make sense of it, I would get a headache. I think I will take your advice and leave the scene of the crime with my accomplice."

We drove the rest of the way to my house in relative silence. One thing is for sure: when it comes to hand-to-hand fighting, Laura really knows her stuff. I really got lucky the night she broke into my house. She could have killed me with her bare hands.

13

THE FRENCH STUDENTS

The desert of Saudi Arabia
Thursday, 10 April, 1:00 AM

The four French university students, Yves, Andre, Michelle, and Jolie, were blindfolded, hooded, and their hands were tied behind their backs. The leg shackles were removed. A single rope yoked them together, tied around Andre's neck, then, after about four meters, around Yves's neck, and similarly around Michelle's and Jolie's necks. The four were led out of the cave and down the hill, stumbling in their blindness.

The nighttime temperature was close to freezing, and the prisoners, who had no outer clothing, shivered in the cold. Heavily armed jihadists guarded them as if they were desperate criminals who might make a break for freedom.

When one man fell, guards beat him until he got to his feet. When one woman fell, they beat her and groped her breasts and crotch until she stood again. Blindfolded and hooded, the captives couldn't see the blows coming. Each strike landed without warning, adding to their torment. With hands tied behind their backs, they struggled to keep their balance or rise after a stumble while blows rained down. Slowly, haltingly, the caravan of pain moved down the hillside toward a waiting pickup truck.

Hakim and three jihadists waited at the truck, all armed with AK-47s. Hakim ordered, "Load them up."

Blindly, the four prisoners climbed up to the bed of the pickup one at a time, the ropes around their necks limiting their movements and causing each other pain. Finally, all four were standing in the back of the truck, the two men on the right, the two women on the left.

"Sit down. Now!" Hakim said.

Jolie was slow to obey, or perhaps she did not understand the Arabic. Majid slammed her behind the knees with the barrel of his rifle, which made her scream and fall in a crumpled heap. Two jihadists, Majid and Tariq, climbed into the back of the pickup to guard the hostages. Hakim and the driver got into the cab.

"East," Hakim ordered, gesturing toward the empty stretch of desert.

The truck moved, picking up speed on the uneven surface. In the back of the truck, Majid, the guard near Jolie, tore her shirt open and exposed her breasts. She screamed in protest, which brought her a punch to the side of her head. Majid twisted Jolie's breasts and pinched her nipples, causing her to cry out in pain. Tariq thought this was hilarious. The other three hostages began yelling in protest about the treatment of their friend.

Hearing the ruckus, Hakim opened the door of the moving truck and stuck his body halfway out of the door, facing the rear. "Stop that noise back there before I get angry."

Majid and Tariq had seen the results of Hakim's anger before and settled down in sullen quiet. Majid's thoughts were swirling about the injustice of not being allowed to have some fun with an infidel-piece-of-shit-whore.

The prisoners endured the cold and the uncertainty of their fate. Whispering to each other in French, they concluded they were on the way to an execution site to be beheaded.

After about an hour, the truck had traveled about forty kilometers into the desert to Wadi Alaf'a at the edge of the Rub al Khali, the Empty Quarter of endless desert. Hakim ordered the driver to stop. "Unload the prisoners," he called.

With maximum cruelty, Majid, using the rope around their necks, pulled each of the prisoners out of the pickup until they were all lying on the ground in a gasping pile of bodies.

"Take off the rope and the hoods," Hakim ordered in Arabic.

The prisoners were forced into a kneeling posture while the rope and the hoods were removed. They were still blindfolded, with their hands tied behind their backs. In this position, each was convinced they were about to be beheaded there in the desert.

No one spoke. With hand motions, Hakim ordered Majid and Tariq back into the back of the pickup. Then he quietly returned to the cab and motioned for the driver to leave the scene.

The prisoners heard the truck drive away. They did not know if they were alone or if there were jihadists guarding them in silence. After about three minutes, Jolie risked a blow from their captors and spoke. "Are we alone?" she said. When no blow came, she got bolder. "I think we are all alone here."

Andre, who spoke a little Arabic, asked, "Is anyone there?" Silence.

"Do you think they have gone and left us here in the desert?" asked Yves.

Michelle said, "I don't sense anyone here but us. I think they drove away and left us here alone to die."

"Fucking animals," said Andre. "I think you are right. We are alone. Let's stand up."

Slowly, awkwardly, they got to their feet. Andre was standing near Michelle. "Michelle, I am going to try to dislodge this blindfold by using the top of your head. Stand still."

"You can try it, but be careful. My head hurts where they hit me." Andre moved behind Michelle and began rubbing the edges of the blindfold against her head.

"I moved the blindfold a little, but I can't get it off," Andre said.

"I have an idea," said Jolie. "One person gets on their knees as tall as they can kneel. Another one of us goes behind and grabs the knot of the blindfold in their teeth and lifts the blindfold upward to get it off."

Within minutes, all four blindfolds were off, and the four students could see that they were indeed alone in the desert blackness. Only the faint light of the desert stars and a sliver of waning moon relieved the total darkness.

"Next thing we have to do is get these ropes off our hands," said Yves. "Are all the knots in the back?"

Andre felt the knots on Yves' hands and said, "Yes, your knots are in the back." Then he went to Michelle and felt her bonds. "Your knots are in back, too." After feeling the ropes on Jolie's hands, he announced, "Jolie's are knotted on the side. I think Michelle's ropes might be loosest. Let's see if we can get her free first."

Michelle stood back-to-back with Andre while he worked on freeing her bonds. Jolie stood with her back to Yves while she tried to undo his knots. They were all desperately cold in the desert air, and their hands shivered as they blindly tried to undo the knots.

After many minutes of frustration, Jolie loosened Yves' knots so he could pull one hand free. A cheer of victory came from all four. Yves, with his hand free, removed the rest of the rope tied to his hands. Quickly, Jolie was freed, and then Yves and Jolie freed Michelle and Andre.

Jolie closed the part of her blouse that still had buttons. "*Merde. That sick bastard really hurt me. I'll have bruises for a month, if we live that long."

Andre laughed, "I just realized that we're going to live long enough to hurt all over. I don't know where we are, but if they set us free, that means the ransom has been paid. And if the ransom has been paid, someone will be looking for us. We need a plan of what to do until we get found."

"We'll die of exposure before anyone finds us," said Jolie. "I'm freezing my ass off. If we live through until daylight, the desert sun will roast us. We have no water, no food, no clothing, no shelter. Nothing."

Yves, who had been quiet for a while, said, "I once read that when you don't have water, put a pebble in your mouth and keep moving it around to stimulate saliva formation. Just don't bite or swallow the pebble."

Michelle added her opinion, "We must do something to help the searchers find us. Maybe we can make an SOS using rocks."

"I like that idea," said Andre. "Gathering the rocks and forming the letters will keep us warmer than we are just sitting still. Having something to do will keep us from worrying too much. Let's get to work. The pebble idea is worth a try, too."

Yves chose an open space about 20 meters wide. The four friends began gathering rocks larger than a fist and laying them out on the sand.

"At least there is no shortage of rocks here," observed Jolie.

Slowly, the letters, about 3 meters high (10 feet), took shape in the sand. About two hours later, the job was done. "It doesn't look like much", observed Michelle. "Maybe we should make the letters two rocks wide."

Yves shook his head. "Let's save our energy and just huddle together to keep warm. Sunrise can't be too far away, and then the problem is going to be how to keep cool. I've been thinking that we could button all our shirts together to make a kind of tent we could hold over our heads. At least we would have some shade from the direct sun."

As the friends sat in a tight circle, holding hands and waiting for the dawn, Michelle said, "Maybe we should say a little prayer to help us get found by someone."

"You can pray for all of us," said Yves. "What I really think we should do is try to sleep while we are sitting here."

Michelle looked alarmed. "I'm afraid if I fall asleep out here, I may never wake up."

"We are in Saudi Arabia. If you die in your sleep, you will awaken in Paradise, and you will have 72 teenage virgin boys at your disposal, including their pimples and bad habits. Isn't that an exciting prospect?" asked Yves.

"You are as sick as the sadists who left us here. If we ever get back to civilization, I am going to forget that I know you."

The moon set, and the stars faded as the dawn approached. In the east, a faint glow appeared below the horizon. Andre was the first to realize the approach of sunrise. "At least now we know which direction is east," he observed.

Thirty minutes later, the air had warmed to a tolerable degree, and the four friends did not fear freezing to death. Another hour later, they were longing for the cool air of the desert night as the sun blasted through the clear sky and began roasting them alive.

The two men removed their shirts and buttoned them together as a partial shelter from the sun. Michelle was wearing a bra, so she took off her shirt. Jolie, who wasn't wearing a bra when they were kidnapped, was allowed to keep her shirt on. Beneath the shade of the three shirts, the four friends kept rotating in a slow circle to keep any one skin surface from getting too much exposure to the sun. Still, they were getting sunburned. The thirst they were feeling was awful, but the pebbles were at least keeping their mouths moist.

Another half hour went by when they heard the faint whump, whump, whump of helicopter blades in the distance. They stopped circling and began looking for the source of the noise. Soon, a slow-moving speck appeared over a distant hill to the northeast. They began waving, shouting, and jumping up and down to attract attention. After two or three minutes, they had apparently been spotted because the speck suddenly changed direction and came directly at them at high speed.

Yves suddenly realized that they were half-naked in Saudi Arabia. "Get the shirts back on. Quickly." Frantic efforts to unbutton the shirts and get dressed again were almost comical. Michelle, as a woman, was most at risk, and they freed her shirt first.

The helicopter, a Saudi military twin-rotor Chinook, arrived within three minutes and hovered over the SOS in the sand. A crewman leaned out the door and waved the four friends away from the landing zone. Then the pilot set the helicopter down right on the SOS. The crewman leaped out of the bird and ran to them.

"We have been searching for you. There is water on the aircraft. We also have a medic if anyone is injured. Stay below the rotors as you go to the copter. Let's go."

They all hunched over and ran to the helicopter door and clambered aboard. The crewman was the last to get aboard.

Once on board the helicopter, before they were even given water, the women were given shawls to cover their hair. Jolie's torn blouse was scandalous, and she was given a military tunic with which to cover herself.

The copilot radioed to Riyadh that they had found the four kidnapped students and suggested that headquarters call off the other searching helicopters.

Sitting in web seats inside the helicopter, drinking water from plastic bottles, the four students were so relieved to be out of the desert sun. Jolie took the pebble from her mouth and said, "I am going to have this made into a necklace so I will never forget the fun I had in Saudi Arabia. This little rock is worth more than a diamond."

Michelle was guzzling a bottle of water and told her friends, "I am never going to waste water again. It is way too precious."

Yves held up his bottle of water toward Michelle and said, "I'll drink to that."

14

JACK

Another restless night. Morning finally came. It has been 17 days since Laura moved in with me, but who is counting? We don't exercise on Sundays to give the body a little rest. I slid out of bed, showered and shaved, then put on undershorts and a terrycloth robe. I intended to make breakfast for Laura and me, but as I came out of my bedroom, I smelled coffee and heard her already in the kitchen. She was wearing the terrycloth robe from the guest bedroom closet. That robe never looked as good as it did on her.

"Good morning, Jack. Would you like eggs for breakfast?"

"Scrambled would be fine. Three eggs, please."

Laura broke five eggs into a bowl and beat them. The pan was heating on the stove. A little butter and salt in the pan, and then the eggs. She stirred and scrambled the eggs in the pan. They were done just as the toaster on the countertop popped up an English muffin.

"Please pour the coffee," she said, as she transferred the eggs to two plates, placing one half of a muffin on each. Then she put a second English muffin in the toaster. We sat down to eat. There were glasses of orange juice already on the table. My knee touched her knee under the table. She didn't move her leg away, so I left my leg there, gently touching hers. The contact felt sexy as hell.

The toaster popped up the second English muffin. We both stood up at the same instant and reached for the muffin. Our right hands touched. We both looked up at the same instant, and our eyes locked. We just stood there looking into each other's souls.

Without conscious thought, I put my left arm around her and drew her to me.

She came to me without any resistance. Laura turned her face up to me, and we kissed. Gently at first, and again and again and again, each time with more passion and yearning. Our bodies pressed together.

I reached down and undid the belts on both robes. The robes fell open. She was wearing a T-shirt and underpants. I felt her breasts against my bare chest through the thin fabric of her T-shirt.

I never wanted any woman in my life as much as I wanted Laura at that moment.

I slid my hands under her shirt and up the smooth skin of her back. She put both arms around my neck and hugged me tightly as we continued to kiss each other. Little moans were coming out of both of us. With my left arm, I kept her pressed against me; my right hand slid under her shirt to cup her left breast. I felt her nipple in my palm, erect and hard. I rubbed my fingertips gently in a circle. We continued kissing, tongues and lips, and hands moving all the time.

Laura took her arms away from my neck and shrugged off her robe. Then she pushed my robe off my shoulders, and it fell to the floor. We kept kissing and touching each other. She reached into my shorts and pulled my rock-hard erection out. I pulled her underpants down a little and rubbed my erection against the pubic hair on her tummy. She had a full triangle of dark hair. I liked that. The excitement kept building.

"Jack," she said in a hoarse whisper, "take me to your room."

Without a word, I scooped her up in my arms and carried her to my bed. I sat her down and stripped off her T-shirt. She lay back and lifted her hips, and I stripped off her panties. I dropped my shorts and got on the bed. I slid into her wet opening as she wrapped her legs tightly around me, pulling me deep inside her. Her passion was so intense, I thought she would break my back.

She thrust her hips upward to meet my downward thrusts. She kept whispering in my ear, "Oh Jack, oh Jack, oh Jack, oh Jack." We both climaxed together.

I was still hard inside her despite having just had an orgasm. Still locked together, I rolled over, so she was on top of me with her legs on either side of my hips. I reached for her hips and started moving them slowly back and forth in a grinding motion. Almost immediately, she picked up the rhythm. I reached up with both my hands, massaging her breasts. She braced her arms against my upstretched arms as we continued to grind against each other, and I pressed and pulled and rubbed her breasts and arched my back to raise myself deeper inside her.

With her eyes closed, she began to speak softly. "Oh Jack, I'm coming, I'm coming, oh Jack, don't stop, don't stop, don't stop, keep going, don't stop, oh Jack, oh Jack!"

I kept repeating her name over and over, and I exploded inside her as she reached a giant shuddering orgasm.

Her orgasm seemed to go on forever, writhing and squirming on top of me.

Finally, Laura fell forward onto my chest, her hands holding my face, kissing my mouth and eyes and nose and ears in hundreds of little kisses. I wrapped my arms around her and held her as close as I possibly could. I never felt so loved or so happy. I wanted to hold her there for the rest of my life.

We lay locked together for almost 15 minutes. Slowly, Laura rolled off me, and we lay beside each other, arms and legs intertwined, exchanging little kisses.

Finally, I said, "You know, I am deeply in love with you."

She laughed, "You silly man. I felt it that first night in your bedroom. Don't you realize that I have been fixated on your beautiful body since that night? Now I'll be fixated on it forever. When you reached out and covered my breast with the cloth of my suit, you proved you were a good man. But that wasn't what I wanted you to do. I wanted you to tear the other side free and make love to me right there. When we first locked eyes that night, I felt an electric shock go through my whole body. I have never felt anything like that before. My emotions were all conflicted at that moment. I hated what you did to my brother and how you messed up my life, but at that instant, I also knew that I wanted you and needed you. I hated you and loved you at the same time. Now, I just love you. You have no idea how hard it has been to pretend we are just platonic business associates doing a job."

"Laura, Laura, Laura. We are so lucky we didn't hurt each other that night."

"Yes, we are lucky. But I am luckier than you. I was hoping you would be a good lover, I never expected you would be such a great lover. I can't wait for you to make love to me again."

Thirty minutes later, Laura's wish came true. We never finished breakfast.

15

LAURA AT LANGLEY

Langley, Virginia
Friday afternoon, 24 April

We finally received word from *Beartrap*, Jack's boss, that the operation was to proceed. Our appointment was set for Friday afternoon. Since Sunday, we had made love so many times we couldn't keep count, nor did we want to. We just wanted it to go on forever. We both agreed that we had to keep our relationship secret from our bosses, or they would never let us go on the op together. Professionals are not supposed to fall in love with each other, especially in the intelligence business.

We showed up at Herb's office at 14:10 (2:10 PM) to receive the formal decision of the top leaders of both services. While Jack was in Herb's office, I was closeted with the agency's top computer geeks. I was showing them where I had discovered the weakness in their firewalls.

A long time back, I had hacked into a seldom-used Chinese military computer in Tibet. I revisited that computer and took it over. Then I repeatedly used the Chinese computer to probe the firewalls until I found a weak spot and could slip in. The agency never suspected I was an Israeli because I was using a Chinese computer, and the Chinese were always trying to break into the CIA computers. Taking over a Chinese computer is a hell of a trick. Just getting into their computer was a bitch because they use a different keyboard than we do. Luckily, numbers are still numbers and icons are still icons.

Then, I had to change the computer's language to English so I could use it, and then change it back to Mandarin when I was done with it. Once I was in the Chinese computer, I had to take over the basic operating system to control the computer. Any CIA suspicions of a break-in attempt were blamed on the Chinese and just appeared to be business as usual. Then, when I finally found a weak spot, I probed for the information I needed and then erased any evidence that I had ever been there. The system is so large that, if you avoid doing any damage, it is possible to enter and exit without being detected.

The agency's people were both embarrassed and grateful and secure enough in their own abilities to appreciate and respect my skills. They now knew what they had to do to protect their computers from me. What they weren't sure about was whether I had left myself a "back door" so I could gain access in the future whenever I wanted to. I tried to convince them I hadn't done that. But spies almost always hedge the truth. In fact, lying is a way of life. The geeks were going to be very busy for the next few months repairing firewalls and looking for a back door that may or may not exist. I hope they won't be able to find mine.

16

JACK

Langley, VA
Herb Watson's Office
Friday, 24 April

Up in Herb's office, he had allotted me about seven minutes of his schedule. He got right to the point. "She's in and the op is on. She is their responsibility, and you are ours. Our people will provide support for both of you unless you need something we cannot provide. We'll finance the overall deal, but she is on their payroll. You leave in three weeks, and you had better stop shaving as of now because you will need a beard again. You'll enter through Egypt and exit through either Egypt or Morocco unless there is a change of plans or there must be an emergency extraction. Any questions?"

"Yes, what passports will we be using?"

"You will have three: Yemeni, Palestinian, and Egyptian passports. The Yemeni passport will be the primary one. Our agency liaisons at our embassies will know you are out there in case you need their assistance. Halevi will have to travel as your unmarried sister, so get used to having her with you all the time. You may have to share a room together sometimes. If she objects to that arrangement, the whole op is off, so you had better do some convincing. I think she will agree because she has a stronger motive than you do. And don't screw around with her or you'll both regret it. She has some powerful friends at Mossad.

"I'll behave if she agrees to the setup. Sleeping with someone who tried to kill me is not something I'm interested in doing just yet. I'll propose the plan to her. If she agrees, we're good to go. Who will brief us about contacts on the ground, and where will we pick up weapons? I assume we'll have to use the usual Russian crap."

"Right. You'll be unarmed on the airlines and when crossing borders. No U.S. or European hardware unless you find it on the scene. You'll get your briefing a week before takeoff. Discuss the arrangements with her. If she agrees, we'll take the next step. Grow a beard. At a minimum, you have to look like that asshole Iranian President Ahmadinejad. Good luck. I will cover your back from here."

"I know you will, Herb. Thanks for all that you did." I got up to leave before I started dancing through the door. I was mister-cool-as-could-be as I left his office.

17

IBRAHIM

The southern hills of Saudi Arabia
Saturday, 25 April

Hakim abu-Jihadi strode into the main area of the cave. "Ibrahim, gather the newer fighters down by the open area for training. Their skills need to be sharper. Some of these men have no skills at all."

Ibrahim, a black-bearded man of about 30 years of age, whose face was weathered and browned by the desert sun and wind, making him appear much older, quickly stood up. He was a skilled trainer and loved to make real jihadis from the basic material of new volunteers. Many of the men he had previously trained were already martyrs. "Yes, Hakim. I will have them there in ten minutes." Ibrahim called out five names and ordered them to get their rifles and gear, then move down the hill to the training area. Three of these men had been in a few fights; two were new recruits. None of them were veterans or experienced fighters.

"Tariq," ordered Ibrahim, "bring a rocket tube and six rockets."

Ten minutes later, the five newer men, led by Ibrahim and Hakim, were standing in a rough circle in the open area used for target practice and infantry skills training. Hakim instructed Ibrahim, "Put them through basic target practice, three magazines each, three-round bursts. No fully automatic fire. Show them how to use and aim the shoulder-mounted rocket launcher. We don't have many extra rockets. Let them each fire one rocket to see if they understand the aiming and to get the feel of it. Then give them grenade training. I will watch and weigh how well they perform."

"It shall be done," Ibrahim said.

The five men were spread out in a loose line about 75 meters from a few scraggly bushes. Ra'if was instructed to spread a cloth with a human outline drawn in black felt-tip marker over the bushes.

Ibrahim looked to the youngest jihadi, a boy of only 15 years. "Qasim, you will shoot first," Ibrahim ordered, "three-round bursts. Shoot a full magazine. When you are done, retrieve the cloth so we can see how well you did."

Qasim knelt on one knee, took aim with his AK-47, and loosed a three-round burst.

Ibrahim was looking downrange through binoculars. "You shot over the target's head. Adjust your aim lower."

Qasim fired another three-round burst. Ibrahim again checked the target.

"Now you are left. You hit the cloth but not the target. And you aren't holding the rifle down. The muzzle is climbing up with every shot."

Qasim was clearly embarrassed. He released another three-round burst.

"You shot the target in the right knee and the right arm. Aim for the body mass."

Qasim fired yet again.

"You went too far to your right," called Ibrahim. "You shot the cloth but not the target." After another three shots, Ibrahim said, "Praise be to Allah! You have finally hit the target. Now finish the magazine and let Khalaf have a turn."

As Qasim kept firing, Ibrahim thought that giving this child real ammunition was a waste. He will never hit anything in a firefight. Maybe in five years, but not now and not soon.

Qasim went downrange and retrieved the cloth. Of the thirty rounds in the magazine, fourteen bullets had hit the cloth; eight were somewhere within the outline of the human drawn on the cloth.

With the black marker, Ibrahim drew a tight circle around each bullet hole. Qasim was instructed to put the target cloth back on the bushes downrange.

Khalaf took his turn on the firing line. Khalaf was a tall, thin Pakistani with a face pockmarked with acne scars. He was a man in his late 30s, angry at life and with a mean disposition. He had been fired from his government job for corruption so far beyond the norm that not even the Pakistanis could tolerate him. This made him determined to show Ibrahim that he could be a killer.

"Fire a three-round burst," ordered Ibrahim.

Khalaf assumed the one-kneed kneeling position and took aim. He silently prayed, "Allah guide my bullets," and pulled the trigger. The entire contents of the thirty-round magazine spewed out of the barrel with the muzzle of the gun climbing skyward. Khalaf's finger froze on the trigger until the magazine was empty.

Ibrahim angrily punched Khalaf on the side of the head. "Fool! Don't you know where the selector is? Can you not tell the difference between three-round bursts and fully automatic? Stand back and let another fighter show you how to shoot! Jibran, your turn. And make sure your selector is set for three rounds."

Jibran nervously knelt on his right knee. The first round hit the target in the right shoulder; the second and third rounds passed through the cloth above the target.

"A little lower and to your right," said Ibrahim. Jibran fired again and hit the target with two of his three bullets. "Hold the barrel down. Don't let the recoil raise the muzzle," ordered Ibrahim.

Jibran fired again. This time with complete success.

"Good," said Ibrahim, "Keep firing three-round bursts until the magazine is empty."

Jibran did as Ibrahim ordered. The cloth was riddled with two dozen holes. The outline of the human was dead many times over.

"You have done well. One day, you will be a warrior who will bring glory to Allah and our cause."

Jibran tried to keep a stern face as he imagined a true warrior would have, but still Ibrahim's praise caused a small smile to raise the corners of his mouth.

Ibrahim unfolded another cloth, also with the black line outline of a man, and told Jibran to replace the old target with the new target.

"Tariq, you are next."

Tariq, at 19, was the shortest man in the entire group, but he was as tough as a tree stump. He was a quiet man, possessed of a cheerful disposition. His beard was just beginning to grow in, and he always made jokes that he might become a martyr before he ever had a beard. Many of the fighters gave him advice and made him their personal mentoring project. Tariq always listened carefully to what he was told. As a result, he had accumulated knowledge, but he was short on real experience.

Tariq carefully sighted his rifle at the belly of the target. His first shot hit the belly, his second, the chest, and his third shot hit the head.

Ibrahim, looking through the binoculars, said, "Good shooting! Give me another burst and try to get a better grip on the rifle to keep it from climbing."

Tariq kept firing and hitting the target.

"You have done well, Tariq. Your friends in the cave will be proud of you. I am proud of you."

Tariq could not control the luminous grin that spread across his face.

"Ra'if you are next. Try to do as well as Tariq," said Ibrahim.

Ra'if knelt with his rifle and fired a three-round burst. The recoil threw the rifle backward and hit him in the cheek, opening a cut.

"You must brace the butt against your shoulder or that will happen every time you fire," said Ibrahim. Ibrahim adjusted the rifle firmly against Ra'if's shoulder. "Try again."

Ra'if fired another three-round burst, and this time the rifle stayed against his shoulder.

"Now aim at the target," commanded Ibrahim.

Again, Ra'if fired three shots with one hit and two misses.

"Better," said Ibrahim. "Keep the muzzle from climbing. Shoot again."

Ra'if took careful aim and fired.

"Three hits! You are getting the idea. Shoot again."

Again, Ra'if loosed a three-round burst.

"Good. Again," said Ibrahim.

Ra'if continued shooting until his magazine was empty.

"Well done. You have shown much improvement," Ibrahim complimented Ra'if. "Now we will fire while lying on the ground. Each man will fire one full magazine in the same order as before. Three-round bursts. Then we will fire while standing. Again, one complete magazine in the same firing order. You will find it is easier to fire from the ground and harder to fire while standing. Concentrate on keeping the muzzle from climbing when you fire."

The clacking of the AK-47s filled the mountain air for the next half hour. Even Khalaf achieved a measure of success.

Ibrahim held up the shoulder rocket launcher and addressed the group. "Now it is time to learn about this gift Allah has sent us. This is a Russian-made (may they all burn in hell) SAM rocket launcher. It is called an RPG-7. With this tube, you can bring down a helicopter, blow up a truck, tank, or house. This is a powerful weapon, and the rockets must be used only at the right times."

Ibrahim held up a rocket in his other hand. "Whatever rockets we have were captured from the Russians and their Communist Yemeni puppets. When this supply is gone, we will have to buy new rockets from those thieving Chinese bastards, may Allah kill them all."

Ibrahim pointed to a nearby hilltop where a large boulder was prominently visible. "That rock is our target. Each of you will get to aim and fire a rocket at that rock. The rock is about 250 meters away. You can fire a rocket at a helicopter that is anywhere from 25 meters to 500 meters away from you and expect to destroy the target. The maximum range of the rocket is 900 meters, but it isn't any good after 700 meters. First, you will practice aiming the launcher at the rock.

Then I will look through the tube to see what you have aimed at. When I think you know how to aim the launcher, then I will let you fire a rocket at the boulder. Always be careful of the blast from the rear of the launcher. That can kill your comrades if you are careless. If you are in a confined space, you can even kill yourself."

Ibrahim held the launcher on his right shoulder and aimed it at the big rock, his right hand held the pistol grip, his forefinger on the trigger. "This is the proper way to hold the launcher," he instructed. "The rocket is in two sections and must be assembled before it is inserted into the front of the launcher. There is the front warhead section and a rear booster section. The trigger must be squeezed with steady pressure. If you jerk the trigger, you will destroy your aim and miss your target. Then the enemy will shoot back, and he will not miss."

Ibrahim continued, "As soon as you pull the trigger and launch the rocket, you must run 15 meters to new cover. The launch of the rocket will give away your location to the enemy. Pick out your new safe position *before* you fire the rocket. Do not reload the launcher; do not stay in the same place. You must be ready to move to a safe position. When you have moved to a safe position, only then should you reload the launcher."

Ibrahim assembled a rocket and loaded it into the front of the launcher. "Watch my movements and how I hold my body." On one knee, launcher on his right shoulder, he aimed at the big rock and squeezed the trigger with steady pressure. The rocket whooshed from the tube with a roar of noise and flame. Ibrahim ran behind a nearby boulder and crouched down. The rocket struck the big rock squarely and chipped off a sizable chunk of stone.

Ibrahim rose and nodded at Tariq, "Tariq, you brought all this equipment here so you can be the first to aim and fire a rocket."

Tariq stepped forward. "Thank you. I am honored."

Ibrahim handed the rocket launcher to Tariq.

Tariq took the RPG-7, hefted it onto his shoulder, and aimed at the big rock. "I think I am ready, Ibrahim."

Ibrahim stooped a little and looked through the launching tube. "Good. We will load a rocket, and you can fire at the rock. First, assemble the rocket warhead to the rocket. Then, load the rocket into the front of the launcher. Before you fire, you must have a safe place to change your position. Pick it out now."

"Would that boulder over there be suitable?" asked Tariq, pointing to his left.

"Yes. Now load your rocket and aim at the big rock up there."

Tariq inserted the rocket into the front of the launcher. Carefully, he aimed at the rock on the hill. He squeezed the trigger. The rocket left the launcher with a blast of noise and smoke. Tariq broke and ran for his new cover just as the rocket glanced off the big rock on the hillside and exploded.

"Tariq was not patient. At the last instant, he jerked the trigger and spoiled his aim. He damaged the enemy instead of sending him to hell," explained Ibrahim. "Ra'if, you are next."

Ra'if carefully assembled a warhead for the booster tube and laid it at his feet. Then he aimed at the rock up on the hill.

Ibrahim sighted through the launcher. "You may fire the rocket, Ra'if".

Ra'if loaded the rocket into the front of the launcher, aimed, and fired. The rocket smashed directly into the rock and exploded.

"Allahu Akhbar," shouted Ra'if.

Ibrahim shook his head in disgust. "Yes, you killed some unbelievers, but the rest of them killed *you* after you fired. You are supposed to change your position by running somewhere away from your firing point. Instead, you stood there and cheered like a fool. If you want to be a jihadi you must first survive. Khalaf, you are next," said Ibrahim.

Khalaf, the Pakistani, aimed at the rock.

Ibrahim gave him permission to fire the rocket. When the rocket fired, his whole body jerked. The rocket smashed into the hillside 30 meters below the target.

"It would be better if you stuck with the rifle," said Ibrahim, "it will be cheaper for our cause to waste bullets instead of rockets."

Khalaf's face burned with humiliation and frustration.

Jibran, on his attempt, hit the rock and scooted to safety as required.

Qasim fired a glancing blow that Ibrahim called a near miss. But at least he ran to a new position after launching his rocket.

Ibrahim gathered the men in a group near the boulder that was the secondary cover position. He held up a hand grenade. "Everyone knows what this is. To make it explode, you must first pull the pin and then throw the hand grenade. When you throw the grenade, the safety handle pops loose. From the instant the safety handle pops loose, the grenade will explode in 3 to 5 seconds. It is supposed to be a 5-second fuse, but this Russian shit is not dependable, and the grenades often explode sooner than 5 seconds. As soon as you throw the grenade, take cover. If there is no place to hide, then fall to the ground. Do not watch the grenade explode, or you will become a casualty of your own weapon. You must never use the grenade pin to attach the grenade to your clothing. If you cannot figure out why this is so, then you are too stupid to be a jihadi."

Ibrahim hooked the grenade to his vest by the handle. "We will first practice by throwing rocks. Each man should find three rocks about the size of a hand grenade. Do it now."

As the men hunted for their three rocks, Ibrahim also chose one rock. The men reassembled with their rocks.

Ibrahim again addressed them. "The grenade can kill in a circle of about 40 meters. Watch as I show you the correct way to throw a grenade. I will throw the grenade and immediately take cover. You have three seconds to take cover after the grenade is thrown." Ibrahim threw the rock in a long arc and immediately dropped behind a boulder, pressing his body against the ground.

Two of the men laughed at his actions.

Hakim called down from his observation point on the hillside, "If you think this is funny, then you are fools. Follow Ibrahim's instructions and you will live to become an effective fighter."

Ibrahim stood up. "I want you each to practice throwing your rocks and dropping behind cover. Estimate the distance to the enemy and make sure you can throw the grenade that far. Do not expose yourself to enemy fire."

The men each took turns throwing their rocks and dropping to the ground behind the boulder.

"You know what to do. Now, each man will get to throw a live grenade. Tariq, you first." Ibrahim handed him the grenade. "Everyone must take cover while the fighter is throwing his grenade."

Ibrahim herded the men behind a large rock. "As soon as Tariq throws his grenade, we all hit the ground until we hear the explosion." Ibrahim called, "Tariq, you can pull the pin and throw the grenade."

Tariq held the grenade in his right hand and pulled the pin with his left hand. He threw the grenade and then threw himself hard on the ground behind the boulder.

Ibrahim hit the ground, and the others followed his example. Five seconds later, Tariq's grenade exploded, sending shrapnel rattling off the rocks.

"Qasim, it is your turn."

Qasim nervously gripped the grenade in his left hand. With his right hand, he reached for the pin.

"Stop!" shouted Ibrahim. "Are you going to throw the grenade with your left hand? You threw the rocks with your right hand. Hold the grenade in your throwing hand and pull the pin with the other hand. Once you pull the pin, you cannot change hands with the grenade."

Sheepishly, Qasim transferred the grenade to his right hand. He pulled the pin with his left hand and threw the grenade in a high arc. Everyone hit the ground and didn't move until ten seconds after the grenade exploded, and the shrapnel stopped pinging the rocks.

"Khalaf, you are next," said Ibrahim.

Khalaf stood behind his covering boulder. He held the grenade in his right hand. His face was covered in sweat. He pulled the pin with his left hand. His right arm shot backward to throw the grenade. The grenade slipped from his sweaty hand, and it rolled three meters away from him. He stood there transfixed, looking at the grenade on the ground.

"Take cover," shouted Ibrahim as he dove to the ground. The others also dove to the ground.

Khalaf sank to a sitting position and cried, "Allah protect me!" as the grenade exploded. Khalaf caught most of the blast on his right side. A fragment of the grenade hit Jibran in his thigh.

Ibrahim ran to Khalaf. He was still alive but severely wounded. His head was cut open, his right arm was shattered, his abdomen was torn open, his right foot was blown off, and he was unconscious. Blood was pouring out of all his wounds, soaking his clothes and the rocky soil.

Hakim ran down the hill from his observation post. His eyes met Ibrahim's. They both knew that Khalaf was not going to survive, and that they had no medical facilities to care for him. Hakim drew his Makarov automatic. "Rest with Allah," he said, and fired one shot into Khalaf's head.

Quietly, Ibrahim said to Hakim, "It is for the best. He would have gotten many of our men killed. We are better off without him. Now he is *shuhada,* he has become a martyr."

"It is *qadar* (fate). Such is the will of Allah," said Hakim. "Khalaf must be cleaned up for burial."

"It shall be done," said Ibrahim.

Hakim motioned toward the men, "Get Jibran up to the cave and patch him up. We have had enough for today.

"It is a shame that we lost a man today," commented Ibrahim.

"He was no loss to our cause. I am not so sure I like Pakistanis anyway," answered Hakim. "Shooting him now saved me the trouble of shooting him later. He never would have been a real jihadi. Get him buried as soon as possible." Hakim turned and started up the hill toward the cave, his mind already working on other matters.

Khalaf was dead, unmourned, and already forgotten.

18

JACK

It was raining heavily, and a crack of lightning and the rumble of thunder shook us awake. We were lying in my bed like a pair of spoons. Laura smelled delicious. She felt even better. The smoothness of her tanned skin and muscles just excited me beyond all reason. We were warm, comfortable, and safe, while the outside world was a soggy mess.

She rolled over to face me. We were holding each other. "I love you, Jack," she whispered. "I have never felt such powerful feelings before. I am so happy with you; I never want to be anywhere else."

"Laura, you make me feel more alive than I have ever been—full of love, want, joy, and peace. I've never felt this way before, and I know you haven't either. This isn't just about sex or physical attraction. What we have is real, and we can't let it slip away. Without you, my life wouldn't make sense. I want you in it—always."

Laura laid her hand on my cheek. "I think about why I came here, Jack. I shudder to think about what I would never have known if I had succeeded in my attempt to get revenge. We live such strange lives. We are not normal people who work at a job and come home for dinner. How can we ever join our lives now that we have found each other?"

"We will find a way, Laura."

"We barely know each other. I don't even know if you have a family, or if they'd approve of me. I don't know where you were born, what school you went to, where you grew up, or who your friends are. I've just started to figure out what you do when you're not on assignment. And the hardest question of all is, could we really change enough to fit into each other's lives? It might mean enormous sacrifices, for both of us just to make it work."

I kissed Laura's fingers and laid them against my chest. "Whatever came before isn't important anymore. Only what we do going forward counts. I'll tell you anything you want to know about me. For you, I will spill everything, as long as it isn't a classified secret."

We lay there for another half hour while the rain drummed on the roof and the windows. The lightning moved away, taking the thunder with it. Slowly, we began to touch each other everywhere. We made love. Gently, sensuously, and tenderly. When we were done, we both dozed off in each other's arms. My last waking thought was, *What a woman I had; she didn't even mind me sleeping with a loaded Browning under my pillow.*

19

AL-NASIRAH HATCHES A PLOT

The Southern Hills of Saudi Arabia,
Wednesday, 29 April

Abu-Basir, the *nom de guerre* of Abdel Karim Washim al-Nasirah, paced the floor of the cave. Hakim stood nearby watching his leader, who was also the leader of all of AQAP in the Arabian Peninsula, with curiosity. Whenever he had seen this behavior before, it usually presaged a plan of operations that would get the world's attention.

Suddenly, Abu-Basir stopped pacing. "We'll do it," he said.

"What attack are you planning?" asked Hakim.

"We need funds for weapons. Kidnapping students gets us nothing but small money. We need millions to get the equipment we need to take on the Yemeni jackals.

"Not enough victims come through our parts of the desert," answered Hakim. "We won't get big money unless we get a big victim."

"Exactly," said al-Nasirah. "That is why we need to catch a big fish. I am planning on taking the U.S. ambassador to Saudi Arabia, his wife, and his whore daughter. I think the Americans will pay $50 million for them. And we can further insult them by demanding payment in euros instead of dollars."

"The Americans don't pay ransoms, and then there is the little matter of how you intend to get them away from their Marine security."

"They don't pay for little people. This one is a personal friend of the Crusader President. He will pay, or we will behead them one at a time and send the videos out on the internet. If they won't pay, I will let our warriors use his daughter before we publicly behead her. Then we will rape his wife before we kill her. If we have to kill the ambassador, it will be very painful for him before we cut off his head. We will let him tell the world how he has enjoyed our Arab hospitality, then he will go to the Devil without his head. They will pay. I assure you, they will pay."

Hakim was quietly pensive. "Kidnapping the U.S. ambassador will bring in hundreds of American SEALs and other special forces. Are you sure you want to do that?"

"Let them come. They almost went bankrupt when they attacked Iraq and Afghanistan and 300 mujahideen can tie up 10,000 of their soldiers. They care about how many of their soldiers die, and they cannot tolerate too many deaths. We do not care how many of our fighters die. The longer we fight them, the more recruits we will get for our cause, the more fighters we have, the more of their soldiers we can kill, and the closer we come to the day of restoring the Caliphate. The way they fight is very expensive. They do not have unlimited money. We can fight them forever with just a few AK-47s. It will be cheaper for them to pay us."

"My sheikh, I have always given you my best counsel, and I am loyal to you until death. Whatever you order, I shall do. But this time, I think your plans are too ambitious. They hunt us now with their drones and spies. We move constantly to stay ahead of them. If we take their ambassador, they will never stop until they get us. The dogs got bin Laden, and he was as carefully hidden as was possible. Still, they got him.

"Bin Laden made the mistake of staying in one place too long. And has his cause suffered? He is a martyr. His death brought us more fighters. We are stronger than ever. Jihad has never been stronger. Our time is coming. The foolish Americans will even finance our war for us. We made so much money from what the Iraqis sent us when Bush and Cheney were trying to buy democracy for Iraq that we didn't have to kidnap anyone. We collected their money and killed their soldiers. Whenever they attacked us, all we had to do was blow up a few women and children and take photos for the world's newspapers. And then their attacks stopped while they arrested their own soldiers. They are such weak fools."

"Still," Hakim persisted, "we must think carefully before doing such a thing. They may be fools, but they are deadly fools. Right now, they have essentially left our Arab lands. I do not want to risk inviting them back."

"It is the easiest way to get a large amount of money," said al-Nasirah.

Hakim resigned himself to his sheikh's decision. "Then let us plan carefully and not rush into this adventure," he said.

"I will make them pay," muttered al-Nasirah, "they will pay."

Hakim quietly wondered who would pay the higher price.

20

UNDERCOVER HUSBAND
AND WIFE

Jack's house
Silver Spring, Maryland
Wednesday, 29 April

Laura and I were about to immerse ourselves in the Muslim culture. In Muslim countries, a wife is her husband's property. All females must belong to some male, like a chattel slave. If the family's honor is involved, a dominant family male, or even any family male, can do anything he wants with any female, including killing her with complete impunity.

Sons are treasured.

Daughters are exploited.

Depending on the particular country, women have almost no rights. A family member, either male or an older female, must accompany unmarried women. Virginity must be preserved until marriage, or the family is dishonored, and that can result in the female's death. Some Muslim societies practice ritual mutilation of the female genitals to diminish female sexuality and desire.

If a woman is raped, it is her fault; she must have behaved like a prostitute. Rapists are rarely punished. Unless the victim of a rape can find four male witnesses who saw the rape happen and will testify against the rapist, the victim of a rape can be stoned to death for having admitted to adultery.

If a married woman is accused of adultery, she is more likely to be stoned to death than the man who was her paramour. The man will most likely get only a flogging of 100 lashes.

Even the stoning of the rape victim is determined by custom. Her hands and feet are first immobilized, presumably by being tied. She is buried up to her neck in a pit with only her head exposed. A circle with a radius of roughly ten paces or more is marked around the sinner. The villagers gather outside the circle, and it is from there that they will throw the stones. By Sharia law, the stones cannot be so large that a direct hit will cause immediate death, but they must be large enough to cause pain and damage. The cumulative damage of less-than-lethal stones is what will eventually cause the rape victim's death.

In effect, the woman is tortured to death by repeated head trauma. The stones are less than lethal in size so that no one throwing the stones can be accused of murder. Because of this state of affairs, rape is seldom reported by the victim, and it is even less likely that the rapist will be punished. An overwhelming majority of Muslims believe that stoning for adultery is a just punishment. Such is justice under Sharia as mandated by Allah the Merciful. So it is written and so it shall be.

The dominant male of the family unit decides who the unmarried female will marry, and he must provide the dowry. Married women have greater freedom of movement and a slightly higher status, especially if the husband is an important man.

Men also dictate how Muslim women dress. The question of the hijab (literally 'the covering' and loosely called 'the veil') is a contentious subject in Western countries, but is fully accepted in most Islamic countries. Sexual modesty and non-arousal of strangers is the goal.

According to a recent survey conducted in Muslim countries by American researchers, 86% of the respondents, both men and women, thought that proper dress for women involved, at a minimum, floor-length dresses, long sleeves, headscarves that were tightly tucked in and covered the hair and ears, but the face could be exposed. Dark-colored scarves were better than light-colored scarves. Some respondents, notably in Saudi Arabia, thought the complete covering provided by the burqa, with the face covered and eyes hidden behind a screen-like veil and gloves on the hands, was an appropriate dress for women.

In Pakistan and Afghanistan, respondents believed that the black-colored niqab, which provides a complete, shapeless covering of the body, head, hair, and face, except for the eyes, was the proper attire for women. Beneath the outer garment, a woman can wear anything she wants as long as it is not visible to strangers.

Some ultra-religious countries, such as Iran, Saudi Arabia, and Pakistan, have religious police, called mutaween, to enforce the dress code. Violations can land a woman in jail charged with immodesty. Many times, a woman who is arrested gets raped by her jailers. The entire system is structured to keep women subjugated to men.

Laura didn't like the idea of being my sister. It would be easier for both of us if we went on the mission as a married couple. For Laura, the extra freedom of movement that married women have would be important. She thought the proposed arrangement was potentially dangerous and silly as well. "I am to be your incestuous sister? You know what the Prophet says about such an arrangement? We could both get stoned to death in the village square. Talk to Watson and get him to send us out as husband and wife. It will be safer for both of us."

I put in a call to Herb. I left a message on his voicemail. Doesn't anyone pick up a ringing telephone anymore? All I ever get is voicemail. Forty minutes later, Herb called me back.

"Herb, Halevi has agreed to everything except she thinks it would be easier to operate in a Muslim country if we went as husband and wife."

Herb thought for a few seconds. "I agree. I'll contact the Israelis, and if they agree, we'll make sure all three of Laura's passports say she is married to you."

We didn't yet know what names we would use, but at least we would be married in the eyes of those who follow Allah. Hopefully, we would find al-Nasirah, the murdering SOB that was the leader of AQAP, and "fix" him permanently or arrange for a drone to neatly blow him (and maybe some of his friends) to Paradise so he could meet the seventy-two virgins eagerly awaiting him there.

21

LAURA

Langley, Virginia
Monday, 11 May

Two weeks later, Jack and I showed up at 8 AM for our pre-op briefing. Establishing our new identities was the most critical phase of our briefing. Jack was now Abdullah (which means 'servant of Allah') abu Al-Farooq, and given the code name *Pogo* and I was Alia (which means 'sublime') bint Zayd Al-Farooq, code named *Koala*. Jack liked Pogo. He associated it with a cartoon character he admired as a child. Koala was a soft and furry, cute little guy from Australia.

In Arabic culture, women keep their own family names and seldom adopt the husband's family name, unless they choose to do so. If a woman adopts her husband's name, it gets added to her maiden name. Our family names, Al-Farooq and Zayd, were ones that actually existed in Yemeni government records, although the living people had long since left Yemen for Western Europe or North Africa, current whereabouts unknown. No known criminal record exists for either name. The best part about Yemeni government records is that no one really seemed to give a damn that they are such a farce.

Our cover story was simple. We were both born in a village near the town of Dhamar, which is on the border between North Yemen and South Yemen, so we could claim allegiance to either side depending upon whom we were dealing with. The Yemeni Civil War had been over since 1997 when the Northern forces conquered the Russian-sponsored communist Democratic Republic of Yemen (South Yemen), but diehards still exist who think the war is ongoing.

Abdullah and Alia are first cousins. My father and his mother were brother and sister. Our marriage was arranged by our families. We are distantly related to the Bakil (Bah-keel') tribe, which is the largest tribe in Yemen, led by Sheikh Mohammed Naji Abdulaziz Al-Shayef. We hate the West, particularly Israel and America, and are pledged to its destruction. The Prophet Mohammed (peace be unto him) guides our every action every day of our lives. We live and die by the holy Koran. The mujahideen are our heroes, and Jack has joined them in jihad against the Great Satan. And if Jack should happen to kill a few Hashed (Hah-shed) tribesmen from the second-largest Yemeni tribe, well, such is the will of Allah.

What we added to our cover story, with slight variations depending upon whom we are using it with, is that Jack went to Pakistan and then hiked into Afghanistan for jihad. I, his faithful wife, accompanied him and waited in Pakistan while Jack went to fight. Jack's father is very ill, and he has summoned Jack home to see him before he dies and goes to Heaven to be with Allah. A Muslim son must obey the wishes of his father, so Jack has a sacred obligation to obey.

We memorized a bunch of recognition passwords and other signals we were to use with our few contacts. If we had to enter Saudi Arabia, our man for supplies was a rug merchant. His name and location would be revealed to us while we were in Egypt. The latest information on al-Nasirah's whereabouts would also be provided to us in Egypt.

But mostly we would be on our own. We would be isolated from any CIA or Mossad assets on the ground, and we were to treat everyone we met as a potential adversary.

Then our briefing officer put us both through several hours of high-pressure interrogations, repeatedly testing us regarding our covers until we had them down perfectly.

We were issued Apple iPhone 6 cell phones, which look identical to the iPhone 5 phones commonly used throughout the Middle East. The language on our phones was Arabic, but we also had a hidden English keyboard. Our phones could be used as regular phones to make calls, but they also have several special features built in.

One feature was that by dialing a coded sequence, we could change our phones into burst transmitters. After entering the code, you text or say your message, and the phone encrypts and records it. You then dial the receiving telephone number and wait for the connection. Then, you dial the second two-digit code, and the phone digitally compresses the message into a one-second transmission, sends it, and then erases your original message. Once the message is sent, it disconnects and reverts to a regular cell phone. This feature can also receive messages using the same process in reverse.

Other variations in our phones include the integration of map and photo apps, which allow us to take a photo of a building or person and obtain exact target longitude and latitude coordinates in degrees, minutes, and seconds. Wherever the camera focusing square is centered, those coordinates appear at the bottom of the screen. That feature will be essential in the event we might have to call in a drone strike on our target, assuming we could ever succeed in finding him. As long as we have our phones in our possession, we can be tracked by satellites passing overhead. Our phones also have IFF (Identification Friend or Foe) capability so that the drones and satellites will know that we are friends and not foes.

The batteries in these phones are special, 96-hour, super-long-life lithium-ion batteries that are not yet commercially available anywhere. We might not always be near a source of power to recharge these batteries. Of course, in any vehicle, we can charge our phones using the cigarette lighter or USB port.

I would have my laptop computer and, once guided by the NSA, could hack into al-Nasirah's email accounts and possibly get a lead on where he is hiding.

One benefit of operating in that part of the world is that almost every male goes around fully armed. Everyone carries a knife. Men carry it in their belts, and women, somewhere on their person. In the cities, every male carries a pistol, and many have rifles as well. It is not unusual to see men on the street or in purely civilian pursuits with automatic rifles on their shoulders. In the countryside or the desert, every male carries an AK-47 and a pistol. An unarmed man is an exception. Every man imagines that he is a warrior from the moment he is born until the moment he dies. So, no one will think it strange if we have the means to attack someone or defend ourselves.

Jack has a two-week growth of beard, and he looks really scruffy. I like to get up close to his beard and whisper, "You have a terminal case of uglies there, big guy." He says the damn beard has an itch like a bitch (is that a song title?).

Once we are off on the assignment, we won't be washing very much. I hope we will be able to tolerate each other.

Yemen is an archaic and anarchic place, essentially free of the rule of law. The government is so weak that it is totally ineffective. Just thinking that Yemen has the same vote at the U.N. as a civilized nation is ludicrous. The only rule respected by everyone in Yemen is what comes out of the muzzle of an AK-47.

The Yemeni army is a complete joke and is fair game for anyone who wants to take potshots at it. Although they are nominally part of the Yemeni government, they are really an independent force that is unwilling to fight for the government and are universally hated by everyone. The hatred directed toward them makes them willing to oppress everyone. Only their commanders get any loyalty from the troops, and that is because they are beset from all sides and they must stick together to survive. Not surprisingly, the army is loaded with AK-47s and rocket launchers, with the occasional armored vehicle or Toyota or Hyundai pickup truck for transport.

Yemen has many tribes ruled by sheikhs who are no better than Bedouin warlords. The tribes do not readily cooperate with each other.

Tribal customs and rules allow for an uneasy coexistence, or there would be constant tribal warfare, but there is no trust or affection between rival tribes. Nothing is sacred. No promise to a member of another tribe counts for anything.

Outside the capital city of Sana'a, every male is armed. Some families have more AK-47s than the teeth in all their mouths. Anyone who owns a toothbrush uses it to clean the small parts of his rifle. The preferred mode of transport is by Toyota pickup truck with an AK-47 poking out each window.

The Yemeni tribes do not get along with al-Qaeda in the Arabian Peninsula. AQAP consists mostly of fundamentalist Islamic fighters from foreign countries. These self-styled mujahideen (holy warriors) are armed to the teeth with AK-47s and rocket launchers and are dedicated to the destruction of the West and the ascendancy of Islam. They are Sunni Muslims and consider the Shi'a Muslims to be non-believers. Death to the nonbeliever is a creed they can live by and happily die by. AQAP wants to rule everyone under strict Sharia law. Anyone who doesn't think as they do is obviously a nonbeliever deserving of death. These guys travel in Toyota or Hyundai pickup trucks with AK-47s poking out the windows. A-Cap is the most dangerous faction in Yemen.

Then there are the few idealists who were inspired by the Arab Spring and who strive for a representative democratic government. These idealists are mostly in the cities and are also armed with Russian and Chinese AK-47s, plus the occasional pickup truck.

In addition to these factions, there are the roving bands of outlaws who earn their livelihood by kidnapping, robbery, and murder. For recreation, they rape and pillage. As usual, they are all armed with AK-47s and use pickup trucks for transport.

Many foreign governments have agents operating in Yemen. There are as many agendas as there are foreign governments. Each group wants to blend in so that it can achieve its aims. The best way to blend in is to provide themselves with AK-47s and (guess what?) pickup trucks.

Between the army, the many tribes, AQAP, the idealists, the foreigners, and the bandits, there are enough AK-47s and pickup trucks to leave you wondering how they all arrived at this one spot on the planet. When a person arrives in Yemen, the first thing he should do is buy an AK-47 and a pickup truck. This gives you parity with every other person or group. At least if attacked, you will go down fighting, or you have the means to escape from any unpleasant situation. Most pre-owned pickup trucks come with their own bullet holes, dirt, and rust. One does not waste water washing a truck (or even your body) in the desert.

One advantage of an AK-47 is the simplicity of operation and maintenance. This rifle, which has been produced in the mega millions, has only eight moving parts. It will work even if the action is full of desert sand, jungle mud, or has never been cleaned at all. Any person who cannot handle an AK-47 is too low on the intelligence scale to be worthy of basic survival.

When we get to Yemen, our first task will be to buy AK-47s and a pickup truck.

Yemenis who desire to live a peaceful, civilized lifestyle leave Yemen as soon as they can scrape up the airfare.

Jack and I are heading into Yemen on our own to do a job. Now that we have each other to live for, it's crazy to go—but we're doing it anyway. Jack still can't believe he was the one who suggested this joint operation. His only defense is that he made the offer before either of us realized we were in love.

Still, I want revenge for my brother, and nothing will stop me from getting it. Neither of us will let the other walk into that ninth-century cesspool alone, so we're going together.

There's something I've never understood about many Muslims from Arab countries who leave home to build better lives in the West. They escape the misery of their old countries—only to recreate the same conditions in their new ones. In France, Holland, England, or America, they work to reestablish the very order that drove them away, as if determined to make themselves unhappy again. I can't explain such thinking—it makes no sense at all.

22

JACK IN PARIS

JFK Airport, New York to Paris
Friday & Saturday, 15-16 May

Laura and I traveled to New York City by Amtrak from Washington. We stayed overnight at an agency safe-house apartment. Between us, we had one piece of beat-up luggage with all the clothes we were going to take with us, which was not much. Happily, the bag had wheels on one end.

The following afternoon, we took a yellow taxi to Terminal One at JFK Airport. The taxi driver, like so many New York taxi drivers, was an Islamic immigrant. Ours happened to be from Algeria in North Africa. We spoke Arabic with him on the ride and told him we were going home to Yemen. He became our best friend on the ride, condemning the Americans and all the Jews and Israelis in New York who controlled all the banks, the government, and the newspapers. Even the taxi he was driving was owned by a Jew.

The standard fare mandated by city ordinance for a New York taxi from Manhattan to JFK is a $35 flat fare. Our new Algerian friend demanded $75 for our ride, $35 for each person, plus $5 for our one piece of luggage. We finally negotiated the price down to $35 when I threatened to call a cop. He departed with a shower of good wishes that our sons, when we have them, should all be cripples and imbeciles, and that our goats should be sterile, and he would be happy if our plane exploded and crashed into the ocean. All delivered in our native Arabic. What a nice guy.

We boarded the Air France flight 17 for Charles de Gaulle Airport. I was dressed in rumpled parts of two different suits. The jacket was gray with pinstripes. The pants were a muted brown plaid, unpressed and sort of faded. My semi-white shirt looked like it hadn't been washed or ironed in a month. I almost looked like Ahmadinejad, the president of Iran, in all his sartorial splendor.

Laura was swallowed by a shapeless dress that dragged to her ankles, hiding every curve of her delicious body. A black scarf bound her hair and ears, tucked in tightly beneath her chin and around her neck.

We flew economy class and were pretty stiff when we finally landed in Paris the next morning, a little after 7 AM. Still, when the lights in the plane were dimmed so the passengers could sleep, we held hands in the dark. We even kissed a few times. Our hands often strayed to erogenous zones. Very un-Islamic.

In Paris, we cleared immigration into the European Union. French law prohibits any outward expression of religious affiliation, so Laura could take off the headscarf. Passengers waited nearly two hours for their luggage, stalled by a wildcat strike from the baggage handlers' union.

The whole airport was in chaos. Departing flights were delayed because the outbound passengers' baggage wasn't being loaded on the planes, and the terminal gates were not being vacated for arriving flights. Rather than have the passengers sitting on planes on the ground, many airlines elected not to load the departing passengers and left them waiting in the terminals. Arriving flights kept landing and were jamming the tarmac taxiways. Passengers from many flights at de Gaulle Airport normally get unloaded onto buses, so those passengers were being brought to the terminals. There were nonstop loudspeaker announcements of flight delays and gate changes. Thousands of passengers from dozens of jumbo jets were jamming the baggage carousel area.

Eventually, the strike was settled, and the baggage handlers went back to work. We finally got our one piece of luggage, cleared customs, and headed for check-in to catch our EgyptAir flight to Cairo. By then, every flight was delayed in a domino effect. French labor unions certainly make life interesting for everyone.

EgyptAir is the national airline of Egypt. It is staffed by government employees who really don't want to work if they can possibly avoid it. They didn't get their jobs because they were capable; they got the jobs because they had connections.

We arrived at the check-in desk looking like poor immigrants and waited behind the stanchions to be called. We were promptly ignored by the clerks. The clerks repeatedly called other travelers to the desk, but they never called us. In keeping with our downtrodden appearance, we waited patiently. After almost 15 minutes, I took a small plastic bag of pistachio nuts out of my pocket. As I ate them, I threw the shells on the floor. Soon, there were quite a few shells littering the floor. I made it a point to step on a few so they would crackle loudly and break into smaller pieces. Then I began loudly humming *suras* from the Koran.

"Don't throw the nut shells on the floor," said the clerk.

I answered, "I am so sorry. We are just killing time until someone gives us our boarding passes."

"Let me see your passports. Just stop throwing the nutshells on the floor."

Laura was having a hard time not giggling at my petty act. In retribution for our annoying existence, the ticketing clerk put us in the last row of the plane. That was OK as long as we were together.

We boarded our flight 90 minutes late. The flight from Paris to Cairo takes 5½ hours. By the time we landed, we were both seriously jet-lagged and out of sync. All we wanted was a bed where Laura and I could collapse into each other's arms.

23

LAURA, CAIRO

Cairo, Egypt
Sunday, 17 May

By the time we reached Egypt, a mental transformation had occurred in both of us. The closer we got to any Arabic-speaking country, the more we morphed into warrior mode. In warrior mode, the only lives that matter are your own and those of the buddies at your side. On this mission, that was Jack and me. Everyone else is a potential enemy and can be considered expendable. The veneer of civilized behavior gradually slips away, exposing survival instincts that, in a civilized world, would appear cruel, but those instincts and thought processes are what will keep us both alive long enough to one day return to a saner existence.

We were directed to stay three days at the Arabian Star Hotel, a ninth-rate hotel on Al Adad Street. This place was so shabby that it was rated at minus five stars (Arabian Stars, of course). The price was 37 Egyptian pounds per night, or approximately 5 U.S. dollars. If this place had ever seen better days, they must have been back when Cleopatra was in charge. Only Arabic-speaking visitors to Cairo stayed at this dive. I was convinced we would exit with fleas or bed bugs, but it didn't happen. How lucky can you get?

Even in what must be the cheapest hotel in Cairo, frequented by the poorest of downtrodden travelers, thieves preyed on the unwary. We carried our money and passports with us when we went out to find some food and locked the door to our room when we left.

When we returned, it was unlocked. Jack's extra pair of pants and my two dresses were gone, but worst of all, Jack's boots and his fighting knife had disappeared. I had removed my Fairbairn-Sykes knife from our luggage and decided I needed it with us before we left the room. But Jack figured we were both really good at unarmed combat, so using a knife for self-defense would only be an invitation to visit the police station if we ran into trouble.

The boots were another story. He'd had them custom-made in Sicily two years ago. They were quite rugged and were very familiar on his feet.

I tried to cheer him up. "Let's go into the souk and buy you a new knife and some pants. I don't know how we can replace the boots, but we can get dresses and pants anywhere."

Jack was really annoyed and still behaving like a grumblefart as we walked. "Those boots were broken in and had served me well through the past two years of trekking through some of the worst Middle Eastern ratholes you can imagine. I am royally pissed off." The complaining continued nonstop for about ten minutes.

We headed out to go shopping. The bazaar was a madhouse of people, donkeys, cars, camels, and noise. The smell remained unchanged for three thousand years. I found some awful dresses that would fit in with our cover. I haggled like a pro. Twice, I began to leave the stall where the dresses were for sale. Each time I tried to leave, the price was reduced again. We bought the dresses at such a cheap price that I felt sorry for the stall owner.

Jack was looking for a suitable knife, so we wandered the market. Down one alley, we came upon an Arab with some interesting wares. The Arabic sign over his booth said: Best Merchandise in Cairo. His tables were wooden planks set up on sawhorses and covered by cloths. There on one table amid an eclectic mix of electric utensils, old tools, small household goods, old clocks, and Russian military hardware, were Jack's knife and his boots. Jack casually examined the knife.

"Very fine knife, American-made," said the Arab.

"Yes, it is. Have you had it for long?" Jack asked. He removed the knife from the sheath and pretended to evaluate the edge and the point. He already knew how sharp it was.

"Ah, about three weeks. A knife like that one will not stay here long. It came to me from a *mujahideen* returned from Afghanistan. Someone—a sheikh or warrior—will surely buy it. If you like the knife, I will let you have it for 300 pounds."

"The boots look interesting, too," Jack said.

"Ah, those belonged to my cousin. Sadly, he is in Paradise now. I can let you have them with the knife for a special price of 700 pounds."

Still holding the knife, Jack reached out across the table and grabbed the merchant's wrist. The point of the knife went to the merchant's throat. "What does the Prophet, peace be unto him, say is the proper punishment for those who deal in stolen goods?" Jack snarled. "I will tell you. The act of selling stolen goods is *haram*. The punishment is the same as for the one who stole the goods. Shall I cut off your right hand? For you are a thief. This is my knife, and those are my boots."

"Please, Effendi, I did not know the goods were stolen. I bought them just today from a traveler."

"Then you are also a liar. I shall cut out your tongue."

"No, Effendi, please. I beg you, take your knife and boots and leave me alone. I am innocent, and I have a wife and many children. Please, Effendi." I thought the poor bastard was going to faint from fright. He looked into Jack's eyes, and I think he saw that Jack was capable of ending his life right then.

"I will take my goods. And I will also leave you a reminder of what happens to those who steal and lie," Jack said. With the knife, he drew a wavy line across the stall owner's forearm. Just enough to cut the skin and cause heavy bleeding, but not enough to cause real damage. "If you make any sound, I will cut deeper", Jack said.

To his credit, the man just moaned in fear. When Jack released his wrist, the owner turned and ran away in a panic, blood dripping from his right arm, the best merchandise in Cairo abandoned.

Jack cleaned his knife on the cloth that covered the table, returned it to the sheath, picked up his boots, and we walked away. The merchant in the adjoining booth, who had seen and heard the entire exchange, never said a word. Jack glared at him and said, "What?" Suddenly, the merchant found the top of his table so interesting that he could look at nothing else.

"Maybe you should have just paid him a few pounds and bought your things back," I said, "but your approach was certainly more interesting."

"I might have bought the stuff back, but his cock-and-bull story pissed me off more than I was before. That creep has probably been selling stolen goods since he was eight years old."

I took his arm under mine and pressed it against my breast. "You are exhibiting a great deal of negative energy. I know a special way to re-channel your thoughts back to positive energy. Let's go back to our rat-trap hotel and get undressed. You can even try on your new boots to see if you like them." Jack is like putty in my hands when I make such illicit proposals. So of course, we went back to our rat-trap hotel and took our clothes off.

Jack never got to try on the boots.

24

JACK, CAIRO

Cairo, Egypt
Tuesday, 19 May

The day dawned like every other day in Cairo: the sun burning down and baking every living and non-living thing to a crisp. The only variation that ever occurred was that on some days the sands of the desert were carried by the wind and filled every orifice and layered every surface of everything that lived.

Today, the winds were quiet; the temperature is expected to reach 110° F (43° C) in the shade by 3 PM. Laura cursed the Islamic customs that required her to wear a long dress with long sleeves and to keep her head covered with a scarf. The only positive was that she could keep her knife strapped to her right calf with no one suspecting she was armed and deadly.

We were scheduled to meet our local intelligence contact today on the tour bus en route to the Great Pyramids on the Giza Plateau. He would look like a German tourist, and he would contact us by asking us to take his picture with the Sphinx in the background. He would have an enameled black, yellow, and red German flag pin in his lapel. The latest information about the location of the leader of AQAP would be in a flattened black aluminum tube attached to the bottom of the camera by a Velcro dot. I was supposed to remove it when taking his picture, return the camera, and break off the contact.

We bought two tickets and boarded the tour bus at El Herara. The Egyptian tour guide was conducting his routine on the bus's public address system, using what might be described as fractured English, and then repeating it in Arabic. His English was so laughably bad that it was far easier for us to understand his Arabic. We spotted our contact, who wore a rumpled linen suit and spoke halting Arabic with a German accent. He was a convincing actor and didn't draw any unnecessary attention to himself. He chose a seat across the aisle, one row ahead of us.

While the bus was working its way to the pyramids through the midday Cairo traffic, our tour guide gave us a short course in the history of Egypt's early pharaohs. Which pharaohs built the pyramids, and what mystical powers have been attributed to them? Of course, he dwelled on the Curse of the Pharaohs and the ill luck that befell Lord Carnarvon after Howard Carter discovered the almost completely undisturbed tomb of an obscure boy-king, Tutankhamen.

For over 3,800 years, the Pyramid of Cheops (also known as Khufu) was the tallest man-made structure in the world, measuring 146.5 meters (481 ft.). The Great Pyramid is the only one of the Seven Wonders of the Ancient World to survive today. It was built over a period of almost 30 years to serve as the tomb of Cheops. Meritites I, Cheops wife, is buried in another nearby pyramid of lesser importance.

The construction required the efforts of hundreds of thousands of laborers. Many theories have been postulated about how the stones were raised into place, but there is no definite knowledge, just theories. What is known is that the orientation of the sides of the Great Pyramid is only 6 minutes away from a true north, east, south, west orientation as measured by modern instruments. The base is almost a perfect square shape. Estimates, assuming the white limestone facing stones were still in place, maintain that the base *is* a perfect square, 755 feet on each side. However, since the facing stones have been almost entirely removed over the centuries to supply building materials for construction in Cairo, this allegation is largely conjecture.

We finally arrived at the Giza Plateau. Leaving the air-conditioned confines of the bus was not my idea of fun. The city of Giza is the third-largest in Egypt, after Cairo and Alexandria. It has grown until it reaches Cairo on one side and the Great Pyramid on the other. I have been here before, but Laura, from the shelter of her Israeli upbringing, has never seen Giza in the flesh, er, I mean in the stone.

The tour's first stop was the Great Pyramid. A limited number of visitors—only 150 visitors in the morning and 150 in the afternoon — are admitted to the burial chamber. Tickets must be bought on site, and they sell out quickly. Everyone on our bus, including us, queued in vain—none reached the window before the last ticket was gone. Laura expressed her displeasure using a few choice Arabic curses.

In Arabic, like the good, obedient wife she was, she said, "Husband, will you take me to see the Sphinx, please?"

All I said was, "Come," and we trekked across broiling sand and broken stones to arrive at the Sphinx.

"Is it true," asked Laura, "that this Sphinx is carved from one piece of stone?"

"That is what the tour guide said, and I believe him," I answered.

At that moment, the German tourist, in his terrible Arabic, asked me, "Would you be kind as to take a photograph with the Sphinx behind me?"

He looked like he was right out of *Raiders of the Lost Ark*. Any tourist who tries to speak the native language of a country he is visiting deserves a little consideration.

"Yes, I will do a photo for you," I said.

I took his camera and posed him with the Sphinx in the background and snapped three photos. A little tube was attached at the bottom with a Velcro dot. I pried it off with my pinky and ring fingers and palmed the tube. "You are from Germany?" I asked.

"Ja," he replied, "Egypt is a very interesting place. Very old."

I handed his camera back to him, and he gave me a 50 piastre coin as a tip for taking his picture. Cheapskate. I took the coin and nodded in thanks. I put the coin and the tube in my pocket. As Laura and I turned to go see the other pyramids, I said, "Maybe one day we will come to see Germany. Are there many Muslims there?"

"Ja," he said, "many Muslims, many Turkos."

What an understatement. Germany is burdened with a large population of Turkish guest workers, originally invited decades ago to fill factory jobs. Now, the German government wants them to return home, but few are leaving, as no comparable jobs await them in Turkey. Many have established poor neighborhoods marked by overcrowding and crime, straining Germany's social and financial systems. Resentment has grown, and the slogan "Turkos Go Home" reflects the hostility they face.

When we were alone, I said to Laura, "You know the Sphinx is responsible for the hump in the camel."

The look she gave me told me that her bullshit antenna was on high alert. "How did that happen, oh Seer of Antiquity?"

"I thought you would never ask. According to the sages, here is how it came to pass:

> The sexual drive of the camel
> is greater than anyone thinks,
> for one in the heat of its passion
> tried to deflower the Sphinx.
> Now, the Sphinx's posterior orifice
> is stuffed with the sands of the Nile,
> which accounts for the hump in the camel,
> and the Sphinx's inscrutable smile."

"That is positively awful. Funny, but awful. You should be ashamed, Abdullah abu Al-Farook. You are lucky the teacher doesn't give you a spanking and make you stand in the corner."

"The corner doesn't sound interesting. But tell me more about the spanking."

Laura giggled, "You have great potential for becoming a complete pervert. Let's get out of here before I melt."

In keeping with our role as tourists, Laura and I went off to see some of the other lesser-known pyramids. Egypt has over 135 pyramids along the Nile, starting at the Giza Plateau and spreading out southwards along the Nile River. We took a quick look at the other two Great Pyramids and called it quits for the day. We found a café and sat down for a Coca-Cola.

The pyramids along the Nile are smaller than those at Giza. Great wealth was required to build a pyramid of any size as a final resting place. These pyramids were the tombs of earlier Egyptian royalty and some of their more important nobles. The ancient Egyptians had great faith in the existence of the afterlife and took great pains to stock their tombs with the earthly comforts they would need when they arrived. All pyramids are known to have been looted. With the advent of Islam, the promises of the hereafter changed to Paradise and virgins, and the earthly misery of daily existence would be replaced by happiness and plenty. The faith in the afterworld is still there, ever longing for something better than the shit of daily living in Egypt, or Syria, or Gaza, or any of ten thousand Islamic hellholes around the world.

After five hours of baking under the desert sun, we finally boarded the bus back to Cairo. Dusty and drained, we grabbed a quick meal at a café before retreating to our hotel. The lone shower down the hall offered little relief, but we scrubbed off what we could. When we returned to our room, Laura slipped into her long dress, wearing nothing beneath it, and I pulled on a simple *thawb*, like the ones worn by Egyptian men.

Later in our room, we opened the little tube and extracted the tiny note inside. The note written in Arabic, read 'Najran/SE' and beneath that was 'Muhammed Ali ben Makhara, Makhara Carpets, Karmis Mushait.' Najran is in the southern desert of Saudi Arabia, just over the border from Yemen.

That means our boy was either intending to make life difficult for the Saudis or he was hiding in the desert southeast of Najran before heading back into Yemen. Our contact for weapons and supplies is Muhammed Ali ben Makhara, who owns Makhara Carpets in Karmis Mushait (Kar-miss Moo-sha-eet), another Saudi city near Najran but a little to the northwest.

"Operating in Saudi Arabia won't be easy," said Laura. "Their government actually functions, and they have pretty excellent control of everything. Their army is trained by the Americans, and the people support them. The Saudi people are relatively content and live well, although they are extreme in matters of religion. Why does A-Cap want to raise hell in Saudi Arabia?"

"I hope he is just hiding out in the desert before attacking again in Yemen. If he has been safely hiding out for a while, he may be sloppy about security. If he is causing trouble, then maybe the Saudis will do our job for us, although I doubt it. If the Saudi military is hunting him, then we have another element of potential problems that we will have to avoid. In Saudi-land you will have to wear the complete burqa or risk arrest by the mutaween (religious police). The good thing is that you can carry all of our hardware under your burqa."

"When did I become your pack mule? Carry your own guns, Mr. Macho Arab Male."

"You forget we are married. It says so on your passport. You must obey me and follow my orders. You will walk three steps behind me at all times, unless we are entering a minefield. Then you must walk twenty steps ahead of me."

"Mr. Macho Arab Male, you will be spending a lot of time playing with yourself. If you want real sex from your enslaved wife, you had better decide you will be a pack mule too. Oh, and a bit of advice: don't put a loaded pistol in the front of your waistband. If it should accidentally go off, then the private parts accidentally come off too." With that, Laura reached out and started making nice by rubbing the front of my *thawb,* which caused my little friend to throb.

"Wife woman, I think it is time for us to be bosom buddies again. I know exactly the bosom I want to be buddies with." I wrapped my arms around this delicious woman I love and hugged her to me while I began kissing her face and neck.

The best thing about being in love with Laura is that she loves me as much as I love her. She encircled my chest with her arms, pressing that delightful body hard against mine. After a few minutes of passionate kissing, she pulled up my *thawb* and reached inside. I had hoisted up her long dress and was caressing her beautiful backside. "Let's get out of these clothes," she said.

Laura ran her hands over my butt. "You have the sexiest ass I have ever beheld, my Macho Arab Husband," she said. "Why don't you roll that sexy ass over on top of me and let me make you happy?"

I slid over on top of Laura. She whispered in my ear, "Go slow, Jack. Make it last and last. Let's set a Guinness World Record for the longest loving in history."

My hips moved slowly on top of her, short motions in and out and around, little grinds against her pubic mound. Her arms and hands never stopped moving on my back and my butt. After what seemed like only a few minutes, she said, "Stop moving or I'll be done in another minute. We have to make this last forever."

I lay still on top of her, trying not to be too heavy. I continued kissing her face. Soon she squeezed my little friend inside her and said, "Slowly, my love, very slowly."

Laura rubbed her feet up and down the backs of my legs as I slowly moved inside her. Whenever she moved her feet upwards, her legs opened wider, and her wetness engulfed me as I slid deeper inside her. My upper body weight was on my elbows. Laura's breasts were in my hands, and I gently squeezed her nipples. A few moments later, I pushed her breasts together and rubbed her nipples against each other. She gave a groan of surrender and raised her legs into the air, so I penetrated all the way inside her. She began thrusting her body upwards, and I abandoned all hope of a world record. I needed Laura so much that I could not hold back any longer. We both came together in an extended shuddering orgasm that seemed to last an eternity.

The loving didn't last long enough for a world record, but maybe that orgasm might make it into the Guinness World Record Book.

25

SANA'A

Jack
Sana'a, Yemen
Thursday, 21 May

Sana'a, the capital of Yemen, is built on a plateau and is the main entry point for international travelers. One would think that Yemeni Air would fly from Cairo to Sana'a, but there are no direct flights. So, for a direct flight without layovers in some other Arab capital, we flew EgyptAir. We used our Yemeni passports, pretending we were returning home. We could just as easily have used our Palestinian passports. Yemen is a big supporter of Hamas. Palestinians shuttle in and out of Yemen regularly for military training and for purchasing arms and rockets and other such incidental necessities of Arab life.

Sana'a is a chaotic, ramshackle, dirty, rundown place. The last time Sana'a was a major metropolis was probably sometime back in the eleventh century. Not much has changed since then.

The buildings are made of baked mud brick and are basically two to five stories high. The city's skyline is dominated by the al-Saleh mosque with its six minarets. Al-Saleh is very large and rises above everything in the city. When looking out across Sana'a, al-Saleh seems to be the only new structure in town. The mosque was built by the former President Ali Abdullah Saleh at a cost in excess of $100 million.

Considering that Yemen is one of the world's poorest countries, this certainly ranks as an essential expenditure of scarce funds, right up there with food and AK-47s. And then President Saleh, in a fit of self-effacing modesty, named the mosque al-Saleh after himself. Some public servants just can't refrain from doing great things for the people they serve.

Modern Yemen is not a user-friendly place. Everyone looks at everyone else with suspicion. Only their own tribesmen can be trusted, and then only a little. You mind your own business and don't make eye contact with anyone. Laughter is for when you get to Paradise. Days are cloudless with temperatures above 100° F; nights are close to freezing. The wind never stops.

Daily life is a very serious business. Disagreements are often settled with gunfire or with knives. Revenge is the motivating factor in a great many deaths. Feuds are common. Electricity is scarce and only available in large cities, and then only part of the day. There is oil and natural gas in the ground, but getting it out is iffy because of frequent attacks on the oil installations. Water is twenty times more valuable than oil.

The country operates in the ninth century with a thin veneer of modern weapons to liven things up. There are more camels and goats than there are people. No two Yemeni citizens agree with anything the other one says or does. The only things that all Yemenis agree on are that Islam is the one true religion and that they hate the West and Israel. There is very little consumption of alcohol because the Prophet, peace be upon him, has forbidden its use. The recreational drug of widest use is the chewing of khat leaves, which gives a mild high.

Roughly 40% of the available irrigation water (in a water-starved country) is devoted to the growing of khat. Men, women, and children all chew khat. Aside from these few quirks, Yemen is a feel-good land with sand. Welcome aboard.

Yemeni politics is a crazy quilt. Nominally, Yemen is a democracy. Practically, whoever controls the army runs the country for his personal profit. The government barely functions. The Yemeni government is not of, by, or *for* the people. The people don't trust the government, and the government looks upon the people as a flock of sheep that must be shorn.

The Saudis and the Americans keep pressure on the government to hunt down al-Qaeda. Tribes keep shifting their allegiances depending upon who is dominating the local scene at the moment, and the tribes don't like each other very much either.

The police are trigger-happy and can kill you or throw anyone in prison with no reason at all. Forget about the courts; the judges are for sale. Corruption, incompetence, and family influence rule the day. Sunnis and Shi'a will fight to the death. Al-Qaeda rules part of southern Yemen and has imposed strict Sharia law there. The government is fighting to get it back so they can control the corruption instead of letting al-Qaeda pocket the cash. Criminal bands roam the countryside and the hills. Hatred runs deep, and everyone has a gun.

At the airport, the Yemeni immigration official wanted to know where we had been after we left a year ago (according to our fake exit stamps in our forged passports). I told him I had been to Afghanistan to fight the infidels. He understood the need for such a journey. But why were we returning when there was still a war going on? I explained my father was ill and had requested that I return before he died. To obey the wishes of your father is a sacred duty for a Muslim. The official stamped the passports and told us to "Go with God. And may your father soon sit at the right hand of Allah, *insallah*." (Hey, asshole, thanks for wishing an early death for my father.)

I thanked him for his kindness and wondered to myself, *Allah must have an enormous crowd on his right-hand side.* There are the martyrs (each with seventy-two virgins in tow), the mothers and fathers of martyrs, the Faithful Followers of the Prophet, peace be unto Him, who heeded the call to jihad, and the innocents who died because they were used as human shields by the Faithful Followers who heeded the call to jihad. Of course, Sunnis believe only Sunnis get to sit on the right hand of Allah, while Shi'as *know* that only Shi'as find favor in the eyes of Allah. Kipling had it wrong. East is East and West is West, and one day they might meet. But Sunnis and Shi'as are very likely to fight it out until no one is left, *insallah.*

Laura was conservatively dressed in a dark, ankle-length dress with long sleeves. Her head was covered, and only her eyes were visible above her veil. We took a taxi into the city from the airport. We went to the Yemen Princess Hotel, an establishment frequented by no one of importance. It was perfect for us. The Yemen Princess didn't even accept credit cards, only cash, in advance, thank you. We paid 35 euros for two nights. There was a discount if you paid in hard currency. Our deluxe room was on the third floor, which was the top floor. There is an elevator that doesn't work even when there is electricity, so you walk up the three flights. The deluxe room features a toilet, bathtub, and shower. The plumbing was Yemeni modern, circa 1920, but at least it worked.

As Laura and I surveyed our digs, I said, "Welcome to the Queen of Sheba Suite."

She laughed and said, "You owe me a real hotel room in a real city instead of one of these sewer pits. I heard that even the rats won't stay here.

"Speaking of rats, the two-legged kind, I don't feel comfortable with just a knife for protection in this town. We need some firepower."

"Do you know your way around Sana'a well enough to get what we need?"

"No, I don't, but I'll bet the desk clerk knows how to score what we need. He'll cooperate for a little *baksheesh.*"

"It will probably be easier if a man does the buying alone. Why don't you go shopping, and I will stay here with our baggage. I don't want a repeat of what happened in Cairo."

"Fair enough. I'll be back as soon as I can." We gave each other a passionate full-body hug and a dozen kisses, and then I left to have a word with the desk clerk. As soon as I was out the door, I heard Laura locking it.

The clerk was dozing in the small office behind the desk in the lobby. A ceiling fan was slowly turning, making a little squeak with each revolution. For all the difference it made in the heat, the fan might as well have saved itself a lot of turning and squeaking for nothing. If the clerk was aware of my presence, he was ignoring me.

I rang the bell on the desk. He opened one eye and looked at me. Slowly, he arose and came out to the desk. "Yes?" he said.

I placed a 20-euro note on the desk. My hand was holding it down. The clerk eyed the note. I said, "I have just returned from Afghanistan. I could not take my weapons through airline security. I feel naked without a gun. Where can I get what I need?"

The clerk again glanced at the money. "For 50 euros, I can give you directions to a friend who will have everything you want."

"Twenty euros is enough for the information I want. If you won't help me, then I will help myself—it will just take longer."

"We are only on the Earth for a short time before we are called to Allah," said the clerk. "As a favor, I will share my connections with you for 40 euros."

"I will give you 20 euros now and 10 later after I return and know the worth of your advice."

"That is acceptable. You will find that everyone knows Rafiq from the Yemen Princess. Mention my name and you will receive a discount." *Terrific,* I thought, *mention this asshole's name so he can collect his commission later for sending a customer.*

I took my hand off the 20-euro note. The clerk made it disappear so fast he could have gotten a job as a magician in Vegas. He took a pen and wrote a name and address on a slip of paper. "There is a small souk about a ten-minute walk from here. Ask for Shaheem. Do not forget to tell him you were sent by Rafiq from the Yemen Princess, and he will give you his best price."

"Where is this place?"

"Truly, it is easy to get there. When you leave the hotel, turn right, go two blocks, then turn right again. After three blocks, you will be at the market. It is a small square with about thirty-five stalls. Ask for Shaheem. Everyone knows him."

"I will go now. If I am pleased with what you have told me, you will get your other 10 euros."

I left the desk and exited the hotel. I turned right. After about 75 feet, I passed an alley, just a space between the hotel and the building next door, about five feet wide. It was dark with shadows, littered with discarded junk, some debris, and sand blown in by the wind. Instinctively, I stepped in and flattened my back against the hotel wall. I was hidden in the shadows.

I watched the pedestrian traffic passing on the street. After about two minutes, a pair of men passed by in a hurry. The larger one was wearing a keffiyeh on his head in the red and white checked pattern of the Palestinians; the smaller one had a slight limp, and he wore a tribal scarf on his head. The gimpy guy was wearing a soiled thwab, the ankle-length robe common to Yemeni men. The big guy with the keffiyeh wore pants, a shirt, and a jacket. Either they were late getting somewhere, or they were trying to catch up with someone.

I waited a little longer. Then I stepped to the edge of the alley so I could see them. I watched as they got to the second intersection and turned right. I don't believe in coincidences. The alley was a dead end with locked doors from the buildings providing the only access. There was no other exit; I would have to go out onto the main street again.

I left the alley and turned left instead of right. I passed the front of the hotel and walked two blocks past it in the wrong direction. Then I crossed the road in a knot of people. I started back in the correct direction. When I got to the second intersection, where I was supposed to turn right, I didn't. I walked another 500 feet past the intersection. Again, I crossed the road with a group of people—three men and a woman. Once on the other side, I walked back to the intersection. I turned left and slowly made my way down the street, blending in with the pedestrians as I ignored the street hawkers and shop owners trying to entice customers into their shops.

Up ahead, I could see the small square with the market stalls lining both sides. It wasn't even a real square, just a wide place in the road. The stalls were on both sides, and the traffic moved between them. All the action was in the middle area. I spotted Gimpy. He was standing between the second and third stalls on my side of the street, smoking a cigarette. Keffiyeh was at the other end, also two stalls in from the end. They were both waiting for someone to show up asking for Shaheem.

I don't think either of these guys had ever seen me. They were looking for someone based on the description they got from Rafiq, my friendly desk clerk. Based on that description, I could be anyone in the northern hemisphere. I knew I had never seen *them* before today, so we weren't exactly old buddies.

Slowly, I made my way down the street on the side where they were waiting. I got to the first stall. All the stalls were iron pipe frames covered with canvas on the sides, backs, and tops. There was a space of about 15 inches between the stall backs and the building walls. I slipped into this space and moved silently past the first two stalls. In the space between the second and third stalls, Gimpy was standing at the opening, lighting another cigarette. The stalls were each approximately 12 feet in length from front to back. There was quite a bit of noise from the people in the market that covered my footsteps.

I slipped up behind him. The point of my knife pressed into the right side of his neck as I whispered in his ear, "Don't say a word or you will die." The point of the knife punctured his skin a little, and a few drops of blood ran down his neck. Smart man, he didn't say a word. I grabbed the cloth of his thwab with my left hand and exerted a backward pressure. "Drop the cigarette and back up slowly, very slowly. Any sudden move and you are on your way to Heaven."

We backed up about eight feet. "Get down on your knees," I ordered.

He knelt.

"Why are you following me? Speak *haq* (truth), or you will die."

"We meant no harm. Rafiq told us to see where you went. He said you had money but no weapons. We were supposed to pick your pocket."

"Stealing my money is the same as no harm to you? What if I didn't want to give you my money?"

"Then we were supposed to convince you to give it to us."

I'd had enough of this. I pressed the nerves on his neck and rendered him unconscious. Then, holding him up by the back of his robe, I chopped down on his right collarbone. I heard the bone break. I did a quick frisk. Gimpy had a 9mm Makarov in his pocket. It looked like he hadn't cleaned it in a year. With a broken collarbone, I was sure he wouldn't be plinking at rabbits in the desert for a while, so I kept the gun.

I dragged Gimpy to the rear end of the stall and propped him against the wall so he looked as if he was asleep. Anyone seeing him would assume he had chewed too much khat and was sleeping it off. Perhaps some other solid citizen would find him and rob him while he slept.

I then continued down the back of the line of stalls until I got to Keffiyeh. There was something about this guy's body language that I didn't like. I've seen too many bad guys and killers. Of the pair, he was the honcho, and if killing needed to be done or torture was required, he was the one who would enjoy doing it. I wouldn't want my sister to go out on a date with this guy.

Again, I approached from behind. This time, Gimpy's Makarov at Keffiyeh's neck was the persuader. "Don't make a sound or you will die," I said. It wasn't a very original thing to say, but at least he had the good sense to be quiet. "Now back up slowly, very slowly." We moved back together. When I figured we were far enough back, I said, "Get down on your knees. Put both hands on top of your head." He did as he was told.

"You will die for this," he said.

I banged the butt of the gun on his fingers on top of his head. Maybe a bone broke. "Do not threaten me, asshole. Answer me. How much of a cut was Rafiq supposed to get from what you were going to steal from me?"

"I will personally cut your heart out," he answered.

"You truly are an asshole of a goat," I said. "Now answer my question: How much of a cut was Rafiq supposed to get from the money you were going to steal from me?"

"Who is Rafiq? I do not know that name," he answered.

I don't like cute answers. I grabbed one of his fingers and bent it back until he was face down in the dirt. Loud voices were coming from the other end of the market. People were yelling for the police and an ambulance. Apparently, someone had found Gimpy and raised an alarm. To add to the general noise, loudspeakers began blasting out the *azen,* the call to midday prayers. There must be a mosque nearby because the sound of the *muezzin's* voice was really loud. *Allahu Akbar. Allahu Akbar. Allahu Akbar. Allahu Akbar. Ash-hadu an la ilaha ill-Allah. Ash-hadu an la ilaha ill-Allah.*

Keffiyeh used the distraction of the loudspeakers in an attempt to disable me. He kicked out at my legs with his right foot. I saw it coming and jumped up above his feet to avoid the kick. I landed with my knee square in the center of his back. There was a cracking noise, and Keffiyeh let out a great whoosh of air and lay still. Pity. I really wanted to know what Rafiq's cut was supposed to be.

I did a quick frisk of Keffiyeh's body. He had a loaded spare magazine in his pants pocket. If there is a spare magazine, then there must be a pistol somewhere, too. I found it in a shoulder holster under his jacket. Another Russian Makarov. He wasn't going to need it. In my head, I crossed two pistols and one spare magazine off my shopping list. It was time to leave.

Keffiyeh could stay where he was. Without any sudden moves, I walked to the back of the stalls and made my way behind the last two stalls until I was out on the street again. Then, I casually walked into the market as any shopper would.

A crowd was gathered at the far end of the market. The stall owners were all standing at the entrances to their stalls, looking up toward the commotion. Although they were as curious as anyone else, they were all unwilling to leave the stalls unattended for fear of being robbed. Someone must have called the police because the oogh-ah, oogh-ah of the police klaxons could be heard in the distance.

I stopped at the first stall and asked the owner, "What is happening there?"

"It seems someone must have been robbed. Maybe they killed him, too."

"Have the police been called? Perhaps they can catch whoever did it."

The stall owner laughed at my naïve faith in the police. "When the police get here, they will only rob him of whatever he has left." He spat on the ground. "That's for the police!"

I looked at the tables in his stall and saw what was for sale. There was an assortment of household goods, some food, an enormous pile of khat leaves, miscellaneous military surplus, knives, guns, a bulletproof vest, and other basic necessities of daily life in Yemen.

I looked at the other end of the market. "The streets are too dangerous these days. Maybe I should buy some more ammunition. Do you have a box of 9mm Makarov ammo? And a spare magazine for a Makarov?"

"I can supply that. It will cost you 50 U.S."

"Do I look like a sheikh or a rich man? Those things are only worth 15."

"40 U.S. is the best I can do," he countered.

"Maybe 20, but no more than 20, or my children will go hungry," I said.

"30 is as low as I can go.

"25 U.S. or I must shop elsewhere," I said and turned as if to leave.

"Done," said the merchant. "25 U.S. Let me see the money."

"First, let me see what you have," I said

At the other end of the market, the police had arrived. Whistles and shouting could be heard as they tried to move the crowd back. The siren of an approaching ambulance could be heard over the general noise. The Muzzein was still calling the faithful to prayer over the loudspeakers, and the noise added to the general chaos.

The stall owner reached under his table and brought out a box of fifty rounds of ammo and a rusty magazine. I picked up the box. There was Chinese writing on it. It felt a little lighter than it should have. "That magazine is not acceptable, and I think this is not a full box of ammo. See if you have something better."

Again, he went under the table. This time, he came up with a magazine that was worn, but not rusty. Another box of 9mm ammunition, this time with Cyrillic printing, was opened to reveal that all the bullets were present. Russian and Chinese ammo were all over the Middle East. As lousy as the Russian stuff was, it was still better than the Chinese junk.

"Good," I said. As an apparent afterthought, I asked, "Do you maybe have a 9mm cleaning brush and a can of oil and some powder solvent?"

"I have what you want, but it will cost another 10 dollars U.S." He rummaged around in a box under his magic table and came up with a cloth bag. He emptied the bag onto the table. It held the cleaning tools I wanted plus a bunch of cotton patches.

"Seven U.S.," I countered.

"Eight dollars or I put it all away," said the merchant.

"Agreed," I said. "Could you put my things in a plastic sack for me?" I hunted in my pocket with my hand. By feel, I pulled out two twenties. I handed them to the merchant. He gave me my change, a rumpled $5 bill that must have been 40 years old and looked like it was left out in the rain, plus two singles. I took them.

The noise from the other end of the market was getting louder, with many people shouting at once—the ambulance had arrived.

The stall owner said, "Now that we have concluded our business, may I offer you a cup of tea?"

"That would be pleasant at another time. Right now, there is too much noise and activity. I think it would be best if I took my purchase and went home to my family."

"You are wise," he said. "Go in peace."

"And peace be unto you," I answered.

I walked out of the souk in the direction I had entered, away from Gimpy and the chaos that was sure to follow when they discovered Keffiyeh's body. I took a circuitous route back to the Yemen Princess.

Rafiq was at the desk when I entered the lobby. I am pretty sure he was surprised to see me. "Did you find Shaheem?" he asked.

"No. There was some kind of police action there and a lot of confusion. I did my shopping elsewhere." I put a 10-euro note on the desktop. As Rafiq reached for the money, I took it back. I looked Rafiq square in the eyes. I said, "You are a very lucky man. At this moment, you are one centimeter away from death. If you try such tricks again, death will surely find you."

He looked into my eyes and then looked away. He knew that I knew, and he was afraid. He opened his mouth to speak, but no words came out.

I turned and walked up the stairs to the third floor, the plastic bag swinging from my hand.

26

LAURA

Sana'a

The same day, Thursday, 21 May

Jack knocked on the door of our room. "It's me, Jack," he said softly. I was standing behind the door with my knife in my hand, ready to attack whoever entered. "I heard you outside the door. I didn't know it was you until you spoke."

I kissed him because I love kissing him, even with that awful beard. He pressed himself against me, and we kissed a few more times.

"Do you always kiss women who are holding knives?" I asked.

"Only the beautiful ones with great boobs," Jack answered.

I kissed him again, then I asked, "How was your shopping expedition? Did you get what we need?"

Jack gave me a detailed narrative of what had happened, starting with Rafiq, then moving on to Gimpy and Keffiyeh, and finally ending with Rafiq.

"You must have ice water in your veins if you could calmly go shopping in the same place where you just killed a man, with his body lying ten meters away from you. And then you take the time to haggle over the prices! If you stayed here a year, you would eliminate half the population of Yemen."

"Would that be a bad thing?"

"Bad for them. But the world would probably be a better place," I said. "Let me see what you have."

Jack produced the two Makarovs and placed the guns, magazines, and cleaning tools on the bed. I looked at the pile. "It is almost junk," I said.

"We'll have to make do with what we have. It is better than nothing. Neither of those animals believed in cleaning their weapons. We'll have to do that, or they might explode in our hands if we try to fire them."

Jack got a towel from the bathroom and spread it on the bed. I began to field strip the pistols so we could clean them. When I released the clip of one of the pistols, a small amount of sand fell out of the gun onto the towel. "I can't believe this would actually work with sand in the action," I muttered. "What pigs!"

Together, we removed the greasy, gritty grime from each piece, ran the brush and patches through the barrels until they shone when held up to the light. Solvent and oil worked wonders. Then we unloaded all the magazines and dumped the bullets Jack had just bought. The Makarov 9x18mm bullets are not the same as 9x19mm Parabellums. They are shorter, 9.22mm in diameter, and carry less powder. Firing a 9mm Parabellum in a Makarov could cause the gun to explode from excessive pressure. Each bullet was wiped with a clean rag, and the four magazines were reloaded. The ammo box was repacked. At least we now believed we had functioning weapons.

Jack said, "The Russian Makarov PM pistol is not a bad weapon if your target is less than 20 feet away, but I would have much preferred my Browning Hi-Power, an accurized Colt 45, or a Glock. Most Makarovs are used at point-blank range, fired into the backs of political prisoners' heads in executions. At that range, who needs accuracy?"

"You have a point," I agreed. Then, changing the subject, I said, "Tomorrow we should head north and connect with our contact. The sooner we do what we came for, the sooner we can leave this cesspool."

"Right on," Jack answered. "The sooner we get out of here, the sooner I can shave off this God-awful beard. Tomorrow, we have to get a pickup truck. Something nice in rust and white, preferably without bullet holes. Laura, you *can* drive a shift, can't you?"

"Of course, you fool, have I not been in the army? If possible, we should get a truck with all-wheel drive. And while we are shopping, two AK-47s wouldn't be so bad either," I added. "I think four magazines each will be sufficient."

"I think another talk with Rafiq is in order to find the best used trucks in town."

"Do you trust him to give you straight advice?

"He knows how close he came to meeting Allah today. By tomorrow, he will know what happened to his buddies. He would not dare mess with me."

I smiled. "Don't jack around with Jack, or Abdullah the Merciful will fry your ass."

27

LAURA

Sana'a
Friday, 22 May

We were up at the crack of dawn, our one bag packed and ready. Jack wore his fighter's garb, complete with his favorite boots. I dressed for the desert in pants, a shirt, and lightweight boots, then pulled an abaya over my clothes. A niqab covered my face and head, leaving only my eyes exposed. I kept cursing the local customs that required me to be fully covered in the desert heat.

Downstairs, Rafiq was at the desk. As Jack approached, Rafiq visibly cringed, but at least he didn't flee from him.

"Have you heard from your friends yet?" Jack quietly asked.

I was toting our one piece of luggage, as a good Muslim wife should. "Y-you are checking out?" he stammered.

"Yes. Also, I need some more information from you. I warn you now, if you play your silly games with me, I promise you a very slow and painful death. Do you fully understand what I am saying?" asked Jack.

"Y-y-yes," said Rafiq. He kept looking around for help from somewhere, anywhere, but we were alone in the lobby, and Allah was otherwise engaged and unavailable. Poor Rafiq was on his own. I thought I smelled urine.

"I need a truck and some AKs. Where can I get them?" The look in Jack's eyes would have frozen a 600-pound tuna on the spot. Rafiq started to shake.

"W-will you be coming back to v-visit m-me?" Tears gathered in the corners of his eyes.

"No. I will spare you, although I really don't know why I am letting you live," Jack hissed. "But I will return if your information is not good."

With obvious relief, Rafiq picked up a pen. With a shaking hand, he wrote a name and address on a piece of paper. "Muhammed ben Amir Kamal-Sidiqi has some trucks for sale. He can get you everything you need."

"Where can I find this man?"

"His place is about 3.5 kilometers west of here. When you get out there, you must ask for the police barracks. He has a space in the sands behind the barracks. His brother is a police lieutenant, and they protect him," said Rafiq.

"I see," Jack said. "I am a cautious man. As the Prophet, *Sal Allaahu Alaiyhi wa Sallam,* is my witness, if the police bother me, you will die as I promised. You had better pray they do not bother me by intent or by chance. Your life is hanging by a thread at this moment."

"There is no trick. If they bother you, tell them you are going to see Muhammed, and they will leave you alone."

"Just so you are aware of what any treachery will bring you," Jack promised.

We turned to go. I dragged our suitcase. We exited the hotel and turned west.

I whispered, "I think he pissed in his pants. I am sure I smelled urine."

"I think so too. Serves the sneaky bastard right."

The sun was already beating down even though it was only 8 a.m. We had been trudging along for about 10 minutes when a farmer passed us with a cart being pulled by a donkey. It was a typical Middle Eastern cart with a wooden platform and seat and four salvaged automobile wheels with tires.

Jack greeted him, "May Allah grant you peace."

"And peace be unto you," he replied.

"We must go to the police barracks up the road. My woman is tired from pulling our bag. What would you charge me to let us ride on your cart until the barracks?"

"That will take me out of my way," he answered. "However, for 50 dinars, I will take you."

"I was hoping for a price of 30 dinars," Jack said.

"40 dinars, or you can keep walking," he countered.

"Done. 40 dinars." Jack hoisted the bag onto the cart, and I climbed up in the back and sat on it. Jack got onto the seat next to the farmer. He paid him the 40 dinars in small bills and coins so the farmer would not think Jack was a rich man who could have paid him more.

"Why do the police wish to see you?" asked the farmer.

"I do not really know. We are going to Pakistan to join the jihad," Jack lied. "Perhaps someone has told them what we plan to do, and they want backsheesh to let us go."

The farmer spat into the dirt. "They are dogs. They do not protect us. All they do is steal from us. May Allah send them all to hell."

The farmer made idle talk with Jack about neighbors he knew who had joined the jihad, and about the prices for barley and wheat, while the donkey plodded along. When we were about 200 meters from the police barracks, he stopped the cart.

"I do not want to get too close to those thieves," he said. "You will have to walk the rest of the way."

"May Allah bless you and give you good harvests," Jack said and climbed down from the cart.

I hadn't said a word during the entire ride, and I continued my silence as I climbed down and hauled our bag off the cart. The farmer said, "May Allah bring you good fortune with those pigs in there." He looked at me in my burqa, "A woman who can hold her tongue is a good woman. You are very lucky." He didn't have a clue how lucky we both really were.

28

A PICKUP TRUCK

We walked behind the police barracks to a littered lot of pickup trucks, vans, bicycles, and farm carts. There was even a beat-up Humvee from the Iraqi army. How the hell it got here must be some story. I fully expected to see an armored personnel carrier somewhere in that mess, maybe a tank. Several vehicles were semi-disassembled. A small cement-block building stood at the back of the lot. A sign over the door read, 'Office.' Finding a usable 4x4 pickup was going to be a challenge here.

We found Muhammed. I wondered why half of the males in Islamic countries are named Muhammed or some variation of it? He was urging a mechanic to fix a truck in a hurry so he could sell it. The mechanic was complaining that the engine was worn out and would not run again. Muhammed was waving his arms as he argued. The mechanic was waving a large open-ended wrench. I was waiting for one of them to strike the other, but then I thought if Muhammed comes out on the short end of this dispute, no one would be able to sell us a truck. I made my presence felt by knocking on a truck fender, and the argument halted, to be resumed later, I am sure.

Muhammed suddenly became all smiles at the prospect of a customer. The mechanic decided his nose needed picking, and he wandered off to do it full-time.

"Welcome, my friend," said Muhammed with a slimy smile, "how can I serve you?"

"I need a pickup truck with all-wheel drive. Something that is not too old or shot up."

"Ah, my friend, I have many beauties in my stock. I am sure we will find just what you need. Step this way, my friend," said Muhammed. He totally ignored Laura's presence; after all, she is just a woman. Used-car salesmen are right down there with lawyers, conmen, slugs, and pond scum when it comes to truthfulness and trust.

Muhammed led us to an antique Ford F-150—rusted, tilting to one side on a broken rear spring, tires balder than Michael Jordan's head, and the tailgate hanging down at a weird angle. "This is a beauty, my friend," oozed Muhammed with that slimy smile again. "It is in excellent condition."

I knew Muhammed was lying to me because his lips were moving. The truck had to be 40 years old. I was amazed that it was still in one piece.

"I will be driving into the desert. I need something better."

"Ah, my friend, I have just what you need over there." He started walking, and I followed. "It was owned by a sheikh who has become a martyr. You will be proud to drive such a truck, my friend. I was saving it for my cousin, but I will let you have it instead." Muhammed gave me another of his patented smiles.

One more "my friend" out of his mouth, and I was thinking about shooting this smarmy prick. Why are used-car salesmen so predictable no matter what part of the world they are in?

Muhammed led me to a Toyota that had seen better days, actually better years. "I want to hear the engine. Start it up," I said.

"Ah, my friend, the engine needs a little work. If you want this beauty, we will have it running like a fine Swiss watch in an hour.

"I don't want this beauty either." I looked around the lot. I saw a truck near the office building, a white Toyota 4x4 with large tires. I pointed at the Toyota. "That truck, how much is it?"

"Ah, my friend, that is my personal truck. It is not for sale."

"If it were for sale, how much would it be?" I asked.

"I would not take less than 10,000 euros, my friend," said my friend Muhammed.

"Let us examine your personal truck to see how it runs."

"But it is not for sale," he protested.

I walked to his personal truck. Muhammed had no choice but to follow me since I was the customer, and presumably, I had the money. The body of the truck had a string of bullet holes from a machine gun stitching a diagonal line across the left side. The rear window of the cab was starred where a bullet had gone through it. It wasn't much, but it was a 4x4. "Start it up," I ordered.

Muhammed got in the truck, leaving the driver's door open, and started the engine. There must have been a hole or two in the muffler because it sounded like a tank roaring into battle at full throttle.

"Release the hood," I commanded. He did, and I opened the hood. The engine compartment was layered with a dusting of sand, but the engine was running smoothly. No strange ticking noises, no parts obviously missing. I closed the hood. "I want to drive it," I said.

"Ah, my friend, but this truck is not for sale," he repeated.

"Everything is for sale when the price is right. I want to drive it." I grasped Muhammed's left arm and gently urged him out of the driver's seat. Well, maybe I squeezed his arm a little too hard because he visibly winced as he got out of the truck. His right hand involuntarily reached up to soothe his left bicep. "My woman will remain here while I test this truck. Treat her with respect," I warned.

"But of course, my friend. I would do nothing less for any woman."

I got in the truck and drove it around the lot and onto the road. The transmission was okay. I shifted into four-wheel drive. That worked too. A roll of duct tape would correct the muffler noise. It had the wheels I wanted. I drove back to Muhammed's Used Truck Emporium – We Only Sell Beauties.

Muhammed was still rubbing his left arm. "I will give you 6,000 euros for this truck," I said.

"My friend, that is my personal truck. I cannot part with it for less than 10,000 euros." Muhammed was now visibly nervous in my presence.

The butt of my Makarov was sticking up over my belt. I let my hand rest on the butt. "Think about your future," I said. "A man such as you will always find another truck as good as this one. In this lot, there are many beauties, as you yourself have said, and you have your pick of any of them. I need this truck now. I will give you 6,500 euros."

Muhammed nervously eyed my hand on the gun. "As a special favor, I will sell it for 9,000 euros."

"7,000 euros is my final offer. I am losing patience."

"Can you at least make it 7,500 euros?" pleaded Muhammed

"For the extra 500 euros, you must include two AK-47s and 500 rounds of ammunition. And then we will have a deal."

My hand was still on the butt of the pistol. Muhammed swallowed hard. "My friend, we have a deal," he said. "Let us go into my office."

We entered his office. There was a table and two chairs, along with a small room added to the back. A curtain covered the entrance to the back room. The place stank of stale food, stale tobacco, and stale people. It hadn't seen a broom in 20 years.

I counted out 7,500 euros in 500-euro bills and laid them on the desk. Muhammed started to reach for the money, but I grabbed his wrist in a vise-like grip before he could touch the bills. "First, I see the two AKs and the ammo, and I want eight 30-round magazines. I prefer the polymer type."

Muhammed looked into my eyes and decided that he would get the guns before he touched the money. A wise decision. He went into the back room through the curtain. I stood in the doorway of the little room with the curtain against my back, watching his every move. He had a regular armory back there. Nervously, he gathered what I wanted and brought the material out and laid it on the desk. The 500 rounds of ammo were in two boxes of 250 rounds each.

I picked up one of the AK-47s, worked the action, and dry-fired it a few times. I examined the barrel and saw no rust or fouling. I dropped the magazine and loaded it with five rounds. Muhammed's level of concern escalated exponentially when I loaded the magazine. I inserted the magazine back into the rifle and fed the five rounds into the breech, and ejected them all onto the desk. The piece was acceptable. I repeated the process with the second rifle. It too was acceptable.

Muhammed watched me nervously as I went through my checking of the AKs. If there had been any loud noise during this process, I am sure he would have shit in his pants. As it was, there was no loud noise, so his dignity remained intact.

"You may write me a receipt for the purchase, and then you may take the money. It was a pleasure doing business with you, my friend." I would not bother to officially register the truck. Almost no one does in Yemen. Registering a vehicle is just an excuse for some petty bureaucrat to collect another bribe. Whatever license number was painted on the bumper of the truck was good enough for me. Muhammed hastily scrawled me a receipt for the purchase of the truck.

I went to the door. "Alia, come help me here." Laura entered the office. I slung the two AKs onto my left shoulder and picked up one box of ammo in my left hand. Three magazines were balanced on top of the ammo box. My right hand was still free if I had to reach for my pistol. Laura picked up the other box of ammo and the remaining five magazines. She went out to the truck and put them in the cab. I followed her. Muhammed remained in the office. I think he was happy to see his new friend leave while he was still alive. His arm and wrist were going to have bruises for a while. Laura loaded our one piece of luggage into the truck bed.

I saw the mechanic at the other end of the lot. I drove the truck to where he was. "I need some duct tape or muffler cloth." It wasn't a request; it was an order. He nodded his understanding and scurried away.

The mechanic returned with a half roll of 2-inch duct tape. I told him, "Get under there and fix the muffler." He crawled under the truck and, in about five minutes, had the holes in the muffler wrapped with duct tape. I gave him a 50-dinar tip.

Muhammed was standing in the doorway of his office, watching us. Without another word, we drove away toward the center of Sana'a. We had wheels, we had guns, and we had some new friends, Rafiq and Muhammed. Life in Yemen was warm and fuzzy.

29

JACK ON THE ROAD

On the road
Friday, 22 May

We headed north out of Sana'a, toward the Saudi border. Both of us wore wraparound sunglasses. Pistols and knives were ready. This was dangerous country. Bandit bands (hey, is that a rock group?) roamed the desert, ambushing the unwary. Kidnapping for fun and profit was a cottage industry. Only Westerners with government connections were suitable victims. If you weren't worth kidnapping, then you would get robbed and killed.

Before leaving Sana'a, we had filled the tank and obtained four 5-gallon jerry cans of extra gas. We had no intention of being out in the desert after dark, and we certainly would not chance running out of gas.

All the clips were loaded. Eight clips at thirty rounds each require 240 rounds. This left us with a full case of ammo plus an extra ten rounds. The AK-47s were between us, leaning against the bench seat of the truck. I decided that once we were out in the desert, we would fire a few rounds from each rifle just to be sure everything was okay. Laura agreed it was a wise move.

After driving for 40 minutes, we arrived at a nice, open area. No hills, no wadis, no large rocks, no trees, no people, just sand. It was a suitable spot to test the rifles.

I stopped the truck, got out, and walked about fifty paces into the desert. I made two mounds of sand, each about 18 inches high, and stuck a fist-sized rock on top of each mound. Then I went back to the truck.

Laura went first. She fired off a single round that knocked the rock off the top of the mound. Then she fired a 3-round burst, which kicked the hell out of the top of the mound. The clacking of the AK's action was loud in the desert air. She then fired off the rest of the magazine on full automatic. The little mound disintegrated into multiple puffs until it was gone. The woman could really shoot.

I went next. My first shot hit the rock, but it glanced off the top. The rock stayed put. The 3-round burst knocked it off. Full-auto fire pounded into the mound. We were satisfied that we could rely on these rifles.

Back in the truck, Laura drove while I reloaded the magazines. She could only drive while we were in the Yemeni desert. Women cannot drive anything with wheels in Yemen or in Saudi Arabia unless it is a baby carriage. A woman driving any motor vehicle would be a dead giveaway that we were foreigners, not Yemenis. But in Yemen, laws were made to be broken. In Saudi Arabia, laws were enforced with religious fervor.

While Laura drove, I sat in the passenger seat on full alert, a rifle in my lap with the muzzle sticking out the window. The truck was not air-conditioned, so we drove with the windows open. We were traveling at about 65 to 70 km per hour, equivalent to 40 to 45 mph. Wind-blown sand often covered the road, sometimes completely hiding it. A low-pitched whistling sound came from the bullet hole in the rear window, sort of the song of the modern desert.

Very few vehicles passed us heading south, maybe one every 40 minutes. Not a single vehicle passed us going north, nor did we overtake any vehicles. There were so few travelers I felt as if we were approaching Dracula's castle in a grade B vampire movie. Only creepy music and the moon hiding behind midnight clouds were missing.

In the desert, water is the key to survival, more so than in any other place on this planet. We had two water bags and some plastic bottles of water. You don't gulp your water; you sip it at regular intervals to conserve it as much as possible. The water is always very warm from the heat, but it is what will keep you alive. Any empty bottles get saved to be refilled and reused.

The Bedouins seem to survive on very little water. Darwin was right about adaptability and the traits that ensure survival of the fittest. This climate was their bailiwick, and they are welcome to every rock and grain of sand in it. Aside from oil, this area has no redeeming features worth possessing.

We were on the road for about an hour and a half when Laura spotted the tops of palm trees in the distance. We did not know whether it was an oasis or a mirage. She pulled over, and we switched places. I got behind the wheel, and she manned the rifle. My rifle lay across my lap with the muzzle out the window. It is an awkward way to drive a truck.

As we continued driving, we saw an oasis up ahead. Where there is water, there are usually people. Sometimes there are actually permanent settlements. When we drew abreast of the oasis, it was clear that this was just a watering hole, not a settlement. The road passed about 100 feet from the edge of the trees. A Bedouin caravan of camels and donkeys was camped here, waiting for the hottest part of the day to pass before continuing to wherever they were going.

We did not need water, but we needed information about whatever they might have seen on their travels. So, I pulled off the road and parked under the patchy shade of a scrubby palm tree. We got out of the truck. I slung my rifle over my shoulder; Laura left hers in the cab. We had a small bag of dates in the cab. Laura said, "Take the dates. They will be a good way to start a conversation. Let's use the story of returning for your sick father." I agreed with her.

I carried the bag of dates in my left hand as we left the truck. Laura carried our four empty plastic bottles so she could refill them. In this society, a man does not fetch water when there is a woman available to do that work. Laura knows how to blend in without arousing any suspicions.

I walked to the group of men who were sitting and smoking. One Bedouin stood up to greet me. I heard the clicks of several safeties being released on the guns of the seated men, but no one raised a weapon at me. There is an unwritten rule that there is to be no fighting at a desert oasis. But there is no rule prohibiting being *ready* to fight. Caution keeps you alive in Yemen these days.

"*As salaam aleikaum*," I said to the standing man.

"And unto you be peace," he replied.

"We are passing by on our way north. We decided to fill our empty bottles."

"You are welcome to do so. Allah put the water there for all to share."

"May I join you in the shade and rest for a short time?" I asked.

"Sit," was all he said. So I sat.

"I have some dates to share." I took one and passed the bag to the man closest to me. He took one and passed it on to the next man. There was a noticeable relaxation in the state of readiness at that point.

"Why do you go north?" asked the leader. "The road is heavy with danger from the bandits."

"I was in Afghanistan fighting the dogs who serve the Americans when I received word that my father was very ill. He requested I return to see him before he died. I cannot disobey my father's request."

There were nods of approval all around me. I scored points for fighting in the jihad and for fulfilling my sacred obligations to my father. These men were warriors by nature and choice. They would rather fight than breathe. I had their respect, if only for a short time.

"Have you seen any bandits or army patrols?" I asked.

"No bandits, but there was one army patrol yesterday. We had to pay the pig lieutenant baksheesh. They are as bad as the bandits."

"So, we must depend upon ourselves. That is how it has always been and how it will always be. I have taught my woman to shoot a rifle. She is not a warrior, but she is better than nothing if trouble comes. She has courage."

"Let her not be talking to our women, or they will get ideas," said the headman.

"She is no fool and knows what she should not say. She listens but rarely speaks."

"A woman like that is a blessing," said the man sitting next to me. We all laughed.

"I thank you for sharing your news with me. It is time for us to get moving again. We do not want to spend the night in the desert."

"Go with God," said the headman, "and stay alert."

"And may you go in peace," I replied. "Your advice is good. We will heed your wisdom."

I rose, slung my rifle over my shoulder, and started back toward the truck. I called "Alia," and Laura left the group of women and came to walk three steps behind me as every good Muslim wife should. She carried the filled water bottles. I got into the driver's seat, and we started off, driving back to the road and then heading north again.

In the truck, I said, "There is an army patrol ahead of us. We have to avoid them."

Laura said, "The women advised that the Saudi border officers are very nosy. We should be prepared to pay baksheesh right away when we get to the border. If we can cross the border without them seeing us, it might be better. They also said they saw signs of al-Qaeda on the Saudi side."

"Baksheesh is probably safer and easier than risking the desert. What signs of al-Qaeda did they see?"

"An oil trailer truck was burned at the side of the road. The driver was dead. He had been tortured. The women guessed it was because he worked for the infidel oil company."

"The men did not say anything about that. I wonder why?"

"The women said that the men took away parts of the burned truck to sell. From what was described, I think they took the valves from under the oil tank. Maybe they were afraid you might report them for stealing the parts. You are a total stranger after all. When you steal something, you don't tell everyone you meet about it. But the women like to gossip."

"You are right. You know, for a woman, you are smarter than you look."

Laura gave me a friendly punch in the arm. "You know, as a man, you are maybe a 3.5 out of 10, just about as long as your putz."

"Touché," I said, "you win." We drove on in friendly silence, constantly scanning ahead and behind us. Man, but I love this woman.

30

CROSSING INTO SAUDI-LAND

At the Saudi Border
Friday, 22 May

Around 2:15, we saw a dust cloud out in the desert. We estimated that four or five vehicles were traveling southwest toward the highway we were on. We couldn't tell how fast they were going because the wind was stirring up everything that was loose.

I told Jack to stop the truck while I scanned the cloud with our binoculars. After half a minute, I said, "I think that is a Yemeni army patrol. Maybe the same one the Bedu were talking about. The sands are very loose here, and the wind is kicking its dust high into the air. They will not get to this road for at least 20 to 30 minutes. If we speed up, we can get away from this area well before they arrive."

"I like your thinking," Jack said. "Let's get out of here." Jack put the truck back in gear, and soon we were clipping along at 110 km per hour. Once we could no longer see the patrol's dust cloud, we slowed down to a more reasonable rate of speed. The wind-blown sand was making the road hard to see.

We reached the Saudi border near the Dammaj Valley at approximatey 2:45. Four men in military uniforms were manning a roadblock with a long barrier made from a pipe blocking the road. They had cloths wrapped around their mouths and noses because of the blowing sand. Two of them were wearing goggles to protect against the sand. The pipe was striped in red and white paint like a railroad crossing barricade. Twenty feet off to the side was a cement-block building, built like a small fort, that looked big enough for fifteen men to live in. If we could see four, were there others inside, away from the blowing sand?

A sergeant was in charge. Three men stood behind the pipe with their guns leveled at our truck. The sergeant motioned for us to get out of the truck. The soldiers relaxed visibly when they saw we were just one man and one woman. We left our rifles in the cab.

The sergeant lowered the cloth away from his mouth. He had a Saddam Hussein mustache and a three-day stubble beard. We stood quietly, with the doors between us and the soldiers. "Let me see your papers," said the sergeant.

Jack produced our two Yemeni passports with a 50 euro bill tucked into his. The sergeant looked at us with hostility. "Where are you going?"

Jack answered, "We are going to Karmis Mushait. My father is very ill. He will not live much longer. He has requested that I visit him before he dies."

"Your passports have stamps from Pakistan. Have you been to Pakistan?" What a detective this guy would have made.

"Yes, we have been there," Jack said. "Then I walked over the mountains to Afghanistan, where the fighting was."

"You are al-Qaeda?"

"No, but I have answered the call for jihad. My wife came with me to Pakistan."

"How long will you be in the kingdom?"

"We will stay two weeks with my father. If Allah should call him while I am here, then we will stay for the period of mourning as well. Then we will return to Pakistan and Afghanistan."

"Raise the gate," shouted the sergeant. He handed Jack the passports. The 50-euro bill had disappeared. "Stop by the corporal. He will stamp your passports."

"Do not make trouble while you are in Saudi Arabia," warned the sergeant. Motioning toward me with his head, he added, "She will need the full burqa if you enter a city. The niqab is allowed in the villages only."

"Thank you, Sergeant. Among our own people, we are very peaceful." Jack put the truck in gear and slowly rolled forward to the corporal. He produced a customs stamp and stamped both of our passports. The pipe gate was lowered behind our truck.

We had officially entered the Kingdom of Saudi Arabia. Hopefully, our quarry was somewhere to be found in the desert.

31

JACK

We were about forty kilometers into Saudi territory when we came to a fork in the road. We, genius operatives that we are, did not have a decent map of the area. Where is a gas station selling road maps when you need it most? "I think the left fork is the one we should take. Karmis Mushait is to the northwest. The right fork might take us deeper into the desert," I stated.

"If we go on the left road, it will take us into the hills," Laura observed. "That might make us targets for the bandits. We should have asked for directions when we were at the border post."

"Real men never ask for directions," I answered. "We just blunder forward against whatever fate throws our way. I vote for the left road."

"I hope you are making the right choice. My feeling is that we should take the right fork."

"Not to worry. As long as we are together, we will be okay."

I swung the wheel left, and we headed more toward the northwest. Forty minutes on this road, and Laura spotted two pickup trucks coming around a dune 1,500 yards away. They were side by side and heading straight for us. Two men stood in the back of each truck with rifles resting on the roof of each cab. They were traveling fast, filling the entire width of the roadway. In the rearview mirror, I saw a cloud of dust behind us as two more pickups with men standing in the beds of the trucks pulled in about 1,200 yards behind us. Somewhere deep inside me, a small voice said, "Oh shit!"

I threw the transmission into all-wheel drive mode and made a hard right turn off the road and into the desert. I spoke rapidly. "When I stop the truck, we will be crosswise to their approach. Get out and use the hood for cover. When the nearest truck gets to about 100 yards away, fire 3-round bursts at the driver's side of the windshield. I'll do the same using the back of the truck for cover. They will be traveling over rough ground and won't be able to shoot straight. Take three extra magazines. Don't waste ammo. Stand by the front wheel to protect your feet."

After about 1,000 yards into the desert, I made a 90-degree left turn and skidded to a stop. The engine was still running. Laura opened her door and got out, positioning her rifle on the hood of the truck. I slid across the seat, got out on the passenger side, and took a position with my AK resting on the pickup body. Laura threw off her burqa. She was ready to fight.

Our attackers swerved off the road and closed in. The nearest trucks were 300 yards out; the closest pickup was already within 200, with another just behind to the left. Two more trailed at 400 yards. "Ten seconds," I called.

At about 110 yards, Laura let loose a 3-round burst. The windshield of the lead pickup took all three bullets. She must have hit the driver because the truck veered hard to its left and overturned. We could hear the screams of the men in the back of the truck as they were thrown forward over the top of the cab. One man lay still. The other got up on his hands and knees. Laura put three rounds into him. He fell flat.

When you fire a three-round burst, the first shot is on target; the recoil raises the muzzle a little, so the second shot goes a bit high. The second recoil raises the barrel further, so the third shot goes even higher or misses completely. It takes great left-arm strength to keep the barrel from moving upwards while firing. Laura held the AK-47 so that all three shots hit in the same area. She was one strong lady.

I took aim at the second truck's driver and let loose three rounds. The truck started weaving left and right, drove sideways for a few yards, and then turned back in the direction it had come from. This exposed the men in the back of the truck. I laid three rounds into the guy on the left. Laura's AK clacked three rounds into the guy on the right. They both fell into the bed of the truck.

The truck had almost stopped moving when the passenger's door flew open and a man dropped to the ground. He got up to run around the front of the truck to use it for cover. Big mistake. The truck was still moving almost as fast as he was running, so he remained exposed. Laura and I both shot him at the same time. He stopped running permanently.

Someone in the flipped-over truck got his gun and raked our truck with a full magazine. Our left front tire took a hit, and the truck tilted in that direction. Most of his shots went high overhead. We had some new bullet holes in the left front fender to match the holes in the body. He must have shoved in a new magazine, and as he poked his head around the end of the truck, ready to fire again, both Laura and I hit him with 3-round bursts. That woman was cool, and she could shoot!

The other two pickups were bearing down on us. "I'll take the gray one; you get the white one on the left," Laura called. "Fire on the count of three! One, two, fire!"

The two trucks were side by side when we fired. We both got hits. The truck on the right veered left and slammed into the other, flipping it over. It rolled once, coming to rest with the passenger side against the ground. The two men in the back got catapulted 40 feet away into the rocky sand.

The passenger-side door of the fourth truck opened, and the occupant jumped out. I put a burst through the window opening of the door, and the man went down. At least one round hit him in the head, maybe two.

Laura spotted movement somewhere and let loose a burst. We heard a scream of pain. Laura said, "There were sixteen of them. I count eleven hits. That leaves five. Three are either dead or unconscious in the sand. I think one is trapped in the cab of truck number three. There is one unaccounted for from the back of the fourth truck. We don't know whether the three men in the sand are dead, injured, or faking. Two of the hits are probably still alive. So, there are at least four live ones, maybe more, out there."

"We'll wait a few minutes and see if anything moves."

Overhead, a vulture began circling. Soon it was joined by two more. A fourth vulture swooped in low and then flew up to join its circling buddies. Within minutes, there had to be 25 birds circling overhead. Luncheon was about to be served in the Royal Saudi Dining Room.

"Let's put a few rounds into the guys lying in the sand," said Laura.

"I'm not so sure we should do that just yet. I think these guys were planning to kidnap us. That means they are probably al-Qaeda. Let's see if we can find anyone alive. They might know where our boy is."

Most of the wreckage was about 80 yards away, but it was quite spread out. A brave vulture landed next to one man in the sand and took a chunk out of the back of his neck. The guy never moved. We were pretty sure we had another dead one there. Another vulture landed and joined the party. The rest kept circling overhead.

We waited. The sun blazed overhead, unforgiving and relentless. Flies gathered on some attackers. Flies didn't mean the man was dead. It just meant he couldn't move to brush them away. Where the hell all those flies came from was a mystery to me.

Laura saw movement in the cab of truck number three, the one that was lying with the passenger's side down. The windshield had three bullet holes in it, but most of the glass remained intact. We could see a man's legs. Laura put a three-round burst into what remained of the windshield. We heard screams of pain coming from the truck. "Load a fresh magazine," I said. We both reloaded.

Ten minutes passed. It felt like an hour. Nothing moved except the flies and the circling vultures. "I'm going over there," I said. "Keep a sharp eye on the bad guys. If anyone makes a threatening move, shoot him.

"Jack, I think we should drive the truck in a large circle around these guys first. If we see any movement, we can then decide what to do. I think we have at least two wounded. They might still be able to fight."

"Laura, I said it before, I'll say it again, you are smarter than you look. That is a good plan."

"And you are a world-class idiot," said Laura. "I'll drive; you keep a sharp eye."

Laura slid into the driver's seat and started the truck. The flat front tire made steering very difficult. In first gear, she made a U-turn so the passenger side would face the battle scene. I had my rifle poised on the passenger door windowsill, ready to shoot anything that moved. She shifted into second and drove about 15 km per hour in a large clockwise circle around the site.

The vultures got spooked and took off again.

The guy in the cab kept calling on Allah to save him. I didn't think Allah was online at the moment.

Nothing was moving except the screamer in the cab of the third truck. We stopped the truck and got out. We approached the first bodies in the sand. Laura and I were about 15 feet apart. One guy was lying on his back, his head at a strange angle. He must have landed headfirst. He was dead. There were three hand grenades clipped to his jacket. He won't be using these anytime soon, so I took them.

The second attacker near him was breathing, but barely. He had landed on the barrel of his rifle, and about six inches of the barrel had punctured his belly. He was bleeding into the sand with a mass of moving flies all over him. This guy was going to die of shock and loss of blood. Shooting him would be an act of kindness. I decided to let him suffer.

The third guy in the sand was alive, but he had compound fractures of his right leg and right arm. He, too, was in shock. Only his eyes were moving, but his vision didn't register anything. Flies were all over his exposed bones, his face, eyes, and head. His rifle was lying ten feet away from him. Laura picked it up and dumped it in the back of our truck. I decided to let him play nicely with his friend, who had the gun barrel sticking into his belly. I thought about putting him out of his misery, but then I changed my mind. I mean, do I look like Florence Nightingale?

We were still short one guy from the fourth truck. I approached the truck cautiously. I found him in the bed of the pickup. He must have been crouched down behind the cab because a round had come through the windshield, exited out through the back window, and hit him in the throat. His days of recreational kidnapping were over. All bad guys were present and accounted for.

Laura said, "I'm going to make some noise." She was over by the second truck. A second later, a shot rang out. "I had to end his suffering," she said. Laura is a much kinder person than I am.

We finished our survey of the destruction. We went over to the truck with the wounded guy screaming for Allah to help him. I stood at the back of the truck. I yelled, "I will help you, but you must first get rid of the weapons. Throw your rifle up through the driver's window. Do it now!"

A few moments later, a rifle was pushed out of the driver's window and fell to the ground. "Now throw out the driver's rifle," I yelled. The other rifle was pushed out and fell to the ground.

"Now, both of your pistols." There was some movement in the truck, and the pistols flew out of the window.

"Now, your knives." One knife flew out the window. "Where is the other knife?" I yelled.

"That was my knife. The driver does not have a knife," came the reply.

"Throw out the other knife, or I will shoot through the roof of the cab. Do it now! You have three seconds." The knife that the wounded guy, or maybe the driver, did not have flew out through the window.

On the ground was a short coil of rope that had fallen out of the overturned truck. The rope was probably intended for tying the hands of the kidnap victims. Also, some black bags that were intended to go over the heads of the victims. I motioned to Laura to get the rope and bags for me.

When I had the rope, I formed a simple lasso with two half hitches. "Put both hands together up through the window," I yelled. Two fists appeared. "Open your hands and place the palms together." When he had the palms together, I walked up on the underside of the truck and dropped the loop of rope around his wrists. Then I pulled it tight. He grunted in pain. I slid the rope between his hands and began hog-tying his wrists together. When his hands were immobilized, I tied the other end of the rope to the outside rearview mirror. I walked around to the roof of the cab and reached inside with a black bag. I put it over his shaggy head.

The injured man, if he cast his eyes downward, could only see his own feet and his shot-up legs. "Let's talk a little," I said. "I need to meet with al-Nasirah."

"Are you not going to help me?" he pleaded.

"Only after you tell me what I want to know."

"I know nothing," he said.

"Then, your ignorance will cause your premature death. I need to meet with al-Nasirah. Where can I find him?"

"He does not tell me where he is going to be. I am just an ordinary soldier for Allah."

"He has a camp in the hills near here. If you were able to kidnap us, you would have taken us there. Where would you have taken us?"

"We would have turned you over to others who would have come to get you."

"How would the others know you had prisoners?"

"We would radio them, and they would come to our camp to take you away."

"Where is the radio?"

"In our camp."

"Where is your camp?"

"Nearby.

"Where nearby?"

"I cannot tell you."

"You want me to help you?"

"I think you are an American spy. An Arab would have killed me without talking. Americans are weak and stupid. They help everyone, even their enemies. They think war is like a game, and a wounded man goes to the sidelines and stops fighting. They even help the wounded men recover so that they can go back to fighting at a later time."

"You are gambling with your life that I will help you, even though you call me weak and stupid. Has it not occurred to you that you are in no position to bargain with me, and worse, you are in no position to *offend* me? Are you not the one who was shot? Are you not the one who is tied to this truck like a goat?"

"Still, you will help me because that is the nature of Americans. You help everyone. You think it will make us like you. It is why Islam shall conquer you. You will help me even though I will never tell you where our camp is. We will kill you for not believing in Allah. All of you and all the Jews."

"You are an asshole. You were born an asshole. You are an asshole today. If you live a thousand years, you will be an asshole until the day you die. Allah will not protect you from me."

I shouted, "Laura, take cover." Then I said to the guy in the cab, "I've had enough of you." I pulled the pin on one of the grenades, but I held on to the handle. "You are truly an asshole. You will not live a thousand years, but I assure you, you will be an asshole until the day you die, which I think will be today. You have five seconds to apologize to me before you die." I pulled the mask off his head so he could see what was coming. I dropped the grenade into the cab of the truck. I ran behind another truck and dropped to the ground.

The guy in the truck called me many bad names as the last five seconds of his life ticked off. The exploding grenade blew the cab apart.

The gas tank exploded, and the whole truck burned. I think my new friend didn't make it. One should not be offensive to Americans when they are willing to help you.

Laura came over to me. "Was that necessary?"

"It wasn't until he promised to kill all the Americans and all the Jews," I said.

Laura frowned. "Well, maybe it *was* necessary." She looked around. "I think it would be a good idea to get out of here. I don't remember seeing a spare tire in the truck. We may need to scavenge one from these other trucks."

I examined our truck and looked under the body. There was no spare tire. I did find a jack and a lug wrench under the seat in the cab.

We moved to the overturned truck, hunting for anything useful. The rear tire still had tread, so that would be our prize. Laura scrambled up the side with the lug wrench while I yanked open the driver's door and yanked on the parking brake, hoping it would hold. Bracing the tire with both arms, I kept it steady as she fought with the lug nuts. Each one screeched as if it hadn't been touched in years. My arms burned, but at last the bolts gave way.

Back at our truck, I worked the lug nuts loose on the shredded front wheel. We propped the jack on a pile of rocks to keep it from sinking into the sand, then cranked the axle high enough to swap the tires. Sweat stung my eyes, and every turn of the wrench felt like a battle, but the new wheel finally locked into place. The tools went back under the seat. We were alive, armed, and, at least for now, ready to roll.

While I had been finishing up mounting the tire, Laura had decided to collect a few AK-47 magazines for our future use. Unless you are swimming in very deep water, you can never have too much ammo on you.

There were now about fifty vultures circling overhead. They would surely be coming in to feast as soon as we left the area. *Bon appétit,* guys.

Dressed again in her burqa, Laura took the wheel, and we got back on the road. She drove with the hem of her burqa hiked up into her lap so it wouldn't interfere with the pedals. Very un-Islamic. We headed south, back toward the fork in the road, to take the right fork that Laura preferred over my chosen route. I sat quietly. The battle was over.

I reflected on how we had done. We came through it without a scratch—sweatier and grimier, but okay. I knew my own abilities in a fight, but now I had seen Laura's as well. Outnumbered sixteen to two, she stayed cool. Her aim matched mine, and under incoming fire, she kept her composure even with adrenaline surging. Tactical improvisation came naturally to her, and when it came to pulling the trigger, she never flinched. She did what had to be done when it had to be done. I would share a foxhole with Laura any day; she was a warrior.

I reached over and held her hand. She met my gaze with a smile. I smiled back. No words were needed; our smiles said it all: we were a team.

32

LAURA

Karmis Mushait
Saturday, 23 May

We spent Friday night in a nameless farming village, little more than a flat clearing in the low hills. Whether or not it had a name, no one told us. The headman offered us shelter, clinging to the old code of hospitality for travelers who appeared on the road. We stuck to our cover story—returning from Afghanistan, bound for Abdullah's ailing father. The villagers accepted it without question, but I wondered what they truly thought behind their guarded eyes.

Karmis Mushait lay farther down the road, a sizable city where faces blur into the crowd. Out here, though, every stranger is remembered.

The right fork was a much more peaceful travel route. But in Jack's defense, that road took us away from the direction in which we wanted to go. At one point, we stopped by the side of the road and sent an incident report regarding our little *tete-a-tete* with the AQAP forces to *Beartrap* in Langley and Yitzhak Nahum in Tel Aviv. I'll bet they were both annoyed that we didn't find out where the AQAP camp was.

We arrived in Karmis Mushait around midday. Saudi Arabia felt hotter than Yemen, if that is possible.

The women were covered up from head to toe; not even their eyes were visible since they had to look through a dark veil in the burqa.

They even wore dark cotton gloves to cover their hands. Because men cannot be trusted to control their passions, women must pay the price. As soon as a girl has her first menstrual flow, she goes under the cover of a burqa.

No scholar can find any direct reference to the hijab (the covering) as a requirement for women to hide their hair and faces in the Koran. The practice came about because of the conservative, retrograde wishes of Islamic clerics who want to control women and keep them subjugated to men. Absolutely archaic. *If men can't control themselves, why not castrate them instead of abusing the women?* I thought.

I was sweating profusely in my burqa. The Saudi royal house insists upon strict adherence to all Koranic orders, even if they aren't actual orders. Jack drove because women are not allowed to drive anywhere in Saudi Arabia. We saw the mutaween, the modesty police, on the streets making sure that every woman was completely covered according to custom and government regulations. No woman was allowed to leave the home without being accompanied by a male family member. Minor infractions could land you in jail, or you could receive a flogging on the soles of your feet. Saudi Arabia is wealthy beyond anyone's dreams, but it is still a lousy place to live.

We found a small, relatively modern guesthouse where we could stay for a few days. We had to contact Muhammed Ali ben Makhara, the proprietor of Makhara Carpets.

When I thought about it, a carpet merchant is indeed an excellent cover. This man does not sell wall-to-wall machine-made carpets. He sells handmade Oriental rugs made by artisans in many countries. He conducts constant importing and exporting; he makes frequent buying trips abroad; he has retail customers who are strangers constantly coming to visit him, and money is always flowing in and out. Moving rugs around is heavy physical labor, so it is natural for him to have some muscular assistants in his shop. Some of his carpets are very expensive, so if he wants firearms to protect his cash, it is reasonable.

And if he is a high-end merchant, he would have a wealthy clientele that includes foreign visitors and top government officials. He will get to know people and hear things that others might not hear. Buying an expensive Oriental rug is not a ten-minute purchase. It could take hours of showing what is in inventory, followed by discussions of many topics unrelated to rugs. Tea and soft drinks are served, social invitations can be extended, and then there is the haggling over prices, which can go on for days until a deal is struck. Yes, upon reflection, a carpet merchant is a brilliant cover.

We don't know where Makhara Carpets has its shop. Jack asked the guest house owner in a way that would not tell him who we were looking for.

"Peace be unto you," Jack said to the proprietor.

"Peace be unto you," he replied.

"I would buy a carpet as a gift for my brother. Where can I find the carpet merchants?"

"Most of them are in the bazaar. A few are on the main roads. Some are in fancy stores. You will get your best prices at the bazaar."

"I am a stranger here. Where will I find the bazaar? Not every city has a bazaar in the center of the town."

"The best bazaar for you will be on Ash Shiykh Saed Ibn Mushayt in Al Khazzan."

"I will need directions, please," said Jack.

The owner took a piece of paper and drew a crude map for him.

"I have heard of a shop run by a man named Makhara. Is that near the bazaar?" asked Jack.

"Ho, my friend. Makhara is one of the fancy shops on King Faysal Road. His prices will steal your eyeballs out of your head. You are better off at the bazaar."

"For that advice, I deeply thank you," Jack said. "The bazaar is the place where I will do my shopping for my brother's gift."

Later in our room, Jack and I made plans to go to King Faysal Road the next day to find Muhammed Ali ben Makhara. I had taken off my burqa and was sitting on the edge of the bed in my underwear. "Let's take a shower," I said. "I think each pore of my body is stuffed with a thousand grains of sand."

We went into the bathroom together and stripped off our grimy clothes. I adjusted the water temperature to my liking, and we got in the shower. We did wet hugs and kisses for a while. Then I soaped Jack's body from the neck down to his feet with special attention to the fun parts. I stood him under the spray and turned and pushed him back and forth until he was no longer soapy.

Jack said, "I love having your hands touch me anywhere, everywhere. Don't stop."

Then it was my turn, and we pretty much followed the same routine except Jack spent a long time soaping my backside and rubbing my soapy, slippery breasts. We were both turned on by our games.

We each washed our own hair. Then I asked, "How do animals mark their own territories and nests?"

Jack said, "Well, mostly they mark their space by spritzing urine on the borders and at selected spots within their space."

I smiled. "I thought so. I want you to mark me for yourself. Then, I want to mark you for myself. This is the perfect place and time to do it."

"Do you mean you want me to spritz on you and then you want to spritz on me?" he asked.

"That's right. And we are going to do it now." I shut off the shower. We stood there, soaking wet and still warm from the hot water.

"Laura, that is the kinkiest thing I've ever heard. I'm willing to do it, but you understand that this will bind us together forever. We will belong to each other in ways that no one else will ever be able to understand. I want to do it. I want to belong to you, and I want you to belong to me."

I said, "Jack, I'm ready. I'll stand by the drain." Jack aimed his penis at my legs and started to urinate. "Higher," I commanded, "do me the right way." So, he aimed at my pubic hair, and the urine ran onto my parts and down my legs. When he was done, I hugged him and said, "Now it is my turn to mark you."

I bent my knees a little and thrust my pelvis forward. A hot stream of urine poured out of me onto Jack's legs. I squeezed hard to stop the flow. "Kneel down on one knee," I told him. Jack knelt down. I relaxed the muscles, aimed, and hit his penis and testicles with my stream. The smell of urine was strong, and the realization of what we were doing and pledging excited both of us so that Jack got an erection while I was marking this man as mine.

When I was finished, Jack came into my arms and clung to me with a ferocious strength I had never felt before.

"You beautiful man," I said, "we belong to each other now. I love you, Jack, until my dying day. I am yours, and you are mine, and nothing can ever come between us."

Jack repeated what I had just said in almost the exact words. "You beautiful woman, I belong to you, and you belong to me. I love you, Laura, until my dying day. I am yours, and you are mine, and nothing can ever come between us."

We stood there in the shower, clinging to each other, both of us understanding that we had just made a vow to each other that was stronger than any marriage vow from any standard religion. I felt happier than any woman ever could be. How many people can marry their lovers while they are naked and seal the pledge in such a primal, spontaneous way? We had mated for life just now. And it felt wonderful.

I shivered from the cool air on my wet body. "Let me turn the water on to warm us up," Jack said.

"I don't want to wash your mark of ownership off me just yet. I like the feeling of being totally yours."

"I don't want you getting a cold on me now that I own you. I'm getting cold, too. Do you want me to catch pneumonia?"

"If you did, I would be your personal nurse, giving you a sponge bath with my tongue and then a sensuous massage." I shivered again. "On second thought, hot water would be just the thing right about now."

Jack turned on the hot water, and we stood under the stream together, one being formed from two people. We held on to each other for a long time. The water washed the urine away, but the ownership and the pledge remained in our hearts and brains. I was his, and he was mine until our dying days.

33

HAKIM ABU-JIHADI

The Southern Hills of Saudi Arabia
Sunday 24 May

The sheikh was raving and stomping around the cave. "How can it be that we lost sixteen fighters and four trucks? Bring the messenger to me!"

The messenger who had brought the news of the losses in the desert was hustled into al- Nasirah's presence.

"Tell me what you have to say!"

"My sheikh," stammered the messenger, "we sent out sixteen men in four trucks to capture hostages for ransom. They never returned. So, several hours later, we sent out two more trucks to search for them. We found them in the desert. All sixteen were together in the desert. They were all dead, and the four trucks were wrecked. We suspect they fell into a trap and were outnumbered by a much larger force. We found no evidence of who the attackers might have been, but only the Saudi army has the men and weapons to have done this. By the time we found them, the vultures had done a great deal of damage to the bodies, so it was hard to tell exactly who had died first or what the battle was like."

"Were there any dead who were not our men?"

"No, my sheikh. Only our fighters were there. One truck was completely blown apart and burned. It must have been hit with a rocket. Two trucks were facing in one direction, and one truck was facing in the other direction. We think that maybe two of the trucks had flipped over at high speed. But only our mujahedin were there."

"That means the enemy took their dead and wounded with them, or perhaps they ambushed our men, and they had no casualties at all. Either way, we need to get revenge on the Saudis for this. I cannot imagine any of the Bedu tribes starting a war with us. It had to be the Saudis."

Hakim had been standing by. He broke his silence. "We must be very certain this was done by the Saudis before we take revenge. They are not sheep, like French college students. And there are many more Saudi soldiers than there are of us at this moment. Their air force is a very potent weapon. They have left us alone until now. But there is another possibility. Could it be that the people we tried to kidnap fought back and won? It would have required a large truckload of armed warriors to kill sixteen of our men, but if we chose the wrong victim, it might be possible—"

Al-Nasirah snorted, "Only the Saudis have enough nerve to do something like this. The Saudi pigs will pay for this. I swear it."

Hakim turned to the messenger, "Leave us," he said.

The messenger was relieved to get away without being punished for bringing bad news. He backed away and left the leaders to deal with the news he had brought.

34

JACK, SHOPPING

Karmis Mushait
Sunday, 24 May

In the Arab world, Sunday is just another regular business day. Friday is the Sabbath day, and most people scratching for a living work on Fridays too; they just make sure that they pray the required five times a day on Fridays.

We retrieved our truck from the lot behind the guesthouse. No one had broken into it or stolen it. The fact is, in Saudi Arabia, you don't steal because if you get caught, they will cut off your right hand with a stroke of the sword. When that happens, it makes it hard to scratch your left armpit.

King Faysal Road is one of the main commercial areas in the town, six lanes wide, and a busy shopping street. We drove over in our bullet-pocked truck. No one gave us a second look. I drove while Laura scanned the stores for Makhara's mega carpet emporium. Of course, 95% of the signs are in Arabic. Fortunately, we both could read the language. After 15 minutes in heavy traffic, Laura spotted Makhara's shop on the other side of the road. We made a U-turn and found a parking spot on a side street near the store.

As we entered the shop, a small bell tinkled on the door. The store was enormous, with carpets folded and rolled everywhere you looked.

There were four large open spaces where the carpets could be spread out for customers to view. This was a top-of-the-line store.

A manager was showing carpets to a male customer in one space. Many rugs were spread on the floor, and four burly men were lugging more carpets for the customer to view. As the customer approved or rejected the carpet, the approved carpet would be left on the floor. The rejected carpet was rolled and lugged away. Some carpets were so heavy that it took two men to move them. There was constant conversation and friendly banter between the customer and the manager. They were obviously in good spirits. There were teacups and soft drink cans in evidence.

A man wearing a Western suit, but no tie, came to greet us. "Salaam," he said, "may I assist you?"

"I would speak to Muhammed Ali ben Makhara. I bring greetings from his cousin Hadi in Afghanistan."

"I shall inquire if Mr. Makhara can see you. He is very busy just now. What name shall I tell Mr. Makhara?"

"I am Abdullah abu Al-Farooq."

The man disappeared into the back. We waited.

The other customer seemed to have narrowed his choices to four rugs that were spread on the floor. We could hear them haggling over the prices. It was a friendly bit of back and forth between them. The customer was obviously a wealthy man, and the sales manager was not willing to make too many concessions, but he had to make some, or the customer would lose face and there would be no deal. Two carpets were eliminated during the bargaining process. The muscle guys took them away, leaving the last two candidates side by side on the floor.

Our guy returned. "Mr. Makhara can see you in his office for a few minutes."

We followed him to an office at the rear. He knocked gently on the door.

"Enter," called a voice from inside.

Our guide opened the door, ushered us inside, and then left us with his boss.

Makhara was seated behind a large antique wooden desk that must have been worth a small fortune by itself. It was carved on the sides and inlaid with mother-of-pearl on the top. It was a beauty. Makhara was a thin man in a Bedouin robe. A neatly trimmed Saudi-style beard fringed his chin. Although he was sitting, I judged him to be of average height. He was sitting in a modern, black, ergonomic office chair. A cup of thick Turkish coffee was on a low table at the corner of his desk. A plate of almond macaroons was next to the cup, and the aroma filled the air. Makhara motioned to two chairs. "Please sit down. You are Hadi's friend Abdullah abu Al-Farooq. He has written to me about how you are his friend and fellow mujahedin. Tell me, how is Hadi faring in the hills of Afghanistan?"

"He is well. He sends greetings to you and hopes you are well also. Hadi often leads the attacks. He is blessed by Allah in that the fighters will follow wherever he leads."

"The Americans make things hot for our men there?"

This was the opening to give the recognition phrase. "Just before I left, Hadi used an RPG to shoot down one of the American drone aircraft."

The recognition answer came next. "Those rocket-propelled grenades are wonderful weapons in the right hands."

"Allah guides Hadi's hands in all things."

Makhara smiled; the formalities were over. "I am pleased that you have arrived safely. I expected you earlier, but it doesn't matter as long as you are both here in one piece. What will you need from me?"

I looked around the room with questioning eyes. Makhara said, "We sweep for bugs every day. And also at night, after the last customers have left, we sweep the sales rooms with more than a broom. No one can hear us."

"We need maps of the surrounding areas, and two RPGs with at least twelve rockets. I will need a night-scoped sniper rifle, preferably a Marine Corps M40A5 if it is available with flash and sound suppression. Second choice would be a civilian Remington 700 rifle, also with a scope. The scope should be a Redfield 3x9 variable. I need at least fifty rounds of 7.62 ammo, must be subsonic loads. The flash and sound suppressor is essential. A bipod for the rifle would be a plus. And of course, we need the latest intel about where to find our target. We have already picked up whatever else we need."

Makhara looked pensive. "The maps and RPGs are no problem. We have those here, and I can have them for you by tomorrow. I will have to get the sniper rifle from the Marine guards at the embassy in Riyadh. It will take some pressure to get them to part with one. Let me have your cell phone numbers. If there are any problems getting what you need, I will call you early tomorrow morning. I will notify you when the repairs to your carpet are completed and when it will be ready for pickup. If you don't hear from me, that means we have been able to get everything you need."

Laura wrote our cell phone numbers and handed them to Makhara. Hidden inside her burqa, she still hadn't said a word. Makhara said to Laura, "Are you always so talkative?"

"I am a good Muslim wife. You cannot see me or hear me."

Makhara laughed. He said to Jack, "If you ever divorce her, send her to me, please."

"I think I'll keep her," Jack answered.

"Make the pickup at 11 AM. When you pick up the RPGs tomorrow, they will be rolled up in a carpet. The rockets, maps, and any rifle ammo will be in a cardboard box. If I succeed in getting the sniper rifle, it will be in the rug as well. I may have to convince someone to bring it down from Riyadh." Makhara nodded over his shoulder. "I have a warehouse directly behind this building. Makhara Carpets is painted over the roll-up door. The loading dock is your pickup point. Ask for Sulamein; he can be trusted. The warehouse also gets swept for bugs twice a day. Despite that, keep the conversation to a minimum."

Makhara turned to a computer terminal behind him and started typing. "I am preparing a pickup order for a carpet repair, so you will have a paper to hand to Sulamein just in case anyone is watching. The rug will be in a long black plastic bag. Sulamein is one of our guys. Most of my employees think I am supplying arms to the mujahideen. Say nothing to anyone that changes that story."

A printer spat out a duplicate order for repairing a carpet that measured 2 meters by 3 meters. "Sulamein will have one copy of this order," Makhara said as he handed me one of the pages. "I suggest you drive by the warehouse as you leave, just to make sure you know where it is."

"Where is our boy hiding?" I asked.

"He is a cautious man and moves his camp every four or five days. He has nine or ten caves, and he moves randomly from one to the other. So far, he has limited his activities to behaving like a bandit, and he hasn't attacked any important Saudi targets. If he does attack them, they will come hunting for him. Right now, he is limiting himself to kidnapping and robbery. We thought we had a solid lead on him a few days ago, but he has moved. However, he is still in the hills southeast of here, near Najran. It is desert country. Some of the Bedouins are afraid of him, and they tip him off to gain favor. I don't know why he is staying out of Yemen. The Yemenis are no threat to him, and he would be safer there."

"We already ran into a few of his people. We got off without injury. The vultures are cleaning up the mess."

"It is nice that you can take care of yourselves. Not everyone has been so lucky. He is getting fat on ransoms." Makhara continued, "If you locate his camp, call in the drones. The Saudis don't care what we do in the desert as long as no one hears about it or sees anything. The hills keep their secrets well out there."

"Understood. Thank you for your help. You have our numbers. If there are any problems, please call us. Otherwise, we will be at the warehouse tomorrow at 11 o'clock."

We all stood at the same time. Makhara shook my hand, and then, in a very un-Muslim-like way, he shook Laura's hand. "God speed to both of you," he said. With that one sentence, he showed us that he was not a Muslim at all.

He pushed a button on his desk and, in an instant, the salesperson who had led us to Makhara was at the door to lead us out. At the street door, he said, "Go in peace."

I replied, "And peace be unto you," as we exited the store.

When we were back in the truck, we took Makhara's advice and drove past the warehouse in the rear. An older man was sitting on a plastic chair near the loading gate. It would be a straightforward pickup if all went as planned.

We spent the rest of the day wandering around Karmis Mushait, getting the layout of the city and the roads in and out of town. The city was much larger than I expected. We found an outdoor supply store and bought some camping gear we would need out in the desert. Sleeping bags, some cooking gear, a propane stove, and some more clothing. Two long aluminum storage boxes for the body of the pickup truck were added to our shopping. The boxes were made of shiny aluminum tread plate. Each box had hasps for two padlocks, so we also bought four locks that were keyed alike. We also bought a camouflage cover for the body of the truck.

Laura suggested we should paint the aluminum tread plate boxes because they were as shiny as mirrors. I liked her idea, so we found a hardware store and bought a liter of paint in a desert sand color and some throwaway brushes. In 30 minutes, our aluminum boxes were no longer an attention grabber. The air in Saudi-land is so hot the paint dried almost immediately as we brushed it on.

Toward dark, we gassed up the truck and filled our spare gas cans too. We ate at a Western café, of which there were a few in town. In an Arab restaurant, Laura and I would have eaten in separate sections for the men and women. In the Western restaurant, we were served at the same table.

After dinner, we headed back to the little hotel where we had our amazing mating ceremony. We were happy in our own skins just being together. Even though we were happy, we never let our guard down. Being careless will get you dead. Right now, we both had a lot to live for.

35

JACK, GEARING UP

Karmis Mushait
Monday, 25 May

I decided I really hate Middle Eastern breakfast food. Diluted yogurt for breakfast sucks. Fava beans and garbanzos for breakfast really sucks. Okra for breakfast really sucks. Lentil soup for breakfast really sucks. No eggs, no ham, no bacon, really sucks. The coffee is strong enough to melt the rust off a bulldozer blade or to cure stomach cancer; not even cancer cells would want to live in that stuff.

Question: How can you tell if Arabic coffee is done brewing?

Answer: Throw a small rock in the brew pot with the coffee. When the rock is soft enough to stick a fork in it, then the coffee is just right.

At least they make decent croissants.

After breakfast, we borrowed a battery-powered drill from the handyman at the hotel, and I screwed the aluminum boxes to the body of the pickup truck. Then we hung around until it was time to go back to Makhara's warehouse to pick up our carpet from Sulamein. There had not been a telephone call telling us not to come.

We drove up to the loading dock at 10:58. The door of the loading dock was rolled up. The same old man from yesterday, with a scruffy white beard, was dressed in a dark beige Bedouin robe and a white keffiyeh, sitting on a plastic folding chair, sipping an unknown liquid from a thermos bottle. He was the guardian of the gate, I guess. Even though he appeared not to be doing much of anything, his eyes were taking everything in and measuring the threat potential we might pose. He was the first person in Karmis Mushait to check out the bullet holes in our truck.

"I would like to speak to Sulamein. I have a pickup order."

"I will get him for you," answered the old man. He took a cell phone from his belt and hit a speed-dial key. He whispered a few words into the phone, then he hung up. "Two minutes," he informed us.

Two minutes later, Sulamein appeared. This guy was big. He had to be 6 feet 5 inches, and he probably weighed 270 pounds. He moved with the grace of an athlete. His face was covered with a short salt-and-pepper beard. His arms were very long, and his hands were huge. He looked like he could stop a tank with his bare hands. Why wasn't he playing in the NFL? He was dressed in a baggy shirt, a vest, and baggy pants. On his head was an olive-green camo-pattern baseball cap with a Quicksilver surfing logo. His eyes were grayish blue, and he appeared to be sharply intelligent. His voice was soft when he spoke, "Your carpet is ready. It has been completely repaired and cleaned to your specifications. You have a work order for me?"

I handed over the paper that Makhara had given us the previous day. Sulamein examined it and nodded with approval. He turned to the old man. "Hamdi, go fetch the cartons for me. I will fetch the carpet."

Hamdi and Sulamein disappeared into the darkness of the warehouse for a few moments. Sulamein emerged with a rolled-up carpet in a black plastic wrapper. The rug was perched on his left shoulder.

I climbed into the bed of the pickup truck, and Sulamein handed the rolled-up carpet to me. The package must have weighed almost 160 pounds. I laid it gently on the floor of the truck.

Hamdi reappeared with a hand truck and two cartons. He handed me one and whispered, "Gently. They might explode."

It was good advice. I stowed the carton in the passenger-side aluminum box. He handed me the second carton and smiled. That one went into the same aluminum box next to the first carton. I don't know if he was happy to be rid of the cartons or if he was happy with what he thought I would do with them. I turned to Sulamein, "Before I leave, I would like to cover the body of the truck. I have a cover."

Sulamein said, "Hamdi, help him with his tarp to cover the truck."

After the camouflaged cover was on the truck body, Sulamein said, "Hamdi, I need the small coil of rope from my office."

Hamdi hustled off. While he was gone, Sulamein said, "We were able to fill your entire order. They would like the special item back when you are done with it."

"I will do my best not to lose it." We were both referring to the sniper rifle.

Hamdi returned with a coil of light rope. Sulamein and I stopped speaking. Hamdi climbed in the truck and helped me tie the rope over the camo tarp covering the rug and the storage boxes, and then tucked the ends of the tarp underneath to prevent it from blowing off. It looked pretty neat, and I was sure it would stay tied until I wanted it untied. Hamdi and I both got out of the truck. He smiled again. "Go with God," he said.

"I thank you for your good wishes. Allah has blessed us." I motioned to Laura, and she got in the passenger seat. I gave a half-wave to Sulamein, who waved back. I got in the truck, and we headed for our hotel to collect our gear and check out. Since we supposedly had everything we asked for, there was no reason to hang around Karmis Mushait any longer. As soon as we could find a private place outdoors, we would inspect the contents of the packages.

At the hotel, we met again with the owner. We paid our bill in U.S. dollars. "Did you find the gift for your brother?" he asked.

"Yes, I did. Thanks to your advice, I got him a beautiful rug and was able to negotiate a good price for cash."

"Cash is always best. There are too many stolen credit cards in circulation."

We turned to go. The owner warned us, "Be careful on the roads. We have almost as many bandits as stolen credit cards."

"We will stay alert for trouble."

"I hope Allah blesses your father, and he returns to good health. I will pray for him today."

"You are kind. May Allah bless you for your kind spirit."

As we left the hotel, Laura spoke to me in a voice the owner could hear, "Husband, the owner of this hotel is a good man. When we say our prayers today, we must ask Allah to bless him." A little flattery to acknowledge his kindness certainly doesn't hurt. I am sure the man was pleased.

36

HAKIM ABU-JIHADI

The Southern Hills of Saudi Arabia
Monday, 25 May

Hakim was seated on the floor of the cave next to Sheikh Abdel Karim Washim al-Nasirah, waiting for al-Nasirah to speak. A battered teapot and two cups sat between them on a low table. The sheikh had been sitting quietly for 20 minutes, occasionally muttering a half-audible prayer. Hakim had seen him like this many times before. The first time was when they had shared a jail cell in a Yemini prison. On that occasion, al-Nasirah had planned a daring escape that freed twenty-two prisoners from the Yemini jail. When the sheikh was done thinking and praying, Hakim knew that the leader of AQAP would reveal the details of his latest plan.

Many more minutes passed. Finally, al-Nasirah said, "*Yalla!* (Let's go!)" He looked at Hakim and gave him a half-smile. "The plan will work."

"Would you share your thoughts, my sheikh?"

"One way to strike back at the Saudis for their attack on our men is simple—humiliate them in front of the Americans. The Saudis love to pretend they are equals. Strip that illusion away, and the Americans will sneer at them.

"I've long considered kidnapping the American ambassador. Take him and his family, and both the Saudis and the Americans are disgraced.

"Keaton always travels in a three-car convoy of armored SUVs—ten armed guards in total. In his own vehicle, he keeps only a driver and one man beside him. Four ride in front, four behind. All Marines. All trained.

"When his wife or daughter accompanies him, they sit alone in the back of the middle car. That is the weakness. All we need is to split the convoy.

"The challenge in such an operation is usually escape. But for us, there is no such problem. Every one of our brothers is ready to die to see it succeed."

"Yes, that is true," replied Hakim, "but we do not want to waste our assets in unnecessary losses."

"Of course not," answered al-Nasirah. "There will be no waste. My plan will succeed."

"Tell me more details."

"Jamal, one of the local people who has worked as a cleaner at the embassy for the past two years, is also a spy for us. The fools trust him, so they are not careful when they speak if he is near. It is from Jamal that I learned the details of how Keaton travels. Jamal has learned that for the past three years, after the infidel school year ends, Keaton's wife and daughter have been flying back to America for something called summer camp during the hot months. The daughter goes to this place, and the wife visits friends and family for a few weeks. Keaton always accompanies them to the airport to say goodbye. Then, near the end of the Christian month of August, Keaton flies back to Washington, and they all return here together.

"The British Airways flight bound for London leaves at 12:35 AM daily, which means they will leave the embassy at about 10 PM. This year, when they are on their way to the airport, we will be waiting for them. They have already done this for three years with no incident.

This year, they will not be expecting any trouble, and we will get them all. The filthy Americans will pay to get them back. The arrogant Saudis will look like the fools they truly are. They will regret attacking our men when I am done with them."

"Where would you expect them to be most vulnerable?" asked Hakim.

Al-Nasirah took out a street map of Riyadh and opened it fully. "When they leave the embassy, they will be very alert. Just before they arrive at King Khaled Airport, they will again be very alert. During the 40 minutes it takes to drive from the embassy to the airport, they will relax their vigilance, and that is when we will take them."

Al-Nasirah leaned forward. "There will be two Saudi motorcycle escorts at the front. None at the rear. The airport road is being widened, and there is construction everywhere on Route 40 and Route 539 is worse than Route 40, so it gets shut down completely, and all the traffic is diverted to Route 40. The work is being done at night under portable lights on both roads.

"We will take control of one of those sites on Route 40. Our men will pose as traffic controllers. All other vehicles will be halted 300 meters back. Only Keaton's convoy will be waved through. They will believe it is a courtesy. In reality, it will be the trap."

He smiled thinly. "The construction company belongs to a Yemeni. I will threaten to kill his entire family. If he cooperates, perhaps they live. If not…well, perhaps they die anyway once our mission succeeds.

"For equipment, we will need two dump trucks already on the construction site. Our own pickups. A truck with a forty-cubic-meter container, a heavy forklift, and a bus. The truck and forklift can be rented. The bus—chartered, or stolen. It makes no difference."

Al-Nasirah's voice stayed calm as he laid out the procedure for the abduction of the Keatons—every detail calculated, every step inevitable.

"What about the prisoners? Where will we take them?" asked Hakim.

"We will rent a warehouse in the desert. The plan is flexible. We can take the 40-meter container truck and hide it inside the warehouse, or we can abandon the big truck and put the prisoners in pickups. Once they are out of their car, I expect to bind them, maybe drug them if they are being difficult, and then transport them to some place in the south."

Al-Nasirah became pensive for a moment. "I don't know how long we will have to keep them. It will depend on the degree of reaction we get from the Saudis. It could be as long as two weeks before we can move them to the hill country. If we get paid sooner, we will then abandon them and tell Al Jazeera where to find them."

"The best place to hide them would be in Yemen," said Hakim. "I would take the risk of moving them immediately out of Saudi Arabia. Even better would be to separate them and hold them in three different places. If they cannot see each other, they will be fearful for the safety of the other family members, and they will then be easier to dominate and control."

"We don't have enough men we can trust to hold them in three different places. One location where we can keep them separate from each other would be best."

"We should videotape their humiliations, and when we broadcast it to the world, more fighters will join us," Hakim said.

"Of course, we will videotape them. We have only three weeks to finish our planning before the Keatons go to the airport. Jamal must get us the exact date of their departure. We must be ready. I will not tolerate failure. We will avenge our 16 brothers who were killed by the Saudi dogs. We will show them to be weak and incapable as they truly are."

"God is with us. *Insha'Allah* (God willing), we will not fail," promised Hakim.

37

LAURA

On the Road, Saudi Desert
Tuesday, 26 May

Jack and I headed southeast from Karmis Mushait toward Najran. We had several days' supply of food and fuel. We camped out in the desert Monday night, taking turns sleeping, two hours on watch, two hours asleep, right through until dawn. It was an awful night's sleep, but with AQAP fighters around, it was vitally necessary.

Without the light pollution from our modern cities, the crystal-clear night sky of the desert was so full of stars it took our breath away. I remembered what an insignificant little place the Earth is in the grand scheme of the universe. The desert air was so dry that there was no moisture to retain the daytime heat. So, the nighttime temperatures drop almost to freezing. Were it not for the cold and the dangerous humans, the desert night sky could be very romantic.

Our idea was to be the bait that would bring the al-Qaeda animals to us and try to capture one who could tell us where al-Nasirah is hiding. We didn't see another living soul in two days. Maybe the al-Qaeda murderers decided not to do any kidnapping for a while since the last attempt cost them sixteen men and a whole lot of equipment. For our part, we didn't even have a clear idea of how many mujahideen al-Nasirah commanded or how he was communicating with them. With all of America's expensive satellites and drones and NSA snooping, we still didn't have a lead on where he was presently hiding.

Come out of your hole, you fanatical bastard. All we want to do is kill you.

38

HAKIM ABU-JIHADI

Sulayyil, Saudi Arabia
Thursday, 4 June

Hakim had been scouting a few warehouses in the southern desert towns. He was dressed like a Saudi businessman in a black Bedouin robe with a black-and-white checkered keffiyeh. He had been forced to trim his beard to make it neater in the Saudi fashion. One of the younger mujahideen, dressed as a domestic servant, was acting as his chauffeur, driving a rented Mercedes limo. Hakim was using the alias Ibn Ali ben Amar to go with his new persona. His AK-47 was left in the trunk of the Mercedes. All he had was his knife in the sash of the robe and a 9mm Makarov pistol in his pocket. He felt naked without his rifle on his shoulder.

Hakim finally settled on a vacant warehouse just a quarter kilometer off the south side of Route 10 in the small city of As Sulayyil. The warehouse had more than enough space to hold all of their vehicles inside and would serve as a good place to keep their kidnap victims. The building was 50 meters wide, 80 meters deep, and 10 meters high. Behind the building was only desert. The nearest neighbor was another vacant warehouse that had been empty for several years. The chosen warehouse exterior was made of corrugated steel, featuring four roll-up loading doors and a truss roof.

The interior was also suitable with a bit of modification. Along one side, it had a small office area on the ground floor, with floor-to-ceiling metal and glass partitions. The second floor had six additional offices directly above the ground floor offices, and a small basement storage area divided into four sections. The basement rooms were made of poured concrete. There was a freight elevator and a stairway to the basement. The only thing that needed to be done to suit their needs was to strengthen three doors with heavy lumber to use as temporary prison cells. A chain-link fence topped by a single strand of barbed wire surrounded a large storage yard. The nearest neighbor, the vacant warehouse, was over 200 meters away. Some small hills were nearby. Hakim was standing on the ground floor with the owner of the warehouse, negotiating the rental.

"We will need the building for eight to nine months," Hakim said. "If we run over, we will need to continue the rental on a month-to-month basis for up to a year."

"What will you be using it for?" the owner asked.

"We will store construction equipment and materials here. The government has plans to improve some small sections of road between Riyadh and Abha. We will be doing the work."

"Those contracts are highly profitable," said the owner.

Hakim snorted, "Building the road is profitable. Only the King's relatives make a profit from building roads. Fixing the roads after they do a shoddy job is not profitable, but it is the only work left for independent contractors. So, do not think we will be rolling in money. We will need a low price on the rental."

Hakim and the owner haggled back and forth for about 20 minutes before finally agreeing on the rental for the warehouse.

The owner said, "I will want a security deposit of two months' rent. When the rental is over, I don't want you to leave piles of dirt and debris in my warehouse. You must leave it as clean as you found it. No damage to the building. If you make any changes inside or build anything in the yard, those improvements must remain with the property. When your lease is over, we will examine the building together to see what part of the security deposit will be needed for repairs or cleaning."

"That is agreeable," said Hakim. In his own thoughts, he estimated they would not need the place past the second week of July. He almost smiled when he thought of how the Saudi police would abuse the poor fool landlord when they discovered what his building had been used for.

The landlord produced a standard Saudi commercial lease for the warehouse. Hakim used the name and Riyadh address of the Yemeni construction company that was working on the airport road improvement project. "We will have a bank draft for the first month's rent and two months' security deposit mailed to you," said Hakim. "I want to start moving equipment here by the 15th of this month, so I will include an extra half month's rent in the bank draft."

"That is acceptable. You can pick up two sets of keys to the gate and warehouse next week."

Both men signed the lease. Hakim signed as Ibn Ali ben Amar. When the formalities were done, Hakim returned to the rented Mercedes limo driven by one of his mujahideen. He sat in the back seat, and the limo departed in the direction of Riyadh.

The warehouse owner was very happy to finally have a tenant for his empty building.

Hakim, too, was very happy to have finally found a good place to keep their prisoners.

39

JACK

Najran, Saudi Arabia
Tuesday 8 June

Laura and I had spent 12 days kicking around from one Saudi desert town to another, and ten nights in the desert trying to draw al-Nasirah's men into attacking us. No luck. Laura thinks that since they are lying low, maybe they are planning a major attack in Yemen. I almost agree with her. Yet kidnapping has been their major source of income, and I cannot see them abandoning it since it is so easy.

Our contacts with Langley and Tel Aviv have been few. They have nothing to tell us, and we have nothing to tell them. Waiting is a bitch. Hanging your ass out in the open, hoping a bad guy will try to bite it, is even worse.

Now and then, we would meet someone in the desert—a caravan, or a traveler. No one reported any danger. It was weird. The world didn't suddenly run out of SOBs.

We drove into Najran for a little civilized R&R. Even mujahideen need some supplies, and Najran was the nearest city to where they were supposed to be hiding. Perhaps we would pick up a lead as to al-Nasirah's whereabouts.

Najran has several Western-style hotels. We checked into the Hyatt Najran Hotel without a problem. Checking in with our arsenal was another story. We locked our RPG-7s and rockets in one of the aluminum boxes along with the sniper rifle, the AK-47s, and all our ammo. Our camping gear was in the other aluminum box. The four padlocks kept the equipment away from prying eyes or sticky fingers. Makhara's carpet, wrapped in its black plastic cover, lay in the body between the two aluminum boxes. The camo cover covered the truck bed, and it was securely tied down. We parked the truck in the hotel garage ourselves.

I can live without everything that modern civilization supplies except for two things: modern medicine and indoor plumbing. A shower can be one of life's greatest luxuries. A shower with Laura is one of Heaven's greatest gifts. We spent one night at the hotel, sleeping in a real bed, eating in a Western-style hotel restaurant. Laura was able to wear a long-sleeved dress and a headscarf instead of a burqa. Some of life's basic pleasures are the truly simple things, like not wearing a burqa.

One night of civilized living, even in Sharia-ruled Saudi Arabia, was a treat, and then it was back on the road again. We restocked our supplies, felt a whole lot cleaner, and then we went back to being bait in a trap. Being in Saudi Arabia had at least one plus: no one messed with our truck while we were at the hotel.

Laura was scrutinizing the map while I drove. "Let's go north toward Yadamah," suggested Laura.

"We don't have any intel that says he is up that way."

"We don't have any intel that says he is anywhere on this planet," she countered. "In two and a half weeks, we have had no inkling of their being anywhere near here. Something is brewing. These guys are bad by nature, and bad guys do bad things all the time. When they suddenly stop doing bad things, it is because they are planning to do something *really* bad."

"I think you are right. They certainly haven't been reformed and decided to become Boy Scouts. I think we should alert the folks back home and see what the analysts have to say."

"Pull over and let's compose a message we can send to both headquarters."

I pulled the truck onto a sandy shoulder. Laura took out her iPhone and started typing a message. After a few minutes, she said, "How does this sound?

> No contact with al-Nasirah elements or any AQAP activity since 22 May. Much too quiet. Suspect a major AQAP operation may be planned. No idea where or when. Most likely will be local. Suggest a heightened alert level. Your opinion?
>
> Pogo & Koala

"Will it sound like we are trying to tell them what to do?" asked Laura.

"We are here on the ground. It is our job to feed them our opinions and suspicions. I think it has the right balance of observation and opinion. Send it to both Mossad and Langley."

Laura pushed a few buttons. "It is sent," she said. "Let's wait and see what the analysts have to say."

I pulled back onto the road, heading north. I don't know why I headed north other than Laura suggested it, and I had no other idea which direction I should head. Trouble usually finds me without my having to do a thing. It is frustrating to go out trolling for fish that refuse to bite when I'm the bait.

Where the hell are they?

40

HERB WATSON, III

Langley, VA
Thursday, 10 June

"What have we got? Pogo and Koala are out there on their own, and we haven't given them anything usable. Not a smidge of guidance." Gathered around a small conference table were Watson, the NSA liaison, and Watson's boss, the Deputy Director of Operations.

The NSA guy shrugged. "We've been checking every rock and sand dune on the satellite images. They've disappeared. They aren't in Saudi Arabia, and there is no trace of them in Yemen."

The DDO said, "Well, I don't think they've reformed and gone straight. Bad guys are programmed to do bad stuff. It's almost like it's in their DNA. Were the losses from that one encounter with Pogo and Koala enough to cause them to stand down and lick their wounds?"

"Based on nothing except my feelings, I don't think so," said Herb. "They don't care how many martyrs they lose. They keep fighting until they die. If they conclude they are going to lose a fight, then they melt into the surrounding population and reappear later. It is the very essence of guerrilla warfare."

The DDO said, "Do you think AQAP knows it was Pogo and Koala that creamed their guys?"

Herb answered, "There is no way they could know unless one of their guys survived. The satellite photos showed vultures lunching on all of them. I am pretty sure they do not know it was us that did this to them."

The NSA guy said, "When there are no little piles of shit around, it is because the bad guys are stockpiling a major load of shit. My gut agrees with what Pogo and Koala think. Something big and bad is about to happen."

"I'm going to send out a heads-up to everyone out there," said Herb. "They keep on their toes as a normal condition. If we get them any higher on their toes, they're going to look like the National Ballet."

The DDO stood up, signaling the end of the meeting. "Do it," he said, and left the room.

The NSA guy said, "That was easy—for him." And he left too.

41

STUART J. KEATON

U.S. Embassy, Riyadh
Thursday, 11 June

Stuart Keaton was sitting at the desk in his daughter's bedroom. "Tomorrow is the last full day of school. Are you getting ready to go? You'll be leaving for home in about two weeks."

Susannah Keaton, eleven years old and mature beyond her years, looked at her father, "It's always the same, Dad. I don't want to leave you and Mom, but when I get to camp and see all my friends again, and there is so much to do, I love being there. When camp is over, we all hug each other and cry like babies, and we don't want it to end. But I don't want to leave my school friends either."

Keaton smiled. "Maybe it's like having two extended families. It isn't a bad state of affairs. You have a variety of friends, and they are everywhere you go. I never went to summer camp, so I'm not sure what it is like, but I know you enjoy it, and Mom loved it when she went to camp, so I guess the best thing to do is accept the inevitable. Camp is worth the trip and the trouble."

"Oh, I'm going for sure. I just don't like leaving you and Mom. But one thing I won't miss is the heat. It really sucks."

"I agree," said Keaton, "just find a more refined way of expressing your opinion."

"Oh, Dad! Don't be such a dweeb."

"That's me: Dweeb Keaton." They both laughed and exchanged high fives.

Keaton stood up to leave her room. "Make sure you have a list of the things you want to take with you. If you forget something, it isn't as if I can drop it in the mail and you'll get it the next day."

"Don't worry, Dad. I'm 'making a list and checking it twice'. I'm sure I'll forget something, but I'm also trying to keep the list shorter than last year."

"Sounds like a plan," said Keaton as he left Susannah's room.

Keaton went to his office on the second floor of the embassy. He encountered Mickey Henderson in the hall. "You look like you've been sucking a lemon. What's up?"

"Let's go inside," he said, motioning toward Keaton's office.

Once inside, with the door closed, Keaton said, "Okay, spill it. What's happening?"

Henderson sat down in a chair in front of the desk. "I just got a heads-up alert from Beartrap. Nothing is happening, and that is causing them some concern. The usual annoying hijackings and kidnappings have suddenly stopped. They think AQAP is planning something big, and they think it will be local. Either Yemen or here. I noticed the quiet and was sort of grateful for it. But I think there is validity in Langley's concerns, and we shouldn't ignore them."

"Our security is pretty good here. The Marines are always alert. The electronics are all working, and the blast barriers are in place and functional. I don't know what more we can do short of putting a dome over the whole building."

"I think we are safe inside the embassy. It is when we go out that we must be extra vigilant."

"I'm happy that Suzy and Adelle will be out of here soon. I don't like having them around when suicide bombers are roaming the neighborhood."

"I don't know why we bother with this place," said Henderson. "It's a society with 21st-century technology living by 9th-century rules. America no longer needs Saudi oil. They don't always cooperate with us. They are openly funding the schools that produce the *jihadists*. We kowtow to the whims of an absolute monarch whose idea of human rights ended its development when Mohammed married a 9-year-old girl. They would like to see us all dead or converted to Islam. The only redeeming thing about them is that they buy their military hardware from us and not China, and I don't know how much longer that is going to last since we don't buy their oil anymore."

"There are lots of times I would like to tell them to go hump a camel, but that isn't our job. Our job is to keep these guys happy with Uncle Sam, despite whatever they may be doing. They give us access to a part of the world where we are fresh out of friends. But as reactionary as they are, they aren't half as bad as the al-Qaeda bastards. They are willing to stand with us against them, so, to quote an Arab proverb, 'The enemy of my enemy is my friend'."

"Since you're doing proverbs, don't forget Don Corleone's proverb, 'Keep your friends close, but your enemies closer.' Sometimes it is hard to tell who is who. I don't see a kid selling scorecards."

Keaton started twiddling a pencil on his desk. "We have been on yellow alert since 9/11. Have they ramped the status up to orange yet?"

"No," said Henderson, "we are still at yellow, but we might want to go to orange on our own. It is up to you and me to decide."

"Not just yet. Let's wait a few days and see what develops. Meanwhile, inform the staff to be extra alert."

"Okay, but I am really leaning heavily toward orange."

"Why not talk to the MI6 guy? See what the Brits are thinking? The French are really pissed off at the moment because they paid the ransom for the college students, so I wouldn't ask them."

"Good idea," said Henderson. "I think I'll invite Gordon to dinner tonight."

"You might even consider talking to the Saudis too. They have the best intel system on the ground here."

"I could talk to them, but then I would have to figure out if they were telling us the truth or trying to mislead us. They've jerked my chain more than once in the past."

Henderson stood up to leave. Just as he was at the door, Keaton said, "Don't forget: 'The enemy of my enemy is my friend.'"

42

HAKIM ABU-JIHADI

As Sulayyil
Saturday, 20 June

Al-Nasirah was nervous. This operation was the most complex he had ever tried to execute. The vital parts of his plan were finally dropping into place. Jamal had informed him that the Keatons were going to the airport on the evening of the 22nd. Two days remained until retribution would descend upon the Saudis.

The 40-meter dump container on its special truck was rented and waiting on an empty lot in Riyadh.

The fighters had abandoned their old hideouts and gathered in the warehouse at As Sulayyil. Now it was no longer just a warehouse; it was a fortress. Supplies were stacked high enough to sustain them for weeks. But it was the prison cells that marked the true transformation.

The doors had been rebuilt only yesterday, reinforced with brutal slabs of lumber. Heavy timber slid into iron brackets on the outside, sealing them tight. Once closed, there would be no escape.

In the basement, a cell waited—black-walled, airless—prepared for Ambassador Stuart Keaton. On the ground floor, an enclosed office had been stripped bare, its single cell reserved for young Suzy Keaton. Upstairs, in a windowless storage room, the last prison stood ready for Mrs. Adelle Keaton. Every interior surface had been painted an unbroken, suffocating black. No light. No distraction. Just darkness and silence.

Hakim worked on his phone with quiet precision. A stolen credit card secured the charter of a bus scheduled to collect passengers outside a mosque near the construction site. But there would be no passengers.

When the unsuspecting driver arrived, two mujahedin would step aboard. He wouldn't survive the first minutes of the trip. His body, wrapped in a black plastic bag, would be shoved into the luggage compartment beneath the bus—out of sight, but not out of mind.

With the driver silenced, the AQAP men would slide into his seat and take the wheel. The bus would roll on, not toward pilgrims or travelers, but toward al-Nasirah's waiting hands. The vehicle was no longer transport. It was a weapon. And now, it was his.

Ibrahim had gone to Riyadh in a pickup truck. At a used equipment dealer, he found a 4,000 kg (approximately 8,800 lbs.) capacity high-lifting forklift. He bought it for cash (courtesy of the French government) and drove it to the empty lot where the dump container sat on its truck. When the forklift was next to the truck, Ibrahim called Hakim on his cell phone. Hakim informed al-Nasirah of the good news. All the necessary parts were in their possession or readily available.

Ibrahim stayed behind at the empty lot, drilling himself on the forklift's controls until every lever, every motion, answered to his touch. His role was too precise for mistakes—one slip could unravel everything. Failure wasn't his alone to bear; if he faltered, the entire operation collapsed.

So he kept at it, hour after hour, until muscle memory replaced thought. He would not leave Riyadh. Not until the day of the attack.

The traffic control equipment was complete. Workers had built large round plywood signs mounted on tall poles—red on one side, green on the other. A speed-limit sign, white with a black "30" inside a circle, would slow vehicles to 30 kilometers per hour—about 18 miles per hour—through the attack zone. A final sign warned of a rough, uneven road ahead.

Everything was in place. The trap was ready.

Al-Nasirah finally relaxed enough to sit down and eat a light meal. The tea he drank was sweet. Almost as sweet as the revenge he was about to visit on the treacherous Saudis.

Al-Nasirah and Hakim had been rehearsing the men for their roles in the upcoming attack. Soon, they all understood what was required of them and the importance of timing for the operation's success. No one could fail in the part he was to play.

The mujahedin would rehearse for several hours today and again for several hours tomorrow, and then one last time before the actual attack.

That evening, they sat in a circle on the warehouse floor, sharing their meal after they had all prayed. Hakim had warned every man of the need for remaining unnoticed by the neighbors, even though the only neighbor was a vacant warehouse. Therefore, there was to be no firing of guns in celebration.

Al-Nasirah stood in his place and addressed his men. "On Monday, we will avenge the deaths of our 16 brothers who were killed by the treacherous Saudis. We will do this by kidnapping the American ambassador and his family. We will show the world what powerless fools the Saudis are. And we will do it right there in their own capital. The ransom we will get for the three Americans will fund our operations for two years. The glory we bring to our cause will attract fighters from across all of Islam. Each of us must perform flawlessly. We may not fail, for Allah is with us. *Allahu Akbar!*"

The men jumped to their feet, shouting and waving their arms, *"Allahu Akbar! Allahu Akbar! Allahu Akbar!"*

Only Hakim remained seated, his thoughts on the impending attack. Some will live and some will die. Success or failure will all be decided by the whim of Allah.

43

LAURA

The Saudi Arabian Desert
Sunday, 21 June

More frustration. We have been driving on the roads in the hill country, and we are easy targets. Still nothing from AQAP. We encountered a small group of bandits who turned away from us without firing a shot. We have been overnighting in a few local hamlets with no leads on where the bad guys are. Maybe the word is out that we are not what we appear to be.

I have been doing half of the driving while Jack scans the hills for signs of life. If anyone were to see me driving, they would know that we are foreigners, but Jack cannot do all the driving. These roads require too much steady concentration, and Jack says it is possible to burn out your brain and make fatal errors.

I was driving along the edge of a wadi when Jack spotted some bones sticking out of the sand. "Come to a stop in a safe place, Laura."

"It is all lousy. How about right here?" I replied.

"Good." Jack and I got out of the truck, AKs ready, and walked back about 40 meters to the bones.

The bones were half-buried in the sand.

Jack was scanning the hills, not looking at the bones. I squatted down and brushed some of the sand away. "These are human. I think it may have been a teenage girl."

Jack scanned the hills around us one last time before he also squatted down next to me. He found the skull in the sand, or more accurately, what was left of the skull. "Some heroic male decided this female represented a major threat. I think she was shot at close range in the left temple. There is an exit wound blowing out most of the right side of the skull."

On a hunch, I pushed the sand away from the left arm bones. "Look, Jack, her hands were tied behind her back. My guess is that this was an honor killing."

Jack and I both knew about honor killings in Islam. The family's honor depends upon the behavior of the women in the family, especially the unmarried ones. There are so many circumstances in which a young woman can be killed by her own family members because she has sullied the honor of the family. Such dishonor can be a major breach, such as falling in love with an inappropriate male from another clan, being seen in the company of any male who is not a family member, or worst of all, having sex with any man who is not her husband. To redeem the family's honor, any male member of the family can kill the offending woman. Most often, the privilege of killing the female goes to the head of the family unit, but her brothers or uncles also have the license to do the deed. No legal prosecutions, penalties, or consequences follow from such a killing. The Prophet, peace be unto Him, has decreed the punishment, and so it shall be.

"Whatever she did," I said, "they didn't even give her a burial in a marked grave. They just left her out in the desert for the vultures and jackals to pick her bones clean."

"What a culture! I'll never be comfortable with Islam. Human life is so cheap as to be worthless to them."

"Jack, unless you want to bury her, I think we should get moving."

"Right. Let's get out of here." Jack placed her skull where it should be on the skeleton and scooped some sand over almost all the bones. I helped him. It wasn't a burial, but at least her bones weren't lying naked in the sun.

I got behind the wheel again and continued driving. Neither of us had anything to say. What can be said when you are confronted with such a waste of a young life?

44

STUART J. KEATON

U. S. Embassy, Riyadh
Monday, 22 June, 9:45 PM

At 9:45 PM, Stu Keaton entered his daughter's bedroom. "Suzy, are you all set to go?"

"Yeah, Dad. All I need is Alfie and I'm set." She picked up Alfie, a small stuffed bear, by his ear and stuffed him in her carry-on case. "I think I'm ready."

"OK. Let's roll, Sweetie. The cars are out front."

Together, they descended the stairs to the front entrance of the embassy. Three black SUVs, heavily armored, stood idling in the driveway. Two Saudi Army MP sergeants on motorcycles with blue flashing lights were waiting to lead the motorcade to the airport. The rear of the middle SUV was full of luggage, but there was a small space available for Suzy's carry-on. Suzy placed it in the back section of the middle SUV and climbed into the rear seat next to her mother. Stuart Keaton climbed in next to Suzy.

In the front seat, two Marine security guards wearing combat fatigues were armed and ready. A Lance Corporal was driving; the other Marine, First Lieutenant Henry "Hank" Newman, handled the radio communications and commanded the motorcade. There were four armed Marines in each of the other two SUVs. A Marine sergeant commanded each of the front and rear SUVs with three additional enlisted men. Weapons comprised M-16s, sidearms, and body armor.

When the Keatons were all seated and belted in, Lieutenant Newman gave the radio command to his motorcade, "Let's move out."

With the two motorcycles leading the way, the motorcade eased its way out of the embassy, heading south on the divided highway. At circle 8, they went a quarter of the way around the roundabout and headed east toward circle 4. At circle 4, another quarter turn onto Amr Ibn Ummiyyah Ad Damri highway, which leads northeast up to Jeddah Rd. (Route 535), a major artery heading north toward the airport. Traffic was light at this hour, and 28 minutes into their journey, they turned east onto King Salman Road (Route 40), heading toward Airport Road and King Khalid International Airport.

Suzy was anticipating her camp adventures. She had no idea what adventures actually lay in wait for her.

45

THE ATTACK

Route 40
Riyadh, Saudi Arabia
Monday, 22 June 9:45 PM

Al-Nasirah's men rolled into the construction site in six pickup trucks, climbing out as though they belonged there—just another night crew reporting for work.

The site itself blazed with light. Thirteen portable generators, each mounted on a wheeled trailer, powered twenty-six floodlights atop tall telescoping poles. The three-lane road was being widened to four lanes, and traffic was funneled eastbound at a crawl through the glare and machinery.

One hundred and twenty meters away, hidden in darkness beyond the reach of the floodlights, the chartered bus waited. Its driver's body lay stuffed in a black plastic bag inside the luggage compartment. Nearby, the 40-cubic-meter dumpster truck and the forklift sat silent, Ibrahim at the controls, their engines cold and lights extinguished. They had waited like predators in the dark for nearly forty-five minutes.

With the pickups' arrival, the bus rumbled forward, easing onto the right shoulder about 100 meters east, past the construction site. Moments later, the dumpster truck lumbered onto the road, edging westward before pulling off onto the left shoulder. The driver killed the headlights but left the engine running, a low growl beneath the floodlights.

Ibrahim followed, guiding the forklift west to the right shoulder, squaring it across from the dumpster truck. Now, at the late hour, traffic crept between them, boxed in by steel and shadow.

The construction workers didn't so much as glance at the new arrivals. No one asked what the machines were doing. And that silence was the last piece of the trap.

The al-Qaeda men quietly approached the men who were working on the site. One by one, they were silently escorted to the bus at pistol point. At the bus, every man was relieved of his cell phone, his tablet, or his computer. There was no possibility of anyone communicating with any authority to raise an alarm. All the workers were loaded onto the bus. One al-Qaeda man stayed on the bus with an AK-47 pointed at the workers.

"Silence! No talking. If anyone tries to make a call or raise an alarm, we will shoot you immediately. Remain calm and quiet. When we are done, everyone will be set free. Right now, you must all sit quietly. If you give us any trouble, we will blow up the bus, and everyone will die."

The workers, mostly Yemenis, Palestinians, and Bangladeshi, were cowed into silence.

Outside the bus, an al-Qaeda fighter was quietly attaching Semtex explosives every 3 meters around the bus, starting at the driver's window and working all the way around the rear to the front entry door. All the explosives were wired together to explode simultaneously. A cell phone was the trigger. The phone number of the trigger was pre-programmed into Hakim's cell phone.

Hakim and three al-Qaeda men, driving on the right shoulder against the flow of traffic, drove a pickup truck 300 meters west, ahead of the construction site. With their red/green traffic control signs, they waited until they saw the flashing lights of the motorcycle escorts. Their AK-47s were left in the pickup truck. To any passing motorist, they looked like construction workers loafing at the side of the road.

Four massive dump trucks stood idle at the construction site, their original drivers now prisoners on the bus. Al-Nasirah chose two of them and barked orders. His men climbed behind the wheels.

The first truck rumbled across to the left shoulder, pulling to a stop directly in front of the dumpster truck, its nose angled across the highway. Headlights off. Engine humming. The second truck—its bed piled high with gravel and broken rock—took position behind the dumpster truck, forming a barricade of steel and stone.

A yellow electric wire, weighted at both ends but connected to nothing, was stretched across the asphalt ten meters in front of the forward truck. It was the trigger line—when the motorcycle escorts crossed it, the ambush would begin.

Beside the wire, a pickup waited with its engine running; three gunmen crouched in the bed under a tarp, weapons ready. Traffic still trickled through the site at forty kilometers an hour, unaware of the trap tightening around them.

Al-Nasirah scanned the road, eyes fixed eastward. Everything was in place. The only thing missing was the Americans.

Then headlights cut into the construction zone. A green Range Rover slowed to a stop. One of the project superintendents climbed out, anger evident in his stride.

"What's going on here? Why has all the work stopped? Where's the foreman?" he demanded, closing in on al-Nasirah.

Al-Nasirah said, "He is over behind that dump truck. I'll take you to him."

When they got there, the superintendent turned on al-Nasirah and demanded, "What the hell is going on? There's no one here."

Al-Nasirah stepped close and said, "Now you are." And shot the superintendent in the heart with his pistol at point-blank range. The sound of the shot was muffled by the proximity of the victim's body and by the traffic noise. Al-Nasirah left the body where it fell and returned to his vantage point, where he could watch the highway.

Four minutes passed, five minutes, six minutes. Al-Nasirah saw red flashing lights. He passed the word, "Get ready." As the flashing lights drew closer, he saw it was an ambulance responding to an emergency call. He passed the word, "Not our target."

Two minutes later, he saw the flashing blue and white lights of the motorcycle escort. Again, he passed the word, "Get ready."

Hakim stood with the traffic control team three hundred meters down the road, watching his men slide into position. At his signal, two stepped into the right and center lanes, raising their red signs to halt traffic. In the left lane, the third man flipped his sign to green, waving vehicles through with a slow, deliberate motion. His hand cut the air in a wavering gesture, warning of the rough road ahead.

The motorcade drew closer, already bunching as the motorcycles throttled down. SUVs closed ranks, steel and glass pressing tight. As the third SUV passed, the left lane controller snapped his sign to red and froze the trailing traffic.

The convoy crawled into the construction zone. Then, the trap snapped shut.

The army motorcycles crossed the yellow wire. In an instant, the pickup truck on the shoulder lurched forward, its tarp ripped back to reveal three gunmen. AK-47s barked, spitting fire. The two sergeants on the bikes went down in a hail of bullets.

The driver of the lead SUV slammed on the brakes, but it was too late. From both sides, the dump trucks roared across the road, slamming broadside into the first and last vehicles. Metal screamed. The SUVs skidded off the asphalt and onto the right shoulder. Airbags exploded in every direction, shrouding the Marines in choking powder and deafening blasts. Vision gone. Ears ringing. Chaos.

Then came the forklift.

Ibrahim drove forward, ramming his forks beneath the middle SUV. The hydraulics groaned as he lifted, raising the vehicle off the ground. Inside, Lieutenant Hank Newman shoved his Beretta through a gun port and fired, emptying the clip. Three rounds punched into

Ibrahim's body. One nicked his aorta. Blood soaked his shirt, but his hands never left the controls.

The SUV kept rising.

Ibrahim rolled forward toward the looming 40-meter dumpster. When the vehicle hung high above the steel container, he lowered the forks onto its edge. The SUV's wheels dangled just twelve inches inside. Then Ibrahim backed away.

Gravity took over.

The SUV tilted and toppled, crashing sideways into the dumpster with a metallic roar. The impact triggered another deafening burst—every airbag detonated at once, suffocating the Keatons in smoke, noise, and blinding white fabric.

The trap had sprung shut.

In the rear seat, Adelle Keaton's skull cracked hard against the steel roof support. A sharp burst of light exploded behind her eyes, and she slumped sideways, dazed and concussed. Beside her, Suzy was crushed between her parents, ribs aching under the pressure, but the bruising pain told her she was still intact. Stuart had been thrown violently against his daughter, his seat belt biting deep into his chest and catching most of his weight, sparing her worse injury.

Up front, the driver's head slammed into the bulletproof glass with a sickening thud. He went limp against the wheel, blood trickling down his temple. The air reeked of burned propellant and acrid smoke from the airbags, stinging every breath.

Lieutenant Newman tore himself free from the deflating fabric, heart pounding, ears ringing. His face was streaked with sweat and dust, but his eyes were alive—sharp, furious. He still had fight left in him.

Outside the dumpster, a heavy canvas cover groaned as it slid forward on two hydraulic arms, stretching over the entire length of the container. With a final metallic clank, the SUV and the screaming chaos inside vanished beneath the tarp.

The massive truck shuddered, gears grinding as it lumbered down the highway, hauling the imprisoned Keatons toward the warehouse in As Sulayyil. In the cab, al-Nasirah sat in the passenger seat; a third fighter squeezed between him and the driver. The air reeked of diesel and sweat; the cab vibrating with every guttural shift of the transmission.

Behind them, the rear dump truck roared. The driver yanked the lever, and with a mechanical whine, the bed began to lift. Tons of gravel, dirt, and jagged rock cascaded onto the asphalt with a thunderous crash. Dust billowed. The road vanished under a mountain of debris— no car would be passing through that barricade tonight. The driver was already leaping from the cab, boots hitting the ground before the first stones struck. Both dump truck drivers sprinted toward a waiting pickup, its engine growling, lights off.

Hakim and his men piled into their own truck and tore up the right shoulder, headlights slicing through the floodlit haze. Within moments, six pickups were speeding away, their engines howling into the night. Shouts of *Allahu Akbar!* split the silence, echoing across the empty highway.

The entire ambush had taken less than two minutes.

As Hakim's truck passed the bus abandoned on the roadside, he braked just long enough to collect the guard posted there. "I told the workers they must wait ten minutes before getting off," the man reported breathlessly.

Hakim grinned, laughter sharp in his throat. His thumb tapped a button on his phone. A heartbeat later, the bus erupted in a fireball— glass, steel, and screams torn apart in a single violent blast. Flames licked at the night sky. The explosion's shockwave rattling windows a mile away.

The AQAP convoy roared into the darkness. Their only loss was Ibrahim, still slumped lifeless over the forklift controls, blood pooling beneath his seat.

46

1ST LT. HENRY NEWMAN

Route 40
Riyadh, Saudi Arabia
Monday, 22 June, 10:12 PM

Lieutenant Hank Newman shoved the deflating airbags away from his face. The driver beside him was slumped unconscious. A quick glance told him the SUV was lying on its left side.

From the back came Suzy Keaton's soft whimpers—stunned, but alive. Adelle Keaton was silent, terrifyingly so. Stuart Keaton groaned, struggling to lift his weight off his daughter. He had switched on the overhead light, casting a harsh glow across the crumpled interior.

Newman reached for the dashboard, flipped open a protective cover, and threw a toggle switch to the *on* position. Instantly, a silent homing beacon began transmitting their exact latitude and longitude to a satellite—alerts would already flash at the American embassy and at NSA headquarters in Bethesda.

His sidearm was gone, lost when the SUV toppled onto its side, but one of the M16s lay within reach. He snatched it up. "Mr. Keaton, are you injured, sir?"

"I'll be all right if I can get my feet under me and out of this belt," Keaton grunted. "My wife isn't moving at all." Bracing himself against the partition, he twisted and shoved his feet against the door now beneath them, finally lifting his weight off Suzy.

"We're moving at a pretty good clip, sir," Newman said grimly. "Obviously, we've been hijacked."

He hit the button to unlock the automatic door locks, then shoved against the front passenger door. The two-inch-thick bulletproof glass made it heavier than expected. With effort, it creaked open about a foot before slamming into resistance. The canvas tarp stretched across the top of the dumpster's body blocked any escape.

In the back seat, Keaton reached down to Adelle to feel for a pulse in her neck. "My wife is alive but unconscious," he informed Newman.

"I'm going to see what I can do, sir. Could you kill that light? There is a canvas cover over the car, and I am going to cut through it and open my door."

"Don't get yourself killed," said Keaton.

Newman said, "They will want you and your family for ransom. They will kill all the Marines, no matter what we do. I'm taking some of these camel fuckers with me when I go. Kill the light, sir."

Keaton shut off the dome light. Lt. Newman pushed open the door again, reached up with his combat knife, and sliced through the canvas cover. Newman pulled himself up and rolled onto the canvas cover. Once he was out of the door, the wind forced the door to shut again. The slit canvas was flapping loudly in the wind.

He quickly understood that they were on a dumpster truck traveling at about 60 or 65 miles per hour. He looked behind him and saw six pickup trucks following the dumpster. They were spread out, filling all three lanes of the highway, blocking any other traffic from passing the dumpster.

Newman crawled to the rear of the dumpster truck, braced himself, and leveled his M16. He squeezed off two short, controlled bursts. The rounds punched through the windshield of the pickup tailing directly behind. The driver lost control—the truck lurched left, sideswiping the pickup in the next lane and shoving it onto the shoulder. A moment later, another vehicle slammed into the damaged pickup's rear bumper. Metal crunched, tires screamed, and both trucks dropped out of the convoy.

The pickup that had been forced aside jerked back onto the road, its occupants firing wildly. Bullets sparked off the steel walls of the dumpster, others whining into the darkness. Newman ducked low, heart hammering, then slid back into position.

He sighted the pickup in the right lane. Another burst of gunfire shattered its windshield. The vehicle swerved hard, fishtailed, and crunched against the guardrail, grinding to a stop.

In one pickup trailing behind, Newman could see one fighter grabbing his phone. *They're going to know I'm behind them at any moment,* he thought. With the rush of wind in his ears and the grind of the truck's engine beneath him, he crawled across the canvas cover toward the cab. The tarp sagged and shifted with each jolt of the road, threatening to spill him off at any moment.

His thoughts stayed locked on the men ahead. The driver had to keep the truck moving—he couldn't abandon the wheel without killing them all. That meant the real danger came from the two passengers riding beside him. They would be armed. They could turn and fire at any second.

Newman gripped the M16 tighter. One magazine. No reloads. Every bullet had to count.

Newman was almost at the cab of the truck. Al-Nasirah could see him through the rear window of the cab.

"When I tell you to stop," al-Nasirah said to the driver, "jam on the brakes. The American will slide off the front of the truck and hit the road. Then step on the gas and run over him."

Newman fired a single shot through the back window into the head of the center passenger.

Al-Nasirah kept looking backward. Just as Newman was taking aim at him, he yelled, "STOP!"

The driver hit the brakes, and Newman catapulted forward at 65 miles an hour, carried by the momentum of the moving vehicle. He hit the pavement 30 feet in front of the truck.

"NOW GO!" yelled al-Nasirah.

The driver hit the accelerator, and the truck surged forward. The truck passed over the form lying in the road. There was no sensation of impact with the tires.

The driver said, "My sheikh, I don't think our tires hit the American."

"Even if we didn't hit him, the fall at the speed we were traveling probably killed him. Maybe one of our pickups will finish him off."

Behind the dumpster, there were now only three pickups. Hakim, in an undamaged pickup, ordered his truck to stop to get the surviving fighters. "Leave the dead men. Make sure no one alive is left behind to tell where we are taking the prisoners. Bring the wounded. Get in the back quickly." By the time Hakim's truck started again, there were eight men in the truck. Two were badly wounded.

Al-Nasirah leaned forward. "Take the next exit."

The dumpster truck rumbled off the highway at Ad Dammam Branch Road, turned twice, and rolled into a vacant lot. The pickups fanned in behind it, engines idling.

"Pull back the canvas," al-Nasirah barked. The driver hit the controls, and the tarp peeled away with a groan of hydraulics. Al-Nasirah jumped down from the cab, waving his men forward.

Gunmen spilled from the pickups, feet thudding against gravel as they scrambled up the sides of the dumpster. The SUV inside lay exposed, its passengers trapped in the wreckage.

"Get them out—quickly," al-Nasirah ordered. "And make sure the driver is dead."

The rear passenger door screeched open. Muzzles thrust into the cabin. Rough hands reached down and dragged Stuart Keaton halfway out.

"Climb out now!" one fighter shouted.

"Do not hurt my family!" Keaton's voice cracked as he obeyed, rising onto the twisted right side of the SUV, weapons trained on his chest.

Another man leaned in with a knife, sawing through Susannah's seat belt. She tumbled against her mother before being yanked free. Arms hauled her up and set her beside her father. Trembling, she clung to him.

"Mommy's dead!" she sobbed.

"No, she's alive," Keaton told her firmly. "She's only unconscious."

Then a fighter slid inside. A single gunshot cracked through the night. The echo bounced off the walls of the surrounding buildings.

Suzy shrieked, her cry piercing. "They shot Mommy! Daddy, they shot Mommy!"

One of the AQAP men clamped a rough hand over her mouth. Keaton's fury exploded—he swung and smashed his fist into the man's temple. The fighter crumpled, dragging Suzy down with him.

Instantly, four gun barrels pressed into Keaton's ribs and back. "Do that again," a voice hissed, "and you will die right here in front of your child."

Keaton pulled a sobbing Suzy to her feet up next to him. The man he punched had a split lip. As he stood up, he swore he would get revenge.

The man inside the car cut Adelle loose and passed her limp form to the hands waiting to haul her out of the car. She was regaining consciousness.

Al-Nasirah shouted, "Get them on the ground. One in each pickup. Tie their hands and hood them. Move quickly."

Adelle and Suzy were passed down to the men waiting on the ground. Keaton climbed down by himself. Guns were constantly pointed at him.

The AQAP men tied the hands of all three Keatons behind their backs and put black canvas bags over their heads. Each Keaton captive was laid face down on the bed of a different pickup truck. The men loaded up. Four men sat with their feet on Stuart Keaton with gun barrels poking into his sides and back. Two men guarded Adelle. Two men kept watch over Suzy. The wounded were loaded onto the truck carrying Suzy.

The three pickups took off heading for As Sulayyil. The dumpster truck, with the SUV sending out its tracking signal, was abandoned on the vacant lot.

47

GENERAL KALIM SURAYAH

Commander, 1ˢᵗ Saudi Army Corps
Riyadh, Saudi Arabia
Monday, June 22, 11:50 PM

General Surayah was royally pissed off. His cell phone interrupted the fun and games with his mistress. He got his slightly portly frame out of bed and dressed quickly. Surayah had a pencil-thin mustache and a pencil-thin beard that trimmed his lower jaw and chin. He left without even tying his shoelaces. His tunic was still unbuttoned.

His mistress came running after him. "Your eyeglasses, Kalim. You will need them."

He grabbed them without a word and stormed out the door. The message on his phone was very disturbing.

- Major explosion at a construction site on Route 40. There are many dead and wounded.

- Two Saudi army motorcycle MPs are dead on Route 40.

- A motorcade carrying the U.S. ambassador and his family to the airport was attacked on Route 40. There is no trace of these people at the site, and the conclusion is that they have been kidnapped.

- The American embassy received an emergency carjacking signal and was sending armed Marines to track the vehicle.

- Two crushed SUVs from the American embassy are on the side of the road near the explosion on Route 40. Three men are dead in their cars; five are seriously injured. All are U.S. military personnel. All injured are being transported to area hospitals.

- An American military man, identified as a Marine, has been found severely injured on Route 40, six kilometers from the blast site. The American was still alive but in very grave condition. He is being transported to the hospital by helicopter at this moment. Paramedics are struggling just to keep him alive. The hospital will notify the American embassy when the Marine arrives. Insignia indicates he is an officer; the name patch on the uniform says his name is Newman.

- A construction worker has been found shot dead on his forklift at the scene of the attack. Another man has also been found shot dead at the construction site.

- Three crashed pickup trucks have been found several kilometers away from the explosion site on Route 40. Three men, possibly attackers, are in these trucks. Two are dead, and one is so severely wounded that he will probably also die. He has been taken to a hospital.

- Route 40 is completely closed to all traffic except police, emergency, and military vehicles.

- The Royal Palace has been alerted to the attack and is demanding immediate action to find the U.S. ambassador and his family. His Royal Highness has placed all military units on high alert until further notice.

- Your presence is requested at the scene.

The general thought, *Allah, what have you done to me?* He finished adjusting his uniform as he hurried down to his car.

The driver had fallen asleep in the driver's seat because he knew from experience that the general would not need him for several hours. He was rudely awakened and ordered to drive to Route 40 at top speed.

Once underway, General Surayah tied his shoelaces, then got on the radio and started ordering army roadblocks to be set up to prevent the kidnappers from escaping from Riyadh. Unfortunately, getting his units in place would take from 10 to 30 minutes due to the late hour and the distance from the barracks.

Unbeknownst to General Surayah he had already missed the three pickup trucks heading south out of Riyadh on Route 65 by five minutes. By the time the roadblocks were to be expanded even further, the AQAP men had cleared Route 10 all the way to As Sulayyil and the safety of their warehouse/converted prison.

When the general reached Route 40, the driver found the highway choked with emergency vehicles. Police cruisers blocked every entrance and exit, their light bars spinning red and blue across the night.

The general's car carried its own authority—hidden flashers pulsed behind the grille and rear window, and small metal flags stamped with his rank snapped on the fenders. The signals cleared a path. Officers waved them toward an exit ramp, and the driver swung the car onto the eastbound lane—heading west, against the flow. The klaxon blared, scattering anyone slow to move aside.

They reached the blast site first. The charred shell of the bus still smoked, its ruin lit by floodlights and fire engines. Ambulances shrieked in and out, ferrying the wounded. In a nearby field, soldiers in gloves laid bodies in rows on plastic sheets—silent, orderly, terrible. Photographers moved among them, shutters clicking, preserving every detail for the investigations that would inevitably follow.

The car stopped; the general got out. "Who is in charge here?" he demanded.

An army major separated himself from the crowd of men, came over to the general, and saluted. "General Surayah, I am Major Manush. This sector is my responsibility. We have twenty-three dead and eleven seriously wounded. They have been triaged, and some have already been transported to hospitals. One survivor told us that these were all workers who were forced onto the bus at gunpoint. The attackers promised to set them free after the attack, but they blew up the bus as they were fleeing the area. It was simply murdering innocents for no reason, sir."

A soldier's shout called the major to the bus. He and the general hurried over. In the luggage compartment, a body had been found stuffed inside a plastic bag.

Even in tatters, the uniform marked him instantly as the bus driver. His throat had been slit.

Both officers stared at the corpse. "What animals they are," the major spat.

The general looked at the major and said, "You have this disaster under control. Where did the kidnapping take place?"

"Over there, where all the work lights are. Brigadier Muhammed Saud, the King's nephew, is in charge there."

The general turned away without a word and returned to his car. They drove a short distance to the site of the attack. The general quickly walked the last 50 meters. Brigadier General Mohammed Ibn Saud was standing in a knot of people comprising military officers, police officers, and three civilians. Two men in business suits were talking to the group. All conversation stopped when the general walked up. Everyone saluted.

General Surayah demanded, "Does anyone know exactly what happened here?"

Brigadier Saud, the highest-ranking man present until the general arrived, answered, "General Surayah, these two men," pointing to the men in business suits, "are crime scene investigators from the Riyadh Public Prosecutor's Office. They believe they have a possible explanation of how this was done. Mr. Henderson, who is from the American embassy," Brig. Saud indicated the third civilian, "believes they are correct."

General Surayah knew Mr. Henderson's true function at the embassy. He nodded at Henderson but said nothing. He turned to the crime scene investigators. "Speak," he said.

The two men were both neatly dressed. One was tall and gaunt—nearly two meters in height—while the other, of average build, carried himself with authority. It was the shorter man who addressed the general.

"Sir, no one here witnessed the entire attack. We're piecing it together from the evidence on site and from questioning motorists who were stopped nearby.

"According to their accounts, three men with red traffic control signs halted all traffic about three hundred meters before the ambush point. Only the left lane was allowed through—that lane carried the ambassador's motorcade.

"The convoy comprised two Saudi Army MP sergeants on motorcycles leading three embassy SUVs. Mr. Henderson confirms that the ambassador and his family were in the middle vehicle.

"It appears the two dump trucks were used to ram and disable the escort SUVs, isolating the ambassador's car between them. From this point, we can only speculate, but evidence suggests a forklift was used to lift the ambassador's SUV and load it onto a flatbed truck, which then departed the scene.

"The motorcycle escorts were gunned down at the start of the attack—both bodies riddled with dozens of bullet wounds. The bus explosion occurred only after the ambassador's vehicle had been taken. The dead man found on the forklift appears to have been one of the attackers, not a construction worker. We believe he was shot by one of the ambassador's bodyguards during the struggle. Until further evidence comes to light, this is the best reconstruction we can provide."

"Hmph!" said the general. "Do we have any clues who the attackers are? This was obviously well organized and financed."

Brigadier Saud answered, "Our best guess is that it was al-Qaeda. Only they have enough men to successfully pull off something like this. Of course, once one of the radicals claims credit for the attack, we will know exactly who to blame for this atrocity."

At that moment, Henderson's cell phone went off. He grabbed it immediately and turned away from the group. He listened for a moment and then said, "Shit." He ended the call and turned back to the group. "That was our Marine detachment following the hijack homing signal. They found the ambassador's SUV in a large dumpster truck several kilometers from here. The ambassador and his family are not there. The driver was executed with a bullet to the head at close range. Apparently, the ambassador's car was dumped into the dumpster by the forklift. Lt. Newman, who is now at the hospital, was in command of the motorcade and apparently could continue fighting after the SUV went into the dumpster. He is probably the one responsible for the casualties to the attackers since all the other escorts were found here at the scene of the attack."

The general said, "The Royal Palace will want results in finding the ambassador quickly. *He* is the important one. *He* represents America. *He* is a friend of the American president. His wife and daughter are of less importance. If we can get them all back alive, even better, but *he* is the prize we must recover. If we fail, it will be our heads that roll."

The assembled group exchanged uneasy glances among themselves. All the Saudis thought the general had assessed the situation correctly.

Only Henderson thought the general was a complete asshole.

The general turned and stalked back to his waiting car.

48

HERBERT WATSON, III

Langley, VA

Monday, 22 June, 5:20 PM

Herb Watson was in attack mode. The word had just come in that the U.S. ambassador to Saudi Arabia and his family had been kidnapped. It was after midnight in Saudi Arabia, but due to the time difference, it was still late afternoon on the East Coast of the U.S.

"Get me a current list of which assets we have in the area. Inform any assets we have on the ground in Saudi Arabia and Yemen of this news. Ordering the recovery of the ambassador and his family is a Priority One effort. Let the director know what we are doing because he will have to answer to the president."

In less than five minutes, Watson's secretary entered with a single sheet of paper. She handed it to Watson. "These are the people we have on the ground right now."

Watson looked at the list. It was much shorter than he would have wanted it to be. Eleven names but only four assets.

Michael Henderson, U.S. Embassy, Riyadh

Stephen Wickham, assistant to Henderson

George Styron, deputy assistant, U.S. Embassy staff

Bonnie Wilson, deputy assistant, U.S. Embassy staff

Eugene Loumis, U.S. Embassy communications clerk

James de Haagen, independent assignment

Jack Miller & Laura Halevi, independent assignment

Muhammed Ali ben Makhara, deep cover

Sulemain bin Kazan, deep cover

Arnold Winston, independent assignment

Willard Sims, independent assignment

"In two minutes, I will have a Priority One message for Henderson, Makhara, de Haagen, Miller, Winston, and Sims. Wait right there, please." Watson took out a message pad and wrote:

Piority one. Ambassador Stuart Keaton, his wife Adelle Keaton, and their daughter Susannah Keaton (11 years old) have been abducted in Riyadh by forces unknown but suspected to be al-Qaeda. The abduction occurred within the past two hours. Rescue of these assets is of the highest priority. All efforts are to be directed toward their recovery. As further details develop, we will inform you. All feedback is critical. Make sure we know what you know. Special Forces will be in place and available within 24-48 hrs. Assign code name *Oilman.*

Beartrap

Watson handed the page to his secretary. "Immediate transmission."

"Yes, sir," and she was gone.

Watson sat at his desk, cursing the Congress that, year after year, kept cutting the agency budgets and the spineless politicians that wouldn't let our intelligence services work within the borders of friendly allies. The bullshit the agency must live with is that Saudi Arabia really isn't a friendly ally, but they have to be treated the same as NATO or Australia or South Korea. Are we a nation of suicidal moronic assholes, or what?

49

JACK

In the southern Saudi Arabian desert
Tuesday, 23 June, 1 AM

Jack was on watch; Laura was asleep on an inflated pad in the bed of the pickup. His AK-47 was ready across his lap. He felt his cell phone vibrate in his pocket. He looked at the screen and knew he was receiving a message from Langley.

When Jack read the message, he immediately woke Laura. "Take a look at this message."

Laura was instantly awake, with adrenaline flowing, anticipating an attack. She visibly relaxed when Jack handed her his telephone. Then she read the message.

"Damn! Now we know why things were so quiet," said Laura. "This is what the bastards were planning."

"Finding the Keatons and getting them out alive is going to take some doing."

"What we need is an internet connection," said Laura.

"OK, but tell me why," Jack said.

"This is a high-profile event. Which means—"

At that moment, a pair of Saudi military jet fighters streaked low overhead. The noises from the engines drowned out Laura's voice. She stopped speaking. When they were gone, she began speaking again.

"As I was saying, this is a high-profile event. Which means they are going to send videos of the captives to Al Jazeera in Doha. I have hacked into Al Jazeera's computers a few times and left myself a backdoor so I can get in whenever I want to. AQAP is not going to mail its videos, and they aren't going to send a messenger with a disk. They will send an email with the video attached. If I am inside Al Jazeera's computers when the message arrives, I can work backward and find the server where the message originated. That will bring us within ten square miles of the location of the sending computer. Because we are in Saudi Arabia with desert everywhere and not too many population centers, we might even have a better chance. My guess is we have at least 24 hours before the first claim of responsibility is made via email."

Jack grabbed the local map of the area. "The closest town is Yadamah. I'm sure the mayor of the town has internet connections to Riyadh. Here's another thought: al-Nasirah wouldn't take his captives north; he would take them south toward Yemen. In Yemen, he has a local support network. So, he is in southern Saudi Arabia, or if he thinks he can get the captives across the border, he'll be in northern Yemen. By now, the Saudi military has sealed the border, and there is already aerial surveillance of the desert areas. Those jets we just heard are out hunting for him. I think he is still in Saudi Arabia. But three captives are a problem to move, so I think he will hole up somewhere for a few weeks while he negotiates the ransom. His only problem is that the U.S. won't pay ransoms. Maybe he is hoping the Saudis will pay up because the kidnapping occurred on their turf."

"Good points," said Laura. I think your analysis is correct. To get the captives into Yemen before the border was sealed, he would have needed some kind of aircraft. I don't think al-Nasirah has any aircraft available. He still thinks in terms of pickup trucks. My guess is that he is somewhere between Yemen and Riyadh. Let's look at the map."

Jack handed Laura the map. After a moment she said, "Jack, he has to be on the civilized side of Route 10. Any hiding place along there would be 400 to 600 miles from any carrier-based aircraft. He would be safe from attacks by SEALs and Delta Force. Everything east and south of Route 10 is the *Rub' al Khali*, The Empty Quarter. There is virtually nothing there except desert for a thousand kilometers. No hills, no caves, no settlements, no people, no oases, nothing, just endless sand dunes. I think somewhere along Route 10 makes sense."

"We both agree he has to be in southern Saudi Arabia. I am pretty sure he has a building somewhere that he has had for a while. He needs a prison for his prisoners."

"Jack, let's get moving to the edge of Yadamah and find a hotel or guesthouse where I can have electricity and keep my computer on all the time."

"No Laura. I think we should wait until dawn before moving for two reasons. First, if we arrive at night, we will arouse suspicion. No one travels at night in this area. Second, the Saudis have scrambled their jets to hunt for the kidnappers. If a Saudi Air Force fighter should spot us moving at night after what just happened, we might get a heat-seeking missile blowing up this truck. It is going to take AQAP a few hours to get organized. I think we'll be okay for another five hours out here. Then we can head for Yadamah."

"I hope you are right. I think we should send our bosses a message telling them what we plan to do. You write it up in English for Herb, and then I will send the exact same message in Hebrew to Yitzhak."

"I'll get to work on it now."

Jack sat at his phone typing a text message to Beartrap with his thumbs:

Oilman alert received. Strong belief act done by AQAP. Heading for Yadamah and steady source of internet for computer. Expect kidnappers to make video claim of responsibility for attack. Expect video will be emailed to Al Jazeera. Koala can access AJ computers and trace email back to sending server. Finding server will greatly narrow geographic territory in which prisoners are being held. Believe it logical that prisoners and perps are in southern SA near Rte 10. Perps need a suitable building to hold prisoners. Once area narrowed, will start search for building. Will keep you posted.

Pogo

Laura copied the message into Hebrew, signed it Koala and we sent both messages at the same time.

Both of us were too wired to sleep. We sat side by side, each of us facing in the opposite direction so no bad guys could sneak up on us. My left hand was holding her left hand. It felt like we were a pair of police cars facing in opposite directions so the two drivers could speak to each other while still watching for speeders.

Two more times we spotted pairs of fighter jets streaking southward across the sky.

Eventually, the sky grew lighter in the east. We stowed our equipment and drove toward Yadamah.

50

HAKIM ABU-JIHADI

As Sulayyil, Saudi Arabia
Tuesday, 23 June

We finally arrived at the warehouse. It was a long, tense drive. I was relieved that we didn't encounter any Saudi army patrols on the drive. The sheikh was upset that we had lost so many fighters. We are reduced to only fifteen men fit to fight. Two men are seriously wounded and not good for any service. They will probably die.

The captives were separated into different cells: the man was locked in the cellar, the little girl confined to the ground floor, and the woman taken upstairs.

Three sentries were sent up to the roof. They would spend two hours up there and then be relieved by three more men. During the day, the sentries would have to stay away from the edge of the roof to avoid detection. We had fifteen men for five shifts of three men each before they repeated. The sheikh and I would not be serving as sentries. I created a rotation list for the fifteen healthy men, including their assigned times for the watch shifts. Some men could not read, so we relied on those who could read to ensure all the men fulfilled their duties. Sentries were not to engage in any prayer while on watch duty. Facing toward Mecca is fine while praying, but we needed sentries with eyes in all directions.

After we got organized, food was prepared and sent up to the roof for the first shift. Later sentry shifts would only eat when inside the warehouse.

The sheikh insisted the video be made at once, showcasing the captives in humiliation.

"Hakim! Prepare a black-curtain room with our flag hanging behind them. Their hands must be tied in front for the camera.

"We will tell the Saudis the Americans were taken in retaliation for their army's attack that killed our sixteen brothers. We will tell the Americans they must pay for the crimes of their puppets—that their riyals and dollars mean nothing to us.

"The ransom will be one hundred million euros. And to deepen their disgrace, we demand that they lower their flag as a sign of submission to our terms."

"It shall be done, my sheikh." I pointed to the two nearest men. "Come do what the sheihk has ordered."

Hakim and the two men went into the second office on the ground floor. "We will set up the camera in here. Get the table and chairs out of here. Then, bring the roll of black cloth from my truck. I will need the black tape as well."

The table and chairs were dragged onto the warehouse floor, leaving the space bare. A roll of black cloth was unrolled, its folds spilling like a funeral shroud.

"Cover three walls," came the command. "The first layer must touch the floor—let it run along every wall like a shadow. Then add the second layer, pressing it tight against the ceiling so no light escapes. Make sure it overlaps, wall to wall, until nothing remains but darkness. Seal it with black tape."

The men worked in silence, their movements precise, almost ritualistic.

"Now," the voice continued, "hang our flag in the center of the middle wall. It must dominate the frame. When the camera rolls, there will be no warehouse, no walls—only the black void, and our banner above the prisoners."

Hakim watched as the two men worked. Finally, they were done, and he was satisfied that their TV studio was ready. He summoned al-Nasirah.

Al-Nasirah looked at the room. "Good. Set up the camera and bring the prisoners. Tie their hands in front so the camera can see their hands."

Suzy Keaton was brought in first and stood quietly. The hood was still on her head. Her hands were untied from behind her back and retied in front. Iron shackles were on her ankles.

Adelle Keaton was brought next. She was still shaky and had trouble standing. The disorienting effect of the hood on her head made her difficulties worse. She also had her hands tied in front of her and had shackles on her legs.

Suzy heard the shuffling footsteps next to her. She asked, "Mom, is that you?"

Hakim was standing near Suzy. In English, he shouted, "No talking!" and hit Suzy on the side of her head.

Adelle heard the impact of the blow and screamed, "Don't hurt her!"

Hakim hit Adelle in the head. "I said, 'No talking!' I mean it. Be quiet!" Suzy stood next to Adelle, sobbing under her hood from fear and the pain of Hakim's blow.

After a minute, a hooded Stuart Keaton was brought into the room, hands tied in front of him. He immediately sensed Adelle and Suzy in the room. They heard him shuffling in his shackles and knew he was with them.

Hakim said, "No talking!" The three of them were lined up in front of the black AQAP flag.

Al-Nasirah was dressed entirely in black and wearing a black balaclava face mask covering his head and face. A black shawl covered the lower part of his face. A black mujahideen headscarf covered his head. Only his eyes and mouth were visible.

Three more mujahideen dressed identically to al-Nasirah entered the room. Each man carried an AK-47. Only their eyes were visible. Each man also carried a short length of rope formed into a noose.

Hakim said in English, "All of you Keatons get down on your knees." The men standing behind them forced them down by pressing on their shoulders. Nooses were placed around each of the prisoners' necks and pulled tight. Then the mujahideen stood with their rifles at port arms, diagonally across their chests. Each one held the end of the rope in his right hand.

The camera operator motioned that he was ready, and the bright light was turned on.

Al-Nasirah began speaking to the camera: "I, Abu-Basir, am the Supreme Leader of al-Qaeda in the Arabian Peninsula. This is the ambassador of the Great Satan, the United States of America, to the puppet Kingdom of Saudi Arabia. Next to him are his prostitute daughter and his whore wife.

"The army of Saudi Arabia has declared war on al-Qaeda in the Arabian Peninsula by attacking and killing sixteen of our mujahideen brothers in a cowardly ambush one month ago. May their martyred souls sit at the right hand of Allah.

"We will not stand idly by. We will avenge our fallen comrades. America has waged war against al-Qaeda. Saudi Arabia has now waged war against al-Qaeda. All of Islam knows who the enemies of Islam are. Allah protects Islam. The Prophet (blessed be his name) has decreed, 'An eye for an eye, blood for blood.' I, Abu-Basir, swear this upon the holy Koran. So, it shall be.

"If the Great Satan or its puppet Saudi King wishes to see these three scum again, then they must pay the blood price. We spit on their dollars and their riyals. The price for the return of these three dogs is 100 million euros."

Al-Nasirah removed his knife from its sheath in his belt and waved it at the prisoners. "If your money is more important than their lives, we will be happy to behead them all and send their filthy souls to hell. If you accept our terms, remove the American flag from the north entrance to the Pentagon for three days.

"We will contact you at a later date.

"Allahu Akbar!"

The bright light was extinguished. Al-Nasirah said, "Take them back to their cells. Keep the shackles on their feet and untie their hands. Take off their hoods. No food or water until I say so."

Suzy said, "Daddy—"

"No talking!" shouted Hakim.

Keaton said, "Be brave, honey."

Hakim punched Stuart Keaton on the side of the head and knocked him down. "When we say no talking, we mean it." To the escorts, he said, "Get them out of my sight before I slit their throats."

Adelle was led away first. Suzy edged over to her father until her shoulder lightly touched his arm. The contact was comforting.

A few minutes after Adelle was gone, Stuart Keaton was led away.

Suzy remained alone for five minutes. Every minute was an eternity. She thought, *These guys are going to kill us all. I will do my best to be strong until the end. If Mom and Dad can be strong, then so can I. I will not cry. I will not beg. I hope someone finds us soon.* " Finally, Suzy was led away to her cell.

Al-Nasirah, satisfied with his performance, removed his costume. "Transfer the video to the computer and send it to Al Jazeera right away."

Hakim turned to the camera operator. "You heard the sheikh. Get it done immediately."

"Yes, Hakim, it shall be sent to Al Jazeera within a few minutes."

51

LAURA

We broke camp at daybreak, heading for Yadamah. We arrived at 8:50 AM and pulled into the first guesthouse we came to. I booted up my computer and picked up a strong internet signal outside the building.

We stepped into the guesthouse and approached the front desk. Above it, a TV mounted high on the wall was broadcasting the nine o'clock news from Al Ekhbariya, the Saudi channel. The kidnapping had been announced earlier that morning, and five men stood transfixed by the screen, waiting for updates.

Al Ekhbariya was replaying a segment first aired an hour earlier on Al Jazeera. Jack and I froze as the footage filled the screen: the three Keatons, forced to their knees, hoods over their heads, ropes around their necks. Broadcast to the world.

From behind the veil of my burqa, my eyes found Jack's. No words were needed. We both knew we had already missed our first chance to trace the prisoners' location. He looked stricken. We had chosen caution—staying hidden in the desert—while the video was sent to Al Jazeera. And now the trail was already cold.

After the al-Qaeda video broadcast was done, everyone watching exploded in conversation. The manager behind the desk said, "The Americans will never agree to those demands. They won't pay anything."

Another person said, "Do you think they will lower their flag? That would really be something to see."

The announcer on the TV set said, "We have a live feed from the north entrance of the Pentagon in Virginia, America. It is now 2:10 AM in the United States. The flag over the entrance remains flying, illuminated by spotlights. We will keep monitoring this flag to see if the Americans agree to the kidnapper's demands. It would be a humiliation to the Americans if they lowered their flag in compliance with the al-Qaeda demands."

"The Americans won't do it," said a man.

"Why not?" said another. "They're weak when it comes to risking their own people. They talk tough, but their actions betray them. If it's one of theirs, they'll do anything to save them."

"We will see," said the first man.

"Has their president said anything yet?" asked a third man.

"Not a word has been heard," said a fourth man. "I am sure they are all putting their heads together to make an announcement that says nothing." There was nervous laughter all around.

"Do you think they might invade us?" asked the second man.

"It would be a good excuse to grab our oil. Who would stop them if they did it? We could wind up like Afghanistan or Iraq," said the man who made the joke. "Not a good thing to look forward to."

The desk clerk finally noticed Jack and me standing quietly. He decided to do some business. "May I help you?"

"I need a room for a week," said Jack. "One with a bath and internet."

We did the formalities of checking in. Passports were photocopied for the police records. Jack paid with a credit card. Unlike Yemen, the Saudi Arabian banking system really worked.

We got our room key, and Jack asked, "How do I access the internet here?"

"You just link into Yadamah Guest House One. Your room number plus five is the password. Your room number is 207. So, your password is 2075."

"Thank you. I understand." Jack turned to me and said, "Bring the bags." He started walking to the stairway, and I followed, carrying the two bags of clothing and gear. It was a perfectly natural scene in any Islamic country. When we were out of sight of the front desk, Jack took the heavier of the two bags, and we continued up to our room.

Once inside, I immediately set up my computer and plugged it into the wall outlet. In less than ten minutes, I was once again inside the Al Jazeera computers. Now, all I had to do was wait for al-Nasirah to send another video. I found the first video in their archives and copied the address from which it had come. Then I set up a tripwire so that anything else coming from that address would sound an alert.

Jack turned on the TV set in the room. The set came on to Saudi One, one of the government-controlled TV stations. They were doing a cooking show. In the upper right corner of the screen was a small rectangle showing an American flag illuminated by spotlights. It was the flag flying over the Pentagon's north entrance. That it was still there meant that the kidnapper's demands were not being met.

52

MICKEY HENDERSON

U. S. Embassy, Riyadh
Tuesday, 23 June, Noon

Twelve hours had passed since the kidnapping, and Mickey still couldn't believe how fast the ransom demand had come. His contact at the General Intelligence Presidency—the Saudi military intelligence service—had been on the line with him almost constantly.

The casualty toll was staggering. Three Marines were dead; Lieutenant Newman was clinging to life. Five more Marines lay in critical condition. Two Saudi MPs had been killed. Among the civilians, the numbers were even worse: the bus driver and twenty-four construction workers were dead, eleven more wounded—four of them unlikely to survive.

Three attackers had been killed in the assault. Another, shot in the head, remained unconscious, and he might not live.

His telephone rang.

"Mr. Henderson, General Surayah here. We have something interesting that we have recovered from one of our traffic monitoring cameras. I am emailing the photo to you as we speak. It's a dumpster truck being followed by three pickup trucks."

"I'm online right now. I have it."

"We have done a quick analysis of how many men are involved and estimate that there are between 15 and 18 attackers in the party. Lt. Newman has just regained consciousness and has spoken to your Marine major at the hospital. My man was also there. He said there were originally six pickup trucks, but that he had caused three to crash and had wounded some of the other attackers."

Mickey's other line flashed with a call waiting. "I think my man is on my other line at this moment," said Mickey.

"One more thing," General Surayah said. "After they abandoned the container truck, they must have proceeded onwards in just the three pickup trucks. Can your people analyze your satellite data to find three pickup trucks traveling together after midnight?"

"I will pass that along to Langley and get back to you. Thank you for calling, General. We'll keep in touch."

Mickey switched to the waiting call. "Henderson," he said.

"Mr. Henderson, Major Compton at the hospital. Lt. Newman has regained consciousness and gave us his oral report, sir."

After hearing all the details, Henderson said, "Write it up in as much detail as he can remember. I want the entire country to know about this man. Is he still awake?"

"Yes, sir, roger that about the country. No, sir, he is asleep. The report required all his energy."

"Thank you for the report, Major. Make sure one of our men is always with him. I don't want him waking up alone."

"Yes, sir. I think he is going to make it, sir. We'll take good care of him. A Navy surgeon is flying in from the Persian Gulf. As soon as he can be transported, we will get him to Germany. He is quite a man, Mr. Henderson, quite a man."

"He's a Marine. That says it all. Please keep me posted, Major. Thank you again."

Henderson snapped the phone shut and went straight to work on a report for Beartrap at Langley. The Saudi traffic-camera photo, Lieutenant Newman's last actions, the casualty list—he laid it all out.

His request was urgent: satellite tracking on three pickup trucks moving together. If the gears of the machine turned fast enough, maybe they could catch a break.

But beneath the formality of cables and summaries, the weight pressed on him. Stuart Keaton wasn't just America's ambassador, and Adelle and Suzy weren't just hostages. They were Mickey's friends. That made it personal.

He wasn't just writing a report. He was fighting to bring his friends back.

53

HERBERT WATSON III

Langley, VA
Tuesday, 23 June, 3:30 AM

Herb was still at his desk. The Middle East was his bailiwick, and the Keaton crisis required 100% commitment. Every news outlet and every talk show in America were focused on the Keatons' ordeal. Never had an American child been held hostage by al-Qaeda. The threat of beheading the father, mother, and daughter had outraged the civilized world. In the six hours since the Al Jazeera broadcast of the AQAP demands, the free world had risen in America's support. Not a word from China, Russia, or any of the Middle East countries. You wouldn't expect their sympathy anyway. Fuck 'em all.

Only Israel and Great Britain were working frantically to help the Americans. Their deep-cover people were all being questioned for leads. So far, nothing had turned up.

A message had come through from Henderson with a grainy photo attached. The photo enhancers and analysts were working on it at this very moment.

Henderson's message gave Watson a ray of hope that the Keatons would be rescued alive.

Watson looked at the TV in the corner of his office. It was tuned to CNN with the sound muted. In the upper right corner, an American flag on a pole was waving in the breeze.

Ever since the al-Qaeda video had surfaced, every major network had parked mobile units outside the Pentagon's north entrance, their cameras locked on the flag above the doorway. The shot ran constantly—shrunk to a small rectangle in the corner of every broadcast across the country.

The effect was electric. Public support for the government surged; prayers for the Keatons poured in from every corner of America. Their faces were everywhere: Stuart Keaton, the steady ambassador; Adelle, striking even in still photographs; and Suzy, whose infectious grin gripped the nation's heart.

And it wasn't just America. Screens in Europe, Asia, Australia, Africa, and South America carried the same small rectangle—the U.S. flag, streaming defiantly over the Pentagon.

One question consumed the world: Would the United States bow to the kidnappers' demands? For now, the flag itself was the answer. It flew in defiance, visible proof of refusal.

But the unspoken question remained: how long before it came down?

Herb's telephone rang. "Watson," he said.

"Herb, this is Jamie in the photo lab. We've done what we can do, and this is our conclusion. There are 17 or 18 attackers. One is definitely wounded. There is evidence of significant bleeding on his clothing. It appears to be a chest wound. He is in the bed of the truck in the left lane. The rearmost truck has nine or ten men in the bed. We can't be exactly sure. We think it may have picked up the survivors from the three crashed pickups."

"Thanks, I will pass that intel to the field. Good job, guys. Get me a written analysis on the double."

Herb's phone rang again. The DDO was on the line. "I just got word the Navy is flying Lieutenant Andrew Keaton to Riyadh. They picked him up from his destroyer and ferried him to a carrier. He is being transported from there."

"Are we going to have to hold his hand?" Herb asked.

"Absolutely not. He is active-duty Navy. Let the embassy Marines take care of him."

Herb began preparing a message for the field operatives.

> Oilman. Urgent. Priority One. Latest intel. Casualty count from attack is four Marines dead, six injured. Two Saudi MPs dead. Three attackers dead, possibly a fourth, one injured. 25 civilians dead, eleven injured. Photo analysis concludes remaining attackers reduced to 17 or 18 in number with one having a chest wound, severity unknown. Attack claimed by al-Qaeda. Attackers traveled in three (3) pickup trucks. Awaiting analysis of satellite images to determine direction of travel. Video sent to Al Jazeera early AM, Saudi time, by kidnappers. Demands will NOT, repeat NOT, be met. C-in-C to address nation later today, estimate 10 PM EDT. Be alert for reactions from attackers.
>
> Beartrap

Watson sat at his desk, dark thoughts running through his mind. He had been here before with hostages in the hands of Islamic radicals. In too many instances, it had ended badly with gruesome beheadings in front of TV cameras. How would this one end?

He buzzed his secretary. When she entered, he handed her the message. "Immediate transmission," he said.

54

LAURA

Yadamah, Saudi Arabia
Tuesday, 23 June, 2 PM Saudi time

Jack and I sat in the hotel room with the air conditioning cranked to the coldest setting. The room was getting so cold that we expected condensation on the mirrors soon. My computer was on the small table that served as a desk. We were waiting for my tripwire to alert us to an incoming al-Qaeda message. The silence was awful.

After we got into the room this morning, Jack took the first shower. He came out wrapped in a towel and sat by the computer. Then it was my turn to get clean. Fresh water is a luxury in most parts of the world. In some countries, there is barely enough to drink. Saudi Arabia, with its abundant oil and solar energy, has built desalination plants, making clean water available to all. Although Western nations often view Saudi Arabia as part of the Third World, in terms of technology, it is on par with Europe. It is their ninth-century religion mixed with their ninth-century politics that drags them down.

I came out of the bathroom naked except for a towel wrapped around me, and a little damp. The cold air in the bedroom immediately chilled my body, and my nipples got hard and erect. Jack took one look at me and said, "The computer can wait."

"No, it cannot wait. I'm getting dressed. And you should get dressed too. Your pogo stick is messing with your towel, Pogo. There will be time for us, but not right now. There is a family with a little girl out there that needs our undivided attention."

"Shit," said Jack, "What a wasted opportunity. You get dressed first. I enjoy watching your body in motion."

"If I didn't like the way you look at me, you could really make me self-conscious," I said. I got dressed in underwear, shorts, and a T-shirt. The burqa can wait until I go out.

Jack took off his towel. His pogo stick was still on high alert. "You could get arrested for super-decent exposure. That is a mighty decent pogo stick, Pogo. Now put on some clothes before he catches a cold."

"What a waste," Jack repeated. "Who knows when I'll ever have another one like this?"

"I know when. And the answer is: anytime you are breathing."

Jack finally laughed and got dressed.

The computer sat there, silent and uncommunicative.

Both of our phones buzzed simultaneously as a message from Beartrap came through.

We each read and digested the messages separately. The loss of life was awful. Too many innocents had died and not enough attackers.

Both of us kept our focus on the seventeen or eighteen men likely to be guarding al-Nasirah. We fully expect to cross paths with the kidnappers—and in our minds, we're already prepared to take them out. Realistically, a SEAL team will probably finish the job if we locate them. But if it comes down to us, the resolve to fight is already there.

We were both satisfied that the ransom would not be paid. We would have been surprised if even a single coin would be exchanged for the captives. If you capture an Israeli or an American and demand a ransom, expect payment in steel-jacketed lead.

We knew the al-Qaeda animals would respond to the president's upcoming speech. It was just a matter of time. And so, we waited.

55

PRESIDENT SAMUEL DECKER

The White House
Washington, D.C.
Tuesday, 23 June

At 10 PM, every major TV station in the United States went blank for a half second before lighting up again with the White House logo on the wall of the White House Press Room. An empty speaker's podium stood in the center of the screen. The Presidential Seal was on the front of the podium. In the upper corner of the screen, a small rectangle showed the American flag flying over the north entrance of the Pentagon.

An announcer off-screen said, "Ladies and gentlemen, the President of the United States."

In complete silence, President Sam Decker walked up to the podium. In his hand was one sheet of paper, which he laid on the podium.

"My fellow Americans. Yesterday at approximately 10 PM in Riyadh —3 o'clock in the afternoon here in Washington—the motorcade carrying our ambassador to Saudi Arabia, Stuart Keaton, his wife Adelle, and their eleven-year-old daughter Susannah, was ambushed by al-Qaeda in the Arabian Peninsula.

"The Keaton family was taken hostage. The attack left devastation in its wake: four United States Marines killed, six critically wounded. Two Saudi soldiers are dead. Twenty-five civilians were murdered in cold blood. Eleven more injured—two are not expected to live through the night.

"The kidnappers have issued a ransom demand: one hundred million euros. Many of you have already seen their video—the humiliation of an American family broadcast for the world to see. Their condition for negotiation is that we lower the American flag over the Pentagon for three days—as a symbol of surrender.

"That flag is not coming down. Not today. Not ever. The United States does not pay ransom. Saudi Arabia does not pay ransom. We will not bow to common criminals masquerading as holy warriors.

"Al-Qaeda justifies its crimes by blaming others for its losses. They claim devotion to the Koran, yet murder innocents and abduct children. No scripture condones such evil. If they truly wish for peace, they should put down their weapons and rejoin the human race.

"Let me be clear: release the Keaton family unharmed and do it now. If a hair on their heads is touched, we will hold every one of you accountable—individually and as an organization.

"The time for barbarism is over. Release the Keatons—or we will come and take them back.

May God protect the Keaton family. And may God bless the United States of America."

The president turned and walked away from the podium.

An announcer said, "Ladies and gentlemen, you have just heard an address from President Samuel Decker at the White House. Good night."

The screens went blank for half a second as the feed from the White House was cut.

No reporters were present, so no questions were asked. The entire speech took less than five minutes of airtime. Immediately, commentators began dissecting the president's words to detect hidden meanings and subtle nuances.

CBS had a panel of five news commentators and analysts hashing out the details of the speech. Finally, Chad Marden, the senior man on the panel, shut them all up with a simple observation: "I think President Decker said what he meant to say and that he meant every word he said. Set the Keatons free, or we are coming after you."

CNN re-broadcast the al-Qaeda video before it let its commentators have their say. It all amounted to much flapping of the gums with little substance.

NBC was not much better. Its talking heads began asking questions of each other that had no answers. "What if al-Qaeda takes other prisoners to complicate the rescue effort?" "What if al-Qaeda separates the prisoners?" "How large a force will be required to rescue the Keatons?" "What price is America willing to pay in spilled blood to rescue three people?"

ABC had three commentators who tried to focus on what the president *did not* say. This meant that they had to say it first and then discuss why the president did not say the same thing. It was a futile exercise.

FOX went with just one anti-Decker commentator, who immediately ascribed political overtones to what the president said in anticipation of the next election. The plight of the Keatons was just an excuse for the president to get more free airtime. The commentator then suggested an invasion of Saudi Arabia would be an appropriate response to al-Qaeda, but he also opined that the president lacked the nerve to protect Americans in trouble.

Their military analyst, a retired Green Beret general, then took over, and he also agreed to the lack of the administration's determination to protect Americans. The retired general stated it would be easy for us to divert forces already in the area to invade Saudi Arabia.

When the talking heads finally fell silent, one image still burned into every television screen across America: a small rectangle in the corner, showing the flag above the north entrance of the Pentagon, snapping defiantly in the wind. In only a few hours, that picture had become more than a broadcast—it was a symbol. A nation's refusal to yield. America was rallying to that flag with a unity and determination not seen since the morning of September 11th.

56

HAKIM ABU-JIHADI

As Sulayyil, Saudi Arabia
Wednesday, 24 June, 5 AM Saudi time

Al-Nasirah had watched President Decker's speech on Al Jazeera with translation subtitles in Arabic. His English was almost nonexistent, so he needed the translation. What he read on the screen made him angry.

Even Al Jazeera was running the little rectangle with the American flag over the Pentagon's north entrance. Would the USA knuckle under to al-Qaeda? Even the Arab world wanted to know. Some in the Arab world wanted the flag to come down as a defeat for the U.S. Others, who longed for liberty, wanted the flag to fly forever as a simple statement of hope and freedom.

Hakim cursed the American president, and then he cursed Al Jazeera for showing the American flag in the corner.

Al-Nasirah was sitting quietly. Such quiet times usually preceded major decisions and operations. Hakim knew something was going on in his sheikh's mind. Hakim left to check on the men and the sentries.

An hour later, al-Nasirah called for tea. The sun was peeking over the horizon. Al-Nasirah had been up all night waiting for the president's speech. He had been disappointed with the content and the brevity. He had expected more of a rant, but it never came. He had made his decision and knew how to carry it out. All that remained was to do it. But first, he needed some sleep.

Hakim had also been awake with al-Nasirah the entire night. If the sheikh was sleeping, that meant Hakim had to remain awake and in command. Hakim checked all the sentries. In only two days, the men were getting weary of the routine of guard duty. They envisioned themselves as fighters, not watchdogs. Each man was on for two hours and off for eight hours. Most of them did guard duty three times a day. The irregular sleep patterns were taking their toll, and several times Hakim had found men dozing while on sentry duty. The longer they kept the Keatons prisoners, the worse it was going to get for the men.

One ground-floor office had been made into a makeshift kitchen. Hakim went inside and discovered they were out of yogurt. "Who ate the last yogurt and did not tell me?" Hakim demanded. "How can we keep supplies unless we know what we run out of?"

Qasim spoke up, "Hakim, you and the sheikh were involved with the TV set and the American president's speech. With respect, telling you about yogurt did not seem very important at the time."

"You are right. We would have chewed your head off if you had done it. The shops will open soon. Check what we need and fill in the missing foods. There is a money purse in my sleeping roll. Take Adnan with you when you go."

"Yes, Hakim."

Hakim went down to the basement to check on the ambassador and looked through a thin horizontal slit in the door. Stuart Keaton was on the floor of his windowless cell, sitting on a thin straw mat, leaning against a wall, asleep. The single light bulb was illuminated 24 hours a day. Keaton's feet were shackled at the ankles. The cell was a bare cement room with absolutely nothing in it. The room was cold during the day and got even colder at night. Keaton had no blanket or cover of any kind. A large tin can in the corner furthest away was his toilet.

He was given only one meal a day, not enough food to keep a starving peasant alive. He had already lost weight, and it was showing on his face. The only thing missing from this cell was rats. Eventually, they would find their way in here when the smell of the filth got stronger. Roaches were visible against the walls near the toilet can. Hakim wondered to himself, how hungry does a man have to get before he will eat the roaches? Soon I will know.

Then Hakim went up to the top floor, where Adele Keaton was being kept. She was also shackled at the ankles. Her windowless cell was right under the roof. During the day, the room became as hot as the desert; at night, it cooled almost as much as the desert. The walls, ceiling, and floor had all been painted black.

Her light was supposed to be on all 24 hours, but a fault in the wiring caused each bulb to flicker constantly and then burn out after a few hours. So she spent much of the day in the total darkness of a black room. She had just a straw sleeping mat like her husband's, no blanket, the same toilet can, and less food than her husband was getting. Why should she get the same food? She was smaller than he was.

She was unable to move her left shoulder without pain. Hakim suspected that she had broken her collarbone in the crash. She probably also had some cracked ribs. Bad luck for her.

The last one to check on was the child on the ground floor. He looked through the slit in the door. Susannah Keaton was shackled at the ankles, like her parents. At 11, she was almost ready to become a woman. She was late. Arab girls started a year sooner, sometimes two years earlier. If we must behead the father and mother, maybe I will take this one for a slave, he thought. She will grow to be a beauty.

Her cell had nothing in it. Not even a sleeping mat, just the toilet can. The men liked to peek through the door slit whenever she was using the toilet can. This room also had no windows. A single light bulb in the ceiling was always illuminated. The walls, floor, and ceiling were painted black. The inside of the door was black. This room remained cooler than the desert during the day and warmer at night. The only way the girl could tell time was by the change in temperature.

Yes, I think I would like this one for a slave girl. The sheikh is my friend, and I have been loyal to him. If I ask, he will give me what I want.

Later in the day, when Sheikh al-Nasirah had awakened, Hakim went to sleep for five hours.

Hakim was sure the sheikh had decided what he would do next with the prisoners, although he did not say a word about his plans. Usually, he discussed such issues with Hakim first. If there was no discussion, it was because the sheik did not want Hakim's advice to change his decision. He was going ahead no matter what advice Hakim might offer. Hakim wondered what course they were all going to be set on by a man who would not consult his closest advisers. There was no sense in thinking too much about it. Obviously, al-Nasirah had made his decision. All he could do was wait.

57

HERBERT WATSON III

A courier was waiting in Herb Watson's outer office when Herb arrived. He had an envelope sealed with a red wax seal. It was from the NSA, and Herb had been waiting for it since Tuesday. Herb signed for the envelope, entered his private office, and opened it. Inside was the analysis he had been awaiting regarding the direction and destination of the kidnappers.

The usual caveats about security and best efforts led off the report. Herb skipped those and got right to what he wanted. Satellite photos of the dumpster truck with the three pickups behind it. The Keatons were standing next to the dumpster at gunpoint. The date and time marked at the bottom is *22-6-15//22:12 Riyadh, Saudi Arabia.*

A series of photos followed in sequence. The first showed the Keatons being loaded in separate pickups, face down in the bed of each truck. The second showed the trucks driving on local streets and going south on the Eastern Ring Road toward Route 65. The photos did not show the pickup trucks arriving at Route 65 because the satellite moved on, and the following satellite did not pick up for 9 minutes. One truck is picked up on the Eastern Ring Road, nearing Route 65, and later again on Route 65. Another photo managed to track the truck continuing south. Later, the satellite picked up a white pickup truck with a canvas cover over the bed, but analysis could not confirm it was one of the AQAP trucks.

Pogo and Koala's hunch that the kidnappers were hiding near Route 10 was looking more likely—if the kidnappers had even gone that far. A whole lot was dependent upon Koala getting into Al Jazeera's computers and hacking back to the source of the video email.

Herb composed a message to his field assets.

> Oilman. Priority One. Satellite photos show AQAP kidnappers splitting up, heading south out of Riyadh with captives. Not traveling as a convoy. Have informed Saudis to concentrate efforts in southern areas. Last confirmed contact on Route 65 southbound. Possibly might go as far as Route 10. Kidnappers have to be in a building large enough to hide three pickups and provide prison space for three captives. Suggest search for unused warehouse or factory or one recently rented.
>
> Beartrap

His secretary had not yet arrived, so Herb took the message directly to the communications room himself. It was all they had, and it wasn't enough.

It had been four days since the kidnapping, and we still didn't have a firm lead on where the Keatons were.

58

AL-NASIRAH

As Sulayyil, Saudi Arabia
Friday, 26 June

Al-Nasirah was up early and dressed in his black costume. When he was ready, he called his video operator. "Put the table back in the video room. I will need three chairs."

"Hakim! Bring the prisoners to the video room in 30 minutes. Hoods and shackles. Hands tied. Gags for all of them."

Al-Nasirah ordered, "Mammudh, get the other two, and all of you get dressed in black. We will need the ropes around their necks for the father and the mother. I need some large nails and a hammer with 3 meters of rope."

Al-Nasirah looked around. "Tariq, bring a small white towel and the first-aid kit. Leave it outside the video room. Find cloth for three gags and bring it to Hakim."

Al-Nasirah stood beside the camera, directing every detail of the scene. "The table goes in the center, one chair behind it. I'll stand to the right. Place the other two chairs off to the left. The father sits on the outside, the mother closer to me.

"When the prisoners arrive, keep the ankle shackles on. Tie each leg to a chair leg. Secure their elbows to the backrest, then fasten their wrists to the rear legs. Loop another rope around their thighs and under the seat. If either parent resists, pull tight on the nooses around their necks. Don't kill them—just choke them until they obey.

"As for the girl, bind her in the same way, but leave her left arm free. She won't need a rope around her neck."

One man brought a hammer and a tin can of large nails into the video room. "Help bring the table and chairs inside. Put the hammer and nails on the table," commanded al-Nasirah.

The sheikh watched as the video room filled with the props he needed. The chairs were set where he wanted them. "Ra'if," said al-Nasirah, "straighten our flag. It is drooping."

"Now, I need the young girl. Bring her."

A few minutes later, Suzy was led in—hooded, shackled, gagged, her hands bound.

Al-Nasirah motioned for her to be placed in the chair behind the table. They lashed her ankles to the chair legs, tied her right elbow to the backrest, and bound her wrist to the rear leg. A rope was looped beneath the seat and cinched hard across her thighs. The work was done in silence.

Suzy sat rigid, refusing to give them the satisfaction of a single tear. Her left arm was forced flat against the table, palm down on the wood. Every instinct screamed danger. She jerked her arm back—too fast for al-Nasirah to block. The response was immediate: a hard fist slammed into the side of her head. She cried out in pain behind her gag. Her arm was grabbed and held firmly down on the table. She sobbed quietly behind her gag under the hood. Humiliation, frustration, and hatred filled her young mind.

Al-Nasirah drove a thick nail into the table, directly in line with Suzy's arm. She flinched at the crack of the hammer, then forced herself still. A rope cinched her wrist to the nail, locking her arm in place.

He spread her fingers wide across the wood. One by one, nails were hammered between them, trapping her hand. Suzy writhed, muffled cries spilling into the gag.

Al-Nasirah struck her twice across the hood, each slap sharp and punishing.

Four more nails were driven into the table, two on each side of Suzy's wrist, set at an angle. A rope was looped tight around her wrist and fastened to the nails, pinning her in place. Another rope cinched her upper arm above the elbow and lashed it to the back of the chair. The bindings cut into her flesh, choking off circulation and leaving her arm throbbing with pain.

When al-Nasirah was satisfied with Suzy's position, he instructed one of his fighters to inform Hakim to bring in the father and mother.

A few minutes later, Stuart Keaton shuffled into the room, ankle shackles clanking. They bound him to the chair—legs strapped to the front, elbows to the backrest, wrists lashed to the rear legs. A rope looped beneath the seat and cinched across his thighs, fusing him to the wood. Then came the noose, slipped over his head, and pulled tight from behind.

A *mujahid* in black—face hidden by balaclava and headscarf—took his place behind Keaton, silent and watchful.

Adelle Keaton was then led in and immobilized in exactly the same way as her husband's. Each Keaton knew the others were in the room and was grateful they were still alive.

All the Keatons were in place, each with a black-clad al-Qaeda man behind them. Al-Nasirah's show was about to start.

"Turn on the lights," ordered al-Nasirah, Let us begin." The video operator turned on the lights and the camera.

Al-Nasirah, standing next to Suzy behind the table, addressed the camera. "I am Abu-Basir! We are al-Qaeda in the Arabian Peninsula. What we do is the work of Allah.

"The Saudi forces that killed sixteen of our brothers last month have not been punished. Blood money is demanded to avenge the deaths of our brothers.

"We are holding the ambassador of the great and powerful United States of America to the puppet Kingdom of Saudi Arabia. We also hold his slutty wife and whore daughter.

"We have demanded a blood payment of 100 million euros for the release of the ambassador and these two whores. On Wednesday morning, the coward President of the United States, Samuel Decker, refused to meet our reasonable demands."

Al- Nasirah turned around and said to his three men, "Remove the hoods." To the man behind Suzy, he said, "Remove her gag."

The Keatons blinked owlishly in the bright lights until they could see clearly. Stu Keaton saw Suzy's hand tied to the table. He knew something very terrible was about to happen to his daughter.

Suzy screamed, "Daddy, what are they doing to me?"

Immediately, Stuart struggled like an insane bear. The man behind him pulled on the rope, choking Keaton until he almost fainted. Hate glared out of his eyes at al-Nasirah. Adelle tried to yell against her gag, but it was useless. She struggled in her chair, but to no avail. The rope on her neck was pulled until she quieted down.

Al-Nasirah looked at Keaton. "I can see in your eyes that you hate me. Well, I hate you even more. Let us see whose hatred is stronger. Let us see whose hate has the love of Allah."

Al-Nasirah turned back to the camera. "You, Mr. President, value your money more than your people. You refuse to deal with us because you think Islam is inferior to your Crusader faith. Allow me to show you what awaits your people when they war with Islam. Al-Qaeda has taken down your World Trade Center. You cannot defeat us. We will reign triumphant!"

Al-Nasirah drew his razor-sharp knife from his belt and held it up for the camera.

Suzy screamed, "STOP! DON'T HURT ME! PLEASE STOP! I NEVER HURT YOU! STOP! STOP! PLEASE DON'T! DON'T HURT ME!!!"

Al-Nasirah bent down and, with a swift slice, severed Suzy's little finger just below the knuckle.

She shrieked from the depths of her soul as blood spurted across the table and collapsed, unconscious.

Her parents thrashed against their restraints, wild with helpless rage. The ropes around their necks drew tighter, choking off their breath. Stuart sagged in his chair, slipping into darkness. Adelle froze at last, tears streaming silently down her cheeks, her sobs strangled before they could escape.

The camera recorded every moment.

Al-Nasirah held up the severed finger to the camera. "President of American dogs, this finger raises the ransom to 110 million euros. This finger is your responsibility. This is on your head. Every two days, we will remove another one of her fingers, and for each finger, the price increases by 10 million euros. All ten of her fingers will double the ransom to 200 million euros. Which do you value more? Her fingers or your sacred money?

"I am Abu-Basir! We are the holy warriors of Allah!" Waving his knife and the severed finger in the air, al-Nasirah shouted, *"Allahu Akbar! Allahu Akbar! Allahu Akbar!"*

Without being told, the cameraman knew the video had come to an end. He shut off the camera and turned off the lights.

"Wrap up her hand," ordered al-Nasirah.

Suzy had finally started breathing again and was conscious.

Adelle was recovering from the shock of her daughter's mutilation. She was untied from her chair and hauled to a standing position. With her shackled foot, she stomped on the instep of the man holding her, and then she head-butted him in the face, breaking his nose. Her hands were free, with ropes dangling from each wrist, and she began punching and clawing at her captors' eyes. Despite her damaged ribs and injured collarbone, she was in such a fury that it took three men to bring her down and hold her until they could tie her up again and get the hood back on her. Through all of this, with the gag in her mouth, she hardly made a sound.

Hakim decided four men should take Stu Keaton back to his cell while he was still tied to his chair.

Al-Nasirah told the cameraman, "Get that video sent to Al Jazeera immediately."

"It shall be done."

Hakim stood outside the video room in shock. *What has happened? How did we go from being warriors to torturers of children? This is insanity. What have we done today? Our sheikh has made a terrible mistake. Now the Americans will come in major force. I wanted that girl for myself. Soon she will be useless to me.*

Al-Nasirah was still walking around with the knife and the finger in his hands. He passed an empty oil drum used for trash and threw the finger in the barrel, then went into the kitchen to clean his knife in the sink.

In ten minutes, the cameraman had emailed the video to Al Jazeera.

59

LAURA

Yadamah, Saudi Arabia
Friday, 26 June

My computer chirped. "The tripwire! They must have sent another video message."

I got right on the keyboard and started working backward from the email. Within minutes, I had the IP address of the server that transmitted the email. I went to the directory of Saudi Arabian server addresses. There it was, in As Sulayyil.

We both knew that As Sulayyil was a sizable city. Finding these guys there was going to be difficult.

Jack had an idea. "Laura, in their first video, they blamed the deaths of the sixteen attackers on the Saudis and said this kidnapping was revenge for that attack."

"Yes, I remember that."

"Could it be that they planned this entire kidnapping after our battle with the AQAP guys?"

"I think that is a real possibility," I said.

"This is what I'm thinking. If they planned this after our battle, then they didn't have the place they are using as a prison until some time after May 22nd. If that is the case, they wouldn't have known what they needed until two or three weeks ago. The Saudis have a multiple listing system for real estate. Could you get into the real estate multiple listing computer, check their backup program for listings 30 days ago, and then check their current listings to see what properties were listed last month but aren't listed this month?"

"Yes, I can do that, but I'll need your help since we don't have a printer. You will have to record the addresses as I read them off. Then we'll have to compare the two lists."

"It won't be that hard. We'll start with the large commercial properties first. My gut feeling is that they would use a warehouse rather than a family home. After the warehouse, we'll look at the factories. Then we'll go check out the buildings for signs that they are in there."

"It's a good plan. But first, I want to see what they sent to Al Jazeera."

I copied the video and sent it to myself as a blind carbon copy. When I had it fully downloaded, we both started watching it together.

The insane cruelty in that video was revolting. That poor little girl being mutilated and her parents being forced to watch the atrocity. Neither Jack nor I ever said a word during the video, and we both felt sick. When it was done, I looked at his face and knew he would never rest until he brought al-Nasirah down.

Several minutes of silence went by. Finally, I said, "Jack, we have to inform Herb and Yitzhak that we know where the server is and that they are most likely in As Sulayyil."

"If we do, they will send in special forces to take these guys down. I want al-Nasirah for myself. He is going to die at my hand for what he has just done."

"Then let's get to work on the lists," I said.

The first thing I did was bring up the current warehouse and factory listings in As Sulayyil. There were twenty-seven properties listed as rentals and thirteen for sale. It was less than I had expected.

Now came the hard part. Getting into the backup program of the multiple listings wasn't as easy as I thought it would be. After twenty minutes, I was still spinning my wheels. I finally tracked down the IP address of the main multiple listing server and went in as *administrator.* The system's security was so lax it didn't even require a password. Just say you are the administrator, and it grants access.

Once I was in, I went back to the day after the battle in the hills and pulled up the listings. There were thirty-one for rent and thirteen for sale. A quick check of the thirteen for sale showed that they were all the same properties. Nothing had sold in the last thirty days. The thirty-one rentals had had some activity. Fourteen had been rented within the last thirty days when we compared the addresses on the old list to the current list. One of those fourteen properties was highly likely to be the place where the Keatons were being held prisoner. As I dictated, Jack wrote the fourteen addresses.

A terrible possibility occurred to me. What if a new property had been listed after the date of our battle with the AQAP force, and the kidnappers had rented that property as their prison? It would not have been on the MLS list thirty days ago, and it would no longer be on the MLS today. I hoped that there wasn't such a property. We had to go with the possibilities we had. If we came up dry, we would have to find some other way to locate these animals. A lot was riding on luck.

We both started packing our gear. We were checking out and going hunting.

60

JACK

We drove into As Sulayyil along Route 10. The trip from Yadamah to As Sulayyil was over 400 kilometers, about 250 miles. It took us over 4 hours to get there. Route 10 is also called King Abdulaziz Road, and it is the only major highway in that part of Saudi Arabia. As Sulayyil is a medium-sized city on the edge of Rub'al Khali, the Empty Quarter of endless desert sands.

I suggested we check into a hotel, get some quick food, and reconnoiter the fourteen properties tonight so we will know what we are doing tomorrow. We had to have the place in our sights on Saturday, or that sadistic bastard was going to cut off another finger on Sunday.

Laura was back in her burqa. I spotted a police officer by the side of the road and asked for directions to the nearest guesthouse. I explained I was very tired from driving. He checked my ID and asked what seemed like a thousand questions before he was satisfied that we weren't allied with the kidnappers. It was nice to see that the local cops were still looking for the AQAP guys, too. The police officer directed me to a small hotel on a side street. We checked in for three nights.

"

We grabbed a quick meal, got a local street map from the hotel, and got back in the truck to go scouting. Laura mapped out each location we had to check on the map. They were all over town. Apparently, zoning was not one of the city fathers' top priorities.

We started at the one nearest the guesthouse. It was a nondescript retail store. Large enough to hold the prisoners, but obviously undergoing reconstruction of the interior. The next address was being used by a food distributor, and six trucks were parked in the yard. And so it went, location after location. While we were driving around town, night fell, with full darkness around 9:30 PM. We continued our search in the dark.

The 11th property on our list was a warehouse, just off Route 10 itself, well back from the road, with desert behind the building. We were about 300 yards from the building, about to turn into the driveway with our lights off, moving slowly, when Laura said, "Someone's there." Instead of turning in, I rolled past the driveway and stopped by letting our momentum drop off until we finally stopped. I didn't want to step on the brake because then the brake lights would give away our presence.

"What did you see?"

"I am pretty sure I saw someone moving on the roof," she said.

"Let's go back on foot."

The cab dome light never worked from the day we bought this truck from my friend Muhammed, so we had no worries about opening the doors. We closed them quietly until they just barely clicked on the latch.

We each carried a rifle and two spare magazines as we eased our way back to the building on the other side of the driveway. Laura's black burqa was almost ghostlike in the dark. She looked up at the roof and stood totally still next to the adjacent building. After a few moments, she whispered, "There's a man with a rifle." A few minutes later, she whispered, "There is another one on the other side. Different silhouette, also armed."

I whispered, "When it is clear, back out slowly."

A minute later, Laura was next to me, and we walked back to our truck.

"I think we found the place. The building appears unoccupied, yet there are armed men patrolling the roof," she said.

"I think so too. But, just to be sure, let's check out the last three addresses. Also, did you notice that the adjacent building is vacant? If we could get up on the roof, we could take out the guards with the sniper rifle from up there."

"The noise would alert them."

"I've done this before. I take the shot when a diesel truck is passing on the highway. The rounds are subsonic. They make noise, but not a lot, and the rifle has some sound suppression, too. No one inside will react to the low pops made by these rounds."

We got back in the truck and drove away slowly. We stayed on the shoulder of Route 10 until we were a good 700 yards away before getting back on the road. The last three addresses proved not to be interesting. They all looked like legitimately occupied business uses for the properties.

We knew where the bastards were hiding.

61

PRESIDENT SAMUEL DECKER

The White House
Washington, D.C.
Friday, 26 June

Once again, at 10 PM, every major TV station in the United States was focused on the White House Press Room. The speaker's podium stood in the center of the screen with the Presidential Seal on the front. The rectangle in the right corner showed the American flag flying over the north entrance of the Pentagon.

The off-screen announcer said, "Ladies and gentlemen, the President of the United States."

President Decker, looking grave and angry, stepped up to the podium. This time, there was no paper in his hand. What he had to say was coming from his heart.

"I come before you tonight with a burden that no person should have to bear. Yet it is mine to bear.

"Almost all of us have seen or heard about the latest video from the kidnappers of Ambassador Keaton and his family in Saudi Arabia. The barbaric mutilation of an innocent little girl by these Islamic fanatics cannot be rewarded. I have met with the Cabinet, with the National Security Advisers, and with the leaders of Congress from both parties.

The consensus of all members of this administration and the members of the House and Senate is that we will not pay the ransom.

"Money is not the issue here. The issue is that if we let this happen, there will never be an end to kidnappings, ransom demands, and mutilations. Any time a radical or criminal group needs money, they will kidnap an American and start mutilating that person to extract money from the United States.

"No human being, certainly not a child, deserves to be tortured and mutilated as Susannah Keaton has been tortured and mutilated. As a parent, as an American, as your President, I will not, I cannot, let it continue.

"Identification of the attacker has been made via voice analysis. His name is Abdel Karim Washim al-Nasirah. He styles himself as a *sheikh*, a leader of warriors. He hides behind the name of Abu-Basir. He calls himself a holy warrior. He is such a coward that he hides his face behind a balaclava and a black scarf so no one can identify him. He mutilates a helpless child. In truth, he is one of history's all-time cowards.

"Watching that video made me sick. That these fanatics forced Susannah's parents to watch while they mutilated their child is one of the most depraved events I have ever witnessed.

"If and when we gain the release of the Keatons, there will be a relentless effort to bring these so-called 'holy warriors' of al-Queada in the Arabian Peninsula to justice. We are counting on the cooperation of the Kingdom of Saudi Arabia to assist us in this effort.

"To the kidnappers who believe in an eye for an eye, I say, you *will* get paid in the *same* manner to which you adhere. I warn you, and I promise you: Do no more harm to any of the Keatons. You have clearly set the terms of repayment for whatever you do. We will hold you to those terms.

"One more thing. Our flag will remain flying at full staff over the north entrance of the Pentagon. By attacking a little girl, you have shown the world what cowards you truly are. If you want that flag to come down, you will have to come and take it down yourselves. There are 330 million Americans ready and willing to stop you before you can succeed.

"That is all I have to say. I cannot say 'Good night' because this has been anything but a good night.

"I end with one thought: There will be justice for Susannah Keaton. You can be assured of that."

The president turned and walked away from the podium.

The off-screen announcer said, "Ladies and gentlemen, you have just heard an address from President Samuel Decker at the White House."

The TV feeds cut back to the respective studios. This time, the talking heads had much more to discuss. Will an American court allow the amputation of the man's finger? Will he be tortured? Will he be executed? Can we even capture him alive?

Assistants were scurrying to find photos of al-Nasirah. Legal consultants were hastily assembled for informal opinions. Ex-generals and special forces veterans were being interviewed.

Man-in-the-street interviews were being conducted in major cities. President Decker's approval rating was being surveyed by Quinipiac pollsters in a telephone survey, and preliminary results showed an approval rating of over 93%.

Two hours later, when all the talking was done, the Keatons were still prisoners of al-Qaeda in Saudi Arabia and not one iota closer to freedom.

62

JACK

As Sulayyil, Saudi Arabia
Saturday, 27 June

Laura and I woke in the cramped double bed of the guesthouse, pressed close by necessity and by choice. The night before, as we lay down, we both knew what tomorrow meant: battle, and the chance that one—or both—of us might not survive. We clung to each other, holding on as if to life itself, and later made love gently, tenderly, as though it might be our last time. Afterwards, we hugged and petted.

Laura said, "Jack, I think you know how much I love you. I want you to know that I am wishing, if one of us gets wounded or killed tomorrow, I want it to be me. I could not bear to live without you."

"Sweet Laura, neither of us is going to die tomorrow. Not if I can help it. Tomorrow night we will be here together again. We are a team, and I expect that team to last until we are too old to be anything but couch potatoes wearing purple shorts and black socks with sandals, walking with a cane, and going out at 3 PM to get the early-bird special."

"You goofus! I'll never wear purple shorts with black socks." We started to laugh and hug and kiss, and suddenly we both relaxed. Soon she was asleep. I fell asleep a few minutes later, holding on to the woman I loved more than life itself.

But morning was here. We had an attack to plan. The only real intel we had was that there were seventeen to eighteen of them versus two of us. They didn't know that we knew where they were, so we had the element of surprise in our favor. Just before I fell asleep, it occurred to me that the Keatons were probably locked in cells and not likely to be accidentally shot during an attack.

We were both up at 7 AM and semi-wired emotionally with the impending attack. We were going to do some shopping, and then we were going to the adjacent vacant building to reconnoiter the warehouse and see what we could learn about the enemy. One thing we knew: the attack was going to take place tonight because on Sunday, al-Nasirah was planning on cutting off another finger.

The guesthouse owner guided us to an outdoor equipment shop. A plan was already forming in my mind. I'm sure Laura had one percolating in her fertile brain as well.

We dressed in the darkest clothing we had, black preferred. Laura had on black cargo pants and a black long-sleeved knit shirt. She was certainly not going to wear her burqa in a firefight, Saudi rules or not. I had on black chinos, a dark blue shirt, and an olive green vest. It was the best we could do at the moment.

On the drive to the shop, Laura dressed in her burqa again, and we discussed our plans. If I could get clear sight lines from the building next door to the roof of the warehouse, I would take out the sentries just before the relief sentries come up to the roof and then take out the relief sentries as well.

Laura thought that was a good approach. I told her about the Keatons being safe in their cells. She wanted to use the RPG to blast down the door, then roll our remaining two grenades inside before we came in shooting.

We would have to get off the roof next door in a hurry. Rappelling would be the fastest way. We would need some rope.

Laura amended her attack plan. We had two RPGs, and there was more than one door into the warehouse. We would each attack a different door. One hand grenade each. With a two-pronged attack, there would be greater confusion inside.

"What time do the guards always change shifts?" I asked.

Laura paused for a second. "No matter what schedule is being used, midnight is always a guard-changing hour."

"Right you are!" I laughed. "I propose we take out the sentries just before midnight. Then, when the relief guys come on the roof, I'll take them out. We'll wait five minutes. If no one comes up to see why the first shift hasn't come downstairs, then we will rappel down and start the ground attack. If anyone does come up, I will take them out, too."

Laura said, "Think about this. Shortly after midnight, almost everyone is bedded down for the night. They might even be asleep. These guys feel safe here. Their guard will be relaxed. The main thing we have to be careful about is not shooting each other."

I had estimated the building next door to be thirty-eight to forty feet high. At the outdoor supply store, we purchased a 250-foot length of mountain climbing rope and the necessary hardware to create two rappelling setups. I wanted black greasepaint for our faces, but all they had was olive green, so that is what we bought. We added two floppy-brimmed canvas hats in camo olive green and two Maglite aluminum penlights. Two long black canvas totes with zippers completed our purchases. The RPGs, AK-47s, and the sniper rifle would fit inside with lots of extra space for ammo.

In the truck, we cut the rope in half. Then we cut one half in half again. We now had one piece, 125 feet long, and two pieces, 62 feet long. We were going to need nourishment while out hunting bad guys, so we bought eight high-energy granola bars.

Next stop was a hardware store for a large bolt cutter. There was a padlock on the adjacent building that would need to be removed. I wasn't in the mood to waste time trying to pick the lock. If we took any prisoners, we would need restraints, so we bought some heavy nylon cable ties, 12 inches long. For all their ninth-century ways, you can buy almost anything you need in Saudi Arabia.

While we were driving to the building adjacent to the warehouse, Laura said, "There is something we must do just before we attack the warehouse."

"What have we forgotten?" I asked.

"Just before we go in, we have to let Herb and Yitzhak know the address and what we are doing."

"If we do that, they'll tell us to wait for backup."

"Not if we tell them we are going in before he cuts off another finger," she observed.

"You are devious. I like that in my best friend."

"It's just in case neither of us gets out alive," Laura said. "They have to continue the chase."

We said little for the rest of the ride to Route 10 and the building next to the warehouse/prison. Laura's last comment had a dampening effect on both of us.

I parked our truck on the property of the adjacent building, as far away from the warehouse as possible

We loaded up the totes while in the truck. Two AK-47s, a sniper rifle with a sound and flash suppressor, a bipod, two RPG launchers, ammo for all the guns, grenades, a bolt cutter, a rope, rockets for the RPGs, Laura's night vision goggles, and my binoculars. Pistols in our pockets, combat knives on our belts. We weren't exactly traveling light. Those totes were heavy!

We approached the side door of the building. The door was on a little landing that was five steps up. A rusty iron handrail ran up the outside of the stairs. The railing had not been touched by anyone's hands for a long time. A hasp and padlock were the owner's idea of security.

I extracted the bolt cutter and snipped the lock. We opened the door and entered. Whew! A musty odor permeated the building. This place hadn't been occupied for years. The daylight was filtered through filthy windows, casting a gloomy mood that added to the awful, stale air. Sand accumulated in the corners. That sand could only have come in through tiny openings, such as under a door or a leaky window. It must have taken a long time to accumulate that much sand through tiny crevices. We heard the pitter-patter of tiny feet scurrying away. This place had rats. Luckily, we weren't planning on staying too long.

Laura shone a penlight around the cavernous innards. Large floodlights were mounted high on the roof trusses. Air conditioning ducts painted black ran across the ceiling. Fire sprinkler pipes were suspended in a grid pattern just under the roof. Electrical cables and conduits ran across the ceiling in all directions. The flashlight cast weird shadows.

About 100 feet away, we saw an open-work steel stairway leading up to a catwalk. The catwalk encircled the entire interior perimeter of the building, approximately 25 feet above the concrete floor.

"Up we go," I said, motioning to the stairway. We lugged our gear bags up the steel grid stairs. The stairs creaked but didn't give way under our weight.

Once we were on the catwalk, Laura said, "Let's leave the bags here and find out how to get to the roof. There has to be a stairway or ladder somewhere."

"You go right; I'll go left. If you find something, whistle and flash your light twice. I'll do the same."

"Good," said Laura.

I got to the corner of the building and made the turn onto the next side, walking cautiously, when I heard Laura's whistle. I looked across the open space and saw two quick flashes of her flashlight. I was almost exactly on the opposite side of the catwalk from her. I whistled and flashed my light twice. Since it was almost the same distance in either direction, I elected to keep walking straight ahead, just to see what might be there.

In fact, there wasn't much to see. A pile of wooden scraps from packing cases was in the next corner. I finally reached Laura, who was standing at the base of an 18-foot steel ladder with skinny, round rungs, shining her light upwards.

"There is a hatch up there, and I think it is locked with a padlock. I can't be sure until I get up there."

"Don't go up just yet. Let's get our gear bags and bring them over here."

We walked back the way Laura had come, collected our heavy totes, and returned to the base of the ladder.

I climbed up to the hatch with the bolt cutter in my hand. Those rungs were filthy, and my hands were covered in dirty smears by the time I got all the way up.

Laura was right: there was a padlock securing the hatch shut. I cut through the lock shackle and removed the lock. I pushed up on the hatch with my hands. It didn't budge. I went up two more rungs and put my shoulder against the hatch, pushing with my legs. There was the tiniest movement, but it didn't swing open.

"We cannot bang on the hatch, or the lookouts on the other roof might hear us," Laura said. "Is that ladder strong enough to hold both of us? I'm coming up, and maybe we can move the hatch if we push with both sets of legs."

Laura climbed until we were both wedged against the bottom of the hatch. If we weren't on a serious mission, Laura's proximity might have been fun. We both pushed up together, straining against the damn hatch. It moved upwards a quarter of an inch, but it still didn't open.

"This doesn't make sense. That damn door should move." She put her forefinger through the U-shaped fitting that once held the padlock and jiggled it back and forth. Suddenly, she pushed backward, and the hatch *slid* open on a track. She looked at me and whispered, "Are you really an engineer?"

It was really embarrassing. I whispered back, "I *am* an engineer. Do you see any transistors there? Any wires? Any electricity? I'm an *electrical* engineer. You want to slide something, call a *mechanical* engineer."

I cautiously poked my head up through the opening. We were at the end of the roof, farthest from the warehouse next door. The bulky housing of the air conditioning unit for this building stood nearby and would provide us with some cover when we exited the hatch onto the roof. The hot wind actually felt good after the stale air inside the building.

"Let's go down and get one of the short sections of rope and haul the bags up using the rope," I whispered.

We climbed down the ladder to the catwalk and tied ropes to the equipment bags—each secured by the handles and a half hitch at the bottom, so they could be hauled up with the narrow end first. I carried both ropes up through the hatch and onto the roof, looping one around my leg to keep it from slipping back down. Then I began hauling while Laura pushed from below. The first bag came up fast. She went back for the second, and together we repeated the process. Moments later, she scuttled through the opening and stretched out beside me on the roof.

I untied and recoiled the ropes. Laura opened the first bag and took out her AK-47, chambering a round. Then she assembled four RPG rounds. Later, when we attack using the RPGs, we probably won't have time or opportunity to fire more than one rocket each. Two rockets each were more than enough. Laura put one RPG and two rockets in each bag, then shoved her AK-47 in one of the bags.

I loaded the scope-sighted M40A5 sniper rifle and attached the bipod. I put ten rounds of 7.62 spare ammo in my right front pocket. I chambered a round in my AK-47 and put it on safe. Then the AK went back in my bag.

It was now around 13:00 (1 PM). We had 11 hours of waiting ahead of us before it was showtime. The roof of the building we were on was about 10 feet higher than the roof of the warehouse. I crawled up to the air conditioner enclosure and took a quick look around. I could not get a good look at the other roof. The metal of the air conditioner was scorching from the sun beating down on it.

"We are going to need the canvas cover from the truck. That metal is too goddamn hot to touch. I'll go down and get it."

"Bring up my burqa too," said Laura. "I can use that for a ground cloth. Don't forget we also have Makhara's rug in case we need it. We can cut it up into small sections."

"I don't want to ruin the rug if we don't have to. I'll be back in 10 to 15 minutes." I headed for the hatch and climbed down inside the building. The stale air was awful, and it was almost as hot inside as it was outside. I walked quickly to the stairway, then down to the truck. The canvas was in one box with Makhara's rug. I left the rug, took the canvas. I picked up the folded burqa from the cab and headed back inside.

The sudden change from glare to gloom was almost welcome. Even though I had been wearing sunglasses, it took a few moments for my eyes to adjust. I stood still and waited. Once I could see properly, I went to the stairs, up to the catwalk, and then climbed up onto the roof again.

Laura had found a tiny patch of shade big enough for just one person, and she was sitting in it, cleaning her pistol again. She cleaned it almost daily. It was the cleanest Makarov in the entire world.

Together, we pulled the canvas cover up and over the air conditioner. The top of the unit was maybe 5 feet high off the roof. I hauled myself up and took a quick look over the top. I could see down onto the other roof. I motioned to Laura to come up. A few seconds later, Laura hauled herself up next to me. My binoculars were on a strap around her neck.

Through the binoculars, she looked at the other roof. She whispered, "I think it is about 800 meters distant."

"I'm glad you said that. I estimated the distance at about 800 to 900 yards, so we are in agreement. Once it gets dark, if we move to the edge of this roof, we will shorten the distance by 90 yards."

Still looking through the binoculars, she said, "The sentries come up through that little enclosure over there. It must be a staircase because a ladder would not require such a large structure. I see boots. There must be a man sitting on the roof."

A few minutes later, two men appeared, walking in opposite directions. They did not walk all the way to the edge of the roof. They walked only as far as was necessary to see the ground without showing too much of themselves. The boots remained where they were in the shade. That indicated there were three sentries.

Laura whispered, "When it gets dark, they must go closer to the edge of the roof. The men I saw last night were easily visible against the sky from the ground." The sentries did their rounds and retreated to the shade again.

Laura whispered, "Jack, if you can kill the three sentries and their replacements, then that will lower the number of A-Caps to eleven or twelve. With them being mostly asleep and surprise and noise in our favor, we have a good chance of successfully pulling this off."

"Sounds good. Except that something almost always goes wrong. But if we can do it, we will have a chance." Jack had been scouting for a suitable anchor for the rappelling ropes. "There is a small vent pipe with a screened top sticking up through the roof over there. It must be a vent for some plumbing drain. I think we can anchor our ropes to that. Those pipes are typically made of galvanized steel or cast iron. That pipe will take the weight of both of us."

The sound of traffic on Route 10 was very audible to us on the roof. Diesel trucks heading south and north made a decent enough racket that we could hear. Now and then, a motorcycle would roar by; some of them were really loud. Jack's idea of using truck traffic to cover the rifle report just might work. Hopefully, there will be a decent amount of long-haul truck traffic around midnight.

"Jack, we will need the bolt cutters to get through the cyclone fence surrounding the property."

Jack nodded and grunted in agreement.

At 2 PM, three sentries came up onto the roof to relieve the group that was already there. The men exchanged a few words with each other for a few minutes, and then the first group entered the warehouse, leaving the newcomers to patrol the roof.

After staring at the warehouse for a few more minutes, Jack whispered, "Let's get out of the sun and get some rest. We're going to have a busy night."

"I am going to need my burqa."

We slid the canvas off the air conditioner and used it to wrap the two gear bags. Laura picked up her burqa and moved to the hatch. Then we climbed down the ladder and the stairs and headed out to the truck.

"First, let's get some food and then go back to the room for a nap. We'll need some bottled water for tonight," Jack said.

"I agree." Then Laura turned to me and said,

But when it comes to slaughter
you will do your work on water,
an' you'll lick the bloomin' boots
of 'im that's got it.'"

"It is true. But what is even more impressive is an Israeli woman knowing an English poet."

"Would you like to hear the entire poem in Hebrew?"

"You can do it for me tomorrow when we're lying in bed hugging and rubbing our naked bodies together."

"I don't think I'll be in the mood for *Gunga Din* under those conditions. I love you, Jack."

"I love you too, Laura."

We drove back to our hotel in silence, each of us lost in our own thoughts about what the night might bring.

64

STUART J. KEATON

As Sulayyil, Saudi Arabia
Saturday, 27 June

Stuart Keaton sat in his cell. A burning hatred and a desire for revenge, such as he had never felt before in his life, were consuming him every second of every minute. Until his dying day, he would hunt al-Nasirah and kill him with his own hands.

Suzy's screams kept reverberating in his memory. He saw it again and again and again, that insane fucker with a knife mutilating his daughter. The way those bastards tied her hand! They all deserve to die painful deaths, slowly, by being cut apart piece by piece. To compound the cruelty, he and Adelle had to watch the butcher at work on their little girl.

How will Suzy ever get past this trauma? Worse, he knew the president could not pay the ransom demanded by these animals. Will Suzy lose more fingers until a rescue comes through? I have to stop him. He cannot do this to my little girl.

He went to the door, and he banged on the inside. The guard outside hit the door with his rifle butt. "Get away from the door!"

"I want to speak to al-Nasirah now," shouted Keaton through the door.

"The sheikh does not want to speak to you. Be quiet!" answered the guard.

"Tell him I have money for the ransom," shouted Keaton

At the mention of money, the guard got on his cell phone and called Hakim. The message was passed to al-Nasirah.

In half an hour, al-Nasirah walked down to Keaton's cell.

The guard banged on the heavy wood of the cell door with his rifle butt. "Keaton, the sheikh is here."

"What do you want, Mr. All-Powerful American Ambassador?" sneered al-Nasirah. The guard laughed at this. Al-Nasirah was speaking through the tiny slit in the door.

On his side of the door, Keaton directed his words toward the other side of the slit. "Do not hurt my daughter again. I have personal wealth of almost 60 million dollars, which I will transfer to any bank you want it to go to. But you must not hurt my daughter or my wife."

Al-Nasirah sneered at the door, "That would only be half of the ransom I demand. Should I only cut off half of your daughter's fingers?"

"Do not harm her anymore. You can cut off my fingers, but not hers."

"The offer is tempting. I don't want your money; I want America's money and America's humiliation. But you have given me an idea. I think I will cut off your finger, your wife's finger, and your daughter's finger. President Decker shall get three fingers for the price of one."

"You sick bastard. You will die slowly for this. I personally will kill you with my hands."

"You are in no position to threaten me. You are my prisoner."

"That was not a threat," answered Keaton, "that was a promise that will follow you forever. To your grave and into hell. Allah cannot protect you from me. I will have my revenge. You said it first: an eye for an eye."

Al-Nasirah broke out laughing. "I do not fear death as you Americans do. Your promise means nothing to me. Goodbye, Mr. All-Powerful American Ambassador. Tomorrow, all the Keatons will contribute a finger for our cause. And you will do it live on television."

Al-Nasirah walked away laughing at the stupidity of the Americans in thinking they could bargain with him.

64

JACK

As Sulayyil, Saudi Arabia
Saturday 27 June

At 7:30 PM we pulled up to the abandoned building just northeast of the warehouse. Laura looked at me and said, "We have to send the message. You compose it."

I pulled out my cell phone and typed:

> Att: Beartrap. Oilman. Urgent. Priority One. Have discovered location of Oilman: As Sulayyil, SA, warehouse at intersection of King Abdulaziz Rd. (Rte 10) and Said bin Sultan Rd. Building is second structure SW of intersection on S side of Rte 10. It is set 500 - 600 yds. off the road. Desert behind bldg. We are going in now before another finger gets cut off. If we do not return, get in here with SEALs. H-Hour for us is midnight local time. Do not call back as telephone ring tones will give our positions away. We are shutting down the phones.
>
> Pogo & Koala

Laura translated the message into Hebrew on her phone.

"We aren't sending that message until about 30 minutes before we attack. Are you in agreement?" I asked.

She slowly nodded her head in agreement.

"Good," I said.

By 19:45 (7:45 PM), we were up on the roof of the building next to the warehouse. The sun had not yet descended. It was the time of year in the northern hemisphere with the longest days of daylight. Darkness would not be here until almost 21:30 (9:30 PM). I took Laura's watch and synchronized it exactly with mine. Then I handed it back to her.

Laura had the binoculars to her eyes, watching the warehouse roof. The three sentries were there, loafing against the stairway covering structure. At a few minutes after 20:00 (8 PM), the replacement sentries came through the doorway. The three men relieved of duty exchanged a few words. One of them laughed, and then they disappeared down the stairs.

Jack was busy with potential sight lines from different parts of this roof to their roof. If he was going to take these guys out, it would require careful shooting. The rifle was a military version of the bolt-action Remington 700, featuring a five-shot magazine and capable of accuracy to a half-minute of angle with the subsonic, match-grade ammunition he had. The sound suppressor was a big plus for us. The scope was night vision capable. Headshots would be the surest means of guaranteeing a kill. It would take an expert to shoot, acquire a new target, and shoot again, and then do it a third time before the second and third targets were even aware they were targets.

Laura continued to observe the sentries' patrol pattern. Every 20 minutes, they would get up and walk to their sections of the roof and look out. They saw nothing unusual, so they walked back to the head of the stairs and sat down again to spend the next 18 minutes smoking cigarettes and chatting with each other until it was time to patrol again. She relayed that information to Jack.

The day dragged on, finally getting fully dark at about 21:45 (9:45 PM). Jack whispered to Laura, "I can get two of them from this part of the roof, but to get the third man, I will have to move about 15 yards to the left to get a clear shot.”

Laura whispered, “If I go with you and make a noise that gets the guard's attention, he will come to the edge to see what it was, and then he is all yours.”

“OK. But only if it is absolutely essential. If one of those guys starts shooting, everyone downstairs will be alerted.”

At 20:00 (10 PM), the sentries changed again. After they made their initial circuit and settled down, both of us relaxed. I ate an energy bar and drank some water. Laura was content with just water.

It was totally dark by now. A slightly more than half moon had risen, and the sky was bright. “That moon is going to be a bitch,” I observed. “I'll have to use the canvas to cover myself when I am lying at the edge of the roof. At least everything has cooled off, and I won't scorch any skin that happens to touch some surface.” Quietly, I slit the canvas cover in half to make it easier for me to handle. Our roof was about 10 feet higher than the other roof, and I only needed to cover the top part of my body and the rifle.

Traffic on Route 10 was sporadic. Every few minutes, a big diesel truck would thunder by, but most of the time it was just automobile traffic. A lot will depend on luck for covering noise from the road with the first shots.

Each of us prepared a rappelling rope. I loaded up my pockets and vest with spare AK magazines. We each had a hand grenade.

23:00 (11 PM) came and went. The sentries made their rounds every 20 minutes. At 23:28, we took out our phones and sent the messages to Herb and Yitzhak. Then we powered off the phones.

At 23:30, I crawled to the edge of the roof and set up my rifle, sitting on the bipod. I covered myself with the half-piece of canvas cover from the truck. Laura crawled to the edge of the roof, 20 yards away from me. In order to shoot down 10 feet onto the other roof, I had to be almost at the very edge. I decided my first target was going to be the guy furthest away from me. The scope with night vision gave me a very clear picture. I waited. I heard trucks passing below, but not as many as I wanted.

23:40. It's showtime. The sentries got up and started their patrol of the roof. I lined up the shot on the far target. He was standing still for a moment. Two and a half pounds of pressure on my index finger, and he was gone. I quickly worked the bolt, feeding another round into the chamber. The noise of the bolt was slightly muffled under the canvas cover. The guy nearest me looked up at the suppressed rifle report as a diesel was approaching us. He got a new hole in the head and fell while looking right at me under the canvas. I scuttled over to Laura when I saw her motioning me to stay put.

The third sentry came running around the stairway entrance. "Ahmed, what was that noise?" Even though he was moving toward me at an angle, I took the shot. We had three down with three shots.

I worked the bolt to reload. I reached into my pocket and took out three new cartridges. With the bolt open, I inserted three additional cartridges into the rifle magazine. I was ready for five more shots.

Apparently, my sound-suppressed subsonic shots raised no alarm within the sleeping warehouse. Low noise is one reason I like subsonic ammo. Bullets traveling faster than 1,100 feet per second break the sound barrier, and the report is really loud. These bullets still made noise, but traveling at about 900 feet per second, they were relatively quiet compared to faster bullets.

We had 20 minutes until the replacement sentries would arrive. Laura looped the ends of the rappelling ropes over the vertical pipe protruding from the roof. She dropped the rope over the edge. I brought the two gear bags to her. She looped the long rope through the handles and tied the end to the pipe. I had the bags at the edge of the roof. She took a turn of rope around the pipe, and I pushed the bags over the edge. She used the rope to control the descent of the bags to the ground. Then she dropped the end she was holding over the edge. It was 23:52. We had 8 minutes to wait until the new guys would appear. We each returned to our positions.

Midnight arrived. I was ready. A heavy diesel was approaching on Route 10. The door to the roof opened. The three replacement sentries came out onto the roof. "Where are Ahmed and Ra'if?" I heard one say. Two of them walked around the stairway enclosure just as the diesel came hammering by. I shot the rearmost guy. As he fell, the guy in front looked back to see what had happened to his comrade. He got his bullet in the back of the head.

I moved over to Laura. The other sentry was looking around for the guy he was replacing. He didn't see him. Laura had her AK aimed and ready to take out the sentry in case I didn't get there soon enough. The sentry took out his folding cell phone and was pushing buttons frantically. The light from the phone illuminated his face. I shot him in the head. The phone fell. The light went out. All was quiet.

We waited five minutes. No one from the warehouse came up to look for the sentries who should have gone below.

"Let's go," said Laura.

I left the sniper rifle on the roof. We hit the ropes. With AK-47s slung across our backs and the rope looped under the right foot and over the left foot, we executed a swift, controlled descent to the ground in 7 seconds. We untied the end of the long rope from our gear bags. AK-47s ready, RPG launchers ready, two rockets each ready, grenades ready. With the bolt cutter, we cut ten of the wires holding the cyclone fence to its supports. The fence sagged open. I held it up and opened it, and Laura crawled underneath. Then she held it up for me, and I crawled underneath. We were on the warehouse grounds.

Laura looked at her watch. It was 8 minutes after midnight. "RPGs at 12:11, fire two rockets."

I nodded in agreement.

Laura was going to take the side door with her RPG. I went around the front to the loading doors. Each of the four loading doors had a Judas door, a smaller door within it for people to enter without opening the larger door. I picked the third door as my target.

My RPG was loaded and ready. My one hand grenade was hanging from my vest. 12:11, the rocket left my launcher. I hit the ground. The explosion was deafening. The entire loading door had fallen inwards.

I reloaded the RPG launcher and fired again through the opening where the door once stood. Again, I hit the ground. Almost simultaneously, Laura's second RPG exploded in the warehouse.

I ran up to the opening, pulled the pin on the grenade, and rolled it inside the warehouse. I flattened myself against the outside wall. Five seconds seemed like forever. Then there were two blasts in quick succession. I came through the door and into the warehouse looking for a target. The entire warehouse space was filled with smoke. Two men were exiting a room with guns ready. I heard Laura's AK-47 clacking away to my left. I took the two men out with half a magazine on full auto.

Anywhere from 9 to 10 A-Cap guys were left. I saw one lying on his back by a wooden door. We were down to 8 to 9 A-Caps. I heard Laura's AK-47 again. Maybe another one is gone. The pickup trucks were behind me.

A grenade came rolling out of one door. "Grenade!" I shouted, dove to the floor, and rolled under a pickup truck. The grenade exploded, and there was momentary silence. I waited a few moments. Then, in Arabic, I called out, "That grenade got them. The attackers are all down." Quiet descended.

Three minutes later, a man cautiously emerged from one room, rifle at the ready. From under the pickup truck, I fired and caught him. My magazine was empty; the bolt locked in the open position. I dropped the spent magazine and inserted a fresh one, working the bolt to load a round. One man I had shot earlier was wounded and moving. He reached for his rifle. I put a three-round burst into him. He lay still.

Silence and smoke filled the warehouse. Nothing moved. I whistled softly. I heard a soft whistle in response. Now came the tough part of any operation. We had to clear the premises. Stragglers can kill you.

I saw four men who weren't moving. I was pretty sure they were dead. I took a spent cartridge case from the floor and tapped it against the truck four times. A moment later I heard three taps. With the six dead upstairs, that accounted for thirteen tangos. There were either four or five more bad guys left. One was supposed to be wounded, but that didn't mean he couldn't kill us.

We waited. Five minutes went by. Ten minutes. Total silence.

A door in the wall at the end of the office area opened a crack. The muzzle of a rifle poked out. Slowly, the door opened a little further. A man's head was visible. He was lying on the floor or on a stairway leading downwards. A second head appeared slightly behind him.

Nothing in the warehouse was moving. Slowly, the two men stood up and moved into the warehouse. They walked into the open area.

One of them whispered, "I don't see the sheikh. Where could he be? Is he alive?"

"Look in his room," the other man whispered. In the total silence, the whispers carried well.

They went to an office made of metal partitions that now had shattered glass. The lead man tapped softly on the door, "My sheikh, are you in there?"

A whispered voice came back at him, "Get away, you fool."

Jack called from behind the men. "If you move, you will die. Put down your guns now." The two men froze.

Jack yelled, "Do it now!"

His voice echoed slightly in the empty warehouse.

One man bent down and laid his rifle on the floor. The other man did the same.

"Knives on the floor. Pistols on the floor."

The men did as they were ordered.

"Now move back three steps, then get down on hands and knees and crawl backward away from the weapons."

They did as ordered.

"Now, lie face down on the floor with your hands on your head."

They did it.

"You in the room! Come to the door and stand still with your hands in the air," Jack ordered. No one appeared. "If you do not show yourself, we will shoot through the walls and glass, and we will let you bleed to death."

A figure stood and came to the door with his hands raised.

"Step out slowly." He stepped out.

"With two fingers of your left hand, lay the hand grenades on the floor. Put your knife and pistol next to the hand grenades."

The man did as ordered.

"Now turn around slowly and face the doorway."

He turned. His hands came off his head. Jack fired a single round that whizzed right over his head and struck the wall the man was facing.

"Take your hands off your head again, and the next bullet goes in your head."

The man placed both hands on his head.

"Now walk backward until I tell you to stop."

The man walked backward until he was past the two men on the floor.

"Lie face down on the floor. Hands on your head."

Jack called, "You on the right, stand up with your hands in the air." The man stood up with his hands in the air.

"How many al-Qaeda fighters are here?"

"Twelve," answered the man. Jack shot him in his right elbow. The man screamed and writhed in pain.

Jack said, "If you lie to me again, I will kill you. How many fighters are here?"

"We are seventeen. Do not shoot me again."

"Put your good hand on your head. If you have lied to me by as much as one man, you will die by bullets to your arms and legs until you bleed to death."

"I have not lied," he said.

"One man is not accounted for. Where is he?"

At that moment, a man appeared at the top of the stairs on the upper floor and started firing wildly from an AK-47. Jack was still under the pickup truck and semi-protected. Laura, who had not made a sound since Jack started dealing with the prisoners, fired two three-round bursts at the new threat. He fell down the stairs and lay still in a crumpled pile at the bottom.

The man who had been standing was lying in a bloody heap. He was still alive, but he had caught some of the wild bullets from his brother, an AQAP fighter.

"Anybody moves and they die!" Jack yelled.

No one moved.

Jack slowly crawled out from under the pickup truck. He walked to the three men on the floor.

Al-Nasirah was on the left. The uninjured fighter was in the middle. The man on the right was bleeding out onto the floor. He was most likely going to die.

Jack took some cable ties from inside his vest. He tied one tightly around al-Nasirah's right wrist and pulled it behind his back. He slid another cable tie under the first one and cinched it firmly around al-Nasirah's left wrist. Then he gave each end an extra tug to tighten them. They were pressing into the flesh of his wrists.

The other prisoner was soon trussed at his wrists. Then Jack went back to al-Nasirah and put one tie around each ankle. He linked them together with a third tie that was cinched all the way down. Al-Nasirah could not possibly walk or move his feet more than a half inch. The other prisoner was also immobilized. Then, to be on the safe side, Jack also trussed the dying man with cable ties.

Laura stepped out of the shadows and came over. She poked the muzzle of her rifle into the back of al-Nasirah's head and pushed his face into the floor.

He grunted in pain.

"So, you are the famous sheikh. You didn't even fight to defend yourself. All you did was hide in that room. Your bravery is only for cutting the fingers off of little girls." She spit a gob of saliva on the side of his face.

Jack had the other prisoner under his rifle. "What is your name?"

"I am B-Badir," he stammered.

"Where are the prisoners, Badir?"

The man, in a quivering voice, said, "The little girl is behind the wooden door over there. The man is in the basement. The woman is up one floor."

Jack looked at Laura, "Get the rope from outside."

She was back in two minutes with the 125-foot section. Jack said, "Cut some shorter sections so we can tie these guys together."

Jack and Laura hauled Badir to his feet. Then they hauled al-Nasirah to his feet. They stood the men back-to-back. The first loop went around their necks and was tied tight. The next loop went around their ankles and was tied tight. The third loop went around their waists and was tied very tightly. The men could hardly breathe.

"If anyone moves, kill him," Jack said. I am going to free Keaton.

With his AK-47 at the ready, he approached the stairs to the basement. No one was there. He went down the stairs. No one was hiding under the stairs. He saw a wooden door. He removed the bar that held the door closed. Keaton was standing near the door.

"Ambassador, you are free."

"Not quite," Keaton said. "I still have these leg shackles on. I cannot walk. Have you found Suzy and Adelle?"

"We came to get you first so that you can free them. There are only two of us, and we have prisoners."

"Al-Nasirah? Have you got that bastard?"

"Yes, he is one of the prisoners."

"I'm going to kill him."

"I can't let you do that. I wanted to kill him, too, but we need his intel to clean out the rest of A-Cap. But I wouldn't mind if you shot out both of his knees."

Keaton didn't say anything.

Jack continued, "I'm going upstairs to find the keys to the shackles. I'll be back as quickly as I can."

Jack moved quickly but carefully up the stairs to the ground floor. He approached the prisoners. "Where is the key to the shackles?"

"Don't answer," said al-Nasirah.

Laura took out her Fairbairn-Sykes knife and placed it under the lobe of al-Nasirah's left ear. She flicked her wrist, and a piece of his ear was severed. He screamed, and the blood flowed freely. "Answer the question. You still have another ear, and I will cut off the entire ear next time."

"The key is on the table in the TV room," answered al-Nasirah. Blood was soaking the shoulder of his shirt, and Badir behind him felt the wetness too.

Jack looked in two rooms before he found the key on the table. He headed back downstairs. By the time he got there, Stu Keaton had shuffled halfway to the stairs. Jack freed him. And handed him the key. "Adelle is on the second floor. Go set her free, and then both of you come to get Suzy out of her cell on the ground floor."

Keaton ran up the stairs. When he got to the warehouse floor, Laura pointed to the stairs leading up to Adelle. Keaton stepped over the dead body crumpled at the base of the stairs and flew up those stairs three at a time.

Minutes later, he and Adelle came down the stairs to the wooden cell door holding Suzy. The screams of joy and the tears were enough to make both Jack and Laura cry while they held their guns on the pair.

Laura said to al-Nasirah, "Where is your telephone?"

"I lost it," he answered.

Laura started patting down his pockets.

"You cannot touch me," he screamed.

"Asshole. I can do anything I want to you, including cutting off your useless cock. Now shut up." Laura found a lump in his pants pocket. With her knife, she cut through his pants and found the phone.

"Now I want your computer," she said. "Where is it?"

"I do not know," but his eyes involuntarily flicked toward the office where he had been hiding. Laura walked into that room and a minute later came out with the computer and a canvas bag full of other documents. She looked at him with disgust. "You are truly a major asshole."

After a few minutes, the three Keatons came out of Suzy's cell. Her left hand was wrapped in a dirty, blood-stained towel with black electrical tape wrapped around it.

They all came to look at al-Nasirah.

Suzy said, "I hope they kill you."

Al-Nasirah barked a fake laugh. "If I haven't died by now, they will not kill me."

Jack took out his Makarov, released the safety, then handed it to Keaton. "Will you do what I offered and not kill him?"

"I promise."

Jack handed Keaton the gun. Keaton was no stranger to firearms. He aimed at al-Nasirah's left leg and shot him in the knee. Al-Nasirah screamed and almost fell over. All his weight was on his right leg, and he was being supported by Badir.

Adelle said, "Shoot him in the balls, Stu."

Keaton took aim at the right knee and pulled the trigger. Al-Nasirah screamed again as he fell forward, and Badir fell on top of him. "Leave them there," Jack said. The bullet had passed through al-Nasiarh's knee and hit Badir's leg. Both men were writhing in pain.

In English, Jack said to Keaton, "We have to leave here. I am obviously an American, and she is a Mossad agent. We cannot be found here. We must gather up our equipment and get moving. Every one of these bastards has a cell phone. Use one of their phones to call the embassy and have them copter down here to pick you up. Let the Saudis take the credit for the rescue. But these guys are your prisoners, so make sure the USA gets to bring them to where we can do the interrogations. Don't let the Saudis keep them. Also, get the Saudis to have this guy, Badir, identify every one of the dead A-Cap guys. We will need the names to know who we can take off our most wanted list."

Laura added, "Oh, we didn't tell you there are six dead jihadis on the roof. Give us 15 minutes to clear all our gear away before you make the call."

"I don't even know your names to thank you," Keaton said.

"We are Pogo and Koala," Jack said. "That is enough ID. One more thing, I don't think that fucker has suffered enough. The comments the ladies made gave me an idea for a good final fix to this holy warrior." Jack whispered the suggestion to Keaton.

Keaton nodded his head. "I think I can arrange that."

Jack smiled. "I wish I had a silver bullet to give you, but I don't. We are going now; give us 15 mintues then call the embassy."

Laura and Jack walked out the side door that Laura had blown in. Actually, there was no door, just a doorway. They picked up Laura's rocket launcher. Jack's launcher was abandoned where he had dropped it in front of the building. They went under the fence, picked up their tote bags, and entered the warehouse next door. They left the tote bags at the doorway to the building. Up on the roof, they retrieved the sniper rifle, cleaned up the six cartridge cases, and hauled up their ropes from the pipe. The two sections of the canvas cover were folded. All their equipment was passed through the hatch, and the cover was slid closed.

Down on the ground, the M40A5 went into one of the tote bags, and they loaded everything into the aluminum boxes.

By the time they were in the truck and moving, about 12 minutes had elapsed

Jack said to Laura, send a message to Beartrap and Yitzhak. Tell them that the Keatons are free, they are holding al-Nasirah, we have his computer and cell phone, and we are leaving town.

Laura sent the message.

We weren't on the road even five minutes before we heard the whump-whump of helicopters coming in from the northeast. When we looked up, there were four military copters making a beeline for Route 10. "I guess Beartrap got the earlier message too," Laura observed.

Laura handed me a bottle of water.

"Thank you, Mrs. Gunga Din. I can really use that."

"What was that comment about the silver bullet supposed to mean?"

"There is a fictional American folk hero of the Old West who used to go around helping people when they were being abused by bad guys. He called himself the Lone Ranger, and he had a faithful Indian companion named Tonto. No one knew the Lone Ranger's name. He was the last survivor of a band of Texas Rangers that was shot up badly by outlaws and left to die. Tonto found him and nursed him back to health, and he dedicated his life to catching bad guys. He rode a white stallion super-horse named Silver, and he used silver bullets in his guns. He wore a mask, so no one ever knew what he looked like. After he and Tonto did their good deeds, he would leave a silver bullet as his calling card. As he rode away, people would always ask, 'Who was that masked man?' And someone else would answer, 'I don't know, but he left this silver bullet.'"

"Does he ever take the ladies he saves to bed?"

"Oh no. He is too pure for sex."

"Then you cannot be the Lone Ranger in this story because I want you in bed with me as soon as we get back to the hotel."

"OK, Tonto, you've got a deal," I promised. And I kept my promise.

65

STUART KEATON

As Sulayyil, Saudi Arabia
Sunday, 28 June, 12:30 AM

The Royal Saudi Army Special Operations Unit of Battalion 85 arrived in force on four helicopters. Two of the choppers hovered overhead, and forty men rappelled to the rooftop. The other two helicopters landed in the front yard, disgorging another forty troops eager to fight. Unfortunately, there was little for them to do.

Outside, the Saudis established a perimeter to prevent any terrorists from escaping from the warehouse. On the roof, the troops were racing down the stairs, spoiling for someone to shoot. Two men checked out the dead jihadists and collected weapons.

Maj. Hamid bin Rasham, in command, was one of the first men through the blown-out loading door. The Keatons were crouching near their prisoners in the center of the warehouse floor.

The first words out of Stu's mouth in Arabic were "Hold your fire! We have prisoners."

Fortunately, discipline held, and no shots were fired.

Major bin Rasham recognized the Keatons. "Get the medic in here," he ordered. "Help the little girl."

Special Operations troops were fanning out throughout the warehouse, collecting weapons, checking for booby traps, and securing the area. The assault team medic approached Suzy. He had seen al-Nasirah's video mutilation of the girl. He said to Keaton, "May I examine her hand?"

"Yes, of course," said Stu. "She will need to have the wound cleaned and a clean dressing."

The medic carefully cut the electrical tape and gently unwrapped the dirty towel from Suzy's hand. Her finger stump was cleaned, and an antibiotic-infused combat dressing was applied.

Adele hovered over Suzy and the medic, ensuring that no further harm befell her little girl, trying to watch without getting in the way. Suzy winced when she saw her hand, but she bravely submitted to the care of the medic without crying in pain.

Major bin Rasham addressed Keaton. "What has happened here? Surely, you three have not done all this damage to the kidnappers."

"I cannot tell you exactly what happened since we were all locked in separate cells during the fight. We were all freed after it was over. As far as I can tell, these are the only two surviving kidnappers. This one on the bottom is al-Nasirah. The one on top is called Badir. They have both been shot in the legs. Please try to keep them alive as they are my prisoners and they have information that we will all want."

"So, who freed you?" asked the major.

"Major, you and I must speak privately. Let's go into one of those offices."

Both men walked into the makeshift TV studio.

"Now tell me who freed you?" said the major.

"I truly do not know who they were, other than it was two Americans. They were on operations in Yemen, searching for al-Nasirah, and were diverted here because of the kidnapping. Were it not for my being one of the victims, they would never have crossed the border into Saudi territory. I don't know what technology they used to locate us, but they found us. They reported back to their base, which summoned you here. I can only guess that they took action immediately to prevent that animal from cutting off another of my daughter's fingers. They would not tell me their names or what department they worked for."

"You are telling me that two men killed these kidnappers? I find that hard to believe, Mr. Ambassador."

"Major, all I can tell you is that I only saw two people. If there were others, they never showed themselves."

"There will be an official protest coming from the Royal Palace to Washington."

"Major, it is your men who will bring us and al-Nasirah back to Riyadh. May I suggest that what I have told you should remain between us? Tell General Surayah, and he will undoubtedly tell the King. But as far as the world is concerned, I would prefer it to be known that the brave men of Saudi Special Operations rescued us. Every one of them was prepared to die to rescue me and my family, and such commitment should be recognized and appreciated."

"This is most irregular. I will leave the decision to my superiors."

"Thank you, Major. May I suggest that the prisoners be put in shackles during transportation to Riyadh. I would not put it past them to commit suicide by jumping out of the helicopters."

"Agreed," said the major as he turned and left the room. Once outside, he called for his radioman. "Send a message to headquarters. Tell them that the ambassador and his family have been rescued and that there are two prisoners. One prisoner is the leader, al-Nasirah. We are transporting all parties back to Riyadh immediately."

The major then turned to the captain. "Captain, stay here with twenty men and two helicopters. Allow no one in or out. Search the building for whatever evidence you can find. Make note of what you find, but do not move anything. Photograph each al-Qaeda man for identification purposes. Be especially careful to gather cell phones and be certain to identify from which body the phone was collected. A crime scene investigation team from Riyadh will be here within the next few hours. Continue to provide whatever security the investigation team needs until you are relieved by regular army units."

Then Major bin Rasham ordered, "Let us get loaded for the return to base. I want the ambassador and his family in my helicopter. The prisoners go in the other chopper. Let's move!"

66

LAURA

Karmis Mushait, Saudi Arabia
Sunday, 28 June

We got back to our hotel at about 1:45 AM. We took a nice hot shower together and fell asleep in each other's arms. We didn't get out of bed until almost 10 o'clock, but first we made the sweetest love I can ever recall. There is something about going into battle and depending upon your partner to cover your ass while you cover his that makes for a very strong bonding experience. And, oh, were we ever bonded!

We checked out of the guesthouse and headed for Karmis Mushait and Makhara Carpets. Jack did most of the driving while I sang him Israeli kibbutz songs. He is picking up a few Hebrew expressions from me. Maybe someday I'll make a *mensch* out of him. Although I kind of like the way he is right now. Nah, why mess with perfection?

On the road, both of our phones vibrated. A message was coming in from Beartrap.

Oilman. Non-priority. Oilman has expressed interest in having you present when he completes your suggestion (whatever that may be). He said you would know how

to contact him. He can assist in transportation arrangements out of SA. He suggests you allow two full days in
Riyadh.

Beartrap

I looked at Jack. "What is this about a suggestion?"

"Oh, it is just an idea I had while we were shooting al-Nasirah in the knees. It is sort of poetic justice."

"What was your suggestion?"

"Since he wants us to be there, maybe I had better not spoil the surprise. I think it will be interesting to see how it all works out."

I punched him on the arm. "You can't do this to me. Are we partners? Are we a team? You had better tell me what is going on."

"No, it's a surprise for Suzy and Adelle. Except Suzy can't know about it for a while."

"You are driving me crazy. You had better tell me, or I will get even with you."

"If getting even with me involves any sexual activity, I eagerly await your revenge."

"You are an impossible man, Jack Miller, and I don't know why I love you. Except that you are slightly better than a vibrating dildo."

Jack laughed. "You certainly do things for my self-esteem."

*   *   *

We arrived in Karmis Mushait around 15:30 (3:30 PM). Jack had done all the driving. We went directly to Makhara Carpets.

We entered the showroom. The same manager type was there to greet us. "Welcome back to Makhara Carpets, Mr. Al-Farooq."

Remembering names like that is an exceptional skill. This guy must be some hell of a salesperson.

"It is nice to be back," Jack said. "Is Mr. Makhara available for a few minutes?"

"Wait just a moment, and I will check." He disappeared into the back of the store. While we waited, I looked around the store. Three of the four selling areas were engaged with customers, and men were hauling rugs in and out. Quite a lot of business must get done here.

The greeter returned with a smile and said, "Mr. Makhara will be happy to see you."

We entered his office, with that magnificent desk. He stood up and shook Jack's hand and then my hand. "I'm sure you know the Keatons have been rescued by the Saudi army and al-Nasirah has been captured. It is all over the news this morning."

"That is good news, especially after what that animal did to the little girl," said Jack.

"To what do I owe the honor of this visit?" asked Makhara.

"We have come to return the things we borrowed from you, including the special item. The special item needs a good cleaning; otherwise, it is in pristine condition. It was all very useful."

"I'm sure it was. Did the ambassador thank you?"

"For what?" Jack asked. Jack actually smiled a little.

"I thought so," said Makhara. "The Saudis cannot rescue a kitten from a tree, much less win a firefight with al-Qaeda."

I said, "All the things we borrowed, less one launcher and a few rockets and bullets, are rolled up in the carpet. Additionally, we acquired some AK-47s and Makarovs from various locations. We left one RPG launcher out there. I think the rug needs to be cleaned again."

Makhara looked at me. "Not only are you a quiet wife, but I get the impression you can be very effective in a tight situation. That makes you even more remarkable."

"Thank you for that compliment." I actually smiled inside my burqa, but Makhara could not see that.

Jack said, "Should we go around back to Sulamein?"

"That would be good but first let me give you a work order." Makhara turned around to his computer and quickly typed a work order. The printer spit out a sheet of paper that he handed to Jack. "Just give this to Sulamein at the warehouse. He'll know what to do with it."

We all rose to say goodbye. Makhara again shook hands with both Jack and me. "If you both ever come back, I would want you to be guests at my home for dinner. You two have done what armies could not do."

"You flatter us," Jack said. "We could have done nothing without your help. If we ever return, and time allows, we would be happy to visit with you."

"Take care of each other," said Makhara. "I wish you good luck and a pleasant journey home."

The manager was outside Makhara's door when we came out. He led us to the outside door and thanked us for coming.

Back in the truck, Jack said, "I wonder how he knew it was us with the ambassador?"

"Maybe he just made a good guess."

"Hmm, maybe."

We drove around back to the warehouse. Hamdi was still at his post in the plastic chair, assessing everything and everyone who came by without appearing to do so.

Jack asked for Sulamein.

Hamdi made his cell phone call. In a few minutes, Sulamein appeared. He hadn't shrunk a bit since we saw him last week. He was a very imposing presence.

I sat in the cab of the truck.

Jack said to Sulamein, "Our rug needs to be cleaned. It is wrapped up in that canvas cover."

Sulamein looked at the old man. "Hamdi, get me the carpet dolly."

Hamdi disappeared into the warehouse.

Jack said, "The special item is in there, too. It just needs cleaning. We didn't even scratch it. Plus, there are some extras that you didn't give us, but we have to get rid of them anyway. I'm sure you'll be able to use them. All the machinery needs to be cleaned."

"We'll take care of it. Thank you for whatever gifts you bring."

Hamdi reappeared with a four-wheeled cart that had a bed of U-shaped pipes for holding a carpet. We placed the canvas cover with the carpet on the dolly. Jack took two cardboard cartons out of the aluminum boxes and gave them to Hamdi. I heard Jack say to Hamdi, "Careful, they might explode." Hamdi laughed a high-pitched cackle at his own joke being returned to him.

After filling our gas tank, we were soon on the road. I took Jack's phone from his shirt pocket. "I'm going to send Beartrap a message that we are coming out through Riyadh."

"Sounds good to me." Jack concentrated on his driving. We kept heading north toward Riyadh and Jack's surprise.

67

GENERAL KALIM SURAYAH

Commander, 1ˢᵗ Saudi Army Corps
Prince Sultan University
Riyadh, Saudi Arabia
Monday, 29 June, 1:00 PM

The news conference was held in the courtyard of Prince Sultan University, beneath a vast green-and-white striped tent, open to the air on all sides. On a small stage stood General Surayah, framed by a bank of microphones.

To his left stood Ambassador Stuart Keaton, sharp in a navy pinstripe suit, with his wife, Adelle, beside him in a long black dress and modest headscarf. To the general's right stood the Minister of Defense and the Foreign Minister, solemn and composed.

In front, two neat rows of chairs held the invited guests. Beyond them, the world's press filled the space—journalists packed into metal folding chairs or clustered at the edges, shifting in the heat, cameras poised, hungry for any word on the fate of the Keaton family.

General Surayah, dressed in freshly pressed combat fatigues, with a maroon beret upon his head, began. "Members of the royal family, Prince Mammudh bin Salman Aziz al Saud, Minister of Defense of the Council of Ministers, Mr. Abdel bin Ammed Al-Jubal, Foreign Minister of the Council of Ministers, honored guests, and members of the press. It is my proud privilege to announce that Ambassador Keaton and his family have been rescued from the clutches of the criminals of al-Qaeda by courageous elements of the Royal Saudi Special Operations Command of Battalion 85. All the kidnappers have been killed except for Abdel Karim Washim al-Nasirah, the group's leader, and one other criminal. Both men were wounded and are currently hospitalized under military guard.

"At the direct orders of His Majesty, King Salman bin Abdulaziz Al Saud, young Susannah Keaton, the ambassador's daughter, is also hospitalized and is being cared for under the direction of the King's personal surgeon. Mrs. Keaton, standing to my left, received multiple injuries during the kidnapping. After receiving treatment for a collarbone fracture and fractured ribs, she has requested to be present today for this press briefing.

"It is now my honor to introduce Prince Mammudh bin Salman Aziz al Saud, Minister of Defense of the Council of Ministers. Prince Aziz al Saud." With those words, General Surayah stepped away from the microphones, and the Prince stepped forward. Polite applause from the two rows of guests greeted the minister. The members of the press were busy scribbling notes and snapping photos.

"Let us all praise Allah for the successful operations carried out by the Saudi Arabian Army's Special Operations units. The outstanding courage and superb training of these brave officers and men have allowed us all to be here today. That only two of the kidnappers have survived is a testament to the professional skills of the Saudi army. Rescuing the ambassador of our good ally, the United States of America, was an all-out effort for every military and law enforcement officer of the Kingdom of Saudi Arabia. By the grace of Allah, the Merciful, we have been granted success, and the ambassador and Mrs. Keaton stand here before all of you.

"Today, I give a warning to any others who might contemplate attacking any person on Saudi soil. We will come in our multitudes, and we will slay all who dare to commit a crime within this kingdom.

The justice of Allah is swift and sure. That is our promise to Allah and to all who would transgress our laws."

Prince Aziz al Saud stepped away from the microphones to vigorous applause from the honored guests. General Surayah again stood before the crowd. "It is now my privilege to introduce Mr. Abdel bin Ammed Al-Jubal, Foreign Minister of the Council of Ministers." The general took a half step backward, turned to his right, and said, "Mr. Foreign Minister." Tepid applause greeted the foreign minister.

"Prince Aziz al Saud, General Surayah, Ambassador Keaton, and honored guests. Al-Qaeda in the Arabian Peninsula attempted to strike a blow against Saudi Arabia and the United States by attacking and kidnapping Ambassador Keaton and his family. Together, our two nations have stood fast against the evil arrayed against us.

"Saudi Arabia and the United States of America have long been allies in the fight for peace and order in the world. It is with the greatest pride that we could safely return Ambassador Keaton to his post as the representative of the United States and as a friend of Saudi Arabia. Let no man lift his hand against our two great nations, for surely Allah will smite you dead. Let us all go forward together to bring peace to the world under the benevolent guidance of Allah." The Minister stepped away from the microphones to mild applause, which was careful not to exceed the applause for the Prince.

General Surayah again approached the microphones. "It is my honor to introduce the Ambassador of the United States of America, Mr. Stuart Keaton." Vigorous applause followed, even from the assembled press corps, which had hitherto been almost silent.

Stu Keaton stepped forward. "Prince Aziz al Saud, Minister Jubal, General Surayah, honored guests, and members of the press. I am most grateful to the government of Saudi Arabia and to the brave officers and men whose mighty efforts have permitted me and my family to once again be free from the grip of a criminal band of fanatics. Let us never doubt that the United States and the Kingdom of Saudi Arabia, working together, are locked in a mortal battle against evil. There is no alternative but for good to triumph over evil. Anything less is unthinkable.

"In the ordeal that my family has suffered, which has cost the lives of many good men, both American and Saudi servicemen, and innocent civilians, lies the determination that we will never yield to evil. My innocent daughter has paid a terrible price for the raving ambitions of a hate-filled madman. No punishment can ever truly balance the scales of justice for what he has done.

"I have seen recorded video of President Decker's addresses to the people of the United States. I applaud his decision not to yield to the kidnappers' demands. It was the right thing to do. I have seen the American flag flying over the north entrance to the Pentagon in the corner of the TV screen while the president was speaking. What an inspiring sight! I am told that the image of that flag appeared in the corner of almost every television screen in the world. My family and I wish to thank everyone who supported us, who prayed for us, who expended massive efforts to free us from our kidnappers, and who finally set us free. That flag is an inspiration to all who love freedom and justice. It stands for courage and liberty. And truly, it is a beacon of hope for all people living under the unbearable yoke of tyranny."

"To the people and armed forces of the Kingdom of Saudi Arabia, Adelle, Susannah, and I thank you for rescuing us. I have been many, many years here in Saudi Arabia, first in the petroleum industry and then as Ambassador of the United States. The ties of friendship that have grown on a personal level and on the official level are strong and enduring. The mutual trust and interests we share shall endure for many years into the future. Perhaps together, we can someday bring peace to the Middle East.

"As soon as Suzy is well enough to travel, we will be going home for a few months. As there are many people in Saudi Arabia, there are also many in America who have earned our gratitude and admiration. We would like to thank them personally.

"I thank you for gathering here today. I am sure you each have many questions you would like answered. However, the technology and the techniques used by our rescuers is classified information, and we must sadly inform everyone that we cannot take questions at this time. Please respect the privacy of my family. Someday, when enough time has gone by, there may come a day when the story will be told. Until then, I ask for your forbearance, and I deeply thank you for all your good wishes."

All the reporters gave Stu Keaton a standing ovation. Even the honored guests in the two front rows joined in.

After the applause died down, General Surayah approached the microphones and announced, "Thank you all for attending today. These proceedings are now concluded."

All the reporters began shouting questions to the men on the platform, questions that were totally ignored.

The four men on the platform held a quiet conversation from which Adelle stayed away. Stu Keaton quietly made a special request to General Surayah and the Minister of Defense. The foreign minister thought the request should be granted and added his vote of approval. The Prince promised to put the idea before the King.

With a final handshake and words of farewell, Stu and Adelle then stepped off the rear of the podium where an embassy limo waited to take them to visit Suzy.

68

JACK

Riyadh, Saudi Arabia
Tuesday, 30 June

Laura and I arrived in Riyadh yesterday. We had a lovely drive through the desert. Lots of impressive sights for tourists to enjoy: sand, sand dunes, blowing sand, dunes, more sand, and sand. Occasionally, we saw rocks too. By the time we reached Riyadh, I had had my fill of sand. I may never go to the beach again. Well, if Laura is there wearing a bikini bottom but no top, I might make an exception.

I telephoned the U.S. Embassy and asked to speak to Ambassador Keaton. When I gave my name as Pogo, the operator thought I was a crank caller. I finally convinced him to ask the ambassador if he wanted to take the call, and I was able to get through.

Suzy was at King Abdulaziz University Hospital on King Abdulaziz Road. (If that name sounds like the name for Route 10 in As Sulayyil, it is because almost every town of any consequence in Saudi Arabia has a King Abdulaziz Road.) Also, being held in the same hospital was Sheikh Abdel Karim Washim al-Nasirah. Suzy had Saudi Arabian Army guards in full combat gear outside her room to protect her. Al-Nasirah had ten Saudi Arabian Army guards, commanded by a major, fully armed for combat, outside his room to ensure no one tried to spring him free. Four reinforced squads of Saudi Arabian Army guards limited access to the elevators and stairways of the hospital in the lobby. Security was ramped up to the maximum. A full bird colonel was in overall command of security. No one who didn't belong in the hospital was getting inside.

Laura, sans burqa, and I had lunch with the ambassador, Adelle, and Andrew at the embassy. Adelle had a fractured left collarbone for which there was nothing to be done except wait for it to heal. Her two cracked ribs were taped from the outside again; there wasn't much to be done. She would heal with time and rest.

After lunch, Laura put on her burqa again. Then we were driven to the hospital with Stu Keaton to visit Suzy. At the hospital, a Saudi corporal accompanied us to the door of Suzy's room.

Suzy was in good spirits. Her left hand was wrapped in clean gauze bandages. She'd had minor cosmetic surgery to cover the finger stump with skin so there would not be scar tissue there. Her spirits were amazingly upbeat. After hugs and kisses, she said, "Dad, did you know that Minnie Mouse only has three fingers on each hand? I could get a job at Disney World and dress up as Minnie Mouse for the little kids."

Keaton choked up when he heard Suzy carrying on.

Suzy hugged Laura and me. Tears were trickling out of the corners of my eyes. Laura was outright crying. This is one gutsy girl.

I said, "The world has enough Minnie Mouses. We need more Suzy Keatons. Even though I am sure you were scared out of your mind, you were still brave, and that means you have real courage. I would be proud to have a girl like you as my daughter. In my mind, you are now 'The Unsinkable Suzy Keaton.' You will come through this terrible experience, and you will still be the good person you were before it all happened."

Now it was Suzy's turn to tear up. Stu was a teary mess throughout the entire visit.

We said our goodbyes with lots of hugs and tears. We had an appointment to keep.

*   *   *

At 14:30 we were due to visit al-Nasirah. We went to the top floor, where he was the only occupant on the entire floor. He was hooked up to monitors and an IV. By order of the King, his wounds were cleaned so that there would be no infection, but no corrective or reconstructive surgery was to be permitted. Al-Nasirah would be unable to walk without great pain and crutches for the rest of his life.

Arrangements had been made to turn him over to the U.S. government. As soon as he was well enough to travel, the Saudis would surrender him to the Americans, and then he would be off to whatever place the agency determined would be the best place to wring his brain dry of any intel he might possess.

Back in As Sulayyil, Badir had identified all the dead jihadists, including Hakim abu-Jihadi, one of the most wanted of the A-Cap group. Badir had been patched up and had already been sent out of Saudi Arabia.

At 14:35, General Kalim Surayah appeared with an entourage of four senior military officers, some of them carrying briefcases. Al-Nasirah's Saudi army guards all snapped to attention and saluted the officers.

The general approached the nurse's station where the doctors and male orderlies in charge of al-Nasirah were waiting. "We are here upon the orders of the King to read the prisoner a proclamation from the Ministry of Justice. We have an army physician with us who will examine the prisoner to assess his ability to travel and be extradited to the custody of the United States Government.

"While we are examining the patient, he will be disconnected from the monitors, so do not be concerned if you are not receiving signals from his machines. The senior legal officer who is present will inform the prisoner of the proclamation handed down regarding his disposition in this matter."

"Mr. Keaton, as ambassador from the United States, you may be present if you wish to witness what transpires."

Keaton said, "General, I would not miss this for the world. Please lead the way."

The general, his four officers, and Keaton as a witness entered al-Nasirah's room.

I did not personally witness what transpired, but later in the car, Keaton told Laura and me what happened:

Al-Nasirah was surprised when the crowd entered his room. General Surayah ordered the two guards in the room to leave. Then he said to the Medical Officer, "Disconnect the monitors." That was done by flipping a few switches. Then the briefcases were opened.

Al-Nasirah was already handcuffed to the bed. Two officers restrained al-Nasirah's arms, they then freed him from his hospital cuffs and clipped new handcuffs on each wrist. The new handcuffs were attached to low points of the iron frame of the hospital bed on each side, stretching out al-Nasirah's arms. The third officer forced a fat plastic bar covered in terry cloth into his mouth to gag him. A strong elastic band attached to each end of the gag was stretched behind al-Nasirah's head.

A long Velcro restraint was circled around each thigh. His legs were spread wide, and the other ends of the Velcro ties were firmly connected to the frame of the hospital bed. His lower legs, beyond his shattered knees, were also similarly restrained with Velcro ties.

The legal officer withdrew a document from his briefcase. This is what he read to the prisoner:

"Abdel Karim Washim al-Nasirah, you have unlawfully entered the Kingdom of Saudi Arabia with a band of outlaws. Therefore, it is the judgment of this court that you are to be expelled from the Kingdom of Saudi Arabia into the custody of the United States of America. Further, you have been found guilty of harming a female child, not yet a woman, a person of 11 years of age, and you have done this act in full view of the entire world. You have used as your excuse for this unlawful act the alleged attack of the Saudi Arabian Army upon your band of outlaw rebels, an attack which has never been perpetrated by the Saudi Arabian Army. You have proclaimed your justification for the harming of the child as 'An eye for an eye, blood for blood,' and you then amputated the child's finger. At no time were you claiming that the child had any part in the alleged attack upon your band of outlaws. The child was innocent, but *you* are not innocent. You are guilty of having caused harm to someone who did you no harm. It is the sentence of the Supreme Court that, in accordance with your own proclamation of 'An eye for an eye, blood for blood,' you are to surrender your finger for a finger. Your crimes against the Kingdom of Saudi Arabia are of such a magnitude that a finger for a finger is insufficient punishment. Therefore, this court has declared, the 'finger' you are to surrender is that you shall be castrated and shall become a eunuch. An eye for an eye, blood for blood, a finger for a finger. Such is the judgment of the Court, and so it shall be. The surgeon here present shall carry out the sentence of the court."

The army surgeon produced latex gloves and put them on. The final snap of the cuff of each glove was like a gunshot in the quiet room. From his briefcase, he extracted a scalpel and other required instruments in sterile protective wrappings. The tearing of the paper covers was a grating noise in the silent room. Everything the surgeon would need was inside that briefcase.

Al-Nasirah thrashed wildly in his bed as the blankets were removed, and his hospital gown was raised. The noises he made deep in his throat behind his gag were ignored. His eyes flashed wildly from side to side. He would crane his neck forward and then throw his head back against the pillows. A thick pad to absorb the blood was placed under his backside. An absorbent blanket was placed over his penis in anticipation of al-Nasirah losing control of his bladder, which he did just a moment later. The smell of urine permeated the room. Some of his urine wet the bed too.

A battery-powered hair clipper was used to remove the pubic hair around the incision site. A vacuum tube attached to the hospital system through a wall fitting sucked up the hair. Then the skin was scrubbed with Betadine to prevent skin bacteria from infecting the incisions. A string tourniquet was wrapped around the base of his penis and drawn tight. It must have been painful because al-Nasirah's eyes almost popped out of their sockets. He was continually grunting and trying to scream behind the gag. The penis was quickly severed almost flush with the abdomen, leaving almost no stump at all. The blood vessels were easily cauterized with an electric cauterizing tool.

The medical term for surgically removing testicles is *orchiectomy*. An incision was made in the center of al-Nasirah's scrotum with a scalpel. The blood vessels and testicular ducts were tied off with surgical thread. The testicles and most of the scrotum were removed, leaving just a flap of skin attached. When the orchiectomy was completed, the surgeon again cauterized the severed blood vessels to stop the bleeding.

Al-Nasirah remained conscious and thrashed through the entire procedure. He screamed nonstop against the gag in his mouth, but very little noise actually escaped.

Two officers were required to lean on al-Nasirah to hold his abdomen relatively still so the surgeon could operate. When the castration was completed, the surgeon held up the severed penis and scrotum so al-Nasirah could see the result of his punishment. That was when he passed out.

A flap of skin was sewn across the penis wound. An opening was created for urine to escape, and a Foley catheter was inserted into the urinary tract to facilitate the flow of urine until the wound had healed. The flap of scrotal skin was stretched and sutured over the wound where the scrotum once was. Antibiotics were injected at the wound sites to prevent infection.

Al-Nasirah's severed penis was placed on a small, kidney-shaped metal tray. Photos of al-Nasirah and his severed organs were taken. And then, upon the orders of the Ministry of Justice, the penis was cut into eight small parts. The testicles were removed from the scrotum and sliced into quarters. An additional photograph of the metal tray was taken to be given to the court as proof that the sentence had been carried out. All the parts were left on the metal tray. Al-Nasirah would have them as souvenirs when he woke up.

The battery-powered hair clipper was again brought out and used to cut off the unconscious al-Nasirah's beard. The hair was again sucked up into the hospital's vacuum system.

Then, a battery-powered electric shaver was used to remove whatever stubble remained until he was smooth shaven. Lacking the hormones produced by his testicles, he would never be able to regrow his beard, and without a beard, no jihadists would ever follow him into battle. This was the final punishment for the prisoner. Al-Nasirah was finished as a leader of holy warriors. Additional photographs of al-Nasirah's "new" face were taken for the court records.

The handcuffs and gag were removed from the limp prisoner. Al-Nasirah's wrists were cut and chafed from where he had struggled against the handcuffs. The surgeon swabbed his wrists with Betadine and applied clean gauze dressings. The original hospital handcuffs were then restored. The Velcro leg restraints were removed. Latex gloves were disposed of. The bloody pad was removed, and a fresh pad was put in its place. The urine-soaked blanket was disposed of. A copy of the Proclamation of Judgment was placed at the foot of the bed. A copy of the Proclamation of Judgment in an envelope was given to Keaton. At that point, Keaton wrote in English on a piece of paper: "An eye for an eye, blood for blood, a finger for a finger. Have a nice day." Then he wrote it again in Arabic. A small "X" shaped hole was torn in the paper, and al-Nasirah's left pinky finger was inserted through the hole. When he awakened, al-Nasirah would be sure to find Keaton's message waiting for him.

The monitors were switched on again. To the staff outside, they indicated al-Nasirah was asleep. The entourage left al-Nasirah's room.

General Surayah said to the hospital staff, "The prisoner is cleared for release to the Americans whenever your judgment says he is fit to travel." Turning to the soldiers present, he said, "Until the prisoner is released to the Americans, I command that he be kept on a nonstop suicide watch to prevent him from taking his own life. Two people must be present with the prisoner at all times."

Keaton shook the general's hand. "My special thanks are owed to all of you gentlemen. I believe that justice has been served today."

"I agree," said the general. "Now let us all depart."

Keaton motioned for Laura and me to follow him as he left the area with the general and the officers.

We all rode down to the lobby in the elevator together. In the lobby, Keaton thanked all the officers again and shook their hands.

We returned to his limo and were driven back to the embassy. In the back of the car, Keaton told us what had transpired in al-Nasirah's room. He read us the proclamation from his copy.

Laura said, "It is fitting. Al-Nasirah demanded revenge. Instead, revenge was meted out against him. He really deserves to die, but I think that right now, he is in a state of suffering that is worse than death. He has earned it."

I sat there content that Keaton had got the Saudis to go along with my suggestion. They had embellished it a little by shaving off the beard, but it was still a fitting penalty for a mad dog human. I imagine that the hospital staff will have their hands full with al-Nasirah when he regains consciousness. He was unstable before; might the castration push him completely over the edge into insanity? On second thought, I really don't give a shit.

When we arrived at the embassy, we were standing outside the limo with Stuart Keaton when Adelle and Lt. Andrew Keaton came out to join us.

Keaton said, "Your luggage is in the trunk of the car. My driver can take you both to the airport. At the airport, a Saudi palace official will be waiting to speed you through all formalities and security. In a few hours, you'll be in London and then on your way to wherever it is they will send you next. You haven't been properly informed of this yet, but you have a private date with President Decker when you get home. I think he wants to pin a medal on both of you. I don't know how that will sit with your bosses since they will want to keep your role in our rescue a secret. So, you'll probably have medals you can never show to anyone but each other. As for me, I will be publicly thanking the Saudis for saving us."

Keaton continued, "There are no words in any language that are adequate to express the gratitude that Adelle and I feel toward you. The debt this family owes you can never be repaid, but if there is ever, and I mean *ever*, a way we can do something for you, then you have but to say the word, and it shall be done. We will always answer a call from Pogo or Koala for assistance. This offer has no end and no limits; it is for life—ours and yours."

"Stu, you are a good man. You, Adelle, Suzy, and Andrew are a great family. Sometimes we do things for people who don't warrant the effort we put forth. Other times the reward we get is the satisfaction of knowing we did something for the good guys. This is one of those times. I hope we never have to call in the favor, but if we do, I know you will be there for us. Thank you."

Jack turned to Andrew Keaton and saluted. "Take good care of your sister; she is a very special young lady," he said.

Andrew Keaton returned Jack's salute. He then said, "The Navy is my life's work. I hope one day I will be more than a lieutenant. That promise my father just made is a promise I will honor as long as I live. I cannot find words to tell you how much what you have done means to me. Literally, you have given me back my entire family." He shook both of our hands.

Jack and I were both choked up.

Jack could hardly speak as he said, "We had better get going before we get all teary and mushy. We're supposed to be the tough guys, and I don't know how much longer we can keep this act up."

Adelle gingerly hugged me with just her right arm; it would be weeks before her shoulder and ribs healed properly. Stu hugged Laura, then Laura hugged Adelle, and Stu and I did a bear hug. Andrew Keaton stood there beaming like a thousand-watt bulb.

It was very emotional and a fitting end to this mission. Laura and I got the guy we came to get. She indirectly got the vengeance she wanted for her twin brother. We had formed a working partnership unlike any I had ever imagined could exist.

Laura and I got back in the limo. Stu, Adelle, and Andrew were waving as the limo pulled out of the driveway. Laura and I held hands in the back seat.

"We're heading back to the U.S.," I said. "I know you would like to go to Israel. I'll go anywhere you want us to go just as long as I can be with you."

"Jack, wherever you are, that is where I want to be. I don't need real estate; I need you. I need us."

We both sat quietly, realizing that as long as we were together, we were both home. And home with Laura felt very good indeed.

ABOUT THE AUTHOR

Murray Eskenazi was born in New York City and raised in the Bronx, where he attended Bronx High School of Science. He went on to Columbia College, where he majored in mathematics with a minor in mechanical engineering, and later earned his MBA in marketing and business law from New York University's Graduate School of Business Administration.

At Columbia, Murray swam competitively under legendary coach Ed Kennedy (although he never scored a point in any swimming meet). He joined Psi Upsilon Fraternity, a lifelong commitment that has led to him serving as president of Psi U's Columbia alumni association and as a member of Psi U's International Executive Council. For his decades of service, he was honored as a Life Member of the Executive Council and as a Distinguished Alumnus.

Murray married Doris Sims. Together they raised two daughters, Lynn and Nancy, and took great pride in their three grandsons, Jake, Noah, and Michael. The couple lived in East Rockaway, NY, for 53 years, during which Murray devoted over four decades to local government, serving as both a volunteer and elected official, including as Trustee and Deputy Mayor. He also enjoyed his work with the East Rockaway Fire Department, where he helped design and purchase firefighting equipment. Sadly, Doris passed away in 2022.

Murray's business career has been as varied as it has been successful—from engineering with International Trucks, managing and designing clothing factories and warehouses, to running his own company for 30 years, providing medical and paramedical services to the life insurance industry.

Now retired in Delray Beach, Florida, Murray spends his time writing, inventing games (he created *Super Scrabble* and holds three U.S. patents), and enjoying life. He is a longtime member of MENSA. Murray believes laughter is the elixir of life.